A DREAM OF SHADOWS

PETER ELIOTT

A Dream of Shadows by Peter Eliott
Published by Further Press, LLC
PO Box 314 Amagansett, NY 11930.

www.PeterEliott.com
Copyright ©2022 Peter Eliott

Cover by: Jeff Brown
Editing by: Sara Kelly
Page Design and Typesetting by: Paul Baillie-Lane
Author photo by: James Asnes

ISBN: 979-8-9867065-0-4
Ebook ISBN: 979-8-9867065-1-1

Printed in USA
First Edition

To Reiko,
who has encouraged and inspired my writing
in every imaginable way

*"Ours is a world of ruthless caution,
where vast treasures remain hidden,
and great profits are earned in shadow."*

~ Beranardos Sherdane
High Lord of Hell's Labyrinth

PART

I

<hr>

1

VAZEER

It's strange the things you remember.

When I call up my story, it always drags with itself a smell, a distinct smell, one that intermittently haunts my memories and dreams with the ghostly provocation of a dead lover's perfume. Ironically, it is the smell of rain.

The thing is, it wasn't raining that twilit evening when I walked away from my moored skiff, crossed the sodden ground of the riverbank, and entered an old, decrepit boathouse that would become the very place where my fortunes changed forever. In fact, the pervasive smell at that time was the usual sulfuric reek of the river Grells, admixed most disagreeably with the stench of urine from the boathouse. The threat of rain wasn't even present on the night of our first meeting. As I said, it's strange the things you remember.

However, I remember other less ironic details. I remember everything, in fact—the sound of the incoming tide lapping like tiny skiff paddles against the outgoing current, ribbons of mist washing all color from the world, black moss, which grew like a sickly beard across the doorframe of the boathouse, making my transition from autumn dusk to candle glow all the gloomier and more oppressive. Indeed, this was a solemn passage if ever there was one. It is not often that a man steps through a doorway knowing that he has just made the best and worst decision of his entire life.

This, I'm afraid, is going to take a few moments to explain.

I will not, at this time, overwhelm you with an extensive recounting of my past; however, some details are necessary to help you understand why I was setting foot inside a piss-stinking boathouse in the autumn of year 213, on the verge of unleashing a cataclysm for which I am still atoning to this day. For starters, my given name is Vazeer, though in the fallen city of Sullward where I have lived my entire life, I am known by a different alias. Vazeer the Lash they call me, and if you think this title hints at sinister things, you are right.

I am, for one thing, an established villain. In an urban landscape nicknamed Hell's Labyrinth for its criminal intricacy—a once magnificent capital city, now teeming with smugglers and brigands, hired killers, and a nefarious cadre of rulers called the Underlords—I had developed a wicked reputation that eventually came to have a life of its own. Men like me must work hard to earn such stature, and believe me, I had. Though at some point I must have lost control of the damned thing, for where mere notoriety would have been sufficient, true infamy was where I landed. Such is life, I suppose. I have only myself to blame.

The dark, burgundy-trimmed cloaks I habitually wore in those days never seemed to hang from my frame with that special air of grandeur I so desperately craved, and yet, when told that I looked all the more villainous and threatening dressed in that manner, I never did a thing about it. I was ultimately driven by vanity, I've since decided. Not confidence, however, as you will see.

These personal failings aside, I dwelled at a unique juncture of our city's underworld hierarchy. There were many names for people like me—bid men, independents, free agents, contract operatives—but most often we were referred to as Shadow Bidders, those who stepped out of the shadows just long enough to bid on a contract, then disappeared again. And there was a good reason we did things in this furtive manner. Every single task we performed was designed to buffer our anonymous employers, known collectively as the Underlords, from the many outside forces that sought to destroy them. Nothing we might confess to the imperial constables after an arrest, and nothing we might blurt out under an enemy's torture knife, would result in relevant information to be used against the person who hired us. We hardly knew each other, let alone the Underlords, and that was the true genius of the system. Like a shadowy fortress, we were the secret barrier that allowed the Sullward elite to sleep safely at night.

Most nights, that was. This evening we would be discussing something entirely different inside that dilapidated old boathouse. I fear there's one more thing I must explain before we step together through that doorway.

On the very rarest of occasions, one of the Underlords contracted a team of Shadow Bidders into a highly unorthodox arrangement that was referred to in Hell's Labyrinth as a "Narrow Bid," and already I despair of explaining the full weight that those two words carried when placed together in the same sentence. Unquestionably, a Narrow Bid was the most hazardous possible extension of the Shadow Bidder's already hazardous profession, and I don't mean to flatter myself by stating that I was one of perhaps a handful of operatives in Sullward who was likely to be considered for such a job.

A Narrow Bid came about when an Underlord chose to make a move against one of his fellows. Unlike "straight bids," which were focused on eluding the authorities and various other parties who tried to interfere with the Underlords' business, the Narrow Bid turned its sights inward towards those who were otherwise untouchable. If you signed on to a Narrow Bid, then you were about to cross one of the Underlords himself.

I realize, of course, that you know very little about these mysterious powerbrokers of Hell's Labyrinth, but for now, believe me when I tell you that one would probably find it easier to move against a Tergonian archduke than an Underlord of Sullward. Their obsession with self-preservation was the stuff of legends.

And if you failed in your bid, you were finished. It was as simple as that. Either the intended target's henchmen would kill you, or your employer's people would hunt you down and reward you for your incompetence. One way or another, if you blew a Narrow Bid, you died.

This, you see, was what I was stepping into as I set foot inside that abandoned boathouse. A Narrow Bid, which I had decided would be my last shadow bid, and therefore the closing act in my long, inglorious drama of criminality. After this bid was finished, I would stow away my weapons, I would take off my dark colors. I'd be filthy rich from the contract, still young enough to reinvent my life, and perhaps unjaded enough to enjoy it. I was grateful to the profession that had kept me in such luxury all these years, but even I knew it couldn't last forever. I would eventually wind up dead or in prison or permanently disabled with little hope of a final payday of this sort. I was rumored to have earned more, in the course of my career, than any other Shadow Bidder in history; however, I had shoveled all of that wealth in one direction—a direction that did not especially lend itself to a secure retirement. The Narrow Bid was the only option if I truly wished to start over, with no financial difficulties that might tempt me back into my old life. I wasn't going to become a damned fisherman after all. This was clearly the right thing to do.

So, there it was, a simple plan. One more bid and Vazeer the Lash was done for good. Now, let's finally step inside that boathouse, and I'll show you how I screwed the whole thing up.

2

SHADOW BIDDERS

The space within the old building was much as it had seemed from the outside: a simple rectangle of stone blocks with a flat roof. There were three thick timber beams running across the ceiling and three posts rising from the floor to meet them. At the far end was a large opening facing the river, a gaping square comparable to what might be found in the wall of a grain barn. The room itself had clearly been swept within the last few hours, and I suspect that a great deal of vagrant bedding and furniture had been tossed out into the river to make the place bearable for our meeting.

There were five figures inside the boathouse when I entered: two leaning up against the left wall, one against the right, another by the large riverside opening, and the fifth figure near the central support post. Four candles burned on the floor, all of them in the proximity of the man in the middle, which made him blazingly visible in contrast to his shadowed companions. He was quite an ugly bastard, with a flabby jaw almost entirely devoid of a chin—just a nubby little bump that separated his face from his squat neck. He wore a red shawl over a belted gray gown with the strap of a shoulder bag slung diagonally across his chest. This was no doubt the Sketcher for the bid.

The man took a step forward and spoke.

"What is your name and function, Shadow Bidder?"

I paused a moment before answering, looking him over, sizing up the figure who would dominate the next hour or so of my life. Sketchers were indispensable icons in the lives of Shadow Bidders, as they were the operative's only link to the proffering employer and also the primary source of information about the bid.

"Vazeer the Lash," I finally replied. "Grell Runner."

"Welcome then, Vazeer the Lash. Wait silently with us until the final Bidder arrives."

I took up a position against the right wall of the boathouse, and there I waited.

The others in the room had remained silent and remarkably still during the admission procedure, yet now the figure who stood nearest to me against the right wall shifted slightly to look in my direction. I recognized him at once.

He was a large man. In fact, he was about as large as a man could be, enough so that in the candle glow I might have questioned whether he was human at all—perhaps a carved tomb guardian brought to life. His features were chiseled as if by a sculptor's tool, and his skin was as dark as lantern oil. The rest of him was draped in a brown cloak that was easily the size of a tapestry.

The man smiled at me in the darkness, his dull teeth showing like flecks of granite, his ebony skin pinching around the eyes and sending creases right up the side of his bald skull. The candle flames cast shadows into the wells of his eye sockets, yet I saw a hint of mirth reflected there.

"Vazeer the Lash," said the huge man quietly. "This *is* a Narrow Bid."

"Finding you here, Helmgrinder, removes any doubt of that."

The man's real name was Coljin, or Col for short, which he generally preferred to his street name. Most Shadow Bidders would have killed for an alias like "Helmgrinder," but Col apparently felt it understated his talents.

The Sketcher swiveled my way with a finger to his lips, his little black eyes stabbing at me through the dusky air. I said nothing more, and Col, too, turned away, though he continued to smile as though he had just solved an irritating riddle that had been bothering him for days.

Against the opposing wall of the boathouse there were further signs of recognition at my arrival. If a riddle had been solved there, then it was accomplished with a bit less pleasure, for the figure directly across from me was glowering venomously. The dim illumination made her features difficult to distinguish, but her posture told all: arms crossed, legs planted defiantly, head shaking slowly in disgust. She was a short, mousy woman with pale skin and brittle auburn hair, which was faintly visible in the gloom. Flerra Tellian she was called. I couldn't remember what might have happened the last time we worked together that would disturb her so much, but I didn't waste much time thinking about it. She had been glowering at me like this for the last thirty years.

Flerra Tellian and I had been raised and trained together since we were children. Our contract broker, Holod Deadskiff, had swooped us up from the same wretched orphanage, along with a handful of other worthless guttersnipes, and the group of us came to be known as the Brood. Holod taught each of us to read, taught us our respective skills, taught us the Labyrinth code, and I must say that Flerra Tellian and I were among the best products from that endeavor. She was also the closest thing

I had ever had to a sibling. I would probably always see her as the foul-mouthed, freckle-faced girl who used to pick the locks to the Harbormaster's warehouse and go on stealing sprees that left the rest of the Brood in a state of jealous disbelief. These days we seldom encountered each other except on the rare occasion that Holod saw fit to contract us both on the same bid.

That was part of what was bothering me at the moment—the thought that Holod had offered this bid to both of us. In theory, I should have seen it as a sign of reassurance that our cagey broker thought this Narrow Bid safe enough that he would risk his two main sources of income on it at the same time. But I didn't. Our combined commissions would be downright obscene on a job like this, and it was clear to me that Holod was looking to sweep his chips from the table and retire on this bid, just as I was, just as I'm sure Flerra was, just as I suppose everybody in that miserable boathouse was. Too many people thinking of this bid as their last made me decidedly uneasy.

But there was something else about the presence of Flerra Tellian that disturbed me, something personal. It was that damned look of scorn on her face! I didn't particularly mind these glowers from the other operatives, but when the disdain came from Flerra, it hurt. The expression was hidden from sight by the dim lighting, though it was as apparent to me as the prevailing stink. I implied earlier that she had been scowling at me in that manner for decades, but this wasn't entirely true. In recent times the frown had grown much worse, and it was obvious that there was more behind it than the customary disapproval that defined this woman, just as there was something more to Col's little jibe about my presence on the bid than dry wit. These two, like so many others in this city, had certain opinions about me that were as indelible as bloodstains.

The source of the problem was the fact that I often went to extreme lengths to perform my unique function in Hell's Labyrinth, and in a few unfortunate incidents this had meant confrontations with other Shadow Bidders. We tried, wherever possible, to avoid this, to adhere to the unwritten code amongst contract operatives that forbade us from doing harm to one another whenever our various nocturnal errands brought us into conflict. To be perfectly honest, I simply couldn't abide by this rule when my cargo was at stake.

A Grell Runner's job was to appraise, negotiate for, and transport the vast hoard of stolen merchandise that flowed to our shores each month, stealthily offloading it from the armada of smuggling ships that docked in our harbor and then ferrying it up the river Grells to secret drop points deep inside the Labyrinth. In the course of one of those runs, there were a whole host of parties that I needed to evade, but unfortunately, evasion wasn't always possible. When confrontations ensued, I tended to be quite the zealot in defense of my payload. While the Underlords greatly valued my fanatical defense of their precious items, my fellow operatives found my behavior baffling and often repugnant.

They would simply never get it. The others weren't idiots, or not completely, but they lacked subtlety, so they didn't realize that as I handled the thousands and thousands of splendorous artifacts that shipped into our harbor each year—the stolen artwork, the jewelry, the ornaments, the books—it wasn't greed that overtook my heart, but longing. Longing for a place and a time that none of us had ever known, but in whose shadow we dwelled every day of our lives. Working my Grell Running bids among the granite ghosts of a world in decline, I couldn't help but feel that in my own small, debased way, I was actually participating in the restoration and that, by extension, abandoning a cargo was somehow tantamount to losing my soul.

In my early adolescence, I had tried several times to entice Flerra Tellian into my visions of antiquity, once even taking her on a winding historical tour of the perilous but magnificent Lower City, where I pointed out the towers and grand halls that I had managed to identify from my reading. Unfortunately, the obsession didn't take hold in her. She was too practical by nature, and Holod's incessant efforts to counter my idealism simply overbore her. Either way, Flerra had never shown much interest in my far-fetched ideas and, at best, seemed to tolerate my pedantic brothering as a harmless annoyance.

Col, at least, found my devotion to my cargos humorous, though I was never quite sure if this was because he considered my loyalty to the Underlords absurd or simply because he found violence entertaining. On more than one occasion he had speculated (a little too eagerly for my liking) on the possible results of a "nocturnal encounter" between himself and the dreaded Vazeer the Lash, one time going so far as to say that facial scars would be the least of my worries. He was referring to the long arcing gash down the left side of my face, the tangible result of my most infamous conflict along the Grells.

I knew firsthand that the ever-taunting Coljin Helmgrinder could back up his threats, having teamed with him on dozens of jobs where I needed to purchase my cargo directly from corsairs, and on a handful of those occasions, his presence had literally made the difference between life and death. Col himself had been a first mate on just such a vessel in his younger years, and he knew the machinations of water-borne riffraff better than anybody in Sullward. I would have liked to consider Col one of my few friends in the city, except for the simple fact that the huge former pirate would willingly, perhaps even enthusiastically, view me as an enemy if it ever served him to do so. This didn't lay the most ideal foundation for friendship, any more than Flerra Tellian's glowering derision lent itself to sibling warmth.

I turned my attention from these two, hoping to observe the remaining figures in the room, but suddenly my gaze was drawn away. Somebody was entering the front door and, having imbibed the lessons of stony quiescence from the Sketcher and the behavior of my cohorts, I hardly moved when the visitor arrived. Stillness reigned on the outside, but something very peculiar happened within.

At first, I could see little of the newcomer, for the lighting in the doorway area was poor, and the individual possessed dark hair that seemed to be covering the features. Only when this person stepped farther into the candlelight did a slender hand rise from the folds of the dark clothing and brush aside what I now saw to be long, full tresses. That was when I caught my first glimpse of the stranger's face.

"What is your name and function, Shadow Bidder?" the Sketcher demanded.

"Nascinthé of Levell," she answered quietly. "Masque."

"Welcome then, Nascinthé of Levell; you are the final Bidder. A moment more and we will begin."

Once again, the Sketcher looked back and made a gesture of some kind towards the river. Nascinthé remained where she was, her hands at her sides, her face half illumined in the candlelight. It is entirely possible that I took a step forward at that moment to improve my view. The fact was, with my eyes now fully adjusted to the dim lighting and Nascinthé's proximity to the brightest spot in the room, I saw her well enough.

Her dark hair fell loosely over her shoulders, back, and chest, appearing in the gloom like a rill of brandy spilling across her travel robe. She looked like she had just come in from a gale. Her high cheekbones appeared flushed and damp while her mouth was open fractionally more than seemed casual, as though she was breathing hard but did not wish to show it. For some reason my gaze was drawn to that mouth, drawn to its oddly half-expressed manner. Her partially open lips were thin but long, stretching rather broadly across such a slender and ethereal face, and this only added to the sense that something important needed to be conveyed from there. I couldn't begin to imagine what it might be, though I found myself hoping I would hear her speak again.

"We do it now," said the Sketcher. "Gather in close."

I was painfully startled by the sound of his voice, as though he were speaking directly into my ear through a reed tube. He waved us all in towards the candles, looking back several times at the river, his eyes restless and severe.

"Closer. I want you all to see each other."

Like pockets of gloom pried loose from the walls, we drew in towards the light source, our faces jittering out of the darkness. This was always a telling moment, to see the others fully, to see their expressions and dispositions and sometimes other things that might make the whole difference when the bid slimmed down to a needle's point. Yet I was distracted. Terrible as it is to admit, on the first Narrow Bid of my career, I began the sketch in a somewhat baffled state of mind, my thoughts still consumed with this peculiar issue of hearing words spoken from a set of partially open lips. I kept gazing at Nascinthé of Levell.

"Good, that's close enough," said the Sketcher, his abrasive voice still rattling my eardrums. "This is a tangled sketch, and you're only going to hear it once. Before I give it, though, I want you to speak your names to each other one at a time. Starting here."

He pointed to one of the two remaining figures I hadn't yet observed.

The man had a stocky frame and a heavily scarred forehead, probably from a scalding of some sort. He was bearded, had small gray streaks through the hair around his temples, and wore a wool seaman's coat, all of these details converging to give him the appearance of being some sort of naval officer, though I suspect that's not what he was at all.

"Fe Gesbon," said the stranger in a stern voice.

He had not been asked to state his function, yet the stiffness in his pose and the clipped manner in which he spoke reflected a little too much effort to achieve an air of authority, and this instantly put me on guard. I suddenly had a very bad feeling that our mysterious proffer on this job had seen it necessary to hire a Line Man—a category of operative that was as unpopular among Shadow Bidders as it was coveted by the Underlords. I had worked only one bid with a Line Man, and the experience had left me in no great hurry to collaborate with another.

The Sketcher pointed to Flerra Tellian next, and she proceeded to speak her own name as she spoke most things, with just the slightest hint of disgusted outrage. Then:

"Nascinthé of Levell."

There was something so intriguing about the way she intoned her own name. It was as though she were reciting it through the fetid air like a hymn, a set of lyrical sounds that might have turned into a melody had they continued just a little longer, and which, yet again, were imbued with the deep weight of the unspoken. A second later she turned to me.

What an odd moment that was. I suddenly felt the full impact of those smooth, damp features shifting around to radiate upon me, awakening in me an abrupt bout of self-consciousness, which rose like a band of stifling sunlight up my body and into my face. The heat throbbed there for several seconds, almost violently.

Candlelight is not the ideal illumination in which to view the nuances of color, though after a few moments in any lighting, one could not help but to note a soft blue glint below the slim arch of Nascinthé's brows. On several occasions I had elicited from Col vivid descriptions of the South Derjian Sea, enticing the former corsair to recall the calm aquamarine waters that were so in contrast with the churning gray and white off the coast of Sullward. Time and again I'd struggled unsuccessfully to picture such places. I don't know why I wasted energy on this sort of reverie, nor why it was so difficult to imagine; what I do know is that on the night of the darkest, most complex sketch of my life, I suddenly saw the illusive aquamarine color at last. It was in the irises of a Shadow Bidder named Nascinthé of Levell.

I snapped my gaze away as though I had been smacked.

"Vazeer the Lash," I said.

In that moment, I truly hated the coarse sound of my own name.

Col spoke next, rescuing the sodden air from the lingering timbre of my voice, the bass rumble of his name drawing out to a tone and a depth that transcended the single syllable that composed it. It helped to ground me. Enough so that when the final member of the group introduced himself, I regained the rest of my senses in a hurry.

Be the factors mystical or simply a combination of having recognized others in the room first and the rotation the Sketcher had chosen, fate had it that I somehow observed this man last. As you will learn in time, many inglorious labels have been heaped upon me since the night of our Narrow Bid, and many rumors of my treachery and machinations have now become part of the Sullward lore. I must tell you, however, that for whatever evil was my part in this whole affair, there is one who should rightfully inherit ten times the blame, if not more, and who deserves to be feared in ways that even the Underlords are not. He is none other than the final Shadow Bidder in our group, and though I will do my best to relay his portrait, I fear that the truly haunting details, the ineffable elements of texture, tone, nuance, and mood, will escape my crude rendition as ever the masterpiece on canvas belies the cheap, sketched copies sold in the bazaar. Still, I will try.

He spoke his name.

"Radrin Blackstar."

Radrin Blackstar. I repeated it silently to myself, struggling as if to remember, though I knew at once that I had never heard the name before. Still, I had the unsettled feeling that I should have known this man. I almost recognized his face, but not quite.

He was, first of all, rather handsome. His good looks were of an improbably neat and unweathered variety: cleanly shaven skin, scarless cheeks and jaw, a well-proportioned nose, firm mouth, and a set of deep green eyes, which were not fierce or penetrating, but rather cool and recessive, like the gloom of a late-day forest. His dark blond hair was carefully combed and untouched by gray, further adding to an appearance of youth, though not boyishness.

One didn't do the dirty work of Hell's Labyrinth and remain so untouched.

Shadow Bidders wore the toll of their profession nakedly in the contours of their faces. Nascinthé, perhaps, had preserved her beauty, which was doable if one made it a priority, yet even she was possessed with a haunting tremor of emotion, which you felt the moment you looked at her, even if you had no idea what that emotion was. As for the rest of us, we hadn't gotten off so easily. A quick pan of the group said it all: Fe Gesbon with his scalded brow, Flerra Tellian, whose visage had molded into the taut, scowling features of a shrew, the massive Col with a head like chiseled rock, and even the Sketcher with an ugly grimace, glazed over by river mist and cold functionality. I, of course, was the severest of them all. My swarthy, hawkish face with its cockeyed nose, its black descending eyebrows, its brutally scarred jaw—ever shrouded in stubble and on the verge of a curse—was the very countenance of Hell's Labyrinth itself. It had even come to attract women in ways that the city sometimes did, drawing to its brutish landscape those who were either too adventurous for their own good or hopelessly self-destructive by blatant admission. Never did I supply such women with the mischief they craved.

And yet none of these qualities, alluring, grotesque, mysterious or otherwise, seemed to quite sum up Radrin Blackstar. Unlike Flerra Tellian, he did not seem to shroud his vulnerabilities in seething hostility, nor did he posture himself stiffly as Fe Gesbon did. He did not even emit the aura of judicious confidence that Col gave off, and certainly he lacked the wicked, skulking air of criminality that seemed to drag along with me perpetually like a pipe-smoker's haze.

Nascinthé of Levell was a mystery, but that very mystery was her recognizable quality—the undelivered communication. The fantasy of more.

Not so with Radrin Blackstar. He emitted nothing. He suggested nothing, yet you knew he was something. He had to be. You simply felt it but couldn't, for the life of you, tell exactly which part of him was ringing the warning bell in the back of your brain. If the words "ominous" and "inconspicuous" could possibly lie together in one illustrative sentence, then they belonged in the description of this man.

"Fine then," said the Sketcher. "Now you know each other. Get your heads ready for the bid. As promised, it's going to be narrow, which is exactly why we picked you. You're the tightest six we could find."

And so he began. This was, of course, the first time a Narrow Bid had ever been sketched for me, yet I found nothing unusual about the format. The Sketcher addressed the identity of the target first, which he accomplished in an extremely tactful manner, never naming names and making sure to get the message across through a series of veiled allusions that had the potential to be conveniently disavowed later in the advent of our capture and interrogation. At first, as I pieced together his references, I felt absolutely certain that I had misunderstood the identity of the target, and also the objective of the bid itself.

A moment later it became grievously apparent that I had not.

"Gueritus?" Flerra Tellian's pale face had now stretched so tightly the bones looked like they were on the verge of poking through the skin. Her fierce brown eyes were wild and incredulous. "The Raving Blade?"

The Sketcher wheeled about, whisking his hand savagely before her face as if trying to erase the words from the sodden air. It was too late; there was now a verbal record of the target, though the far more important issue was to avoid speaking the proffer's name out loud. Still, the Sketcher was enraged.

"You reckless little witch!" he snarled. "I could have you killed for that!"

"Go on then!" Flerra shrieked. "That's what this bid will amount to anyway, you hideous troll. Six Shadow Bidders! Just six? Why doesn't your damned boss—"

"Flerra!" I practically roared her name, raising a hand in warning and siphoning the full murderous energy of my own rising despair straight at her. Anything to keep her from crossing that line.

Much to my amazement, she stopped. Flerra Tellian literally clamped her mouth shut and crossed her wiry arms over her chest as if forcing down the explosive disapprobation that yearned to ruin her if only she would give it a chance. The Sketcher was obviously riled, rocking back and forth on his stubby legs and scouring unconsciously at the hem of his shawl as if still attempting to cleanse the space of this disgraceful breach of etiquette. Col surprised me by speaking up.

"No harm done, Sketcher," he said in his bass rumble. "That is, if we execute the bid properly."

"Yes, if you do it properly, Shadow Bidder!" the Sketcher snapped. "That's the whole point, isn't it? I was warned about her...told that she does this."

Flerra's arms came uncrossed, and her mouth started to open, forcing me, once again, to rescue her from herself.

"Yes," I said loudly. "During the sketch she sometimes causes trouble. But only the sketch. After that, she works her trade better than any Locksmith out there. Why don't you continue, Sketcher? As Col said, no harm's been done."

For several seconds, the Sketcher seemed almost too distracted to go on. His eyes stirred about in distress as if searching for the lost cotter pin that had suddenly slipped from his plans, making them too hazardous to operate. He seemed incapable of accommodating for Flerra's mistake.

"Fine then," he muttered, glancing back quickly over his shoulder towards the river opening. "No more slips...I warn you. This isn't Grell Running or cargo pinching or other wide dirt bids you've worked. You figured out who the target is. We don't fiddle around here. We work it tight, like I told you at the beginning. Tight."

He repeated the word "tight" several more times and continued to scrub compulsively at his shawl. I could see his mind scrambling as he attempted to stall in this manner, obviously calculating a whole new set of circumstances, which had him entirely baffled. I might have been more perplexed by the Sketcher's behavior had I not been so consumed by what had to be the single most chilling name in all of Hell's Labyrinth: *Gueritus*.

Now I had really gone and done it.

In actuality, it was Gueritus's other name—the one often rasped in a queer, inebriated cross-resonance between fear, admiration, and loathing in the taverns of Sullward and several other North Derjian cities as well—that had carried his infamy far and wide: The Raving Blade of Hell's Labyrinth.

Never had an alias been so thoroughly deserved.

I cannot take the time now, nor the considerable mental and emotional energy necessary, to relay the stories, the many stories, which circulated like the flu through the serpentine alleys, dank cellars, and curtained tavern booths of the nefarious underworld capital known as Hell's Labyrinth, the ones which at once depicted a man of mad, unbridled genius and terrifying sadism— that unique fusion of character traits that appears once or twice in a generation and breeds human wickedness that leaves the rest of us petty villains looking like justices of the peace. I simply cannot bear the recounting.

What I can and must do is explain why I, Vazeer, criminal though I am by my own admission, am suddenly mentioning the name of this cold-blooded demon named Gueritus. The answer is simple. On the 26th day of the autumn month known as Dekharven, in the 213th year of the new Sullward calendar, I was offered a colossal sum of money to kill him.

I and five others. Six Shadow Bidders sent out into the autumn night, sent out to murder the darkness itself.

In the underworld feudal system upon which Hell's Labyrinth was founded, Gueritus had been granted peerage—officially he was Count Ulan Gueritus—and he was one of only three direct vassals to the most powerful criminal figure in our city, a man known simply as the High Lord. By virtue of sheer military might, he was considered the number two man in the Labyrinth, and while his army was perhaps half the size of the High Lord's, it still contained scores of soldiers and a network of vassals and sub vassals who each commanded armies of their own. Even more disturbing was the Raving Blade's propensity for deviltry; for ingenious schemes, which were uncanny in their knack for preemptively spoiling moves against him. I had received my education on this subject from a handful of witnesses to those wild intrigues—men and women whom the Count had permitted to live on as a warning to others, and who were thereafter dubbed with the most regrettable of titles. "The Raved" they were called, those who had been bankrupted, ruined, or out-and-out maimed by the dreaded Ulan Gueritus. The man's impish delight in torturing prisoners had been well documented.

And so, as I stood silently inside the candle-lit boathouse, staring at the peculiar antics of the Sketcher, watching Flerra Tellian's face grow whiter, and sensing a subdued demeanor creeping over the group as a whole, I found myself disturbed, most of all, by my own degeneracy of character. One defect in particular had me disgusted.

I had ignored all the damned signs.

From the start, the fee for this bid had been too high. Holod had seemed too eager. Even in the boathouse, before the bid was sketched, there were little clues that should have caused me to bolt. Flerra Tellian shouldn't have been there, but she was because Holod didn't want her left behind to figure out that he had deceived me. He had obviously deceived her too because she would never agree to a job like this if she had any idea what it entailed. And Radrin Blackstar, there was another clue. Damned if I didn't know what he was without ever hearing him state his function. He certainly hadn't come along to help row a skiff.

According to bid etiquette, I could have fled just before hearing the sketch, and while it was true that no Underlord would ever hire me again after such an incident, I had to ask myself, "so what?" At least I would avoid joining the ghastly legions of the Raved, a fate far worse than dying. Most of the Raved became gibbering, dismembered things, broken men and women left to crawl through the sewers in search of others' scraps. I had seen them occasionally in the streets of Sullward, sometimes retaining only a single useful limb, and always branded upon the forehead with the two coiling blades of the Gueritus crest. I remember encountering one as a teen near the banks of the Grells, and as I watched him drag himself along with his one remaining arm, I recall thinking that I never, ever wanted to meet the person who could transform a speaking, thinking, functioning human being into a creature that was lower than a toad.

Well, I was going to meet him. Whether I liked it or not, it was now officially my job to kill him.

"All right," the Sketcher said. "All right then, let's get on with it. And as I said, no more slips."

It was clearly a formidable act of self-control for him to rein in his agitation and push on with the sketch. He accomplished it, however, and laid the whole thing out for us with an impressive degree of detail. I had to admit, despite the alarming identity of the target, the plan was a good one. So good, in fact, that a few of us might actually live.

"You see, Tellian," the Sketcher muttered when it was over, with something vaguely resembling satisfaction. "Six will be enough, just enough, if you work this thing tight. It's your personal job to get them in and out of there, so I hope, for all your sakes, that the Lash is right about you."

The Sketcher turned back towards the river opening, and this time there was something to see. A ladder had been raised from below, and its top three rungs were now bobbing in the opening. The tide was low enough that the skiff and its rowers were hidden from sight, but I guessed there were a bunch of them down there to hold the vessel steady and keep the ladder straight. The Sketcher turned back to us, and for the first time that night, he grinned—a leering smirk that curdled the puttyish skin at the tops of his cheeks. The expression aged him at least twenty years.

"My part's over," he said. "The rest is up to you. As detailed, you do this thing in two nights' time, on 28 Dekharven. Not sooner, not later. Forty-eight hours should be enough time for you to make your preparations. Of course, there's one more thing, the part that makes it all worth it. As promised, the payment comes in full. It's all in here, easy to transport."

The Sketcher pulled back his shawl, revealing a belt laden with small pouches. He unslung it and removed six cloth bags, tossing one to each of us. I snatched mine, then quickly peeked inside, noting instantly the soft, purple-red sparkle, like drops of dew refracting the light of the rising sun.

Gosian Diamonds.

The most precious stones of all. More wealth than I'd accumulated in the last five years, and all of it contained in a purse smaller than my fist.

"Be warned, however," said the Sketcher. "If this seems like a fine moment to scatter without performing the job, think carefully about one thing. Look at the wealth in your hands and then try to picture how much the proffer will pay to have you tracked down if you break the contract. There are no lengths to which he will not go. Bear that in mind as I descend that ladder and leave you to your own devices. There's only one option now. You all know what it is."

And with that, he waddled to the far end of the boathouse, swung himself heavily onto the ladder, and descended into the night. As his puffing exhalations faded away, the only sounds that remained were the hushed murmuring of the river and the intermittent cawing of frogs from the marsh.

"How do we work it, Vazeer?" Flerra asked once the Sketcher was gone. Her arms were again crossed, though her defiance looked muted.

"By following the sketch, precisely," Fe Gesbon answered in my stead, stepping into the center of the circle and taking on his role as our ostensible leader. "It'll work if it's executed precisely as it was given to us, with no spur-of-the-moment changes."

"No, Fe Gesbon, in this matter you are wrong."

I didn't realize how much I'd utterly forgotten Radrin Blackstar until he spoke those words. He seemed to have dematerialized for a time, then re-formed as sounds exited his lips. The others must have had a similar experience, for all turned to look at him in that quick, jerking rhythm that bespoke surprise.

"It's all spur-of-the-moment changes."

Gesbon seemed as startled as the rest of us, though he regained his composure quickly.

"That approach means death," he said definitively. "Following the sketch gives us a chance. A good chance. I won't work with a Finisher who won't work with the plan."

"I'll work with the plan, Fe Gesbon," Radrin answered calmly. "Until the plan no longer works with me. The sketch is but a memory now, already dissipated like vapors in the wind. Bidders who don't understand that are the ones for whom death is a guarantee."

"Pull out on us, Finisher, and I have a guarantee for you."

Fe Gesbon planted himself firmly, hands on hips, and seemed intent on provoking a staring contest with the enigmatic Finisher of the bid. This display had little effect on Radrin Blackstar, however, who stared past Gesbon as if he were a section of air and, somewhat startlingly, locked gazes with me.

"Well then, Vazeer the Lash," Radrin said, his expression unruffled. "You never did answer Flerra Tellian's question. How do we work it?"

For a moment I just gazed at him. I stared at that clean, untouched face with the perfectly straight nose, scarless cheeks, and relaxed green eyes. That misplaced array of handsome features reached out to my much grittier ones, to all that had gone into shaping them, to my Labyrinth-twisted mind. Radrin Blackstar was looking for something just then and, strangely, I felt inclined to give it to him.

"How do we work it?" I asked, posing the question to myself for the first time. "The only way you ever work a bid in this city. By setting out with the genuine intention of following the sketch. After that...improvise like hell."

3

HOMECOMING

I arrived back at the harbor that night just after Ninth Bell, bewildered, anxious, and deeply exhausted. This was the hour when my nocturnal activities usually began, not ended, yet still, I felt as though I had appraised and transported three loads of stolen merchandise, so mentally drained was I from the evening's discussion. The group of six had remained at the boathouse a full two and a half hours after the Sketcher left, debating the plan, rehearsing our respective roles, talking through the potential pitfalls, of which there were many. But none of it helped. None of it gave me the slightest confidence that this was anything other than a brilliantly conceived and morally justified suicide mission. The thought of fleeing for my damned life was still very much on my mind.

When we finally left the meeting site that night, Fe Gesbon insisted that we depart individually, spaced fifteen minutes apart. Breaking the group up was a wise precaution, I suppose, though I think Gesbon was most interested in showing off his ability to track time internally, just as he had enjoyed reciting every single word that the Sketcher had spoken. These were just some of the skills that made a Line Man valuable—the ability to record time, conversations, all manner of detail, without ever needing to write any of it down, or without measuring instruments of any kind. At the end of the bid, he would meet with the Sketcher one last time to report all that had transpired. I'm fairly certain that Fe Gesbon was the only one among us who believed he would live long enough to fulfill that portion of his duty.

Morbid pessimism notwithstanding, I ended the evening's activities in much the same manner that I concluded most of my working nights. I rowed quietly down the last portion of the Grells, through the wide misty river delta and into Sullward Harbor. My safety was not entirely guaranteed at this point in the journey (in the rarest of instances, troublemakers could still accost me here) but for all intents and purposes, I was home free. And it was a rather stunning experience, no matter how many times I had traveled this route.

The mist in Sullward Harbor is always thick in the dark hours, creating a soft, moist blanket for the senses, muffling noises, stealing the sharp edges from the world. And shrouded in this way, one approaches the docks as if in a dream. The first thing you experience is the briny reek of the harbor water, which is a little different than the sulfuric tang of the marsh, and this tells you that the cool, saline currents of the sea are flowing here. Then you catch your first clear sight, which is usually the looming dark hulls, lilting softly upon black waters. But at other times, if the mists above have parted briefly before the moon, shredding like torn silk, you see the masts first. Rising spectrally in the fog, the high slender crosses seem impossibly tall from the water's surface. A lantern or two always glints dully from the random cabin window even in the darkest hours of the night, but there is seldom any human activity. The only sounds are the taut squeaking of ropes and the distant grumble of breakers rolling against the sea wall. It is almost a place of profound serenity. Almost, but not quite.

That night as I paddled stealthily behind the sterncastle of an enormous galleon, I could faintly hear the low thrumming of voices within one of the dimly lit cabin windows. I knew what sort of ship this was, sensed it without needing to climb aboard and meet the fine inhabitants therein. The choice of dark colors, the algae creeping like a disease up the sides, the barnacles adhering to the planks like ticks on a dog, all told me this was a Derjian pirate vessel, which I could spot in far dimmer lighting than this. It was a damned big one too, and rather poorly disguised, which was likely to draw some attention from the imperial constables. But that didn't concern me. I would not be hoisting myself up a discreet rope ladder dropped from the rear of this ship. I would not be introducing myself to the honorable and thoroughly murderous captain so-and-so and his distinguished cutthroat of a first mate. Nor would I be warily eyeing a stinking rabble of drunken malcontents, each more stubbled and scarred than the next, and with clothing and weaponry so mixed and matched it seemed to have been dumped out of a theater troop's costume chest. Let some other poor bastard of a Grell Runner have that distinguished privilege. I had something much worse to do in the next forty-eight hours.

I rowed past three other large ships—two merchant carracks and a low, sleek whaling schooner, the latter making itself known by smell long before I could see it. There was a certain acrid stink of whale blood and burnt blubber that was always unmistakable, and I found myself holding my breath as I passed.

But this boat, stench and all, was the sort of vessel that had brought me the bulk of my good fortune in the last twenty years. All of these ships had. Inside the oil barrels of that reeking whaler, and beneath the false planks of those merchant carracks, and strewn throughout every corner of that enormous pirate ship came my livelihood. Sullward wasn't just another run-down haven of petty crime. It was the largest and most complex fencing operation that our world had ever known, an outlet for all manner of pirating and theft within the territories, client states, and protectorates of the vast political behemoth known as the Tergonian Empire. The goods came from every corner of the realm, funneling in across the Derjian Sea in the fat hulls of corsair vessels and rogue galleons, in the catch bays of fishing doggers—in dozens of forms originating from every breed of unfortunate property owner, from the illimitable merchant class to landed gentry to the very upper reaches of the Tergonian aristocracy. And the goods were stolen by every possible means: waylaid on highways, lifted on the high seas, taken at sword's point in an opera house, or at knife point in one's own home, cat burgled, cut-pursed, swindled, switched with fakes, looted by feuding lords or (and this happened more often than one might imagine) pocketed by family members and lovers who wished to profit from misplaced trust.

We who worked the Labyrinth committed none of these crimes, yet we benefited from all of them, which was precisely why I could stomach it. I never had to witness the baroness in her dressing chamber, sobbing abjectly over the precious family heirloom that had been lifted while she was sleeping, nor did I have to watch the honest merchant being dragged off to debtor's prison after losing the shipment that would have finally cleared his books. Most of all, I never had to see the decks of a passenger galley, awash with blood and littered with torn women's clothing after a ship like the one currently inhabiting Berth Four had gotten hold of it.

No, I never had to see any of that. If I had, if I had witnessed the grim reality of it even once, then perhaps I would have turned out to be a very different man indeed.

But that's not what happened, and I never became that other man, the one whose face always eludes me yet whose subtle buzzings disquiet me like the blind bumping of a fly against my window. Instead, I went on to become other things—some worse than I might have wanted, but others far better. I was, after all, a highly educated person, one who could identify, appraise, and appreciate every last item that lay in the secret bays of these illicit vessels, including the fine artwork, which had become a passion of mine.

Holod, the man who had raised and mentored me, often expressed profound regrets about my education. My *over*-education, that was. I almost can't think of a funnier concept. Responding to a dramatic upsurge in the quality and quantity of items that began arriving at our shores when I was a boy, Holod came up with the clever idea of hiring a cultural historian to teach me the intricacies of artifact appraisal. This historian, a house tutor named Esmond, had apparently deflowered a teenage marchioness under his care, and he was hiding out destitute in our city when Holod put him on my case. Not content to merely teach me monetary appraisal, Esmond wanted to unload so much more into my susceptible brain. He explained everything to me: why the pieces were special in the first place, the subtle facets of artistic style. He insisted I understand the various political and cultural currents that were moving in those societies when the art was created, none of which was truly necessary to figure out what it was worth. Finally, he harangued me with his own personal love of history and architecture, which was way beyond the purview for which he was hired. Even at that young age, I could see that Esmond was a blustering ass, a man who took undue pride in his ability to overawe an orphan from the slums. But I drank up what he taught me like a dry bar cloth mopping up a spill.

Holod was busy at that time instructing the older children, and he simply didn't catch wind of what was happening in those tutorial sessions until it was too late. By then the damage was done, and while he did quickly bounce Esmond out of the Labyrinth via his bloody face, he could not bounce the knowledge out of my head, nor could he remove the newly engendered desire to learn more. It only got worse from there until, by my late teens, I had become a sort of academic abomination in Holod's eyes. These days he viewed me more as an unbearable snob, a Shadow Bidder far too obsessed with the finer things in life, and while all of this did, in fact, make me a much better Grell Runner, the whole topic exasperated him to no end.

Sorry, Holod, but you created this snobby monster. Maybe I *am* delusional, with my fancy clothing, my luxurious townhouse, my books, my artwork, my ludicrous dreams of Sullward revival…but even you have to admit, I've certainly crawled to the top of the misty pile of crap where I was born.

Up ahead I saw the tight crisscrossed section of low docks where smaller craft like mine were tied off. The whaler had been docked in the adjoining berth, so, being careful to breathe through my mouth, I made my way quickly to the area in the back where my small armada of skiffs lived. A couple of people were moving about among the boats, and one slender figure was sitting on the dock, slowly tilting forward and back in a rocking chair. He was a tall, scruffy-haired lad, wrapped in a thick cloak, humming to himself quietly. When he saw me pulling into my bay, he raised his chin slightly in acknowledgment.

"Sorry about the stink, Leddy," I said once I had tied off and climbed onto the dock.

"Bastard Harbormaster berths it there on purpose," Leddy said. "He and Droden are at it again about docking fees."

"Droden's got leverage; he'll get his way."

Leddy merely shrugged.

"Listen," I said. "Tell him I need to speak with him. Will he be here tomorrow afternoon?"

"If it's you asking, he'll be here. What time?"

"Fourth Bell, give or take a few minutes."

Leddy nodded and gave a slight wave, and then I was off.

The buildings surrounding the wharf were mostly tall, wide warehouses, with big barn-style doors. All of these were locked at this hour, though I could see the lantern glow coming from a few of the windows. This area was often desolate after sundown when the loading and unloading ceased, though tonight I did see two men in dark blue cloaks standing up against the grain depository, conferring quietly. Their clothing was well coordinated, and I saw the dull glint of armor at their necks. It wasn't hard to recognize a Tergonian constable even for a layperson, and for a man like me, the capacity to spot such individuals quickly was as essential to my livelihood as the ability to row a skiff. I cut a wide margin to avoid this pair, but still they drilled me with inimical glares as I passed. I couldn't tell whether they recognized me individually or simply understood that a relatively well-dressed individual such as myself, emerging from the docks at this hour, probably wasn't disembarking from a fishing expedition. Over the years, I had done a remarkably good job of eluding these constables, though my record wasn't perfect and, like all Grell Runners of any longevity, I had done some prison time. That memory was dreadful enough that I was absolutely determined never to repeat the experience.

Moving northwest out of the heart of the wharf area, the warehouses gave way to a smattering of residential buildings, and here the desolate feeling of the night wharf slowly transformed.

I could hear the clanking of pots coming from above, and in a lower apartment a woman was calling to one of her children. I turned onto the wide thoroughfare known as Cargo Street, and immediately the sights, sounds, and smells of night revelry enveloped me. There was fiddle music emerging from an open doorway, along with some poorly timed clapping and stomping. Light flooded out of doors and windows on both sides of the street, and I smelled a strong mixture of ale and sweat, with the tiniest hint of sewage underlying it all. Cargo Street was the heart of the Dockside neighborhood, and it was here that most of the waterborne visitors to our shores came to drink and lodge. It was a geographically large district, threaded with tight, crooked streets and interspersed with a heavy supply of taverns, shops, boarding houses, and brothels. It was also home to the majority of Sullward's working people, who lived in the hundreds of cramped apartments that filled these tall buildings.

I had no need to linger tonight, so I made my way quickly down Cargo Street, avoiding a handful of drunken mariners along the way and politely refusing the catcalls that erupted from a brothel. When I was passing an alleyway near the border of the neighborhood, I detected the slightest blur of a dark shape in my peripheral vision, and this caused me to stop and retrace my steps. I didn't often do this. Drunkards and vagrants of all sorts inhabited the alleys of Dockside, and I paid them no mind as long as they remained in their crevices. But, having just seen the Tergonian constables at the dock, and being quite a bit more paranoid than usual, I felt the need to check. When I walked back, I saw nothing, leading me to believe that I had simply spied a skittish pickpocket who thought better of targeting me.

Not long after that, I turned left, making my way towards a part of town with an even grittier character than Dockside. About a half mile north of the wharf lay a tight knot of streets and back alleys where the city's poorer merchants set up makeshift stalls to display their wares. Nicknamed "the Wags" for the incessant wagging of merchant tongues, the area was congested and noisy, rife with haggling, litter of all varieties, and petty crime. Even in the days of the Old Calendar, the Wags had been the poorest section of the city, possessing none of the grand stone buildings that were so prevalent in the Lower City, or even the character-rich, timber-framed dwellings of Dockside. Instead, this region was composed largely of ramshackle wattle and daub structures built by the residents themselves and clogged with an obstacle course of patchwork tables, crooked wagons, and makeshift tents. The sounds and smells of this squalid warren stirred feelings and memories in me that are almost too deep to describe.

Four decades earlier, I had been unceremoniously dumped here like a bag of garbage, left in the care of a horrid little orphanage at the end of a horrid little courtyard, where the stink of rotting vegetables and the beatings of the house matron were among my earliest memories. Since nobody at the orphanage gave a damn about records, and few if any of those people are alive today, the mystery of my blood parentage will likely never be solved. However, I have one clear parental memory that holds no mystery at all. I distinctly recall the scowling man who came and plucked me and several of my fellow ragamuffins from our filthy barracks and made every day thereafter a brutal exercise in survival. Under the so-called care of this man, I learned how to fight, I learned how to read and write, how to manage a skiff, how to estimate the price of a cargo, how to hide from authorities, how to ambush other scoundrels…basically, I learned every single skill I would ever need to be a successful Grell Runner. I even learned to hold my breath under the frigid waters of the

Grells for several minutes at a time, an invaluable skill that has literally meant the difference between life and death on several occasions. But those lessons, like most of my training, were far from pleasant, and I can clearly recall the distorted image of a skiff paddle hovering a few feet above me, ready to crack my skull were I to come up for air too early.

My Broodmates received similar attentions, and while we weren't all groomed for the same function in the Labyrinth, there was always some form of hell that could be brought to bear in the education process. Day by day, that scowling man transformed our haphazard propensities towards juvenile mischief into true practiced criminality. He was not a good man. He was certainly not a kind man. But, because of this man, I am for better or for worse all that I am today. It was to his residence that I was headed on this cool, moon-brightened evening.

The night market was fully up and running by the time I walked a highly crooked route along Scutter's Way, one of the few paths in the Wags that might legitimately be called a street. There were only a handful of streetlamps; however, the residents more than made up for this with an abundance of strung lanterns, creating shifting puddles of sallow light. While the night market lacked the yelling street hawkers and jostling bargain-hunters that made daytime passage difficult, the clouds of pungent smoke from the cooking vats had me aggressively fanning the air in front of my face. All manner of formerly living, questionably edible thing was transfixed by skewers here, stinking away over spitting flames. The lively crowd milled about, many of them eating as they walked.

While the fog was generally thickest in the neighborhoods closest to the harbor and river, there was a fair amount lingering in the Wags tonight, mixing with the smoke and making it hard to see into the surrounding alleys. As I passed one of these, I had the sense that somebody was watching from within, and I found myself stopping and retracing my steps for a second time. Yet, as before, when I stared down the warped little space, I saw nothing there. I pulled the brim of my hat a little lower, then resumed my winding path through mist and smoke towards my boyhood home.

The "Broodhouse," as it was popularly known, was a good deal larger and more substantial than the other buildings in the neighborhood. While thick wooden supports were visible in the walls, the bulk of the construction was made of grouted black stone, and this had served to keep the building in relatively good shape over the years. But damn if it wasn't the ugliest building in all of Sullward. I could see that now, having long ago exited the derelict world of the Wags where permanence could be mistaken for beauty. Sitting like a fat block in the constricted core of the neighborhood, there was absolutely zero embellishment to the black, mildewed exterior. Its sloped gray roof had no dormers or crenellations or decorative features of any kind, and even the two plaster chimneys set in the ridgeline were particularly squat and inelegant, looking more like stout support posts that had accidentally poked through the ceiling. The homespun whimsy that made many of the structures in the Wags both ludicrous and interesting was entirely missing in the Broodhouse. It was a place of practicality and survival, just like its owner.

I knocked on the door, and after a few moments I was greeted by one of Holod's young urchins. This pale-faced boy of about nine years must have known who I was, since he did not question my presence there and quickly ushered me inside. I had not visited the Broodhouse in a while, as my dealings with Holod were usually conducted in outside establishments—a circuit of taverns, ale gardens, and even a few outdoor spaces where we met to negotiate fees for the latest bid. Therefore, I found myself in a strange netherworld of disquiet and nostalgia as I was led through the old dark building where I had spent my youth. Time away from the Broodhouse always intensified my reactions to the musty heaviness of the stone interior, the cool dampness of the air. I had taken no more than five steps on the gray flagstone floor before a part of me became the same age as the boy leading me, and I could viscerally remember scampering through the stools and tables of the large common room, past the massive sooty fireplace where we tried to warm ourselves throughout the winter and occasionally hid in the summer months. As I passed the door to the kitchen, I noted that it was quiet and dark. However, I could powerfully recall the smell of watered-down stew and over-cooked vegetables and hear the clanging of the other children as they prepared a meal. I could also feel the sharp crack of Holod's belt across my back and face, a reward for stealing a piece of bread from the pantry.

The boy led me past the two dorm rooms all the way to the back section, which had always been off-limits when I was a child. I had, in my adulthood, visited Holod's private area, though not for several years, and I gazed around with interest at this hidden section of the Broodhouse. Holod Deadskiff was decidedly rich by Sullward standards, even by Derjian standards, yet there was an almost fanatical commitment to austerity in his personal suite that I had always found peculiar. I saw that the same worn books I had read as a child were arrayed on his bookshelves, and his simple desk was empty of papers or keepsakes. There was no artwork, though he had a large taxidermy Cod on one of the walls and a map of the city on another. The space smelled of pipe weed.

I approached one of the doors on the far wall and knocked.

I heard a gruff voice mutter from beyond, and I pushed my way inside, closing the door behind me. There was a large flame burning in the wood stove, and the room was stuffy, with pipe smoke drifting like a sheer tapestry near the ceiling joists and saturating the chamber with a fruity reek.

I wasn't surprised to see two figures inside. Flerra Tellian and I had already agreed that we would meet here, and since she had left the boathouse before me (not to mention she was one of the most maniacally impatient people I'd ever known), it only stood to reason that she'd get here first. She and Holod sat across from each other near the fireplace, and it was hard to say which of them looked like they were in a worse mood. Flerra appeared positively depleted, with little splotchy bags under her eyes and a general pastiness to her freckled features, which told me that her refreshing walk from the boathouse had done nothing to dispel her apprehension. Holod looked as he always did—severe, disapproving, and on the verge of calling one or the other of us an idiot.

He sat in a wooden armchair, close to the fire, in a posture that was oddly upright. His graying beard was well combed, and his thick eyebrows were a bit less chaotic than usual, as if he had combed them too. The characteristic angry intensity was in his face, though I thought I detected the slightest hint of unease. His eyes were jittering a bit, and I saw him look over at Flerra several times, as if concerned about what she might say or do now that I was in the room.

I walked slowly forward and stopped in the middle of the space, staring down at him. I didn't speak at first, so he prodded me.

"Go on, you pompous hoodlum. Ask your questions."

"Did you know?" I asked.

"Know what?" he snapped. "Speak in full sentences, you over-educated thug. I taught you the Derjian language, didn't I?"

Holod squinted up at me suspiciously. His brown eyes were narrowed, with an array of lines splintering over his broad cheeks, and his mustached upper lip was curled back ever so slightly in an expression that looked like a sneer. But it wasn't, as I knew all of Holod's expressions quite well. He was agitated.

"Did you know who the target was?"

He took a long drag on his pipe, then blew the smoke up at me in a thin, swirling jet.

"Of course I knew," he said. "Who the hell else would cost that much to kill?"

I was, for several seconds, genuinely speechless. I'm sure my face displayed the full spectrum of my shock and bafflement, for Holod almost laughed at the sight. But he twisted up his lips and controlled the impulse.

"You would knowingly send us against the Raving Blade?"

"I would. And did."

"He doesn't care, Vazeer!" Flerra cried from where she sat. "He's happy to sacrifice us both."

At this, Holod leapt upright out of his chair, his broad frame looming over Flerra Tellian.

"You little burglar rat!" he snarled at her. "I'll tell you about sacrifice! Sacrifice is paying half my silver to that damned orphanage thirty years ago, with no clear promise of a return. Sacrifice is sweeping up a bunch of discarded, lice-ridden street vermin, worthless rejects too malnourished to be press-ganged, too goddamned ugly to be whores. Sacrifice is feeding and educating you for a whole ten years, all of it without a single iron diven coming back to me. What do you think it cost me to have a Locksmith teach you the trade, you little scamp? And you, you pseudo-intellectual swine…what do you think it cost me to educate you? I hired those teachers and that goddamned tutor so that you could read ship manifests and appraise cargos, not so you could become some sort of delinquent librarian, holed up in that ridiculous art museum of yours. All of this cost me a fortune. So, in the bloody name of hell, don't talk to me about sacrifice, because sacrifice is all I've known for thirty years!"

Holod's face had grown increasingly flushed throughout his diatribe. The grimacing leather of his skin had developed furrows I didn't ever remember seeing—little gouges at the edges of his jaw, and a new spidery forehead wrinkle that shot straight into the silver tangle of his hair. Outbursts of this sort were not uncommon with Holod Deadskiff; however, I again had the distinct impression that something else was going on here. My safety as a child had often depended on learning to read the moods and impulses of this man, and I sensed a disturbance hiding just below his irate exterior.

I glanced over at Flerra, who had remained seated throughout the explosion, and she seemed sullen and rather chastened. Flerra Tellian did not submit easily to anybody, but often under the weight of Holod Deadskiff's derision, she became the morose little girl I had first met at the orphanage. That hurt expression affected me, and I had a strong impulse to spit back at my mentor and contract broker that he should thank the gods that Flerra did not turn out to be a prostitute. For a dozen reasons. But we could start with the fact that even before she became an independent Shadow Bidder, teenage Flerra Tellian had pilfered so much merchandise from the Harbormaster's warehouses on Holod's behalf that she had probably paid off all of our debts several times over. She alone had made the investment worthwhile.

But I said none of this, for Holod Deadskiff was not a man to be trifled with at such moments. Hulking there in front of me, his thick shoulders bulging, this belligerent former Grell Runner was capable of delivering a dirty, close-quarters blow that would leave me in no shape to conduct the Narrow Bid the following evening. It simply wasn't worth the risk.

So, I took another tact.

"I don't think Holod would send us to our deaths, Flerra," I said. "I'm sure he has a high degree of confidence in this contract."

Then I said to him, "Holod, maybe you could explain your reasoning to us."

One of Holod's thick brows arched slightly, as if he were observing a subtle change in the current of the Grells or assessing a gathering cloud pattern on the horizon. He studied my face carefully for a few seconds, then grunted.

"So, you're a stinking Masque now too? Since when did you learn to be reasonable?"

"At this point I don't have a choice."

Holod muttered something I couldn't quite make out, then gestured for me to sit down in one of the two empty armchairs, and soon we were all seated together around the tea table. Flerra's mood didn't seem much improved, but there was the slightest hint of anticipation on her narrow features.

"No, Tellian," Holod said to her, "I'm not sacrificing you for this bid. Neither of you. You're going to live…all of you will probably live, and I already told you why."

"But you're only guessing," Flerra shot back.

"It's a damned well-informed guess, you pilfering tart!" Holod snapped, and I could see instantly that we were in danger of another outburst, so I jumped in.

"Why don't you tell me, Holod. What's this well-informed guess you've made?"

It took Holod a moment to compose himself, but he managed to lay his theory out succinctly.

"After the Sketcher gave me the gist of the bid, I knew that only one man in the entire Labyrinth would have put out that particular contract. And since I was certain that he was the proffer, I knew the plan would be a good one…a great plan, in fact, and there will be no reason for him to tie up loose ends afterwards. Sherdane doesn't want to lose his top Grell Runner, and Sullward's finest Locksmith, and the best Contract Blade…all on this one bid. He intends for you to live."

I sat there a moment and let it sink in. It wasn't as if the thought never crossed my mind, but, like Flerra, I had my doubts.

"I'm told that there isn't a single Underlord in all the Labyrinth who likes Gueritus. They say he is by far the most despised figure in the hierarchy. Why couldn't it be his own vassals who turned on him? How do you know we weren't hired by a patchwork alliance of various resentful parties?"

"Never!" Holod spat. "They would never do this without authorization. The Raving Blade is his chief vassal. This is too bold a move to make without the High Lord being directly involved."

This, I had to admit, had some logic to it. Holod Deadskiff knew a great deal more about Underlord politics than I ever would, and he had a good instinct for these things, which started to give me some optimism. We would be in far better shape if we were taking this action on behalf of the most powerful man in all of Sullward. Truly, the most powerful criminal figure anywhere in the Tergonian Empire.

High Lord Beranardos Sherdane was not a terrifying bogeyman like his chief vassal, Gueritus. He was, in many ways, our true sovereign, since few Sullwardians gave a damn about the government in far-off Tergon. Unlike the Raving Blade, Sherdane was sometimes seen in public. He was a striking figure physically, and also a man of stunning vision, for it was he who had created the ingenious system in which I now worked. It was under Sherdane's rule that the code of the Shadow Bidder was first implemented to stave off an unrelenting crackdown by the previous Emperor—an aggressive prosecutorial campaign that had placed the prior High Lord's neck on the chopping block and that pushed the Labyrinth to the brink of dissolution. Sherdane was the one who elevated the hitherto marginal role of the contract operative into an indispensable piece of the Sullward puzzle. He demanded the use of unaffiliated men and women to accomplish those tasks that most endangered Sullward's elite, the jobs that readily linked the Underlords to the inconceivably vast fortune of stolen merchandise that flowed through their city each year. Proof of the plan's success was now evident in almost four straight decades of unparalleled abundance and immunity for the Underlords.

While Sherdane was certainly a ruthless individual, capable of inflicting terrible retribution on anyone who opposed him, he was also known to be levelheaded and meticulous in his planning. And, more than any of his fellow Underlords, he respected and appreciated the Shadow Bidders. If Holod was right, and the High Lord really was the proffer for this contract, then the chances were good that we were not being sent into a death trap.

"Did Flerra tell you about the letter?" I asked.

"She did."

"What does it say about our target?"

"It says that if the sick bastard was a menace before, he now deserves to die a hundred times over. I'm impressed by the High Lord's patience and cunning on this revenge."

On a certain level, I had to agree. Every element of Sullward's criminal enterprise was founded on a policy of secrecy and evasion, of appearing disorganized and never falling into the costly pitfall of cocksurety that kept the lifespans of lesser criminals in lesser cities relatively short. The current High Lord of Hell's Labyrinth had gone to great lengths to enforce his policy of "Ruthless Caution," a phrase he had coined years ago and a principle that, like the ruler himself, had now dominated Sullward for almost four decades.

Among the chief governing tenets of this policy was a rule that nobody, not even the High Lord himself, would dare to break. Simply stated: we were never to forget that the world effectively ended outside of Sullward Harbor. In the unlikely event that any of us passed beyond the city's borders, then we walked there as civilians, with no affiliation of any kind to the Underlords. Even the Underlords themselves were strictly forbidden from extending their criminal reach into the rest of the Empire. This bore exception only when Finishers needed to be hired to track down other denizens of the Labyrinth—such as ourselves, for instance, if any of us were to decide to break the contract and run without performing the deed. Other than that one deviation, the High Lord adamantly forbade any exertion of power or criminal influence over the broader populace beyond the dark borders of our rigorously guarded world. This, more than anything else, kept the Emperor out of our affairs.

Therefore, it was truly a shocking revelation to learn that Count Ulan Gueritus had actually gone out and blackmailed a member of one of the Empire's most distinguished political families. He had targeted the Countess Shaeyin of House Odel, daughter of Archduke Vodun III of Odel, Chief Legate to the Emperor himself.

This, in itself, was already a horrific breach of the code, yet true to form, Count Ulan Gueritus had found a way to push his exploits beyond the borders of madness itself. The Sketcher had showed us a copy of a letter from the victim to her tormentor, which had been intercepted, carefully transcribed, then allowed to continue on its way. It read:

I have agreed to your terms and am already making preparations to fulfill them. I will give myself to you for a single night and no more, and for this favor I expect you to honor your side of the agreement, thereby freeing me from this painful circumstance and ensuring that you will never again attempt to exert control over my life. I trust you to be a man of your word in this matter.

Expect my arrival in Sullward on or shortly after the date of Twenty-Eight Dekharven. I shall meet your Legate at the three-sided bay, which you described in your letter, though I will arrive there by my own means and insist on coming after dark. I fear discredit to my family's name a great deal more than I fear harm to my own person, which, as you so deviously know, is the only reason I have agreed to this.

Let this be the end of it!

Shaeyin of House Odel

After reading this letter that evening, I was, I confess, possessed with an unsettling and rather baffling case of moral outrage. As far as I could tell, this was a first for me. Understand, it had nothing to do with the idea of this grotesque, ignoble, and ultimately faux count going out and terrorizing a real countess for his own pleasure, nor did it have anything to do with protecting the reputable House of Odel. Instead, it had everything to do with protecting Sullward.

It would take so little to destroy us, you see. Just a single hint of this scheme to one of Sullward's long list of political enemies, then an alert to Chief Legate Vodun Odel, and before you knew it, we would be watching an armada of Tergonian galleons sailing into Sullward Harbor carrying papers effectively stating that enough was finally enough. The remote city of Sullward had been a protectorate of the Tergonian Empire for the last two hundred years, not an actual possession. And while a miniscule garrison of imperial soldiers and less than a dozen constables were stationed in our city, our protectorate status allowed our governor and state senate large measures of autonomy in matters of law enforcement. Tergonian constables, for instance, were only permitted to examine ship manifests and inspect cargos as they came off the ships that docked in our harbor; however, they were not allowed to indiscriminately board those same vessels. Therefore, the only chance the constables had of seizing the illegal merchandise was to catch men like me in the act of sneaking on and off those ships in the dead of the night. Or, as was more often their intention, to nab me as I ferried those goods up the dark, misty Grells, to the secret drop sites that lay deep in the heart of the Lower City. This is what our protectorate status bought us. This is what would be lost if Ulan Gueritus's perverse blackmail were to be discovered by outside forces. No wonder the High Lord was commissioning this execution.

Even if I chose to retire in two days' time, I did not want to see this happen to our city. I did not want Sullward to become a mere imperial possession, or even a client state, which would, I was absolutely certain, turn us into a characterless military outpost. I had dreams for this city, crazy, wonderful, asinine dreams, and while continuing to believe in them bordered on lunacy, I did not want to be robbed of this private fantasy.

However, at this moment, that was not my primary concern. What I really wanted to know from Holod Deadskiff was his opinion about the second part of what we had learned.

"What about the Sketcher's plan, Holod?" I asked. "What do you think of it?"

"The plan?" he said, taking a long drag on his pipe, then releasing it slowly. "I think the plan is a goddamned work of genius. It only confirms my confidence."

"I stinking hate it!" Flerra suddenly shrieked. "I'm not dressing up like a maid. I'm no good at play-acting. I'm not the right one for this bid!"

"You're perfect for the bid, girl!" Holod snapped back. "You're both perfect, and the Sketcher knew it."

"He chose well," I conceded. "But you feel confident it will work?"

"Of course it will work."

Holod nodded a few times affirmatively, as if agreeing with himself, and then his grizzled hands came forward and beat the tea table twice for emphasis.

"It will work," he repeated. "It will work…if your Masque does her part. Does she seem talented, this foreign woman?"

I gave it a moment's thought, then shrugged. I wasn't sure how to answer that, so Holod decided to answer for me.

"She must be. She must be, or else Sherdane's Sketcher

wouldn't have chosen her. If she can become Shaeyin Odel, even for a few minutes, then the rest of it will fall into place."

Perhaps you are starting to get the plan. Possibly you are realizing that our strategy was not the most original in the long, gruesome history of subterfuge. It was going to rely on a fairly convincing act of masquerade by Nascinthé of Levell. Yet that didn't make it any less clever and, to my initial surface-level estimate, any less likely to succeed. In fact, barring a poorly timed appearance by the real Shaeyin Odel, our Finisher was likely to get remarkably close to a target whose paranoid defenses were legendary. And truly, we did not expect the real Countess to be on time, for this had been a particularly difficult autumn for shipping, with virtually every arriving captain complaining about foul weather delays and stubborn fog banks that had made navigation a nightmare. I had a long list of worries about this bid, but that wasn't one of them.

Flerra, it seemed, had an even longer list than mine.

"It's not just her, Holod," said Flerra. "We all have to be Masques on this bid. Maybe the foreign girl can act, but what about me? What about the rest of us? I was bloody trained to pick locks!"

"You're going to pick locks, Flerra," I said. If you can't get us inside, then the bid is a bust, and we're all probably dead. We've been over it a dozen times already."

And we had. We had spent hours discussing it earlier. The Sketcher had laid out the probable scenarios, and the group of us had largely agreed. Now Holod concurred, and this all painted a reasonably clear picture of what was likely to unfold in two nights' time.

The overwhelming belief was that Ulan Gueritus would wish to conduct his tryst in a private location, to minimize the number of parties who might bear witness to this dreadful breach of the

Labyrinth code. I was well acquainted with the three-sided bay mentioned in the Countess's letter, and it was located in a portion of the Lower City surrounded by exceptionally tall buildings. My guess was that the Raving Blade had taken possession of one of these and had turned it into a place where he could feel both secure and private as he enjoyed his prize. Our arriving party was almost certain to be met by the minimal number of the Count's retainers—probably just the Legate mentioned in the letter and a few highly trusted bodyguards, but no one else. The moment Gueritus brought his common soldiers into the picture, every last one of them became a liability. Were such men to report what they had seen to the High Lord, they would not be viewed as traitors to their own lord, but as heroes of the Labyrinth, and this was the detail that gave us our greatest confidence of success.

Col and I would eventually be recognized for what we were; we knew that going in. But we had a good explanation for this. The story went like this:

Shaeyin's steward, played by Radrin Blackstar, would purportedly have gone straight to the Dockside neighborhood upon arrival in Sullward and there made inquiries regarding a tough and reliable Labyrinth guide who could bring him and a few others into the dangerous Lower City. It was entirely plausible that such inquiries would have led him to the notorious Coljin Helmgrinder, who was a highly visible presence in the taverns of Dockside. In fact, Col was one of a handful of Shadow Bidders who did not employ a contract broker—he simply made it easy for the Sketchers and other interested parties to find him, and thereby saved himself the fifteen percent broker's commission.

Once hired, Col would have insisted to the steward that the best way to reach the Three Bay, as it was called by the few who knew of it, was to paddle there in a skiff. And the best operative to help in this regard was none other than yours truly. Hence, the two of us were hired by the Countess's party to bring the group to the rendezvous point. It was fairly believable.

While the Countess would not insist on bringing Col and me into Gueritus's secure locale, she would at least demand that we be allowed to wait outside for her return. As for the three other Shadow Bidders in the group, they were not recognizable figures to the Underlords' retainers, so their cover stories were likely to be believed. Nascinthé would leave her steward and her lady's maid (played very reluctantly by Flerra Tellian) outside with the Shadow Bidders and simply insist on bringing her personal bodyguard, Fe Gesbon, with her inside the building. While none of us imagined that Gesbon would be permitted into the private chambers where Gueritus planned on satisfying his desires, he would at least have time to ascertain and memorize the layout of the building. He was also Nascinthé's only line of defense once the two of them were alone with Gueritus and his handful of staff.

At that point, much of the success or failure of the bid would fall on the knotted little shoulders of Flerra Tellian. Flerra needed to get the door to the building open, then eventually the door to Gueritus's restricted chambers, and she would need to do all of this in record time. Once Col and I were inside, we could neutralize whatever guards were about, and once Radrin was inside the bed chamber, he could eliminate the target.

Thus, we had our plan. And while I'll admit it was a good idea in concept, I couldn't help feeling that there were far too many things that could go wrong.

"Gueritus is not going to be happy when he sees Shadow Bidders," I said after we had bandied the details around one more time. "Why should he trust us to keep our mouths shut?"

Holod grunted and rubbed his bearded jaw for a moment.

"He won't like it," he finally said. "But it shouldn't be a complete surprise to him. How else would the Countess get to the Three Bay? Shadow Bidders are a hell of a lot more trustworthy than Underlord soldiers."

I was not entirely assuaged.

"The whole thing seems too risky," I said. "Too risky for *him*. Why conduct this exploit in Sullward at all? Why not some other town? A remote manor house somewhere? He's really tempting fate here. Does that sound like the Raving Blade to you?"

Again, Holod grunted, and this time he leaned back in his chair and stroked the thick column of his neck. He truly did appear to be thinking.

"I can't really say what 'sounds like the Raving Blade,' Scuff. He's a damned mystery to me, and everybody else in the Labyrinth."

It was unusual for Holod to call me by my childhood nickname. "Scuff" was short for scuffle, and Holod only hauled it out when he was either trying to be exceptionally reasonable or when his guard came down, exposing some sort of rare vulnerability. Usually, I was appreciative of these moments, but not today. Today I wanted him to be his dismissive, stubborn, pathologically certain self.

"I'm only assuming," Holod continued thoughtfully, "that this is some sort of chauvinist power play for him, a way to degrade and humiliate the woman—make her crawl into his dirty world on her hands and knees."

This, at least, struck a chord of truth. While the Empire's ruling class was technically patriarchal in structure, there had been many powerful female rulers over time, and women held positions of great prominence in the Tergonian Court. But this was not true among the Underlords, who were a last holdout of male dominance. Despite his assorted nasty qualities, Holod Deadskiff had always rejected this bigotry in his own dealings. While he steered the Brood girls towards trades that favored intelligence, artistry, and finesse over brute strength, he insisted that such qualities were far more precious and lucrative than what the boys generally brought to bear. Growing up under his tutelage, I was reminded regularly that the girls were going to turn out better, which, for the most part, they had.

"I heard them say Gueritus is a split-head," Flerra said, leaning forward and gripping the edge of the table with the spindly pallor of her fingers. "That he has two personalities, maybe more."

Instead of brushing this aside with some derisive comment, Holod looked over at Flerra with what could only be interpreted as thoughtful consideration. His briny cheeks scrunched further, and his lips compressed into something resembling sadness, giving him a much softer look than I had seen in years. He did not take his eyes off of Flerra for several seconds, and I again found his behavior strange and unnerving.

"Could be, girl. Could be," he muttered. "I've heard such tales myself, and a dozen other things that make the picture a muddle. I've met several of the Underlords in my day, but not this one. Never even seen him."

"Who has?" I asked. "Do you know anybody who can describe what this bastard looks like? Otherwise, how do we know who to kill?"

At this, a touch of the old Holod Deadskiff returned.

"Doesn't matter what he looks like, fool. Just kill the grunting pig that's screwing the Countess."

We continued to discuss details of the plan until I heard the faint droning of the Midnight Bell, at which point Flerra felt the need to go home to sleep, and I wanted to get along to my next errand. We all stood, and Holod walked us to the door of his chamber. Flerra exited first, and as I was about to step out, I felt my mentor's fierce grip on the collar of my cloak. He yanked me back into the room and spun me around, then hooked his fingers down the top of my chest cuirass and pulled my face within inches of his. I instantly smelled his stale breath and the musky Deadskiff odor that I had known all my life. His squinted brown eyes were fierce and almost possessed in that moment.

"Now you listen to me, Scuff," he hissed quietly under his breath. "If this thing goes bad…if it doesn't work out…"

"Why shouldn't it work out, Holod?" I said in an equally quiet voice.

"I'm just saying *if*, Scuff, if it doesn't work out…"

"Are you doubtful, Holod?"

"Shut up, you stinking whore's son, and listen to me! For once, just listen."

Holod craned around to make sure that Flerra had continued on her way through the next room, and then he leaned in so close that he was literally breathing into my ear.

"If it goes bad, Scuff, you don't worry about the others. Your friend Helmgrinder can take care of himself. Ditch the Line Man and the Finisher. And don't get blinded by a pretty set of tits, you understand? Flerra tells me you ogled that foreign Masque like she was the second coming of Giradera of Azmoul! Don't get stupid to all that, you hear me, Scuff?"

I nodded, scraping my ear against Holod's mustache.

"You just focus on one and only one thing," Holod continued, and now he pulled his face back a little so that he was staring me directly in the eyes.

"Whatever happens, no matter how bad it goes," he said, his eyes suddenly glistening with emotion, "you get our little Flerra out of there! You understand me, Scuff? You bring her home to me. No matter what happens, you bring her home."

4

GHOSTS

I must admit, I'm not a good Shadow Bidder.

It isn't that I'm deficient at my job. In fact, I perform my particular contracted function better than anybody else in the entire Labyrinth. I am better acquainted with the merchandise that comes into our docks than most of the other Grell Runners, often able to identify, for instance, the exact craftsman who designed a custom piece of jewelry or, barring that, certainly the region where it was created. And don't even get me started about the artwork. I know all of it and can authenticate the stolen artifacts and appraise them with far greater skill than any of my cohorts. I am also better at running the Grells than the rest of them combined, with an almost preternatural ability to get through scrapes out there in the misty darkness. Add to all of this the impressive network of informants and spies that I have carefully cultivated over the years, and you can see that I have left no stone unturned when it comes to my job. Therefore, I'll acknowledge that I am a very, very good Grell Runner. But I am not a good Shadow Bidder.

Leaving the Broodhouse that night, I was uncomfortably present to that reality, feeling it as a strange self-pitying malaise that spread outward from my chest and into the rest of my body.

As I made my way through the thinning crowd on Scutter's Way, weaving past the makeshift tables and greasy carts, my mind was elsewhere.

I turned left onto a small shut between buildings that had more or less existed since I was a child. The residents of the Wags engaged in an almost constant campaign of repair and renovation to their humble dwellings, which had the effect of altering the landscape of narrow streets and alleyways on a shockingly regular basis. Every time I visited the Wags, I noted that some familiar pass-through had either expanded or contracted or changed shape entirely. On occasion, a path that had once existed no longer existed, and on other occasions the opposite was true. The municipal government took no note of these changes, for nobody had ever bothered to diagram the area in the first place (city maps simply showed a gray block with a single squiggly line through it to represent the Wags). I had just moved off of that squiggly line, but I didn't need a map to find my way here, which was fortunate, for my thoughts were still lost in my final discussion with Holod Deadskiff.

Everything about that last encounter was disturbing, and were I truly possessed of a good Shadow Bidder's mind, the part that should have concerned me most was my own safety. After all, there was no question that Holod was harboring serious doubts about the Narrow Bid. I'm certain that by the time Flerra and I had sketched the whole elaborate thing for him, he was wondering what the hell he had gotten us into. Perhaps he knew or understood things about the plan, about the players involved, about the target himself, that he was too nervous or horrified to share. But that wasn't the thing that gripped my thoughts as I threaded my way through the twisted Wags. I was consumed by far pettier material.

It was okay that Holod Deadskiff had never understood me. I accepted that he found my obsession with books and artwork and fine clothing a thing of comical idiocy. I also accepted his resistance to my fantasies of Sullward revival, given that he was a man utterly committed to our city as a run-down criminal purgatory where figures such as himself could thrive. An individual who was incapable of empathizing with anyone other than himself could not be expected to appreciate the finer points in another, even if that other person was, for all intents and purposes, his adopted son.

However, when I saw the terrified, beseeching look in his watery eyes that evening, when I realized that he was, in fact, capable of caring deeply, caring with every last crooked fiber in his crooked being, it did beg a most basic question: why was it Flerra he treasured, and not me?

I slipped down a series of ever twistier little passageways, hooking right, then left, then right again. While these improvised lanes were dark, they weren't pitch black, for light spilled out of surrounding dwellings via windows, open doorways, and gaping cracks in the daub. More than once I needed to duck below protrusions in the exterior walls. Some of these were crude bay windows, while others were mere extensions to the space inside—a highly inconvenient contrivance that the resident had framed out in rough timber and sloppily daubed in plaster. These homespun carpenters at least had the decency to leave a small, dank tunnel below, so that stooping pedestrians could continue on their way.

There were still a few figures moving about in the crooked warrens at this hour, and several times I came face-to-face with people who had to back up to let me through. At one point, a rather hostile-looking man in a leather apron tried to get me to retreat, but then I lifted the brim of my hat and he quickly, and rather apologetically, scurried back the way he had come. Even after all these years, I was still a recognizable figure in this neighborhood.

At last, I pushed through into a section of the maze where a few dull beams of moonlight filtered down through mist and poorly vented smoke from the nearby houses. There was a fair amount of space in this area, and while calling it a yard was a stretch, it was one of only a handful of spots in the Wags that had perennially remained vacant. The smells from the Scutter's Way frying vats were still present here, along with the composite smoke from the neighboring chimneys, but I could not help but detect another smell too. Terrible as it is to say, this was the very first odor that I consciously registered in this life. It was the sweet, rancid stink of rotting vegetables.

I slowly entered the vacant lot, absorbing the familiar details. I had not been back here in years, and while there were certainly small changes to the grimy wooden walls that defined this triangular area, much of it had remained the same. The first and most obvious thing was the incongruent abundance of plant life—weeds and vines, bushes, and even a few stunted trees growing anywhere they could get a foothold, which was pretty much everywhere, for this little improvised park was a dumping ground for the produce merchants from Scutter's Way. The odd effect of this was generations of composted material that allowed every manner of inadvertent vegetation to take root. Creepers twisted like green and red worms up the walls, and thorny bushes had entirely consumed the three main corners of the space. The center of the yard was dominated by poison ivy and thistle, along with errant cabbages, corn stalks, onion plants, and a bunch of non-producing fruit trees. The Orphan Grove it was named, and some of my first memories as a child were of crawling through this jungle of discarded flora, hiding in the ragweed and thorns.

There were a few clearly worn trails, and one of these led straight to the back, where an old ruin squatted in the rank stillness. I made my way there, avoiding thorn bushes and stepping over rotting melons. Like the Broodhouse, this was one of the rare buildings in the Wags that had incorporated some stone into its construction, though this had not protected it from the ravages of time. Only three of the four timber-framed stone walls were standing, and it was clear from the gaping holes in what remained that neighborhood residents had carted off many of the most transportable blocks for their own use. Two of the original joists still ran across the top, and it appeared that vagrants had nailed a haphazard patchwork of boards to these supports, creating the semblance of a roof. Vines grew on virtually every square inch of this decomposing carcass.

The North Derjian Children's Compassionate Sanctuary was the official name. There had been a sign once over the front door, but it was long gone now, as was the wall where it hung. Here, at last, I reaffirmed the answer to my self-pitying question.

Holod Deadskiff had plucked me and Flerra and eight other discarded wastrels from this forlorn place and, in return for his benevolent kidnapping, he had really only asked a few things of us: that we do absolutely everything he told us to do, learn everything he instructed us to learn, and ultimately become everything he demanded we become. Flerra did that. In addition to being Sullward's finest Locksmith, she spent her time and money between bids exactly where she was supposed to—on alcohol and narcotics, on prostitutes (female, if my memory served me) and gambling, just like most of the other Shadow Bidders. The rest of the money she squirreled away, so that she could invest it one day in some enterprise that would sustain her in her older years. This was what Holod had taught us, for it was what he himself had done. But somehow, I failed at all of these lessons. I found little interest in typical Shadow Bidder pastimes, and instead of placing my money in the Sullward Civilian Vaults, I had invested every last iron diven into that pretty art museum of mine, filled to the brim with things that I would never sell.

So, no, I could not become what Holod Deadskiff wanted me to become or, more accurately, I became too many other things at the same time—grandiose, impractical things—which rebuked him to his core. Holod had tromped across this reeking Orphan Grove thirty years ago with the intention of creating the best Shadow Bidders the Labyrinth had ever known. He was pleased with some of his creations. Others, less so.

Ahead of me I heard a faint, gurgling moan emerging from the dim opening that had once been the front wall of the orphanage. There was at least one light source pulsing inside, and I could tell that something was moving slowly behind those tangled creepers, just out of the path of the dingy moonlight. Another sound followed, this one a high-pitched wheeze, which eventually transformed into a shrill giggle. I drew a dirk from my belt and shifted forward to the entrance, parting the vines with the blade. I had come to this old, haunted crypt tonight for a reason, for two reasons really, and neither had to do with reminiscence or melancholy introspection. There was actual business to be done in this place.

I stepped inside, crossing a threshold of crumbled stones and broken glass, keeping the blade out in front of me the whole time, as the sorry residents of this place were well beyond recognizing my face. There was a small campfire in the middle, and its radiance was sufficient to reveal the frail, malformed shapes— some lying on the ground, others twitching and slithering about amidst the rubble.

Like many of the old ruins in this city, the North Derjian Children's Compassionate Sanctuary had become a makeshift shelter for the crippled and insane. These poor wretches were too infirm to engage in crime, and their only means of sustenance was begging and scavenging. I jingled my purse, and that promising timbre drew all eyes to me instantly.

There were nine of them, at least that I could see in the immediate vicinity of the front opening. The interior walls had long ago decayed into rotted heaps, and when I gazed back into the farthest recesses, I did not see any human figures there—just piles of debris and perhaps a few mean possessions. I began to scan the desolate faces, searching.

The closest to me was an old man who was propping himself upright on a set of mismatched poles that he had roped together to create an awkward tripod. He was badly stooped, and when he heard the jingling of my purse, he lurched forward, scraping his tripod through the rubble, his extended hand shaking terribly. Just to the right of him, a gibbering woman crawled on the ground, dragging her withered legs behind her. I couldn't tell what age she was, but I noted that there were some signs of youth in that twitching face, which made the sight all the more disturbing. I looked beyond these two and saw several who were missing limbs. Others were whole of body, but the wild look in their eyes told a tale of deep, impenetrable madness. Still, I kept searching, looking for that one hopeless face that could help me. And then I saw it.

He was sitting silently in the back of the group, leaning up against a pile of filthy sacks. He appeared to be a man in his late fifties, with thinning silver-brown hair that hung around his face like brittle fibers. He was wrapped in a cloak, and while he did appear to be staring at me, there seemed to be something wrong with his eyes, which, even in that dim lighting, were a little too dark and lifeless. It was the thing that lay just above those eyes, however, that grabbed my attention. Faintly visible between the thin strands of his hair, I saw a branded symbol on his forehead with two wicked blades that coiled and interlocked with each other like a pair of coupling serpents. The emblem seemed to radiate at me like a dirty beacon in the gloom.

I sheathed my weapon, then reached into my purse and scooped out three copper poltets, clinking them noisily in the process. I tossed them each into a different area of the room, where they chimed in the dirt. The effect was immediate, as six of the sad creatures went lunging on a mad hunt for the coins. The one place I did not throw the poltets was in the vicinity of the man with the brand, and once the way was clear, I quickly approached him.

When the man looked up at me, I was greeted with the terrible sight of two black holes where his eyes had been. Those dark, empty sockets were set in a deeply worn face that had once been, it seemed to me, rather dignified, with strong, elevated cheekbones and a square jaw. I stared down at him for a moment, waiting to see if he would speak, waiting to see if he would acknowledge the odd presence of a stranger coming to visit this dreadful place. He did not.

"You, man," I said quietly, kicking the decrepit bottom of his shoe with my boot. "Can you recognize the feel of a silver tolgen?"

For a moment the man simply gawked up at me sightlessly, but eventually he made a slight nod.

I reached into my purse and fished out one of the silver coins, and then I squatted down and placed it into his dirty palm. I spoke to him in a whisper.

"Another will follow if you do one simple thing for me. All you have to do is tell me about the man who put that brand on your forehead. Can you do that?"

More sightless gawking. Then, slowly, ever so slowly, his mouth cracked open, the lips splitting apart as if he were breaking a seal or unlocking an old tomb. His mouth widened into a gaping black hole, and from that hole emerged a low, guttural groaning, which then transformed into a phlegmy warble, all of it originating from the very back of his throat. Something actually drew me to stare inside that gaping mouth, and after a moment I understood what I was seeing, or rather, what I was not seeing and should have. The man had no tongue.

I snarled out a low curse under my breath.

"Great sir," said a shaky voice at my right shoulder. "He can't talk none at all. Can't see, can't talk, can't do much…but think, I s'pose. And even the thinking ain't quite right no more."

I turned to see one of the men who had not lunged for the copper poltets. He was quite old, with long straggly white hair and skeletally thin arms, but he seemed otherwise able of body. There also appeared to be the glint of sanity in his eyes.

"You're telling me that I'm trying to talk to a blind, dumb half-wit, is that right?" I said.

"Partial true, I s'pose," the old man replied. "But his wit's more than half. Just that he visions things all like a dream. In the end I understand it, most of it."

"He communicates with you?"

"Aye, though it's hard. But he gets his point across, and I translate. Don't know what he'll do once I'm gone, 'cause none of the others understands his signals. And they don't care to try."

"Do you know this man's story?"

"Precious little," the old man replied. "Don't even know his name, since that ain't the sort of thing I can understand with his signals. I just call him 'Brand.' I'm pretty sure he don't know letters, and I can't read, so we can't talk that way. But over time he makes these different signals to me, and I sing out what I think it means. He nods or shakes his head, and now he's got this way to talk to me. He's a good man, Brand. Terrible thing what was done to him."

The others in the space had started to crowd around, and I shooed them away. When they failed to back off sufficiently, I promised that there would be more poltets if they gave me some room, which they did. In fact, I kept waving and waving them back until they were out of easy earshot.

"What is your name, old man?" I asked once we had a little privacy.

"Pippen," he replied, "though here they call me Pip."

"Okay, Pippen, I'll cut you in on the deal I offered Brand. A tolgen for each of you if you can be his translator. I've got a bunch of questions to ask him, and you need to get the best answer possible. Can you do that?"

"Indeed, sir! That I can do."

"And keep your voice down with the answers, understood?"

He nodded dutifully.

I turned back to Brand and again tapped his shoe.

"Brand," I said, "describe the man who scalded that mark into your brow."

For a few moments, Brand was motionless. His mouth had closed again, but there was a slight hint of expectancy in his worn features, as if he were looking forward to this game of questions and answers. Finally, he raised his hands up before him and made a series of quick gestures. I saw his fingers go into a triangle, then his palms were open and upright, then he pointed to his own forehead, and then his hands moved fluidly through a bunch of motions that I couldn't begin to identify. Pippen, however, seemed to grasp the essence of what was being said, though he asked Brand to repeat one gesture.

"I think he's saying that the one who did this to him was a terrible demon. But noble. A demon and a nobleman both, I think."

"What about a description?" I asked. "What does he look like, this noble demon?"

Brand again made his symbols, and Pippen again tried his best to translate.

"A mad swordsman, I think," said Pippen. "Or maybe a mad sword, which don't really make no sense."

I squatted down again and leaned in close to Brand's ear.

"The Raving Blade?" I asked too quietly for even Pippen to hear.

At the mention of this name, Brand's lips suddenly opened. Not a slow, hesitant parting, but rather a snapping yawn, like the mouth of a brook trout. And the warble was back, this time of a higher pitch and resounding like the outlandish notes of some exotic instrument. He began to flap his arms, and it took me a moment to realize that Brand was also making exaggerated gestures as he flailed, so I backed off to allow Pippen to read the peculiar symbols.

"Whoa, whoa there, Brand!" he said. "Slow down, will ya? Can't read all of this at once."

"What is he saying?"

"I think," said Pippen, "I think he's trying to say what kind of demon this 'mad sword' really is."

I put a finger to my lips, then gestured for him to go on translating.

"He says…he says the terrible, noble demon lives in a hole," Pippen continued quietly. "A dreadful hole…but, oh, this is strange. Also a beautiful hole. Terrible, but filled with beauty… with jewels and splendors, I think. And the noble demon is also a madman. He wears something…he wears two things. Slow down, Brand! I can't understand this thing you keep saying."

Pippen was leaning in, and his face had become intense with the exchange. I had the sense that these strange dialogues with Brand were meaningful to him, perhaps giving him a sense of purpose in this otherwise hopeless place. He appeared committed to getting the words right.

"Ah, okay, now I see," said Pippen. "The madman wears two faces. Yes, he wears two—one is the noble face. One is the demon face. And it were the demon face that ruined our friend Brand, here. Cut out his tongue and plucked out his eyes. The demon did that. But it were the noble face that lured him in. That's it, ain't it, Brand?"

Brand made a series of screeching noises, then he nodded his head several times, and finally, he appeared to relax. His mouth closed and his hands stopped flapping, while Pippen smiled broadly, seeming tremendously pleased with himself.

"This is very nice…that you two are communicating so beautifully," I said, making no effort to disguise my annoyance, "but this doesn't help me much. What does this demon look like? Can't you give me a description?"

"Descriptions are hard," Pippen said. "He might say such things as the man has long hair or a beard an such…but those things can change. And the lasting things, like colors…he's no good with colors."

"Maybe I can help you, sir!" I heard a croaking voice from behind. "I knows everything. If ya give me some coin, I'll tell ya whatever it is ya wants to know."

"Me too! I know it too!" came another voice.

I glanced over my shoulder, and the old man with the tripod and a woman with a blighted discoloration all over her face had come forward a few paces. Behind them, others were starting to shuffle in our direction, evidently sensing the opportunity that lay in my game of questions and answers.

"Very helpful of you all," I said, projecting my voice a bit. "But I seek an old friend who is a foreigner and is unknown to all but a few in this city. I was told that this man alone knows him, and he does. I was just having a little trouble understanding which land my friend sailed to. I'll get it eventually. Now, please back off and give me room, or else none of you will get those poltets I promised."

There was some muttering, but eventually they retreated to their various corners and turned away. Even if these infirm creatures managed to pick up bits of my conversation, there was little chance that they would understand what I was truly asking, and even less chance that they would be able to convey the information to the appropriate parties in the next twenty-four hours. Still, it paid to be cautious.

"Okay," I murmured under my breath. "This is your last chance to earn that tolgen. Give me something I can use. Describe the demon to me."

The same pantomime ensued, with Brand making gestures and Pippen earnestly attempting to translate. At last, Pippen spoke.

"The noble demon is not tall, not broad neither. But he is fast…fast like a cat. And he speaks clever words. His words are clever, and they contain…traps. His words are clever traps. Yes, I think that's it."

"What color are his eyes? What color is his hair?" I snapped. "Is his nose big or small? For hell's sake, can he not remember the look of the bastard who maimed him?"

Pippen leaned in and tried to coax Brand to give this information, but he clearly wasn't happy with the result.

"I'll be honest with you, sir," Pippen said softly. "Brand can't recall all of that. I don't want to spin ya false, on account of you being a serious sort. I do think what I said already is about the long and short of it. Any more beyond that an I got my own doubts about how much he recalls."

I stood fully upright and straightened my clothes. I brushed my hands over the fabric a number of times, trying, unsuccessfully, to clear away the stink and disappointment.

"Okay, so it goes," I said to the two of them. "At least now I know I'm looking for a quick, two-faced demon who lives in a pretty hole and speaks in traps. I'll also bear in mind that he's medium-sized, and at least partially insane."

"I'm sorry, sir, if ya didn't find what ya hoped here," Pippen replied with some obvious dejection.

"I still might," I replied, remembering the second errand I had come here to accomplish. "And it's also possible some of what Brand said will prove useful. I need to sort it out a bit. Time will tell."

Then I leaned in close to Pippen and lowered my voice even further.

"Listen, Pippen, I'm sure you didn't understand much of what you just heard, but it's still dangerous information. Do you understand me?"

Pippen's features crinkled into a pinched and rather nervous expression, and he nodded quickly.

"If somebody were to come here after I left and ask you about our conversation, you are to repeat to them the same thing I told your fellows there. You tell them that I was asking after a friend named Jergen, from the city of Tergon. And that I was told that the man with the brand on his forehead would know some answers. I came looking to find out where my friend had gone, and Brand here thinks Jergen returned to Tergon. Understood?"

Pippen nodded.

"For your trouble so far, and as a down payment on spinning the tale I want told, here are two tolgens for you. Does that seem like a fair deal?"

Pippen's eyes widened considerably, and he let out a small breath.

"'Tis generous beyond what I deserve, sir. I thank ya from the bottom of my heart."

I leaned in close and grasped Pippen's old hand, inconspicuously transferring the coins to him that way. But I did not let go of his hand, and I clenched it to the point that must have been painful for the old man.

"I can be generous, Pippen," I said. "But I can also be very dangerous. If you fail me in this, if you end up relaying what actually happened here, I will come back and find you. I will see to it that you and Brand are in a similar condition. Do you understand me?"

Pippen let out a tiny squeak at the pressure in his hand, and he nodded fervently.

"I understand, sir," he whimpered. "Only a fool would cross Vazeer the Lash. An I didn't survive this long by being a fool. Your secret won't never be revealed by me."

I pulled my head back and glared at Pippen, and he smiled weakly in return. Finally, I released his hand, and he quickly stuffed the coins into his clothing, then proceeded to massage his sore fingers.

"Doubt the others know ya, but I been in the Wags a long time," Pippen said sheepishly. "Seen ya from afar. And I certain know yer reputation. I'll take my chances under a torture blade before I go ratting on the likes of you."

"It shouldn't come to that, not if you're persuasive. And, needless to say, my identity is another thing you don't discuss."

"That secret's on the house."

After that, I asked Pippen which of the others in the building had not managed to secure a poltet in their last mad scramble. Not surprisingly, Pippen knew, and he pointed them out. To each of these I tossed two copper coins, and then I threw a single coin to each of the winners from the last hunt. It was an impressive haul for these people, though not the stunning windfall I had just paid to Pippen. Of course, there was one more reward to be given.

I squatted down and took Brand's grubby hand. As I held it, I transferred three tolgens to him, making his total payment four silver coins. Prudently spent, it could feed him for the next six months.

"Hear me, Brand," I whispered. "I am going to hunt the two-faced demon that did this terrible thing to you. I'm going to hunt him and I'm going to kill him. And once he's dead, I will come back and tell you about it, so that perhaps in that small way you might have some peace."

Brand was entirely motionless as I spoke. He did not sing out his eerie, tongueless song, nor did he make his hand symbols. He just sat there for a moment, and then slowly, ever so subtly, the corners of his lips turned up into the vaguest hint of a grin. His eyes were still black holes, but somehow that shadow of a smile gave life to his lusterless face.

I stood up and said to Pippen, "Where is your secret exit from this place?"

Again, he showed his value by leading me through the debris into the dark back section, which was clogged with piles of wreckage and a few indigent treasures—a broken vegetable cart, a collection of crude cups and bowls, a rake, and a cracked mirror. The rear doorway that I remembered from childhood had been boarded up long ago and piled with rubble; however, there was a discreet opening in the rear side wall that had clearly been chiseled out for purposes of egress. I knew that street people would never dwell in a place that had only one exit, and this escape route was particularly clever in that it was entirely screened by vines on the outside.

I turned and gave a final nod to Pippen.

"Sir Lash," he said, uttering one of the strangest oxymorons I had heard in a long time. "What sort of man might it be that comes asking me questions?"

I pondered it a moment, then shrugged.

"That's what I'm about to find out, Pip," I said. "The skulking bastard has been tailing me all evening, and he shadowed me here. I can pretty much guarantee he is crouching in the weeds of the Orphan Grove, trying to get close enough to listen."

Pippen seemed truly alarmed, and he craned around to look towards the opening, as if he might spot the tail, which was useless. The man who had been shadowing me was a highly trained professional.

"What's your plan, Lash?" Pippen whispered.

"My plan?" I asked, giving it a moment's thought. "Simple, I guess. I'm going to creep out of this hole and go get the bastard. I have a better chance of doing it here than anywhere else. Now, go back to your friend and enjoy your new wealth. You don't want any part of what comes next."

And with that, I stepped carefully through the curtain of vines and into the dull, smoky moonlight of the world outside. The residents of this building had chosen their secret door wisely, as this western edge of the orphanage was flanked by a narrow side yard that was not directly connected with the Orphan Grove. I was able to make it out of the building and around to the back without being seen from the front. I climbed over the crumbling rear yard wall and moved quickly through the knot of alleys and shuts, circling around to approach the Orphan Grove from the same entrance I had used earlier.

I didn't know the identity of the man who was following me, but his skill so far in the pursuit told me a lot. I'm definitely not easy to track. It's an essential part of my profession that I am able to spot pursuit quickly, and were you to ask the Tergonian constables or the marsh brigands or even my fellow Shadow Bidders, they'd tell you that it's bloody impossible to get the drop on me. So, the fact that I couldn't catch sight of this tail earlier in Dockside or while en route to the Broodhouse made it clear that I was not being pursued by a common street thug. I did, at last, manage to spot him for a second after I exited Holod's home, and the figure was a mere blur, moving so quickly out the back side of a shut that I had to close my eyes and consciously conjure up what I had just seen to try to glean any small details. About the only thing I could determine was the fact that he was decidedly thick of build, therefore probably a man.

As such, I had led this quick, thick, stealthy son of a bitch to the Orphan Grove, where I intended to make a more formal introduction. There were several places in the city of Sullward where I was likely to find one of the Raved, some of them a better bet than the North Derjian Children's Compassionate Sanctuary. However, I chose my earliest home because it was highly familiar territory for me and, quite honestly, I'm more effective in a woodland environment than in the world of twisting streets, pedestrian crowds, and back alleys. The Orphan Grove was a sad excuse for true nature; however, it was sufficient for my needs.

I began my hunt. Upon reaching the grove, I crouched down, slipped around to the right, and, avoiding the larger beaten paths, moved instead towards a hidden trail that I had created as a boy. Luckily, a hint of it still existed today, for back in my childhood I had put some real effort into this secret thorough-fare—my chipped fingernails turning dark from scraping the soil, painful scratches on my gaunt arms and hands as I plucked out inconvenient thorn bushes. But it had been worth it, for that hidden trail did not get reclaimed each spring by the explosion of growth, and it became the main highway that Flerra and I took when sneaking out of the orphanage to perform mis-chief. We must have traversed it together a hundred times in our early years, hunched with fear, breathless with anticipation, our minds whirling with whatever juvenile subterfuge we had just concocted. I felt a fondness for it now as I again found myself stealing along that narrow furrow, through a kinked nest of briars and browning weeds.

I stayed low and made my way quickly towards the spot where I was confident my tail was hiding. Because of the sun's southern path, the vegetation had always been thickest on this northern side of the Orphan Grove, and in the place where an adjoining wall intersected the orphanage, the vegetation simply erupted, spilling out into a huge gnarly tangle of tall bushes, ragweed, and scrub willows. Thirty-some-odd years ago it had been a brilliant refuge for a child seeking to avoid a strap across his backside. On this day, it had become a shelter of a different sort, or so I suspected.

This was really a good choice for my spy. Ensconced there, he would have had the best chance of creeping in close to the big front opening of the orphanage without being seen, and had I conducted my conversations inside at a normal speaking volume, he might have picked up quite a bit of the dialogue. In any event, it was only a matter of time before any self-respecting tail would figure out that I had exited by another means, and I needed to get to him before that happened.

I unclasped my cloak and quickly folded it up into a tight ball, then shoved it into my satchel. I drew the longer of my two stilettos and held it in a thrust grip. I kept the other hand free, to help with the parting of vegetation and also to allow me to grab my quarry once I got close enough. Slowly and very warily, I slipped inside the thicket.

This is not my specialty. The great majority of my skills are centered around eluding troublemakers, not hunting them, but I am exceptionally quiet, and I move very well through exactly this sort of tangled undergrowth. I know which twigs and leaves will snap under my weight and which will bend in silent compliance. I had started my training in this very grove (in this very spot in fact), and while the subsequent years that I had spent under Holod Deadskiff's tutelage had made me a master smuggler, I still think the true origin of my talents lay here.

I had traveled a mere ten feet into the gnarled copse when I discovered my first piece of confirmation: a small clump of ragweed was trampled down, with a tiny smear of rotted melon glistening in the stalks. Somebody had recently stepped in one of the produce piles from the center of the grove and then tracked it in here. Since the vagrants from the orphanage had little reason to enter these bushes, and likely had not done so in the last two hours, I felt certain that I was closing in. As I proceeded a bit farther into the under-brush, however, I started to grow concerned. I peered ahead through the gaps in the branches and leaves, and I saw no sign of him. I didn't see a thick, squatting form nestled in the weeds like an ornery badger, nor did I see him pressed back into the intersection of the two buildings, melting away into the gloom. After moving forward a few more yards, I became convinced that he was no longer there, which meant he had either left already or, far more troubling, he had detected my presence and was actually stalking me in turn.

I spun, searching to the rear, then to the side of me...I even looked above, having the sudden, frightened thought that perhaps this skulk had managed to climb one of the spindly scrub willows and was staring down like some hungry jungle cat. He wasn't. He was nowhere to be seen.

Yet, in my gut I knew he was close. It occurred to me then, wouldn't this slippery son of a bitch eventually creep out of the thicket and take the risk of peeking inside the orphanage? That's what I would do. I'd want to know if my mark was still in the building, or what he was doing in there, and since there were a lot of vines hanging in front of the opening, I'd sneak over and very carefully peer through the screen. So, I pressed on with my hunt, making my way to the southern end of the thicket where I could squint out into the dim moonlight and get a glance at the entrance to the orphanage.

When I stared out through the bushes, I saw, for a few seconds, only what was supposed to be there—the crumbling, run-down front of the dark building, heaped with vines and weeds. And then...then I noticed something that wasn't quite right. Among the creepers on the near side of the entrance, there was a dark form woven into the vegetation, nestled in it like a beetle that had crawled into someone's hair. There was no mistaking it; a man was hiding in the vines. And what a stealthy one he was, with a dark cloak that blended well with the surrounding walls and a cowl over his head. He had also made expert use of those plants, worming his way behind them and slithering right up to the edge of the opening. I saw him start to lean ever so subtly into the gap to get a look, and I knew I wouldn't get a better opportunity than this. I made my move.

Craftiness had served me well in the hunt, but quite frankly, I was sick of it. So, I erupted from the brush in a sudden burst, charging straight at my target like an angry boar, and I moved so rapidly that despite hearing me, he simply couldn't spin around and disentangle himself from those vines in time. I managed to get a hand on his cloak, and I jammed my stiletto up against his collar. There was quite a bit of fabric in the way of my blade, but I'd make it work, and at the same time, I slammed his body against the wall of the orphanage. In this way, our face-off began.

I had already expected that this tail was tough. I guessed it from his thick frame and the simple fact that he was assigned to following me (proffers generally didn't put the lightweights on my case). If these hired sneaks weren't stealthy enough to avoid detection, then they had better damned well come prepared to fight.

And this one was. There was more than a little Contract Blade in his makeup, as he had managed to draw a dirk as I ran him down, and he had even gotten it pointed at the region of my lower ribs as we slammed up against each other. His other hand had come up around the back of my neck, gripping me in turn, so that we shuffled together in an awkward dance. This went on for a few seconds, and then we both went still, breathing into each other's faces amidst the tangle of vines.

"I have a steel plate woven into my cuirass where your dirk is pointed," I said to the lower half of his cowled face. "Even if you slip around it, it's a mere flesh wound. By contrast, I'll spill your neck open quicker than you can blink and leave you rotting here with the melons. Sheath your goddamned blade."

"Ya lie like a dog, Bidder," he rasped back with a heavy Dockside brogue. "Grell Runners don't use metal in their armor. My blade is just fine where it is."

Because of the hood, I could only see the stubbled bottom half of his face, which was heavily creased, telling me that this man was a veteran. There was also something vaguely familiar about that jaw, and the sound of his voice.

"Hear me well, Eye," I said. "If you really want to trade wounds in this position, I'll oblige. But since you've been assigned to my tail, you damned well know who I am and what I'm capable of. The barter will not go well for you."

He took a small shallow breath, which told me he was absorbing the truth of what I had said. I'm sure this veteran operative wanted to come back with another tough rejoinder, but in the end, he showed his Shadow Bidder bonafides by being a pragmatist. Win or lose, nothing useful would be accomplished by trading blows with the man he had been assigned to follow.

"All right, Lash," he finally breathed. "I'll stand down, if ya do. Neither of us can benefit from this."

And with that, he loosened his grip on the back of my neck slightly and I felt the dirk lighten up on my side. I pulled my stiletto back in turn, and then a moment later we both simultaneously sheathed our blades. I did not have to ask him to pull back his cowl; he reached up and drew it back on his own.

The face that was revealed was stout and rather hard edged, with cheeks that were wide and rutted, and a nose that was almost as crooked as mine. The moonlight didn't allow me to pick out too many colors, but it seemed to me that his curly hair was free of gray, or mostly so. His eyes were dark and suspicious, and they were hooded by strong brows.

"I know you, don't I?" I said after scanning his features. "Bez… something."

"Bevin Slywell," the man replied.

"We worked together once."

"We did," Bevin replied. "And if ya recall, I did ya right."

I took a moment to scour back through my memory, and sure

enough, I did recall the job. The bid had come very early in my career, perhaps a full sixteen or seventeen years earlier, and it involved a rather dangerous jewelry buy aboard a rogue shipper's schooner. Grell Runners were rarely teamed with Contract Eyes, who were the spies and information-gathering operatives of Hell's Labyrinth (most often we were paired with Contract Blades, and sometimes with Masques, who, in addition to their skills at imper-sonation, were practiced negotiators). But, on occasion, when a Sketcher felt there were just too many unknowns for a particular buy, he decided it was worth paying for a bit more scouting just prior to and during the bid. In the case of this particular job, Bevin Slywell did a commendable job with his reconnaissance, climbing the rigging of a neighboring ship and spotting more mercenaries on board the schooner than had first been reported. This prompted me to quickly hire a third Blade out of the purchase funds and bring all three of them onto the schooner during the negotiation, instead of leaving someone to guard the skiff. Throughout the buy, Bevin remained in the rigging of that neighboring ship, prepared to make signals to me if he saw those auxiliary soldiers coming up from below. They never did, and whether or not this was because of my extra show of force, I would never know. Either way, the bid went off smoothly, and I certainly had no complaints about Bevin Slywell's performance.

"As I recall it," I said, "your paranoia cost me the price of an extra Blade on that job. Just as your filthy skulking tonight has cost me a whole tunic full of nettles."

For a moment, Bevin's expression darkened, and a harsh gleam ignited in his hooded eyes.

"It's a joke, Slywell," I said. "You did me solid back then, and you've been a damned clever sneak tonight. When'd you pick me up, as I rowed into the wharf, or before that?"

Bevin was a very good Contract Eye, but he was certainly no Masque, and I saw his rough features twitch through a series of confused reactions that started with harsh indignation, then relief that I had not insulted him, followed by a hint of a grin at my joke, and finally a slight shake of the head that he had to cut off abruptly. But it was too late. I knew what that headshake meant.

"Aye, at the wharf," he lied.

"I see," I replied, understanding now that he had picked me up at the boathouse, which made it pretty clear who had contracted him. "Well, it's pointless to ask who hired you, because you probably have less idea than me."

"That's how it works."

"But maybe, without compromising your bid, you could just nod or shake your head. You're supposed to report on all my movements?"

Bevin took a deep breath, then gave a slight nod.

"And you'll want to note whom I spoke to and, if possible, what I spoke about?"

Bevin nodded again.

"And finally, you'll particularly want to report if I make any moves to leave the city; is that right?"

Bevin did not move his head, but his expression became extremely grim.

"I don't know what yer involved in, Lash," he said. "And I don't wanna know. But take some advice from a colleague and don't screw around with whoever it was that hired me. I got a sense ya know who that is."

I contemplated this for a moment.

"They paid you well, didn't they?"

"Aye."

A covetous little sparkle appeared in the hooded wells of his eyes. He smiled, rather unpleasantly.

"And I intend to earn it."

I nodded and glanced up at the illumined sky, which, with the moon only a few days past full, painted the city's foggy ceiling with a silvery sheen. I had heard the First Bell earlier when I was in the orphanage, and now I noted the muffled single tone of the Half Bell. Meanwhile, the inhabitants of the North Derjian Children's Compassionate Sanctuary had gone completely silent. I could only guess that they had retreated farther back into the building once the scuffle began, and perhaps some had fled entirely, which would be wise. Bevin Slywell had just revealed that he would want to gather information after I left.

"Okay, Bevin," I said. "I appreciate the advice, and I also understand you are simply doing your job. Just know, I'm also doing mine."

And suddenly, with all my might, I drilled my fist straight into Bevin's solar plexus. Contract Eyes never wear much in the way of armor, and though this one was a particularly tough specimen, I caught him largely by surprise. He crumpled forward, and as his shoulders came down, I grabbed them and then drove my knee straight up into his stomach. I kneed him so hard that his feet actually bounced a few inches off the ground. He fell against me in a heap, but I still wasn't done with him.

Taking things too far is a problem of mine. In this very orphanage, decades ago, exasperated adult figures had tried desperately to control me, to whip and subdue me, to get me to stop whatever excessive pursuit I had grabbed hold of with the tenacity of a rabid dog. But it never worked. Even Holod couldn't completely control me, though he did better than most. These days he hauled out the name "Scuff" when he was trying to reason with me, but the ferocious boyhood scuffles that had earned me the nickname, often against much older boys and usually several at once, were anything but reasonable. Sometimes I could only remember a fraction of what happened afterwards, and on rare occasions, I went into a total blackout of pure rage. Reason, it is fair to say, played no part once that thing took over.

So, as I held tough old Bevin Slywell in a crumpled position against my body, then raised my right elbow and brought it down hard on the base of his skull—probably not injuring him permanently, but certainly taking that risk—I was simply doing that excessive, exasperating thing again. Why? Ostensibly it was to dissuade Bevin from continuing his assignment. Also, it was to ensure that he was in no condition tonight to interview the inhabitants of this crumbling building. But possibly the true reason was the fact that I was in this awful, reeking place again, and I felt the ghosts of a past that no man wants to claim as his own. Add to that the lingering memory of my conversation with Holod Deadskiff, the one where his mouth said I was not about to walk into a deathtrap but his eyes told me I probably was.

Most of all, I think I clubbed Bevin Slywell unconscious into the stinking dirt because of another conversation I had just had. It was my dialogue with a nice fellow who had black holes where his eyes should have been and a gaping chasm in place of a tongue.

If the goddamned Sketcher for this bid and his vainglorious employer saw fit to send me out to kill the two-faced demon psychopath who gouged out eyes and cut out tongues, then the least they could do was trust me to do my job. I did not need to be watched. I could walk into the pretty deathtrap all on my own, with no coaxing from the likes of them.

And so, to send that message, I harmed a fellow operative, did it in an excessive and brutish manner, which was the very thing the other Shadow Bidders loathed about me. Even my own Brood sister couldn't stomach it. But I did it because I wanted them all to know—Bevin, the other Shadow Bidders, the Underlords… perhaps, on some subconscious level, the Raving Blade himself— that Vazeer the Lash was not a man to be trifled with.

As I said, I am not a good Shadow Bidder.

However, I am rather good at getting my point across.

5

VOLUMES

It was always a tangible relief when I crossed Stenneck and moved from the snarled congestion of the Wags into a lovely residential neighborhood known as White Hill. While it was generally taboo to ask another Shadow Bidder where they lived (we valued our privacy almost as much as our ill-gotten silver), I do believe I was one of the few among us who had chosen this neighborhood as a place of residence.

White Hill was a quiet, relatively lawful district that housed many of the city's wealthiest merchants, landholders, and government officials. Named after the light-colored granite used in the construction of its buildings, the entire neighborhood was on an elevated piece of ground that provided views of the sea. While one must avoid exaggerating this idea of a "view" given the ubiquitous nature of the fog, I am happy to report that at midday, when most of the mist burned off, I was often able to see the gray band of the Derjian Sea from my third-floor window. To be sure, this was a very nice place to return each night after committing my illicit deeds.

The intersection of Fletcher and Gale was often the spot where I first laid eyes upon my home, and tonight as I reached the oblique junction and saw the smooth white-gray façade, I was, for several seconds, set free from my underlying sense of foreboding. Twenty-seven Fletcher Street was a grand beauty dating back three centuries before the start of the new Sullward calendar. It was well graced with the swan statuary and bay windows that made that particular period so elegant. The Kaennamin family ruled then, and in addition to being great patrons of art and culture, they were particularly devoted to fine architecture. The monarch of that time, Queen Sarien I, went on a mad building spree from 311 O.C. through 289 O.C. and was responsible for commissioning almost the entire White Hill area, which is the neighborhood most notably marked by Sarentine constructions. Sarien, who was quite a skilled architect herself, went above and beyond in a few cases and personally drafted the detail work, then inscribed her own name into the granite at the building's threshold. Through the dark grace of my wildly lucrative criminal profession, I was privileged enough to own one of these rare jewels.

It took me a while to fish my keys from the deepest safety pocket inside my leather cuirass, after which I began work on the four locks that made up the preliminary defenses of my building. It required the better part of a half minute, but at last I opened the door.

I've described a number of smells so far, most of them quite horrible, and yet there is one that has the power to temporarily dispel the memory of all the others. Mountain elm is among the most aromatic building materials available to those of us in the North, and its abundance in my entry hallway as octagonal wall paneling would have made a fragrant impression on its own. But underlying the mountain elm is the mild leather scent of the twin settees, along with the faint mustiness of the three-hundred-year-old Kaszian rug, and also that basic, ever-present pungency of wet Derjian granite, which all Sullwardians come to know even better than the odor of their own skin. Add to all of this the minute threads of smoke still rising from the wall braziers, and you have a singular bouquet that can ease almost any dark anxiety that might afflict my soul. I don't even know how good a smell it actually is. I just knew, each time I breathed it, that I had once again returned to myself.

I headed into my kitchen and looked around for something to eat. My cook wouldn't be back for a few days, but she had left me an assortment of options, and I gratefully pulled half a smoked game hen and a bowl of steamed potatoes and greens from the ice chest and placed them on the bar. Cold though I was, I couldn't be bothered to heat the food, so I just stood there and shoveled it all down in that chilled condition. A few minutes later I exited the kitchen and approached the great engineering feat of my dwelling—a circular balustrade stone staircase that ran from the first floor all the way to the third, graced at regular intervals with thin stained-glass windows. I began to climb.

Holod had once named this stunning granite spiral my "Staircase to Grandiosity," and on a certain level, I had to agree with him. I really was a snob. Not a faker, though, or at least I don't think so, since the things inside my home truly did mean everything to me. When I mounted this grandiose staircase, I felt justified in all I had done over the years to reach this place, and at the same time I tangibly experienced an ascent through my own intrinsic needs. If sustenance and the rarest of social interactions occurred on the first floor, then it was the second floor where my spirit truly began to soar. There I had joined two of the guest rooms and converted them into a large gallery, and this double space had become the repository for my sizable collection of artwork.

I didn't know, or particularly care, what the other Shadow Bidders did with their prodigious wealth. They had trinkets and baubles perhaps; they had, I'm sure, Dockside apartments or Lower City dwellings of some quality. But none of them possessed two works by the famous Tergonian landscape painter Ashland Nuce. And I doubt there was a single other citizen in all of Sullward to possess a masterwork by the great Engoliese sculptor, Emalia Zeltier. My Zeltier was a gorgeous life-sized depiction of the ancient battle queen, Giradera of Azmoul (remember that insulting comment Holod made about ogling— this is who he was talking about). Queen Giradera, possibly the most awe-inspiring ruler of all time, had been rendered widely by artists of all disciplines; however, I had yet to find a version to equal this masterpiece by Zeltier. A veritable eruption of bronze, my sculpture portrayed the lithe battle queen in her full war regalia, cocking her arm back to its farthest extent to throw a javelin.

Even the Underlords did not own such things. They stockpiled them perhaps, locking their many stolen treasures in giant warehouses known as Ripening Halls. These secret fortified bunkers were the ultimate hub of Underlord power, and the place where the vast hoard of purloined merchandise was kept out of circulation until the various statutes of limitations expired. But locking a Zeltier or a Nuce in such a place was not true ownership. It couldn't even be called possession. It was storage.

I climbed the final flight and stepped off into what was far and away the largest and most pleasing room of the whole house— my third-floor library. I had been told once or twice by my rare visitors that this massive rectangular space, with its tall, vaulted ceiling, its glorious Sarentine crown molding, the domed skylight, polished hardwood floor, six clear glass windows, should have been my art gallery, not a display hall for rows upon rows of old leather-bound books. They were right, of course. I'm not a complete idiot.

The issue was I couldn't help feeling that the books demanded this space. When I craved their friendly intimacy…well, that's what my adjoining study was for, with lamps that could be turned up for ideal illumination, and a wood-burning stove that kept the temperature constant. In between sessions of cerebral wandering, these troves of wisdom needed to affirm their substance, needed to stand like proud bricks in great walls of intellective solidarity. So, I viewed them at a distance. I employed a chamber large enough to contain them on its four walls, while leaving the middle open and free of shelving. Several times a week I would stand in the dead center of that hall, bathed in the dull glow of the skylight, and gaze slowly around the mighty circumference, hunting. Hunting for that one engraved leather binding that would whisper to me through the wide-open expanse, calling me across a field of polished hardwood to draw forth yet another piece of the great puzzle. For some men it was women that filled the emptiness, for others it was hard drink. For me, the great siren call emerged from that which could be ascertained, for better or for worse, from a vast sea of esoteric memories and reflections transcribed into the written word.

A short time later, I slid aside the books on one of the shelves in my library and opened the false panel hidden there. Behind that panel was a heavy, welded safe, and I securely locked the pouch of Gosian diamonds inside. After that I returned to the second floor, removed my damp clothing, and drew water for a bath. The houses on my end of Fletcher Street all shared a common well, and it lay so far beneath the bedrock of the city that issues of flooding, sewage spills, and backsurges simply didn't affect it. Tonight, the water came out of the pump clean, as always, and I quickly retrieved some smoldering embers from the bath chamber wood stove, sparked a fire in the grill beneath the tub, and within minutes I was gratefully banishing the chill from my body.

At last, I exited the bath, re-stoked the stove in my personal chambers, and finally collapsed into bed. For a few, restful moments, I stared around at the sheer homey elegance of my own bed chamber: the paintings, the ornate weaponry, the busts and tapestries, the tiled fireplace adorned above with a figurine of a leaping stag, a small model galley, and one of the original Kaennamin maps of the city. As was my nightly ritual, I stared at that faded brown and gray map for several minutes before going to sleep, my eyes following the dark dimensions of the harbor and the river Grells, tracing over the winding contours of streets and neighborhoods. What a masterpiece it was. Written in faded but fluid script in the border below the map was a quotation:

*"The maddest and grandest of dreams
shall summon forth the means."*

This simple line was, very likely, my favorite quote of all time, and it was authored by unquestionably my favorite historical figure of all time, a man whose outlandish vision inspired me on a daily basis. The wonderful madman had actually written the quote in his own hand on this lovely map, and he had done so six hundred years ago at a time when the artistic city-state was just a dream. There was no more meaningful artifact in my entire home.

Aurellis Kaennamin was Sarien Kaennamin's grandfather, and he was the visionary mastermind, artist, lunatic who had taken it upon himself to transform a busy but otherwise insignificant fishing port into the dominant city of the North. In his fledgling city-state he envisioned a cultural nexus, which he said would become the artistic center of power for all of Derjia. The painters and musicians, the architects and sculptors would come, he said. The wealthy merchants and the Tergonian nobility would make pilgrimages, he assured his family and retainers. They thought him mad, obviously. But he wasn't mad, not entirely. He was inspired.

For some reason I draw great strength from this story. Aurellis had to make enormous sacrifices to achieve his vision, and he caused a lot of trouble with the local population in order to push forward with this dream. But the means did present themselves, and one by one the hurdles were overcome, which is exactly why I love that quote.

The Kaennamins are but a memory now, as are the two other Sullward dynasties who followed. The great cultural heyday of our city, which Aurellis accurately predicted and which his family personally nurtured, has long since come and gone. And I grieve for it all. I, who know of these things only through my reading and my obsessive collecting, grieve deeply for all that once was, and all that has been destroyed along the way. I cannot help feeling that the enormity of that loss is somehow my loss and that if it could ever be made right again, then perhaps I could be made right again, which I admit makes very little sense. Still, I continue to imagine a world that, against all laws of reason and sanity, might someday be. With that hopeful thought still reverberating within me, I closed my eyes and let the warm darkness overtake me.

⸙

I awakened just before noon the next day and, after a hearty meal of eggs, sourdough bread, and cheese, I returned to my bedroom to get ready for the day's errands. It was there, as usual, that I faced the daily conundrum that was my wardrobe.

As previously noted, I have a stubborn case of vanity, which is a most inconvenient failing for a man with my anti-social qualities. It would have been much easier if I didn't give a damn how I looked.

Like most Shadow Bidders, I tended towards the darker spectrum of colors; however, I devoted an embarrassing proportion of my energy to such inspired pursuits as finding creative shades of dark purple and scarlet to accentuate my innately swarthy skin tones (a legacy from one or the other of my anonymous Kaszian parents, or perhaps both) without looking like some sort of pompous Midland aristocrat. I do believe I got the balance right sometimes. On the good days, I appeared to myself like one of the tough but cultured lords from the founding days of the city-state. I dressed as though I were a member of that hallowed Kaennamin court, where even the regional gentry were expected to know their way around the latest artistic trends.

But other times, mornings when my black hair was just a little too unkempt, or there was some new bruise darkening my stubbled features, or my existing scar was, for some irritating reason, particularly livid…in those instances the effect didn't turn out quite right. I no longer looked like the rugged northern gentleman that I aspired to be, and I instead slid down into arch-criminal territory.

So it was that day as I sought for balance. I picked through a closet lined with long raven and burgundy capes, tunics trimmed with patterned stitch, high, finely crafted boots, trousers crisscrossed with iron buckles—an entire wardrobe composed of garments inspired by records and paintings from days long past, when the beautifully crafted swords and daggers slung at one's belt were worn to defend honor, not boatloads of stolen goods. The great crimes from Sarien Kaennamin's day were the pilfering of ideas and artistic technique that did, in fact, lead to duels on a regular basis, a practice at which I would have failed miserably. I'm the first to admit that I'm quite mediocre in a fair fight.

Vanity aside, today was simply not a day where I wanted to be noticed. I enforced a degree of subtlety on myself and chose portions of a Grell Running outfit, albeit with an attractive blue silk tunic and a short gray cloak thrown on top to lighten the effect. I also strapped on the full weapons belt, and I didn't neglect several auxiliary jacks and razors inserted into hidden pockets and sheaths. Then I was off, sweeping out into the mild midday air, with a soft brimmed leather hat drawn down low to mask my face. The time was a little before Second Bell, and I did not anticipate returning home until evening.

As I moved down Fletcher Street, I saw a portly figure approaching and recognized Mogrin Deen, the owner of the Broad Street Silk Market who lived in 35 Fletcher. He twitched his head slightly as I passed, which was the curtest and least personable gesture a neighbor could get away with, shy of a total snub. This didn't surprise me, though it did somewhat amuse me, for the merchants, local government officials, and other wealthy lay people who dwelled here made a conscious habit of "not seeing" the Shadow Bidder who resided quietly among them. The joke of it was that the true origin of the city's wealth was known to all, and to a certain degree enjoyed by all, so an intelligent man such as Mogrin Deen could not possibly justify his success in any other way. Why else did he have a steady stream of moneyed customers in this gods forsaken North Derjian outpost?

I was never particularly bothered by the silent derision of my neighbors, and this was largely because I had outclassed them all at this point, despite my humble upbringing. Not to mention, my home was much better than any of theirs. Mogrin, for instance, did own a reasonably large house on my block; however, 35 Fletcher was not one of Queen Sarien's lovely masterpieces.

Funny story, but the architect for 35 Fletcher, in an effort to show up the other swan statuary in the neighborhood, created stone specimens that projected halfway off the face of the building. I understand what he was after, as I've seen some drawings of the original building, and the birds did indeed appear to be taking flight. The problem was those long slender necks eventually broke off, and when a subsequent owner had them repaired, a good deal of reinforcement was required. Hence, graceful, curving shapes became stout, straight ones, and all of the majesty was lost. These days, when you strolled past 35 Fletcher, you felt like you were walking beneath a bevy of fat, squawking geese.

So, go on and snub away, Mogrin Deen. I now have enough money to buy a majority stake in that market of yours. And your hideous swans are an embarrassment to the entire neighborhood.

On the outskirts of White Hill there was a magical little street called the Virtuoso, which was, without exception, my favorite spot in all of Sullward. In the current era, as in the days of old, this was a street inhabited by art dealers, book sellers, and traders in antiquities, though before the change of the Sullward calendar, the Virtuoso was an entire neighborhood, comprised of six interconnected streets adjoining White Hill. Now only one of those streets retained its original identity.

While the Underlords worked hard to redistribute their immense hoard of stolen merchandise out into far corners of Derjia, ensuring that it was largely untraceable, there was simply too much to offload in this manner. Consequently, a portion of the items were often filtered out to local merchants after a suitable period of "ripening" had elapsed, which usually meant that the appropriate statute of limitations had expired. The more practical merchandise went to the Dockside bazaar, and even the Wags, while the finer collectibles came to the Virtuoso, where enough of us coveted items of cultural significance to keep eleven dealers employed.

The Virtuoso was not only one of the most charming streets in Sullward, a twisting cobble lane through eccentric townhouses and handsome stone and timber merchant dwellings, but it was also home to most of the stores where I spent my ill-gotten fortune. On a given afternoon I might find myself in any one of these shops, perusing the latest batch of paintings, sculptures, furnishings, musical instruments, antiquities, and books released back into the marketplace. Many of the items were recognizable to me instantly, and, I must say, coming across a familiar crested shield, or bust, or Derjian map that I had carefully appraised and ferried up the Grells, now in the homey confines of a store along the Virtuoso, was among the most gratifying reunions I was privileged to experience on a regular basis. The dealers on this street all knew to alert me when certain items arrived. While most of them were simply friendly acquaintances, there was one individual with whom I had formed a particularly close bond.

It was just after Second Bell when I approached Merejin's Books. The shop was located in a stately townhouse constructed from ocher-colored sandstone, its facade festooned with the carved griffins and celestial musicians, which were common throughout the neighborhood. There was a pretty scrollwork sign hanging over the front door, showing an open tome with the shop's name written in golden script across the pages. I ascended the five brown steps and rapped the knocker loudly.

It usually took Merejin some time to get to the door, and in that interval, I glanced down the winding length of the Virtuoso.

This street always saw its highest concentration of foot traffic at this hour, which today amounted to about a dozen nicely dressed pedestrians strolling in that idle manner that bespoke leisure, not necessity. While cloud cover retained its grip on the Sullward sky, the late afternoon fog had not yet rolled in from the harbor, so I could clearly see all the stores along the cobbled street. It was really the most wonderful of sights. All of the shops had beautifully painted signs that hung out from the walls on decorative brackets, most with an elaborately detailed image—a violin, a settee, a statue in front of a painting, a partially unfurled rug. The majority of the shops were outfitted with clear glass front windows, reinforced with iron mullions. I saw Annaliese, the pretty young owner of Wind and Strings, crouching and cleaning her exterior glass. When she glanced up, I waved to her, and she smiled in return.

I was personally incapable of producing a single tolerable note on a musical instrument of any kind. However, I had purchased several beautiful specimens over the years from Wind and Strings, including a rather exotic harbeen, this because the long, curved, heavily inscribed item was a thing of wonder to behold. I had tried blowing in it a few times when I first purchased it, and the ungodly racket had been enough to dissuade me from further attempts. Annaliese had offered to switch it out with something easier to play, but for some reason I greatly valued it, and now it was mounted out of harm's reach on the wall of my study, making a nice showpiece between a crested plate and a painting of Sullward Harbor.

I heard quiet footfalls approaching from inside the book shop, and this prompted me to straighten my cloak and remove my hat. A moment later the heavy, double paneled door swung inward.

I allowed a couple seconds for old eyes to register my identity.

"My dear lad," she said in a light, pleased voice. "Back so soon?"

Merejin's plump form filled the doorway. Her graying black hair was set in braids, which were coiled up in a bun, and she squinted up at me through narrow spectacles. Though I could see her dark fingers twitching on the doorframe, she seemed in her typical good health.

"Is it so soon, Mera? Only my second visit this week…which shows that I am learning the rudiments of self-restraint."

She wheezed out a laugh, then gestured emphatically for me to enter. She wore a brown blouse, and I could see that the sleeves were crumpled, no doubt from sorting through a new shipment of books and scrolls. These items rarely even made it into a Ripening Hall, sometimes sitting with the Underlords for a mere month or two before moving back out into the market-place (stolen books, no matter how rare, simply did not garner much interest from law enforcement). I hadn't ferried volumes of any sort up the Grells in almost a year, so it must have been another lucky Runner who had won that bid.

"May you never learn restraint, lad." She chuckled over her shoulder. "When that day comes, I will certainly go bankrupt."

Merejin took my cloak and hat once we were inside and began to utter words about tea and cakes, but I gently stopped her.

"I can't stay long. I'm going to need your expertise today to find what I'm looking for."

"As if it's ever otherwise!" She wheezed loudly. "Your bumbling jaunts through my shelves always lead you in a dozen non-sensical directions."

"There's some truth to that. But there can be quite a bit of fun in bumbling."

"And quite a bit of money for old Merejin!" she replied, and she laughed again happily. Then she tugged me along towards the library.

Merejin's beautiful townhouse was not as old as mine, coming a hundred and fifty years after Sarien Kaennamin's building spree. It belonged to the much more haphazard Angiérs period when the new ruling family allowed a whole array of eclectic homes and public halls to spring up in whatever order they chose. The bulk of the Virtuoso was built during the Angiérs, which explained the cockeyed nature of the street and the asymmetry of its buildings.

The initial views inside Merejin's building were pleasing but undramatic, lacking the stunning detail of the sweeping balustrade staircase that dominated my entry foyer. Her vestibule was actually quite small, and her staircase was set back near the kitchen out of view. However, this building lent itself well to Merejin's needs, for directly adjoining the foyer was a massive drawing room that she had converted into her main vending library. Unlike me, she had been economical with her book storage, creating orderly rows of shelves that were nearly as tall as the elevated ceilings. The library was nicely lit by regularly spaced steel and glass lanterns, assisted by a window in the back that faced a small courtyard. In the center of the room there was a square, fifteen-foot break in the shelving where a decorative wooden desk sat with chairs on either side, facing each other.

Despite what I had said to Merejin about needing assistance, I walked straight past the desk and began to wander through the rows upon rows of leather-bound volumes. Their rich, cracked spines almost seemed to smile at me, and I felt the familiar sense of buoyant wonder that always overtook me here. This library, and another smaller one upstairs, were truly among my favorite places in existence. It was from these shelves that I had purchased the overwhelming bulk of my own collection, and the urge towards discovery that marked my time here was impossible to quantify.

"Ahhhh, old habits die hard, lad," said Merejin, who had ambled along behind me. "My expertise, indeed!"

Merejin had only the slightest hint of an accent after all these years living in Sullward, but it sometimes came out as a lilting exaggeration of certain words, especially when she was chiding me. Her "indeed" stretched out a little longer and deeper than necessary, just to make her point.

I waved my hand in good-natured dismissal and continued working my way towards a section of the library that I didn't know quite as well as the others. I stopped at last in front of a large set of shelves near the back, where Merejin kept her volumes on the noble families of Tergon. I squatted down, running my fingers along the cool, smooth surfaces, smelling the deep muskiness of the aged leather. I kept searching.

"Which house?" asked Merejin from behind.

"Odel."

"Bah, you're wasting your time. Nothing here on them. Too obscure a family."

I turned and looked up at her. Merejin's creased, charcoal-colored skin was slightly flushed, and her dark eyes were clearly amused behind the slender gleam of her spectacles. There was a chubbiness to her cheeks and overall shape that belied her age, and which seemed better suited to a baker than one of Sullward's preeminent scholars. Like Col, she was from a distant southwestern region of the Derjian basin known as Gosia, which was mountainous, rich in natural resources, and (through some brilliant act of negotiation or bribery) had managed to retain a highly favorable protectorate status within the Empire. Gosians rarely made their way this far north; however, when they did, they tended to make their mark, as Coljin

Helmgrinder had done. They were also notoriously superior in their demeanor, which, again, described Col, but not necessarily Merejin.

"A joke?" I asked, not entirely sure.

"Oh, for the love of the nonexistent gods, lad! Of course it's a joke. Is there a single more prominent house, apart from the imperial dynasty? Now go get the ladder in the next row and let Merejin's expertise take over."

And I complied. I brought her one of the room's two hook ladders, and once it was secured to the high iron rail, she began to climb. Years ago, I had given up trying to spare her these ascents. If I requested her help, then she was the one who went up the ladder.

"This one," she said, and she handed down a thick, tan leather volume. I glanced at the title, *Codex of Noble Tergonian Lineages*.

"And this one."

The next tome was bound in dark red cloth and was very wide and somewhat thin.

Arms and Crests of the Empire.

"It's better than it sounds," said Merejin. "With quite a bit more than emblems. There are some sketches of prominent figures, including a few of the Odels."

Merejin kept searching, at one point leaning so far to the right that I put my hands up just in case she slipped.

"And finally…this one. It came in last year and was only written a couple years before that. It's definitely the most current."

When she handed it down to me, the leather was relatively free of cracking, and the embossed gold lettering was in excellent condition.

Splendors of the Tergonian Court, it read. In this case, there was actually an author listed, which was unusual for tomes that chronicled the aristocracy: Hendjick Pinsar II.

"An insufferable elitist, that Hendjick!" Merejin said as she began to descend. "Quite elevated snobbery for such a minor noble. But I'll admit he does a good job with court gossip, and my recollection is that this book ruffled quite a few highborn feathers when it first made the rounds. A lot of copies were scribed."

Merejin stepped off the ladder and tugged my sleeve.

"Come," she said, and she led me to the desk.

Once we were seated in the two comfortably upholstered chairs, Merejin had me spread the three books out on the wide desk.

"Okay, lad," she said. "What's this all about?"

I was ready for this.

"It's for a friend," I replied. "She will be playing Countess Odel in an upcoming theater production, and she asked me to find her some reference material to help her assume the character."

Merejin had been in the process of reaching for the *Codex*, and she stopped with her hand resting on the thick volume.

"I see," she said, looking at me over the top of her spectacles. "I'll leave it at that, then. No need to say more. You can ask your questions now."

I couldn't help smiling. Perhaps it was my reference to a "friend" that had tipped her off, seeing as I had never so much as mentioned another acquaintance in the decade and a half of our relationship. Or perhaps she knew enough about stage plays to understand that my so-called "theater production," featuring such a prominent noble, was rather unlikely within the confines of the Empire. Merejin and I had never spent much time discussing the nefarious industry that subsidized our city, nor the true rulers who presided there. And we had never so much as hinted at my particular role in the enterprise. She didn't ask, and I had no wish to mention it myself, but the truth was more than obvious to a sharp woman such as Merejin, who had arrived in this city as a young woman and had been in her prime during the ascendancy of the Shadow Bidders. She knew full well where her books came from. She also knew that a scar-faced rake such as myself, with no obvious form of employment and a seemingly unlimited fount of silver in his purse, could only belong to one possible strata of the society.

"The Countess," I said. "Might you have a sketch of her in one of these volumes? Perhaps in the book of crests?"

"I'm afraid not, dear," she said, and she reached for the wide, flat red book, which she opened before us both. "This is a rather old volume, and there isn't even a sketch of her father…though I believe there is a sketch of his father, Vodun II."

I nodded. I was fairly certain that Vodun II had been Chief Legate to the prior Emperor, and also briefly to the current one at the start of his reign. If I went back any further than that I would be out of my depth. I had never given much attention to the broader Empire's ruling class, as almost all of my expertise focused on the history of my own city. And, of course, there was a much darker and far more relevant aristocracy for me to contend with here. Merejin began to thumb through the book, presumably looking for the section on House Odel.

"How about the women in the family? Are there any sketches of them?"

"Indeed," Merejin replied. "Shaeyin's great- or possibly great-great-grandmother is drawn here somewhere…maybe…ah, got it. Here she is. Lady Derabel of House Rengiér. And, let me see… hmm…yes…looks like we must add two 'greats' to this one."

Merejin spun the book about so it was facing me, and I stared down at the spot where her finger was tapping. There I saw a black and white ink drawing of a stiffly posed, heavily adorned patrician woman wearing a fur coat and a large courtier's hat replete with an enormous feather. It was difficult to determine the woman's true features from this sketch, which I ultimately saw as a positive sign.

"In your estimation, Merejin, what are the chances that there is a portrait of Shaeyin Odel somewhere in this city?"

"Zero, lad," she replied. "I doubt there is more than a single portrait of her anywhere, and that one would be found hanging in the Odel ancestral home. The lady is known to be both beautiful and very modest at the same time. A rather rare and pleasing combination."

I'm sure Merejin thought she was disappointing me with the news about the portrait, but in fact I was quite relieved. I had promised my fellows at the boathouse the night before that I would look into this issue and try to determine if there was any way that the Raving Blade possessed such a painting, which would be an obvious danger to our entire endeavor.

"The *Codex* and the book of crests will provide the best overview of the family," Merejin continued. "You can read ad infinitum about the lineage, the estates, the family exploits…etc. However, Pinsar's book has the only references to Shaeyin herself."

She slid that one towards me.

"You'll have to comb through it a bit, as he mentions her throughout. But, just in case you were hoping for salacious details, you can forget it. While I'm certain that pompous Hendjick understood enough about self-preservation not to denigrate the heir of Odel, I actually believe there isn't much bad that can be said of the girl. My foreign buyers bring me plenty of news from Tergon, and by all accounts this woman is both fiercely intelligent and level-headed, another rare combination. She will almost certainly succeed her father as Chief Legate. And then…even greater things are likely."

This gave me pause. Merejin was dangling something, and I decided to bite.

"You think Shaeyin might one day become Empress?"

"I do, lad. The current Emperor is in poor health and has no heir. The Odels are next in line, and while Vodun is hardly old, he won't live forever. The whispers I hear are that the Emperor views Shaeyin like a daughter. He works with her personally and often jokes that she is far smarter than her father. So yes, I think we may very well see the rise of another great Empress in our lifetime. In yours at least."

Interestingly, upon hearing this, I had the first real pang of sympathy for the Countess herself. Whatever compromising material Ulan Gueritus had on Shaeyin Odel, it obviously threatened to bring down the reputation of her entire family and, by extension, a potential future that enthralled my dear friend Merejin. I myself cared little about who reigned in Tergon, but I couldn't help but be intrigued by the vision she laid out. It was well known that in the last seven hundred years, the handful of empresses who had sat on the Tergonian throne had been among the best rulers of all.

Of course, there was also the dreadful price that the Raving Blade was exacting, which, now that I truly thought about it, made me sick to my stomach. I wasn't really looking for more reasons to want to kill this bastard, but somehow the incentives just kept piling up.

"What about a physical description, Merejin?" I asked. "Are there details written in Pinsar's book?"

"Some, I seem to remember. The girl is in her thirty-sixth year now, if my math holds up. Much about her beauty and her classic Odel features—blue eyes, fair hair, like her father. Some exaggerated imagery: sparkling like a fairy princess, tall, lithe, and majestic like a celestial nymph…this sort of thing."

I thought of Nascinthé as Merejin spoke and felt she was quite a good match to this description, minus the fair hair. Perhaps Gueritus wouldn't look too closely at the color in the dim light of torches, entranced as he was likely to be by the rest of her. But physical features weren't the entire puzzle.

"Anything else about her, about her personally?" I asked.

"There's a good amount contained in that book," Merejin replied. "You'll need to read through it to pluck out all the interesting tidbits. A strong person, I garner, though apparently not headstrong. Just independent, which will make her a valuable advisor to the Emperor when that day comes. She remains unmarried, which has raised eyebrows and left many a besotted suiter heartbroken."

"How does she come by the title Countess?"

I had always found the topic of titles and peerage more than a little confusing.

"Ah," replied Merejin. "Countess is merely an honorary title, bequeathed to her by her father, from one of his lesser holdings. But, in keeping with the customs of the Tergonian aristocracy, she will become an archduchess upon Vodun's death, seeing as he has no male heirs. I do recall that she shares her father's strong antipathy for piracy, and also religion. Pirates and gods. Are there two more wretched things in all the world?"

A caustic little smile formed on Merejin's wrinkled lips, and I had to chuckle.

Merejin knew damned well that piracy supplied as much as half the goods that entered our city, which certainly included books, so she was clearly being facetious. As for religion, that sentiment was genuine. The Tergonian Empire had been officially irreligious for almost four hundred years, ever since the philosophical movement known as the Dawn of Reason, which banished all formal denominations from the land. As a counterreaction to over three hundred years of unrelenting religious strife, the ruler of that time, Empress Asadeissia of the Besidian Dynasty, fresh off a series of political victories and in position of unmatched military power, declared the end of all organized sects. The names of the many emperors and the details of their various reigns were largely a blur to me, but even the most illiterate peasant knew about Asadeissia. She had not only put a stop to what she termed the "deadly poison of factionalism," but she ushered in an age dominated by reason, philosophy, and virtue, or at least that was the intention. The experiment had not been quite as successful as hoped.

Still, by all accounts, the last four centuries had been significantly better than the three that came before that, and while rebellious religious movements did arise on occasion, the Emperor always had plenty of support to put them down. After all, people were free to worship whatever god they chose in their own homes. They were entitled to snarl out a curse or declaration using the name of a divine entity or a demon, or the gods as a whole. They simply could not organize and proselytize, as that had always marked the start of trouble in the past. I, for instance, occasionally said a prayer to Gudros, the North Derjian god of smugglers, before I set out on a Grell Run, and while I had about as much conviction that these prayers helped me as I did in the promise, or threat, of an afterlife—which wasn't much—it didn't hurt to cover all bases.

Outside, I heard the muffled drone of Third Bell, and with that I let out an apologetic sigh.

"I would love to sit here all afternoon, Mera, discussing the finer points of the Tergonian nobility, but that bell signals my next appointment."

"As you wish, lad. Which of these do you want?"

I reached over and flipped briefly through the book of crests. While I could see that this book had value for a person doing deep research into the subject, it was overkill for my purposes. Besides, it was by far the most ungainly of the three and would be the most difficult to hide.

"Just these two," I said, tapping the *Codex* and Hendjick Pinsar's book. "And please include one of your felt bags to protect them."

"Neither book is cheap. I could loan them to you instead."

"Since when did you start a lending library?"

This elicited yet another laugh, and with that she leaned down and pulled a soft brown sack from the drawer of the desk.

"In all seriousness, I appreciate the offer," I said, "which I know you don't make to many customers."

Merejin smiled and gave a little shrug as if to say it was a small price to pay for my business. Also, perhaps, my friendship.

"But," I continued, somewhat hesitantly, "I couldn't promise I would be returning these…anytime soon."

I'm not entirely sure why I said this. I could have phrased it a dozen different ways, said some highly plausible thing about fleshing out my own knowledge and my collection, which was arguably deficient in volumes of this nature. But I didn't. I spoke this cryptic, faltering sentence, which hinted at things, puffed out just the faintest whiff of the threatening unknown, and this was not likely to escape my host. Merejin continued to place the two books into their bag, but her movements slowed, and she tilted her head down so that she could look at me over her spectacles.

"Okay then, lad. It should be twenty-one for the pair, but I will make it eighteen as a courtesy…since I know you are doing someone a favor."

I thanked her and reached into my purse to fish out the tolgens.

"And do tell your friend that I wish her well in her production," Merejin continued. "Playing the Countess is sure to be fraught with hazards…in a theatrical sense. Will you be attending this particular production, Vazeer?"

This, in turn, caused me to pause in my own movements, with sixteen coins counted out on the table. It was extremely rare for Merejin to use my name. I sometimes sensed that she associated it too closely with the alias that usually accompanied it, a moniker that I suspect she had heard by now. I was quite certain that she was purposely referencing my work.

"Yes, I'll be in attendance," I replied. "And it's hard to say exactly where this production will lead. It could be a big success, or perhaps a terrible failure. Only the nonexistent gods can say."

Merejin smiled sadly, then leaned forward and patted my hand affectionately.

"I think I will start that lending library today," she said in a voice that could not entirely disguise the heaviness. "Keep your tolgens…for your travels. And return the books to me when you get back. This puts the onus on you, my dearest and least restrained customer. Now off with you, before you make havoc of your next appointment."

6

THE EMPORIUM

A short time later, I found myself strolling briskly down the Virtuoso, my gaze meandering over the stone and plaster storefronts I knew so well. The first traces of the afternoon fog had already started to creep in, though the familiar North Derjian grayness had not yet stifled colors and dispelled details. There were still quite a few pedestrians ambling the brown cobbles, often in pairs, and it was easy to note that more than half of them were foreigners. People of the North Derjian coastline were generally ruddy of skin, stocky of build, with hair color that ranged from dirty blond to chestnut brown. Additionally, Sullward locals, whatever their bloodline, tended towards practical clothing at the duller end of the spectrum. Thus, whenever I saw alternately dark or pale skin, draped in gaudy, colorful attire, I usually knew I was looking at somebody from the Mid or South Derjian, or even from one of the Inland Kingdoms. The great joke was that I could almost be mistaken for one of them. With my swarthy skin tones, my overt Western features, and my penchant for fancier clothing, one might think me a Kaszian merchant in search of a bargain. But nobody ever thought that.

Looking at these foreign buyers, wandering the twisting path of the marvelously asymmetric Virtuoso in their red and blue and green velvet cloaks, trimmed with patterned silk, I saw an innocence, a pleasantness, or, at times, a haughty affectation that simply was not Sullwardian. I didn't need to look in a mirror to understand the severity of the contrast.

Still, I never disparaged the outsiders, nor did I resent their intrusion, as some of my less enlightened fellows were known to do. I was grateful for them. If not for the steady stream of foreign buyers, the Virtuoso would be down to perhaps five measly stores, comprised of a paltry inventory, since most of the locals who shopped here were either landlords, large business owners, or members of the local government. Those men and women were certainly well off, but they lacked any true refinement. They could not support the likes of Merejin or Annaliese or even Jasper Marzan, whose shop I was headed to at the moment. So, I might be required to move quickly sometimes to beat out an Engoliese collector, or a merchant from Tergon, but the competition was worth it if it kept these vendors employed.

When I arrived at Marzan's Exotic Emporium of Fine Collectibles, I saw what I had expected and hoped to see: a sizeable crowd milling about in the large gallery of artifacts. The Emporium, as we called it, was one of the most successful stores on the Virtuoso. It was here that some of the truly prize inventory from the Underlord Ripening Halls made its way out to market. Jaspar was a highly ambitious and rather unlikable son of a bitch, who had clearly worked out some sort of favorable deal with the agents of the Underlords, for he consistently had the best merchandise in the entire city. I was certain, in fact, that he had figured out a way to jump the queue.

The primary clients for the Underlords' ripened merchandise, and by far the most reliable path of redistribution, were the big southern trading companies who, on roughly a biyearly basis, sailed into Sullward Harbor with massive galleons protected by armed escort. These conglomerates were powerful enough to be nations in their own right, and when they bought in force, they could clear out several Ripening Halls in one load. From there they sold the goods to the appropriate merchants in numerous affluent cities, and since they could effectively set the markets on those items, they made even more money from the whole venture than the Underlords. Additionally, prestigious auction houses held annual events in towns neighboring Sullward, attracting some of the wealthiest citizens in the Empire, and this moved a whole other swath of the ripened merchandise. Both parties—the trading conglomerates, and the auction houses—had become powerful de facto allies to our city, and their formidable lobbying efforts in Tergon ensured that key legal provisions, such as the statute of limitations for stolen goods, were kept in place.

The fact that Jaspar Marzan was able to step in front of these behemoths and fill his sizable Emporium with the choicest of artistic splendors showed a dogged determination and a certain degree of risk-taking that I had to admire, even if I didn't care for the man himself. After all, if not for Jaspar's aggressive dealing, Ashland Nuce would never have made it to the walls of my gallery, and Giradera of Azmoul would right now be some other man's silent bronze love interest.

I entered the Emporium and instantly smelled the light sweet smoke of incense, which burned from dawn until dusk in the place. An impeccably dressed guardsman in a polished breastplate and plumed helmet waited just within the door, and he gave a slight bow as I entered. Jaspar certainly knew how to set the mood. As I strolled into the grand, high-ceilinged space, dodging around shoppers and statuary alike, perusing glass display cases filled with ballroom masks, exotic fans, and antique weaponry, I was, as always, enchanted. Even more pleasing was the fact that I recognized much of it. I had negotiated for and smuggled at least two of the fans in the glass case, as well as a magnificent longsword set in a jeweled scabbard. The longsword was just one piece in a very pricey buy from a rogue shipper, and I remember wishing I could simply swipe the damned thing for myself. I didn't, of course, just as I would never skim a single silver tolgen from the purchase funds provided by a Sketcher, since such practices were always eventually discovered by the Underlords. Once that happened, you were finished, in every sense of the word.

The Emporium also contained plenty of items I didn't recognize: tapestries, exotic pieces of furniture, and even a royal scepter from one of the Inland Kingdoms, protected inside an ornamented steel cage. Additionally, I spotted a painting of the Sullward Clock Tower, which must have come out of the Ripening Halls recently, for it hadn't been here on my last visit. I gave it a quick look but knew immediately that it wasn't going to make it to any of the walls of my home. It was a work by Nedier Odgey, a lesser Midland painter who did a decent job with mood and tone but who always seemed to lack a driving theme in his work. One glance at this depiction of the iconic Sullward Clock Tower and I knew that he had missed the thing entirely.

The Clock Tower, officially "The King Aurellis Kaennamin Inaugural Bell Tower," was the first building commissioned by Aurellis Kaennamin upon his coronation. It was the construction that launched all the others, the Kaennamins' grand declaration that the region would now be ruled by an official monarchy, as opposed to a disparate collection of regional lords. Boldly ambitious in scope, the project initiated an even more ambitious political plan, and there was much opposition to that towering structure at first, just as there was near rebellion at the new, self-appointed monarchy. For this reason, I suppose, King Aurellis chose to have his famous quotation inscribed over the southern door of the building, where it could be read even on the mistiest of days.

*"The maddest and grandest of dreams
shall summon forth the means."*

Those words were ostensibly his clarion call to the architects and painters, sculptors and performers, that he officially welcomed the best and most creative of them into his new city-state. The Kaennamins themselves would be the means, for they were intent on becoming the greatest patrons of the arts that Derjia had ever known. And yet, the tower was really Aurellis's statement to the world that his dream was now being realized, that he had won. By inscribing that quote, he told them that the sheer power of his vision had made it happen.

In this painting, however, Odgey had foolishly chosen to backlight the building with the moon, thereby forfeiting any hope of legibility for the inscription. He did a reasonably good job capturing the soaring fortress shape, with its sharp point piercing the moon-laced mists, but it wasn't enough. Without the inscription, the painting was worthless, at least to my eyes. In my vestibule I possessed a wonderful painting of the Clock Tower, a work by Haedria Denneker, which managed to capture the heavy atmosphere of the city, while still allowing the inscription to be read. Denneker herself was from the North, and she understood the great importance of that building and exactly how to depict it. In time I would probably find another similar image to grace my home, but in the meantime, this work by Nedier Odgey certainly wasn't it.

I turned and browsed the many other items in the crowded, sweet-smelling room. As always, I had to work hard to maintain my stoic face. Jaspar Marzan was as quick to detect and exploit customer delight as a wild dog sniffing carrion; however, I was in no real danger of getting fleeced today because I wasn't there to shop. As an added lucky break, the proprietor was rather engaged at the moment with a pair of customers in silk coats, and it appeared that he was in the act of trying to sell them a pair of decorative, gold-inlaid halberds. I could see his gangling frame waving energetically and his balding brow scrunching and releasing in exaggerated fashion, as if alternating between sympathy and indignation with every question or counteroffer his customers made. I turned my back on that familiar and somewhat distasteful spectacle and moved towards the back room of the Emporium where some of my favorite items were displayed. There, another smartly dressed guardsman stood at the door.

"Hello, Ottavar," I said as I drew near. "Keeping awake today?"

"Barely, Vazeer," he replied. "Just barely."

Ottavar was tall and slender like Jaspar, and in fact they bore similar features—long narrow noses, sharp chins, and the hint of olive in their complexions, which made sense since they were both from the same region of the Northwestern Derjian, known as Upper Kaszia. Jaspar had been living in Sullward for decades, but Ottavar was a more recent arrival, and I could only assume that he had landed this job on account of being Marzan's fellow countryman.

"As I told you last time, Otto, you'd get a lot more excitement guarding a warehouse down at the wharf. Those guards spend the whole day drunk, and there's roughly one break-in a week."

"Ahhhh," Ottavar moaned. "I should consider this. In five years, I grab three idiot shoplifters, one spoilt Engoliese brat who try to fire crossbow, and this terrible time I have to toss hobo who think this place is toilet. Fancy people doesn't cause enough troubles."

I gave a good chuckle, in part because I always enjoyed Ottavar's disjointed use of the Derjian language. Upper Kaszia had been slow to adopt the Empire's tongue, and some Upper Kaszians who remained on the western side of the ocean rarely spoke it at all.

I patted Ottavar on the shoulder.

"Well, I'm not likely to do any of those things today, so you're out of luck."

Ottavar laughed and nodded, then turned back towards the main room. I entered the smaller showroom, where Jaspar kept a whole range of beautiful goods that could fill out the lesser rooms of a house. The big space at the front of the store was where the most dramatic pieces were displayed—items for the foyer or salon or living room. But in the back room one found a plethora of beautiful rarities that could embellish every last inch of a dwelling—a glistening copper bathtub with gold inlay around the border, a gem-encrusted bath chamber mirror, a whole set of brand-new Tethsian steel cooking pots and cutlery, ornate porcelain flatware, vases made of glass, ceramic, and bronze, gold scissors, pearl-handled pens with similarly clad ink wells, gem-encrusted jewel boxes, silver servant bells, glass lanterns of every manner of workmanship, ornate candle sticks, and a whole array of idiosyncratic items such as models and figurines. Here, too, I recognized perhaps ten percent of the merchandise from my various nocturnal errands. The only category Jaspar Marzan did not deal in was books, for which my old friend Merejin was very grateful. And today so was I, as it was going to make my ploy here much safer.

Ottavar wasn't particularly worried about thieves preying upon the back room since the smaller items were all locked in thick glass cases, reinforced with steel, while the larger items—the bathtub, various mirrors, the biggest of the lanterns—were simply too cumbersome to cart past him without notice. So, he stared back into the main room where he stood his best chance of encountering a disturbance, and this left me quite free to conduct my business.

There were a half dozen other browsers in this section: four women and two men, and all but one of them appeared to be foreigners. I dipped my chin cordially to the one Sullwardian I recognized, an older woman whose name escaped me but whom I encountered regularly on the Virtuoso. She gave the weakest of nods, then went quickly back to her intense perusal of a porcelain tea set, hovering over the glass case as if to block her many competitors, of whom I saw none. I scanned the others but didn't recognize any of them. The two men each seemed to be accompanied by a woman—one couple with fair features most likely from Tethsia or thereabouts, and the other couple with dark skin, likely from the Southwest corner of the Derjian Sea. They didn't quite look Gosian, but my guess was that they hailed from somewhere close. The remaining woman was wearing an angled patrician's hat, and I could only see a hint of coppery Western skin tones beneath that hat and at her forearms. She limped slowly through the merchandise with a silver-handled cane.

I made my way over to the very back corner where there was a display case containing lovely blown-glass sculptures of every imaginable color. Only the best artisans from the East Derjian were capable of creating these figures—running animals, female dancers, breaking waves, small landscapes—beautifully colored using a wide palette of metal oxides. The nicest of them could fetch more than their weight in gold, and I myself had only been able to afford two so far in my years of home embellishment, though I had smuggled dozens in my day. However, it was the object on the wall above the sculpture display case that grabbed my attention. Hanging grandly there, between two Middle Kaszian tapestries, was the true prize of the back room—a large, wooden-framed wall clock, with a swinging brass pendulum. The face of the clock was a sheet of mother of pearl, and the hands and numbers matched the shiny brass of the pendulum. Only the wealthiest of citizens had a clock inside their own home, for such devices were exorbitant to produce, and the internal mechanisms were so complex that the best clockmakers were required to create a piece that would remain accurate throughout the day. Despite my many years of prodigious earning, I had not yet found the right moment to lay down forty-five gold suldots, which is what Jasper was asking for this beauty.

"Iz very nice, this one, yes?" came a raspy female voice to my right. I turned to observe the foreign woman with the cane standing next to me, gazing up at the wall clock. The angle of her hat was such that I could only see the lower part of her tanned jaw, which appeared somewhat wrinkled from age. Her heavy accent marked her as somebody from the far Western Inlands, and therefore probably not even a resident of the Tergonian Empire. I wasn't particularly given to chatting with strangers; however, being inside the Emporium always made me more sociable, and the sight of that magnificent wall clock definitely lifted my spirits.

"It is," I replied. "But you can set your sights elsewhere, because it's mine. Or it will be…in time."

"Ooohh," said the woman, her coppery skin wrinkling further, and then she giggled a few times hoarsely. "You make joke, I think. About time?"

"Not a very good one. It's probably funnier in your language."

Out of the corner of my eye I saw the woman's narrow lips smile subtly.

"So, this thing…how you call it?"

"It's a clock," I replied. "A house clock specifically, which is very rare."

"House clock," she repeated somewhat awkwardly. "When will be right time for you to buy this house clock?"

"At a time when I can afford it," I replied. "Did you happen to see the price?"

The woman went silent for a moment. Then she spoke almost under her breath, "I am not so good with numbers, but I am believe one full pouch of Gosian diamonds could buy you house clock…along with entire store."

The muscles in my neck twitched, and I had to exert tremendous restraint not to swivel and glare at this woman. A second later I relaxed, and then I had to work hard not to smile like a complete imbecile.

"You enjoyed that, didn't you?"

"Quite a bit," replied Nascinthé of Levell, and the subtle smile again graced her long, slender mouth.

It is difficult to describe, or accurately quantify, the strange feelings that came up in me while in the presence of this woman. The night before there had been the added embarrassment of faltering before my fellows, of distraction overtaking me at exactly the moment I needed to be sharp. Though my face was disguised by torchlight then, my unseemly inner swoon was clearly apparent to Flerra Tellian, perhaps to the others as well. Maybe to Nascinthé herself.

As I stood there in the back room of the Emporium, I felt the same hot flush rippling up my torso and into my cheeks, and my face seemed as if it were on the verge of some truly idiotic expression that would be entirely ruinous to my reputation, were anyone to see it. As such, I turned away and glanced around the room to assess what the other occupants were up to. The old Sullward woman was still hovering in the vicinity of the tea set, and now, in fact, she did appear to have some competition, for the Tethsian couple had arrived at that end of the space, and they were clearly taking some interest in that particular display case. The other couple had divided, and the man was examining a set of crystal wine decanters, while the woman appeared to be thoroughly entranced by the bathtub. Ottavar was still facing the main room, and his slouching posture suggested that he had made little headway in his battle against boredom.

I turned back to Nascinthé, and she, in kind, turned towards me. While her patrician's hat was shading her eyes, there was now a blue glint just below the angled brim that was unmistakable, which was helpful, for in every other way she was unrecognizable from the beautiful young woman who had showed up at the boathouse. Her skin appeared sun-darkened and wrinkled, as if it had spent too many years journeying under the desert sun. Her nose had a notable bump on the bridge, which further skewed her appearance in the direction of being an old matron. Added to this overall effect was a flabby jowl just below her slightly bulbous chin, plus a rather unsightly blemish that ran down her jaw and onto her neck, and all of this made a figure upon whom no man wished to rest his eyes. Truly, it was a remarkable disguise, surpassing the handiwork of any Masque I had ever seen.

Grell Runners worked with Masques fairly often, for those of Nascinthé's trade were the premier diplomats and empaths of the Labyrinth. They were brought in to spearhead negotiations on particularly difficult buy operations, and also to ferret out the intentions of new shippers looking to establish relationships with the Underlords. Masques could be absolutely uncanny in their abilities to guess at motives, sniff duplicity, and spot disguised Tergonian constables conducting sting operations. By doing their job well, they could prevent untold trouble for the rest of us.

While, theoretically, all Masques were good at assuming personas, only a select few could convincingly impersonate specific individuals, and fewer still were trained in the advanced art of physical disguise. Nascinthé of Levell, it now appeared, belonged to this last and most elite category of Masque.

"Well, at least one of my concerns is now laid to rest," I mumbled. "Shaeyin is apparently blonde. But I'm guessing that's not going to be a problem for you."

"It's not," Nascinthé agreed. "You met with your scholar?"

"I did. I have two books for you. Come closer."

As soon as I said it, I regretted my tone. I had spoken to her with the gruff bossiness I used when commanding my fellow operatives during a bid.

"Please," I added, though even that word sounded unintentionally sarcastic.

Nascinthé complied and came very close. I don't know if she made a habit of addressing all the physical senses when assuming a disguise, but I found the soft hint of jasmine in her perfume rather delicate and entirely too feminine for a gimp-legged desert crone. She slid her satchel over so that it was close to mine, and all the while our bodies pressed each other lightly at the sides, effectively obscuring the bags from view. It was easy enough to slide the brown sack containing the books out of my bag and deposit it into hers.

"On occasion the front door guard will check the bag of a person he doesn't recognize. But this place doesn't deal in books, so he'll wave you along."

Nascinthé nodded. I remained close to her for another moment, and then I pulled away, before it would seem strange to the others. A quick glance around indicated that nobody was even remotely looking in our direction. This brought up another issue.

"Did you happen to notice if you were tailed?" I asked.

Nascinthé had tilted her head down, as if examining the glass sculptures. She spoke quietly from below the brim of her hat.

"I was tailed this morning. I am not tailed now."

"How can you be sure?" I asked, feeling quite certain that Nascinthé had not dealt with her tail in the same manner that I handled mine.

"Because the tail followed a relatively young, fair-skinned, able-bodied woman to a tavern in Dockside. I suspect he is still waiting for her to emerge from the women's privy."

Again, I had to resist the urge to turn and glare at her.

"You put on…all of this in the time it takes a woman to relieve herself?"

"It's better when I'm not in such a rush," Nascinthé replied. "Thus, the hat, and relying on an overt gimmick like the limp. A good Eye should be on alert for these things, especially when he knows he's tailing a Masque, but this one didn't seem to be. The cane is collapsible and fits in my bag."

During the prior night's conversation with Holod Deadskiff, he had asked me if I thought our mysterious Masque was up to the job. I couldn't answer the question then, and I suppose I didn't know quite enough to answer it now. However, my confidence was certainly rising.

"If I'd known you'd shake off your tail so easily," I said, "I would have brought you to meet my scholar yourself. You could have asked her whatever questions you wanted. But I was…it seemed risky."

And my voice trailed off.

The truth was I had no obligation to introduce any of my cohorts to Merejin and, if I was being honest about it, I absolutely abhorred the idea. In most cases, that was. For some reason, I did not hate the thought of Nascinthé of Levell inside that most sacred of buildings. This was strange really, for what did I know about her? I didn't have a clue who she was, where she had actually come from, how long she had been working in our city, and, perhaps most of all, what the hell she was thinking joining a Narrow Bid. And yet, for all of that, despite her obvious aptitude for deception, I sensed that she was different from the others. She might, in fact, appreciate a room stacked with rows upon rows of rare volumes and scrolls, presided over by a brilliant old woman whose passion it was to unlock the abstract secrets of the world. Something in Nascinthé's quick eyes, in her newly revealed penchant for dramatic surprises, something in the whole intriguing puzzle that composed this mysterious Shadow Bidder, told me she would be right at home in Merejin's Books. So, yes, if not for the risk of leading a man like Bevin Slywell straight to my dear friend's doorstep, I might actually have considered it.

Nascinthé raised the brim of her hat slightly, then stared at me directly. And I, seeing the gentle curvature of her eyebrows, her soft eyelashes, and, most of all, that incredible blue-green color once again revealed (this time in the light of day) forgot all about the disguise. I truly didn't see it. What I saw instead was the strangely intimate act of this woman seeing me; fully seeing me. I'm not sure how else to describe it.

I had been read by Masques before, felt their inquisitive eyes roving over my face, searching out my moods and motives and intentions. But I had never felt anything like this. Nascinthé did not appear to be observing little clues in my expression, or my body language, or miniscule changes in my breathing—all of which I had experienced in the past. She just gazed into my eyes, absorbing whatever it was that she saw there, and I, in turn, allowed it. For about three seconds. After that I abruptly turned away and resumed staring at my overpriced house clock.

"I understand," I heard Nascinthé say.

I shrugged dismissively.

But really…she did? Understand what? Was it, perhaps, the fact that I was a pretentious, split-headed thug? That, despite my nice clothing and my little bundle of scholarly books, I had clubbed a fellow Shadow Bidder unconscious to the dirt the prior night, beat him bloody just for doing his job? Did Nascinthé see all of that? How else did I get rid of my tail, she must have wondered? Certainly not by playing dress-up in an alehouse toilet. Perhaps, when she stared at me that way, she saw the whole wretched tangle of the Wags displayed behind my eyes, or maybe she sniffed the fetid Orphan's Grove just under the subtle scent of her own jasmine perfume. The woman understood things now, or so she said. I wasn't at all sure that this was a welcome development.

"We should get on with this," I said curtly. "I have other appointments after this one."

Nascinthé nodded.

"There's a lot to read in these two books. Do you think you can glean what you need in the next twenty-four hours?"

"That's not a problem," she replied. "But if your scholar had additional information, that would be useful."

And so I quickly relayed it. I conveyed the handful of details that Merejin had provided, and I noted the respective uses for the *Codex* and Pinsar's book. As a final point, I mentioned that I had interviewed one of the Raved the prior night, and I recounted the disjointed muddle of descriptions I had received during that encounter.

"I'm sorry it's not more helpful," I said. "I suppose there could still be time to hunt down another one of these unfortunates and try again."

"Don't," said Nascinthé with an edge of firmness. "It's an unnecessary risk. I will know the target when I see him."

I didn't argue with that. Having just been stared through like a polished storefront window, I suspected that this was yet another thing that wouldn't be a problem for her.

"Well, that's it then," I said, still gazing at the clock. "The next time I see you, you will look quite a bit different, I imagine."

"I will," she agreed. "And you will appear very much the same."

And with that she turned her head to look at me once again, but I did not return the gaze. Not directly at least. I could detect the soft intensity of that stare out of the corner of my eye, and the mere hint of it reignited the weird heat in my face. I was concerned that my cheeks had gone red.

"Perhaps someday," she said very softly, "when nobody is following either of us, you could bring me to meet your scholar, and to see her many books."

To this I offered another one of my careless shrugs, as if it didn't matter to me either way. Inside, I felt decidedly light-headed.

"I just wanted you to know," she said, "that I would like that very much."

7

FOG AND LIES

A half hour later I was standing at the edge of the wharf, listening to the baying of offload foremen, inhaling the stink of the returning fishing boats, and watching the distant blasts of white spray as waves crashed against the sea wall. And beyond that, beyond the crumbling stone barrier that divided our still waters from the vast heaving anger of the Derjian Sea, an ominous wave approached. How slowly and silently it came. How inexorably, like the passage of time or the relentless fluctuation between human good fortune and bereavement. I had watched the onset of this foreboding wave an uncountable number of times, often from this very spot, sometimes from my third-floor balcony, but usually from the skiff docks, where the view was most dramatic and always eeriest. Onward it came. Onward rolled the soundless gray wall of the North Derjian fog.

It was not simply a poetic turn of phrase to call us Shadow Bidders. Every afternoon the gray wave arrived, burying our city in a shroud of obscuring vapors, and it only thickened once the sun went down somewhere behind all of that massless mass. Not until late the next morning did the dissipation begin, and even then, the wisps and trails often lingered, as if holding their place in the queue and reminding us that clear vision was a rare, fleeting privilege not to be squandered. Of course, the opposite was also true. When the nebulous veil dropped over the eyes of our city, when concealment and opacity reigned, men such as me needed to be about our business. Civilized things must be cast aside. The hour of the Shadow Bidder had arrived.

"That's a mighty fine get-up for a little row in your skiff, Wharfie."

I had seen him coming out of the corner of my eye, but I hadn't imagined he would speak to me. Most of the time they just glared.

"Good afternoon to you, Constable," I said and tipped my hat slightly.

Lieutenant Constable Vestién D'jaen was a dangerous-looking man. He had fierce hazel eyes and a manicured black goatee that gave such severity to his mouth that even a casual expression had the appearance of a frown. He was not particularly large, but one could sense the strength and intense conditioning that had molded the body beneath his chainmail hauberk. In our brief unpleasant exchanges, we never referred to each other by name.

"Gerard, wouldn't you say that this man is incredibly well dressed for a wharfie?"

I hadn't seen Constable Gerard coming up behind me until Vestién called out to him, which was a grave lapse. I now also noticed another constable making his way down the wharf from the other direction. This new one had only joined the garrison in the last year, and he looked like quite a bruiser, with a heavy frame that seemed to bulge out of his armor and a dark beard that was so thick it appeared to be foaming out of his face. Gerard, who stalked up right behind me, was also burly, and even though I didn't turn around to look at him, I could sense his hulking animosity radiating onto my back.

"Yes, Lieutenant, that's a mighty fine cape," replied Gerard. "The boots are nice too. It really makes you wonder how a wharf rat comes by such fine clothing."

"It does indeed," replied Vestién. "Hail there, Rogiért, perhaps you could weigh in on this matter."

The big ugly one with the thick beard had now come quite close, and a moment later I was pressed in on all sides by these three.

"Gerard and I were just speculating how this man, who is clearly some sort of harborside loiterer, how this man possibly comes by his fine clothing. I don't possess clothing this nice, and I am a Lieutenant Constable in the Tergonian Forces."

"Might be he stole it," growled Rogiért.

I saw a brief flash of irritation cross Vestién's features, as it became obvious that ugly Rogiért did not possess the subtlety to play this game.

"No, I doubt it's the clothing that's stolen," Vestién said, quickly putting the sport back on track. "But one wonders what, exactly, *is* stolen. I suspect something must be, for I don't remember seeing this particular man running any sort of legitimate business here in this loathsome city. And nothing in his look or demeanor suggests nobility."

"It might pay to keep an eye on him, Lieutenant," said Gerard from behind, and I could literally feel the puff of his breath on my neck. "That's the best way to figure out which part is the stolen part."

At this point I turned around so that I could face them all, and I must say the sight was formidable. I myself am relatively tall, but Rogiért was even taller, and both he and Gerard outweighed me by a comfortable margin. Gerard was the only one of the three who had North Derjian features—dirty blond hair (cut very short), a weather-beaten complexion free of facial hair, and an angry set of blue eyes that looked threatening enough to belong on the face of one of the Underlords' soldiers. Adding his hostile glare to the sight of Rogiért's big foaming face and Vestién's dangerous severity, I was growing increasingly desperate to extricate myself from this situation.

"Good men of the Tergonian Forces," I said with a polite nod, "let me quickly remove your confusion on this matter. I had a rather wealthy uncle living in Kaszia who passed on a few years ago, and I was the sole beneficiary of his estate. So, while I do miss my dear uncle Jathrin, I have certainly seen quite an improvement in my finances as a result of his passing. The clothing is a bit of an extravagance, I'll admit."

"Oh, isn't that a bittersweet story," said Vestién with a malicious glare, "but it's ultimately not the clothing that concerns me. Rather, it's the things hidden underneath. Like this for instance."

And with that, the Lieutenant reached forward and grabbed my right wrist, and with his other hand he pulled back the sleeve of my tunic, exposing a few inches of my forearm, just before the start of the leather cuirass. There, a small section of branded black numerals was visible. It took an intense act of will for me not to jerk away.

"Now this is a curious tattoo for the heir to a wealthy Kaszian estate," exclaimed Vestién.

He did not let go of my wrist, and there was a fractional moment when I feared something terrible was about to happen. For just that instant I forgot about consequences; I forgot about my own future. I felt only that contemptuous hand on my wrist, heard the derisive grunts of the two ill-tempered brutes, and, perhaps most of all, saw that hateful tattoo on my wrist, exposed to the open air like the sudden dropping of my pants. I came close to snapping. The flush of humiliation washed up through me like a backsurge of latrine water in a listing ship. Lieutenant Vestién D'jaen appeared to sense the reaction he had achieved, and his eyes glinted in triumph.

"Your fancy clothes might temporarily cover that mark, criminal, but they can never make it go away."

To my right and left I saw the twin beasts put their hands on the hilts of their broadswords. Additionally, Gerard put his other hand on the grip of his stiletto, in true North Derjian fashion, and I could see in an instant where this would go if I did not bring my emotions under control. I knew from firsthand experience that Tergonian constables were among the best trained soldiers in the entire Empire. Even if I were similarly trained (and I most certainly was not) disaster was the only possible outcome of failing to submit in this situation. I took a deep breath, then spoke.

"Yes, Lieutenant Constable," I said as politely as I could. "I am not proud of that mark, which signifies the indiscretions of my youth. But I have paid for those indiscretions, with eighteen hard months in the dungeons, and also on the labor gang. I have not covered the brand with another tattoo, as specified by the magistrate…"

"Because we'd lock you up right now if you did, criminal!" snarled Rogiért.

"Indeed, Constable," I replied, still polite. "I have tried to remain on a law-abiding path since those days of my youth, and I hope to use my newfound wealth—"

"Oh, shut your filthy mouth, smuggler!" Vestién snapped, and he tossed my wrist back at me like a piece of trash.

"I can't take another douse of the perfumed sewage spewing out of your face. Imperial constables aren't the spineless, bribable half-wits that make up your city watch. You can't work us with your horseshit."

And it was true. It was so terribly true; Lieutenant D'jaen was not making idle threats. Understaffed though they were, these three constables, and their half dozen cohorts in the Imperial Garrison, were dead serious about their jobs. They couldn't be bribed or intimidated. And they weren't drunken fools either, like our city watchmen. They were a constant, terrifying threat in the lives of all Shadow Bidders, particularly those of us who ran the Grells. The lengths I went to avoid these men, through a whole complicated array of tactics and devices, could fill out an entire anthology on the art of smuggling (I had even joked to Holod once that authoring such a series was my eventual exit strategy from Grell Running). This was the main reason I was looking to sweep my chips from the table; this was why I dared to consider a Narrow Bid. I might wear that humiliating tattoo on my fore-arm forever, but I no longer wanted to live the life it signified. I wanted to spend all of my days wandering the lovely Virtuoso, or occasionally the safer streets of the majestic Lower City, and then retire each evening to 27 Fletcher Street at a decent hour. I feared that if I didn't make this change soon, I would eventually fall a mere half-step behind one night, and then these men would have me at last. Lieutenant Vestién D'jaen seemed to share this view.

"Understand, Grell Turd," he said with calm menace, "those dark dungeons and that chain gang are not just your past; they are also your future. I will personally see to it that you live out the remainder of your days in such places. The wretched mists can only hide you for so long."

And with that he signaled his companions, and the three of them turned and continued their way along the gnarled wooden planks of the wharf. All the while, the world around me slowly disappeared, banished inch by inch into the formless gray prison of the North Derjian fog.

<hr>

I would like to tell you that I easily brushed off the effects of my encounter with the Tergonian constables, but that would be a lie. A foolish, image-painting lie, designed to present myself as a man possessed of infinite (ultimately inhuman) aplomb. I am not, not even close. As I made my way down the final stretch of wharf before the skiff docks, watching the hazy forms moving up and down the gangplanks, seeing the pivoting black steeples of the dock cranes hoisting their bulging nets through the grounded clouds, I felt a brittleness in my psyche that was not going to be easy to dispel. I swerved around a mule-drawn cart overloaded with sacks and crates as it creaked heavily away from Berth Nine. A clerk was just visible, reviewing a manifest at the gangplank of that berth, where an Engoliese barque was docked, and while his features were too blurry to see, I spotted the imperial blue surcoat easily enough. There might be only nine constables in the Sullward Imperial Garrison, but they certainly brought a boat-load of clerks with them from Tergon. If not for men like this one, I could use the goddamned gangplank for once. Instead, these fastidious little bastards (nearly as incorruptible as the constables), saw to it that only legitimate merchandise came off the ships in the conventional fashion. Everything else needed to be lowered over the back in the dead of night by prison-branded Grell Turds like me.

I stepped down onto the skiff docks and made my way towards Droden's marina, passing a bunch of local fishermen hoisting their heavy catch bags on their shoulders. When I arrived in the area where my collection of skiffs was stored, I found Droden himself waiting for me, and at once he detected my disturbed frame of mind.

"Some little birds told me you had a nice chat with Vestién and his imperial knuckle-draggers," Droden said by way of greeting. He was a tall wiry man in his late forties, with long graying hair, which he always wore loose. He also sported a thick gray-brown mustache, which gave him a rather wise look, and this was no deception. Droden Sailwain was a very wise man, and, after Holod Deadskiff, he was the single most important resource in my Grell Running profession.

"Aye," I replied. I clasped his forearm, and he mine, in traditional maritime greeting. "It was a particularly bad one."

Droden smiled wryly, and there was a fair measure of sympathy in that expression. He understood very well what it was to live under the threat of the imperial constables. Were I to pull back the sleeve of his tunic, I would a find a tattoo similar to mine on his right forearm.

Droden had been a Grell Runner once, and, as an added connection, he was also one of Holod Deadskiff's Brood. Being a good seven or eight years my senior, he had largely ignored me during our brief time together in the Broodhouse, and by the time I entered my teen years, he was already out of the house contracting bids. We shared a few concurrent years Grell Running and we did get paired together on about a half dozen jobs. While Droden had been a reasonably capable Grell Runner, his true passion lay in the building and maintenance of boats, something for which he had always shown great proclivity. So, after a decade out there on the deadly river, living under the constant threat of incarceration and death, he took his solid stockpile of earnings and converted it into his current enterprise, which had netted him significantly greater gains than he had ever achieved as a smuggler. In this way, he was a fine example of what my mentor and contract broker hoped to see happen to all his highly trained little felons.

"Don't give those imperial bastards any further thought, Lash," Droden said, clearly sensing the durability of my poor state of mind. "Vestién only worked you because he's under-staffed, over-commissioned, and his own Emperor is far more interested in collecting our bribes disguised as tax revenues than in stopping some harmless smuggling. Remember, the venomless snake hisses extra loud to make up for his harmless bite."

I had to smile at Droden's valiant effort, but I was not mollified.

"No offense, old friend," I said, "but I think there's quite a bit of venom in that bite."

Droden snorted, then pulled me by the shoulder towards the eastern end of the dock. We strode together through a patch of spilled fish blood, around a half dozen upright barrels, and over a huge, coiled length of rope, until we were at the very edge of the dock. There he pointed towards the lower berths and, foggy though it was, the first thing I noted (by both sight and smell) was the merciful absence of that whaling schooner from Berth Seven. Beyond the empty berth I saw what Droden presumably wished to show me—the faint but unmistakable shape of the huge pirate galleon that I had passed in my skiff the prior night.

"See that monster?"

"Hard to miss."

"It's one of Kaszivar's flag galleons," said Droden, "which is pretty ballsy, even for her."

There were literally dozens of unaffiliated pirate vessels oper-ating in the Derjian Sea at any given time. However, only one individual I knew of had managed to assemble an actual fleet of these raiders. Her name was Lave Kaszivar, and she was a living legend to all who dwelled in our city. To my knowledge, Kaszivar had never set foot on our shores, but the tales of her exploits and her extraordinary riches were known to all. She was said to be a tactical genius of the highest order and had simultaneously taken over large swaths of the West Derjian coastline, while keeping both regional and imperial authorities at bay.

Rumor had it that the woman had come from a wealthy Middle Kaszian merchant family, although I had also heard it said that she was actually from the East Derjian Midlands, and that the whole "Lave Kaszivar" identity was an assumed persona. Either way, it was well established that she had somehow managed to maintain a semi-legal trading business at the same time she ran her pirate empire, and this provided extraordinary cover for her unlawful activities. It also allowed her to bring plundered goods into Sullward Harbor via legitimate merchant vessels. Given the great efficacy of this approach, it did seem odd to find one of her prize war ships sitting conspicuously in our port.

"Constables are all in a tizzy over this boat," Droden continued. "My boys have seen them skittering back and forth all day like bilge rats, counting heads aboard, taking note of the markings, probably trying to come up with a plan of how to handle it. But there isn't a plan, nothing that'll work. Knowing Vestién, though, he'll try something. Zealous lunatic might even attempt a few arrests in the taverns…and the dark hells only know how that will go."

Droden clapped me hard on the shoulder.

"You can trust me, Lash. There won't be any constables out on the water while this monster's in port."

"And did your little birds tell you how long that might be?"

"I heard some chirping," Droden said with a chuckle. "Let's just say that any contracts you take this week will be entirely constable-free. Can't promise they will be brigand-free, or Bidder-free…

or even pirate-free. But you won't see hair nor hide of those nice gentlemen you were speaking with earlier."

And with this I did, in fact, relax. Droden was not merely speculating here. He had garnered this information through a complex network of harborside informants—some who worked for him directly, like Leddy and a half dozen other dockhands—and several other individuals who were posted in useful places, such as the Harbormaster's staff, warehouse guardsmen, and members of the eminently bribable city watch. I, too, had a network of moles, and each had their uses, but when I wanted the definitive word on the activities of the Tergonian constables, nobody could match the intelligence provided by Droden Sailwain.

In truth, this was where most of his money came from. Droden certainly did a solid business selling and repairing boats for fishermen and local traders. However, his true coin minter was his role as the preeminent service provider for Grell Runners—selling and renting them skiffs, repairing their vessels after bids, providing priceless information on the activities of all potential threats, particularly the constables, and even arranging to have skiffs discreetly moved to safe launch points to further confuse law enforcement. In recent years I had stopped purchasing new vessels altogether. Instead, I had simply entered a long-term lease agreement with Droden, and I could, on any given day, swap out any of my current boats for a specialty craft, such as a barge for large cargo hauls, or a multi-seat passenger craft like the one I was going to need the following night to get our group to the drop site. Yes, I paid a bloody fortune every month for all of these services, but the man was worth every last iron diven.

"So, what are your needs?" asked Droden as we walked away from the eastern end of the dock, back towards the armada of small boats that constituted the marina's inventory.

"A well-balanced six-seater with rows of two. Primary steering will need to be from the front. Four paddles."

"Steering from the front can be tricky at that size, but if you're not carting a heavy load, I think I have something that will meet your needs."

"No payload. Just the six passengers."

At this, Droden squinted slightly, and he turned to me with more than a little curiosity in his clever brown eyes.

"Not my business, Lash, but sounds like a strange bid to me."

"The less you know, the better."

Droden nodded, then led me past several bridge docks to a place where we could view the boat he had in mind. I could see at a glance that he was spot-on, as usual. Like most smuggling vessels, it was relatively narrow, with a sharp front and a tapered rear, which allowed for speed and maneuverability. Three of the four benches had sufficient width to allow two passengers to sit abreast. I worked out the critical front seating quickly, mentally placing myself in the narrow single bench at the prow of the boat, with Col on the double bench just behind me.

"That'll do it," I said.

"Where and when?"

"Tomorrow evening before Sixth Bell. Nestle it into the weeds near the split oak."

"Done," said Droden. "Do you want one of my boys to keep an eye on it until you arrive?"

"Better if he doesn't. In fact, make sure the kid is gone by the bell…for his sake. Just camouflage the hell out of it."

Droden again looked at me curiously, but he didn't say anything.

We stepped away from the boat and started back towards the location where we had first met up. I saw one of Droden's dockhands hurrying down the wharf, presumably to report something to his boss, and I stopped where I was. Droden did the same.

"There's one more thing."

Something in my tone must have alerted Droden to the fact that this was going to be a sensitive topic, for he subtly raised a hand to his approaching messenger, halting him in his tracks.

"Go on."

"That caravel of yours—do you still have it docked at Eastcove?"

"The Elena's Guile. She's there, along with all my favorites. Why?"

I took a long breath, then spoke very quietly.

"Can you load her up for an ocean crossing, and have a discreet crew ready to set sail tomorrow night, if necessary?"

Another one of Droden's dock boys was now approaching out of the mist from the other direction, and Droden shooed him away. My former Broodmate stepped in very close and spoke in a murmur.

"'If necessary,' Lash? What the hell have you gotten yourself into?"

"As I said, the less you know, the better. You can name your price."

"Oh, believe me, I will," Droden replied. "But I still need to know what sort of backlash I might face with this peculiar bid of yours."

"Shouldn't touch you at all."

"No?" Droden said, and now there was the first trace of irritation in his voice. "So, I'm to expect you'll come strolling peacefully along in the dead of the night and shove off then, with only the buoy bells to guide you through the pitch-black fog? And you'll do all of this only 'if necessary'? Sorry, Lash, money alone won't buy you this. You need to tell me who's going to be on your tail. I'm not prepared for a showdown with Underlord soldiers."

This, I'm afraid, was the one drawback of working with Droden Sailwain. He was simply too smart. I had hoped to get through this with minimal probing, but I could see now that it wasn't going to happen.

"What I've gotten myself into, Sailwain, is my bloody retirement package. Not all of us planned as well as you."

"I appreciate that, and I wish you many happy years drunk in a rocking chair. But that still doesn't answer my question. Who's going to be coming after you in the dead of night?"

I took another weighty breath, gave him a grim, painful smile, then nodded, indicating that he was right. He deserved to know the truth, which was the least I owed him. After that, I opened my mouth, and the lies spewed out like reeking sewer water.

I'm not at all proud of the statements that followed. It is fundamental to the Shadow Bidder code that we honor our word, and, from a personal standpoint, I particularly loathed telling lies to Droden Sailwain, with whom I had a bond of trust upon which my life and freedom habitually depended. In any given week, the man could sell me out to any of a number of parties, telling them where I'd be picking up a skiff, how many co-operatives I'd probably have on board, and a list of the two or three ships in port that were the best candidates for that night's buy operation. I knew with a high degree of certainty that he would never do this, and not just because his business insulated him from capture and coercion by the Tergonian Forces. He honored the code. He was a former Shadow Bidder himself, and also a Broodmate, and (I would like to venture to think) one of my few friends. All of this ensured that I could depend on this man with my life.

But the same was not true in reverse, I now saw. I was not

equally trustworthy. Nor did I thoroughly honor the Shadow Bidder code, as poor Bevin Slywell could attest; as could many others before him. When the threats squeezed in from all sides and my personal agenda conflicted with the needs, principles, and safety of my fellows, only Vazeer mattered. The only code I knew at such moments was my own.

"The target is a vassal of a vassal," I lied. "Rather low in the hierarchy. And it likely won't be a termination. But there's a chance of that, if he doesn't see reason. Either way, we were told to make ourselves scarce for a few weeks afterwards, just as a precaution."

Droden brushed back a few strands of his long graying hair and squinted at me carefully.

"Before, you said, 'if necessary.' Why did you say that, if this is definitely the plan?"

Droden seemed particularly fixated on this one line, which meant that further sewage was required.

"Because I have a far easier route planned," I said. "Only a few miles out of town, where I can keep an eye on things at home as I wait for my signal to return. The Elena's Guile is merely the backup plan, in case I really screw things up."

For a few moments, Droden appeared to be weighing all of this.

"This 'vassal of a vassal'...do you have a head count on his soldiers?"

"About six. No more than that."

The crap was really piling up now and starting to stink. Only the pettiest of Underlords had garrisons this small (one really needed to add another "of a vassal" to get to a figure that insignificant). These troops existed primarily to protect the Underlords from each other, but there was always a danger that the likes of Lave Kaszivar, or some other marauder, might storm the Lower

City and attempt to seize the staggering wealth that was stored there. For this reason, the Underlords paid out a good portion of their earnings to keep sizable armies at the ready. However, this was not Droden Sailwain's area of expertise. It wasn't exactly mine either, but I had been to many more drop sites in my day, and I was consistently contracted by the top figures in the Labyrinth. Based on the offload crews I encountered at the end of my runs, I had a rough sense of the sort of muscle these figures brought to bear, and the news wasn't good. If everything did go to hell on this Narrow Bid, there was a chance that as many as two dozen soldiers could be chasing me along the east side of the river to the secret, protected cove where Droden kept his best vessels. Maybe more than that.

So, I just kept lying. I lied because were I to so much as utter the name "Gueritus," the conversation would be over. No Elena's Guile, no exit plan. In fact, Droden might actually demand that I settle all accounts with him right then and there. In our profession, an "area of expertise" was not required to understand the implications of crossing the Raving Blade. By lying in this manner, I was putting everything Droden had worked so hard for in jeopardy, including his life.

"Okay, Lash," he said. "Just you, or some passengers?"

I paused here, as if pondering. But really there was nothing to ponder, for I had thought this through extensively. It's merely that I had never uttered it out loud, never heard my own voice proclaim the suggestive head count that would send Holod into a tantrum. Just a simple number, but it said so much.

"Four," I replied. "Four in total."

Here's how I got there. The Line Man and the Finisher meant nothing to me, so dispensing with them was easy. It also went without saying that I was making room for Flerra (I would even cover her retreat and send her to the launch point alone if it came down to it). But beyond that, I had trouble editing my manifest. I had known Col for close to two decades now, and while I can't really say that we were friends, I couldn't imagine leaving him behind if that boat meant the difference between life and death. And then finally there was the woman I had known for a mere twenty-four hours, whom, if I was being honest about it, I didn't know at all. Despite Holod's warning, I was making room for her too, and while this might all seem like prudent planning, even I knew it signaled a degree of attachment that had no place on our Narrow Bid. It was split-headed Vazeer up to his exasperating tricks again—willing to hoodwink and jeopardize the man who had dealt with him faithfully for the bulk of his career, while turning sentimental about one of the most callous mercenaries in the entire Labyrinth, along with a complete stranger who made her entire living by lying. Well done, Lash. Now go and try to make money a compensation for this betrayal.

"I'll pay you two suldots to prep the Guile for the four of us," I said. "That money's yours either way. And another eight if the crossing is made, no matter how many passengers show. Does that sound fair?"

Of course it was fair. I had offered at least double what these services were worth, and I really had to wonder if in some subtle way I was tipping my hand. Was I perhaps trying to warn him that he should sever all ties with me immediately and send me packing to a place where shadowy armies could chase me forever into the dreary fog, never coming close to his beloved caravel? Droden Sailwain was not a Masque. He was a very smart man, yes, but not one who could differentiate between a nervous but grateful Vazeer and a poisonously guilty friend who knew he had, at the very least, just created a breach in their trust that might never be repaired. If Droden sensed that something was wrong with this plan, he didn't show it.

"The price is more than fair; however, if any of these three passengers arrive without you, make sure they come with the eight suldots. I won't launch without payment in full. If they've got the money, and they say you sent them, that's good enough for me."

I reached in my purse, slipped two gold coins into my palm to pay for prepping the boat, and Droden and I shook on the deal. As I clasped his tough, weathered hand, I stared him in the eye and smiled, holding his grasp a moment longer than probably seemed appropriate. It was a strange thing to know that he and I might never shake hands in this manner again.

"Thank you, Droden, for all of it."

"Of course, my friend," he replied. "And may luck be with you tomorrow night. While I'm never averse to this sort of financial windfall, that's eight pieces of gold that I sincerely hope I don't need to earn."

8

DARK THREATS

It was fully dark by the time I reached the small, dimly lit tavern known as the Gilded Razor. Located on a narrow Dockside street called Heker's Way, the Razor was far removed from the raucous ale houses of Cargo Street, and while foreign mariners occasionally found their way to it, they tread there carefully, leaving their loud songs, foolish drinking games, and messy brawls outside. With a nondescript step-down doorway, in a rather nondescript stone building, the only thing that marked this place was a faded etching of a Derjian slip blade in the heavy wooden door. The paint had long ago worn away. There was but a single lantern to the side of the door, which often burned down to a tiny sputter. The sum of this conspired to create the least assuming drinking establishment in all of Dockside, and this was entirely deliberate. The Gilded Razor was Sullward's most notorious haunt for contract operatives.

I stepped down the short flight and instantly smelled the nithrin smoke. The sounds within were muted, with the low murmuring of voices and the occasional pouring of a pitcher and the thud of a tankard. The lighting here was exceptionally dim, provided by only a handful of lanterns around the walls and a single open-flame candle on each of the two dozen tables,

143

though nobody who drank here wanted it otherwise. We were men and women who had grown used to conducting all of our business under a cloak of darkness.

I threaded my way through the tables, nodding to several individuals I spotted along the way. There were perhaps a dozen people visible to me in the common space, including four at the bar, and I recognized at least half of them. But no pleasantries were exchanged. We did not ask after the others' families, or business or health; a simple nod was all, if that. There were other Shadow Bidder establishments—some here in Dockside, more on the fringes of the Lower City—where my fellows dumped out their silver between bids on lively dice games, strong drink, and narcotics far heavier than nithrin. Those were the places where the latest rumors flowed, where the occasional vendetta was settled, but not in the Gilded Razor. The Razor was a place for business.

I made my way to the back of the tavern where there were curtained booths lining the walls, eight in total. The ceiling in the Razor was quite low, with bulky, heavily knotted overhead beams, and the ceilings in the booths were even lower, making them feel almost like the sleeping cubbies on a ship. However, there was room enough once you were sitting comfortably behind the thick black curtain, and they did offer quite a bit of privacy from both eyes and ears. In these back booths Sketchers held initial meetings with brokers, then later sketched full jobs to Shadow Bidders. Contracts were negotiated, money exchanged, and bid details planned by co-operatives. The gods only knew how many hundreds of hours I had spent talking in a hushed voice behind those eight illicit black curtains.

As I approached one of the closed booths in the back-left corner, I skirted a table with two men and a woman conferring over a bottle of wine. The woman, along with one of the men, glanced up at me briefly, and I was quite certain that their expressions slid past lukewarm indifference into cold disapproval. The man was a Masque I had worked with many years ago, and the woman was either a Locksmith or an Eye who had never joined me on a bid but who was a regular presence in this tavern. These two, like many of the other Shadow Bidders sitting at the center tables, had dispensed with contract brokers altogether and merely spent their evenings in the Gilded Razor waiting for a Sketcher to come and propose a bid to them. That likely explained this cozy little meeting over a bottle of wine, for the third man had sketched perhaps a dozen bids to me in the last decade. What wasn't exactly clear was why they were scowling at me so brazenly.

I knew I wasn't particularly liked in this tavern, but usually the denizens did a better job of keeping it off their faces. This was, unfortunately, yet another thing that I needed to brush off in life, like the constables' icy malice, and Holod's crotchety disappointment. The funny thing was I almost enjoyed the irony of it. Any one of these people might get paired with me next week, and when that happened, their demeanor would change immediately. Suddenly, all of my objectionable qualities would be working in their favor, and they would become quite appreciative of my threatening reputation, my tough negotiating tactics, and, most of all, the considerable fees allotted to my jobs. All of this would make them richer, and ultimately safer. So, my Bidder comrades, you can scowl as much as you like as you sit there negotiating your thankless, pauper's bid. Once you get paid to work one of my contracts, I promise you'll be smiling like a giddy fool.

I reached out and rapped quietly on the wooden divider to the corner booth.

"Come in."

The voice was low and deep and decidedly self-assured. If, as a general point, the Gilded Razor was dominated by Shadow Bidders, then there was one bid operative in particular who ruled here, and this one individual alone was sufficient to ensure that no bouncer was ever required. His fees were perhaps double that of his closest competitor, and his capabilities were probably four times that of any other who shared his skillset. He was, I feel quite certain, one of the few Shadow Bidders in Hell's Labyrinth possessed of even greater notoriety than myself, which was a good thing, for he was coming with me tomorrow night on this mad, quasi-suicidal mission to kill Count Ulan Gueritus.

Coljin Helmgrinder was leaning back casually in the corner of the booth when I entered, his pitcher of ale already half empty. In his right hand he held an ornate brass pipe, which emitted lazy indigo threads of smoke that coiled up against the low wooden ceiling and smelled vaguely like cumin. The exotic herbal mixture known as nithrin was a mild stimulant that was extremely popular in the Gilded Razor. I had tried it a few times in my day and found the taste too brackish to form a habit, though my fellows insisted it helped to sharpen the mind. Col pushed one of the two tankards towards me, and I poured myself half a cup of ale.

"How did it go today?" I asked, taking a sip of the cool amber liquid. I'm not much of a drinker, but I could tell instantly that Col had ordered the very best brew in the Razor, which probably meant the best in the city, for, despite the unassuming appearance of this tavern, there were no lower shelf beverages here. Shadow Bidders (and the Sketchers who wooed them) never drank the cheap stuff.

"Straight to business, eh, Vazeer?"

Col had a much stronger Gosian accent than Merejin, with greatly elongated "ee" sounds, particularly when he uttered my name. However, like all of his countrymen, Col spoke the Derjian language perfectly, as centuries earlier the Gosians had willingly (and rather diplomatically) adopted the common tongue of the Empire. Col remained in his relaxed posture, and he took a deep drag on his nithrin pipe, expelling the light purple vapors into the translucent smoke web that was already pressing against the ceiling. I was always surprised at the size of Col no matter how many times I saw him (and over the years that had been quite a lot). He more or less filled his entire side of the booth, and the top of his bald head touched the nithrin clouds. He had on a custom leather vest with thin steel plates sewn prominently throughout, and the tight, finely woven crimson shirt underneath did little to disguise the extraordinary musculature of his arms. I could see the hilt of a spade protruding from his waist, which, in the hands of Col, was more like a dagger than a short sword. His deeply chiseled features wore their usual expression of sagacious confidence.

"Okay, Col, I suppose you're right," I replied. "Some personal niceties tend to get a meeting started off right. Let's see, how is your bevvy of whores lately? Any new ones you'd like to tell me about? And, on a related topic, any more bastard children scampering around the Wags because of you? If so, Holod is sure to be grateful. Gosian blood is almost impossible to find this far north. Now...having gotten all of that out of the way, how the hell did it go today?"

For a moment Col just stared at me with the same mildly amused expression, then his thick mouth broke into a wide grin, with his brown, granite teeth shining in the light of the booth's single candle.

"You didn't let me answer any of your niceties," he said with a sonorous chuckle. "I have much to report on all of those topics."

"I know you do, Col," I replied, "and I could go on about Daegan Ugentis's strange use of light and perspective in the Colonnades of Audlin Park, but I'm pretty sure we don't have time for it. So, if it wouldn't be too much of an inconvenience, too taxing on your delicate sensibilities, could you kindly report what you and that stick-up-his-ass Line Man discovered today?"

Col took another long drag on his nithrin pipe, and this time he expelled it out the side of the curtain. Then he leaned forward, placing his huge arms on the table.

"I have always appreciated this about you, Vazeer," he said. "The other Bidders, and sometimes the Sketchers, they try to be my friends. They think if they talk nice to me, if they show an interest in the things that interest me, then I will like them, and hopefully protect them if things go bad. But I won't. I won't like them, and I won't protect them, not unless the bid calls for it. You and I seem to be the same in this way."

I took a rather large gulp from my tankard, then shrugged.

"Nobody shows an interest in the things that interest me, Col. Which is probably the source of most of my problems."

Col seemed to give this some thought. Then he shook his big granite head slowly but definitively.

"No, I don't think it is. Your problems come from somewhere else."

Damn. I didn't like where this was going.

I slouched back in my seat and let my eyes wander up to the ceiling where the nithrin slowly coiled. How tired I was of this topic, the hints of which often filtered into Col's little offhand comments, and whether the big, condescending bastard actually wished to teach me something, or if (far more likely) he simply wished to needle me, I always counted the seconds until we could move on. Col knew all the stories about my zealous behavior on my bids, but he had also experienced it directly. Despite the dozens of successful contracts we had worked together over the years, he tended to focus on the handful that had turned violent. Turned violent, he asserted, because of me.

There was one bid in particular, aboard a small pirate carrack, that drew most of Col's attention. After aggressive negotiations with the captain, I settled on a favorable price, and the man happily took my bags of silver. However, as we prepared to load the crates of fine Azzerian weaponry into our skiff, I noticed that some of the boxes didn't feel and sound quite right. So I opened them and discovered that beneath the top layer of blades there was a pile of wooden poles filling the bulk of three crates. It was only three boxes out of ten, for the others were as promised. After the fact, Col insisted that the shortfall was something we could, and should, have accepted, for while it made the price less favorable for our Underlord employers, it was still within a workable margin for that buy. That was all true, and excellent Shadow Bidder logic. Unfortunately, I simply couldn't tolerate it, for it reflected poorly upon my negotiating skills, as well as a lapse in judgement for failing to thoroughly check all of the crates before paying for them. Of course, there was also the added factor of those insolent smirks on the faces of the captain and his crew, which perhaps motivated me most of all.

So, I grumbled but played along. We loaded the crates into our skiff and then, just before Col and the other Blade on the job could go over the rail, I launched myself at the captain, cracking my elbow into that hateful smile so hard I knocked out half his teeth. But I didn't stop there. I sprinted to the bags of silver where they were piled and rammed the rogue who was straddling them straight over the side of the boat. I swept up all three of the sacks and ran them back towards the rope ladder, bowling into pirates and dodging cutlasses along the way until I could toss the bags overboard, where they exploded into the bottom of our skiff. After that it was sheer chaos.

I honestly can't recall many details from the fight that followed, as I sometimes obscure such memories from myself. However, what I do know is that the ensuing melee left six pirates dead, almost got our accompanying Blade killed, and furnished me and Col with sufficient injuries that we both had to convalesce for several weeks before taking additional jobs. But the Underlords were overjoyed. They had gotten the entire cache of Azzerian weaponry for free, while sending a sharp message to all duplicitous shippers going forward. The other Blade retired shortly thereafter with a permanently injured leg, but also a very hefty bonus for his efforts. And both Col and I saw our reputations greatly enhanced. Our fees went up a good twenty percent after that, though Col never mentioned that part. All he ever discussed was the fact that I had no ability to gauge odds, no capacity to abide an acceptable loss in the service of avoiding a much greater risk, the fact that my own pride was always in danger of taking control of the moment. And this definitely wasn't the only incident of this nature.

However, if I'm being entirely honest about it, these episodes weren't always as spontaneous as they appeared. It was true that I possessed a violent temper, and in the most extreme cases I did, without question, lose control of myself, but the rest of the time I tended to choose when I wished to let the creature off the leash. For instance, when Coljin Helmgrinder was standing a few feet behind me, that was a good time. After all, I couldn't boast Col's skill with a sword, and I certainly lacked his physical size, so I made up for these shortcomings with something else. I fostered a reputation as a dangerous hothead, a man whose violent moods were so unpredictable that it was best to tread delicately in his presence. I wanted the ship captains, marsh brigands, off-load crews, and even other Shadow Bidders to live in a certain degree of fear that they might inadvertently set me off, and that no matter what the odds or what the cost, Vazeer the Lash would settle the score if they were stupid enough to cross him. Yes, there was a blood price to be paid for my eruptions. But over time, I sincerely believe that they had protected more Shadow Bidders than they had harmed. Of course, I could never tell Col any of this, so whenever he raised this matter, my strategy was to simply move on to the next topic.

"All right, Col, I have an idea," I said, reaching forward to pour myself another cup of ale. "Let me tell you all about my day. You seem to be in the listening mood."

Col didn't protest, so I quickly related the relevant details from my various errands, including those from the prior evening. The only thing I avoided mentioning was my encounter with Bevin Slywell, since I didn't think this would be well received. As to whether Col himself had been tailed, it didn't really matter at this point. What was done was done.

Col leaned back in his seat and remained largely impassive throughout the telling, asking no questions. When I was done, he simply nodded, then launched into his own recounting.

"The Line Man and I set out at dawn in one of Droden's little sailbirds. Made it to Lothrum by Tenth Bell. I found our ship within a few minutes."

Col and Fe Gesbon's job on our off day was to find a suitable vessel in a nearby town that we could claim was the craft that had brought Countess Odel to our shores. Despite the paranoid assertions of some, the Underlords did not have spies watching every last occurrence in our world. However, if there was one thing the Underlords did, in fact, scour with the attention of hounds waiting for scraps beneath a banquet table, it was the many ships that arrived at our port each week. Any one of them could be a big score, and the agents for the Underlords always swept in quickly to make discreet inquiries with the captains of all arriving vessels. Therefore, it was simply too risky to claim the Countess's ship had put in at Sullward Harbor.

However, there were a couple of neighboring towns where some of our shippers docked if they had reason to be particularly skittish—corsairs with the biggest bounties on their heads, as well as honest merchants engaged in a one-time act of malfeasance. For this reason, the Underlords kept a few lesser agents in those towns, and these individuals intermittently sent reports back to Sullward concerning new arrivals. Since most of the vessels docking in the neighboring towns were either fishing boats, local merchants, or passenger craft, the Underlord scrutiny there was never particularly intense, making them great candidates for our purposes.

"A good-sized merchant caravel called Venture's Gain arrived yesterday," said Col.

"From?"

"Abelein. I have been there once or twice. Not far from Tergon."

"Did your contact let you see the manifest?"

"He did. Spices, tools, cloth…a few other things. All legal cargo. Seven crew. Five passengers, I think. Underlords won't give it a second thought. And seemed big enough to leave room for four travelers not on the manifest."

I grunted, and it was hard to keep the sound of approval out of my voice, for this did sound promising. Years ago, Col had been first mate on a high-bounty pirate vessel, and the ship had regularly put in at the neighboring ports to avoid imperial attention. Even after leaving that calling over a decade earlier, he had retained several of his key harbor contacts. They were certainly proving useful now.

"How did the Line Man do?" I asked.

Col took a swig from his cup of ale, sloshed it around in his mouth for a second, then gulped it down.

"The man knew how to handle a boat," he answered after a pause.

"I mean the relevant skills."

"Let's see," said Col thoughtfully. "He took one look at the manifest and memorized it—every piece of cargo. Along with the names of all the passengers and crew. He can describe every detail of the ship, plus the harbor. Maybe more than we need, but then again, when you spend a few weeks at sea, you get to know everything about a ship and all aboard. Could help if the target is particularly paranoid."

"And the man, personally? What's your take?"

At this, Col cocked an eyebrow at me, which pulled his heavy, dark features up to the left in an expression that looked like a peculiar hybrid between humor and disdain. If there was an actual smile somewhere in there, it was deeply sardonic.

"Personally? What do I care about anybody personally?"

I leaned forward on the table, as if sheer proximity might help to suck the information out of him.

"Will he be trouble, you goddamned lofty bastard? That's what I care about. Personally."

"Ahhhh," said Col, and now both of his eyebrows raised, freeing his big, sculpted face of the irritating hybrid expression. Unfortunately, the new openly mocking one was worse.

"You seem to be concerned, Vazeer, about a Shadow Bidder causing trouble on our bid. I'm glad you raise this topic, because I have a similar concern."

And now Col also leaned forward, and in doing so, our heads were almost touching. I could smell the ale and nithrin emitting from him, and I could see the cold, derisive glint in his bloodshot eyes. In that moment, I suddenly remembered the two Shadow Bidders at the table outside, both of whom were possessed of a similar icy scorn, which radiated from them like a northern wind. Aversion and judgement and disdain, all coalescing in this corner of the Gilded Razor. At last, it made some sense.

"Bevin Slywell came here?"

"About an hour before you arrived," Col replied.

"And he made some overt inquiries about me?"

"I've seen the man be more subtle."

"Did he reveal anything that compromises us?"

Col now slid his face even closer so that we were literally butting heads. I could feel the cool, rough surface of his forehead grinding against mine like a stone pestle.

"The only secret he revealed was the one that everybody here already knows."

"And what secret is that, Col?" I muttered under my breath, pressing back against his forehead until it actually became painful. The irony of the man's namesake, apropos this awkward standoff, was not lost on me.

"What he revealed," Col continued, "was the simple fact that Vazeer the Lash is not really governed by our code at all. Instead, he follows his whims. His pride, his anger…his feelings. All things that have no place in the world of a contract operative. I lived with this foolishness for decades on the high seas, and it is part of why I left that world for this one."

"Please tell me, Col, when have I ever failed to get the job done?"

"You meet your own agenda. But there are times when your agenda is not the bid's agenda. Which means it is not my agenda."

I pulled my head back a few inches, freeing us from our uncomfortable deadlock, and glared at him outright.

"And you deduce all of this simply because I was a little rough shaking a tail?"

"You were reckless. You created an unnecessary problem, as well as a true enemy. Slywell was a Blade once, and a fairly good one. Plus, he's stealthy. He will come after you, perhaps as soon as tonight. But even more than that, I suspect that you have now made the proffer anxious. He probably thinks you are hiding something. He wonders if you have some secret agenda on this bid."

I experienced an unpleasant flush in my chest, which quickly moved up my neck and into my cheeks. The sensation was identical to what I had experienced earlier while talking to Nascinthé of Levell, and realizing that, I suddenly felt stifled and claustrophobic inside that smoky booth.

"Okay, Col, your admonition on behalf of the so-called 'proffer' is duly noted. Are we done here?"

I sensed that Col was not done, and sure enough, he shook his head.

"For the most part, I do not believe in things that I cannot touch and see," he said pensively, and his gaze did appear to go a little unfocused, as if he was staring just past me at the back of the booth. "However, there is one thing I do believe in that is not visible to the naked eye. I believe in it because it has saved my life many times before. In both professions."

I couldn't imagine where this was going; however, in the interest of getting Col to wrap up quickly, I bit back all sarcastic commentary and remained quiet.

"What I believe in are my own instincts. Particularly when they give warnings, which they are doing right now. And here is what they are telling me. They are telling me that if I do, in fact, wind up spilling out my blood on this job, it won't be because of the 'stick-up-his-ass' Line Man, as you call him. Nor will it be because Flerra Tellian has one of her fits and refuses to play a convincing maid servant. It won't even be because the Finisher decides he's going off script and wants to 'improvise.' I'll wind up bloodied, Vazeer, because you suddenly decide to pull one of your interesting maneuvers on this bid. It'll be because that thing inside of you snaps, and your emotions suddenly take over. Like I say, it's just an instinct, but I can't help feeling it's right."

I would have liked to come back at him just then with some snide criticism or witty retort, but suddenly the hot, flushed feeling became utterly intolerable. It was like a blanket over my defiance, and more than anything else I just wanted to get the hell out of there. Col quickly moved into that opening.

"I want you to know that if I sense you are about to do that thing, about to flip the whole bid on its head because of some personal impulse you are having…I want you to know that I will stop you. In fact, I will cut you down where you stand, and I won't give it a second's thought. Do you understand me? I will not hesitate in that moment."

I didn't answer and simply glared at him in the dim smoky light of the booth. All the while I saw a number inside my mind. It was a simple number, but it said so much.

Three.

Three was now the number of potential passengers on the Elena's Guile. Because, as the dark, stinking, largely indifferent gods were my witness, there was no chance in hell that this menacing son of a bitch was ever setting foot on my escape boat.

9

SHADOW

It was but minutes after leaving the Gilded Razor, well before the crooked lanes of Dockside gave way to the calm, softly lit dignity of White Hill, that I became aware of the shadow. That is the word I must use, for there is no other term that comes close to describing it. If, in a virtually lightless place, one could generate a dusky, ever-so-subtle distortion somewhere behind one's back, or at times to the side, and if this vague interruption in the field of vision was so elusive as to seem like it existed beyond sight altogether, like a silhouette spawned by mere thought, then this would start to approximate what I experienced. Maybe the heavy nithrin smoke in Col's booth had tampered with my senses. Perhaps it was the ale. Whatever the cause, I knew with a strange, nervous certainty that someone—or something—was following me.

I veered north onto a small Dockside street called the Scratch, a tight little connector lane that would lead me to Trader's Way, and from there into one of the darkest sections of Dockside. How badly I wanted to go home. How deeply I wanted safety and comfort and food and warmth, but I dared not drag that skulking shadow to 27 Fletcher. I needed to address the problem here, before it entered my personal domain.

I could only assume that my clandestine pursuer was Bevin Slywell. He had likely reclaimed my trail at the Gilded Razor, and while it was possible that he would simply tail me for the remainder of his contract, I suspected that observation was no longer his intention. I had seen it in Col's expression, seen it in the faces of those two Shadow Bidders who couldn't keep the disdain out of their eyes. Slywell's paid bid was bust; he was now out for revenge.

The man, of course, had no idea what sort of problems he would cause if he acted on his revenge tonight, no understanding of the larger contract in which he was playing but a miniscule role. This was, I now understood, the very thing that Col meant when he accused me of causing an unnecessary problem. I had drawn first blood, which meant that Slywell was within his rights to settle the score, something that would likely lead to injury or worse for the lone Grell Runner on our Narrow Bid, the man charged with the critical task of getting the group to the bid site.

It hadn't been a terrible idea to drop Slywell the prior night, but as usual I had pushed things too far. A man with better restraint would have simply hit Bevin once in the stomach, then pressed a pouch of tolgens into his hand and promised to owe him a favor in the future. Slywell would have been chagrined and angry, but it could have been repaired. Instead, I had caused him real harm, given him nothing in return, and left him (and his pride) like a piece of trash in the dirt. He was going to seek redress immediately, which is exactly what I would have done.

Therefore, guilty though I was in the affair, I needed to put an end to it tonight. This Contract Eye was a messy loose end, hanging out there, ready to cause a problem at some inopportune moment—perhaps tonight, or maybe tomorrow en route to the launch site, or possibly even on the bid itself. I couldn't allow this. It was now my job to clean up the mess that I had created.

I turned left off the Scratch onto Trader's Way. This was a street largely devoid of taverns or other night establishments, and thus particularly deserted at this hour. There were streetlamps spread every hundred feet, and in the middle of one of the lightless gulfs, I made a quick right down a nameless alley. I threaded my way through the tight, dirty passage until I found myself in a small courtyard created from the back side of four buildings. I had used this particular space several times in the past for quick meetings with Sketchers and co-operatives, as it was remarkably private for an outdoor area. There were only a couple of barred upper-story windows facing it, and while drunks and addicts sometimes passed out here, they were usually too far gone to listen in on my meetings. Tonight, the small courtyard was empty, furnished with just a couple of broken crates and some shattered glass.

Behind the thick blanket of fog, a gibbous moon was providing only a trace of illumination, but my sight, like that of most Shadow Bidders, had grown so proficient in darkness that I found the lighting more than adequate. This would be true for my enemy as well. I knew there was little chance that I could catch Bevin off guard a second time, so I dispensed with trickery and decided I would make one attempt to resolve this conflict peacefully.

"Okay, Slywell, you can come out now," I said. There were three alleys leading into the courtyard, and I didn't have a clue which one he would use. I kept my right hand on the hilt of my short sword and my left on a stiletto and made ready to respond to an attack from either direction.

"If you're willing to deal, Bevin," I continued, "I'm sure we can come up with a reasonable compensation. If you're not, then let's get on with this."

I heard no answer. There was a light scratching down one of the alleys, which was almost certainly a rat. I also heard the faint echo of boisterous laughter several streets away, but nothing in my immediate vicinity. In fact, the quiet in my little courtyard was so pervasive as to seem unnatural, as if the darkness itself was muzzling this small section of Dockside, drawing curtains around the coming violence. I realized then that my opponent probably wasn't going to show his face at all, that he would likely play to his strengths and come at me from behind. I eased backwards until I was but a couple feet from one of the plaster walls, and I quietly drew the two blades and held them pointing out to either side.

"Bevin Slywell," I said, making one last attempt. "Are you willing to deal or not?"

"There is nobody here by that name, Vazeer the Lash," came the calm reply from the darkness. "You and I are entirely alone."

There are times when a sound is so familiar that it hardly registers as a sound at all. I have several acquaintances who reside in close proximity to the Sullward Clock Tower, and they tell me that throughout the night the hourly drones and Half Bells are as routine to them as the sound of their own snores and rarely disturb their slumber. And then, there are sounds even more familiar than that. Sometimes, the listener and the source are so intertwined as to beg the question whether it was the physical ears or the most attuned recesses of mind that heard it first. Such, it seemed to me, was the case with that calm, strangely intimate voice emerging from the darkness.

I did not see fit to answer this voice immediately, and likely it was the redundancy of the whole business that threw me—this weird concept of responding to a noise inside my own head. Then logic reasserted itself, and I was hit with the alarming thought that I had spontaneously lost my mind. A second later I saw him.

Through the churning, moon-painted coils of fog, the eerie man-shadow approached. He was like a figment, though a figment of what I could only wonder, for I was fairly certain that he was actually there with me in that courtyard. That voice was so recognizable that it sounded like it had come from the mouth of a family member.

How shocking it was when I recognized him a moment later and realized that nothing could have been further from the truth.

"You?"

That was all I could muster.

"Would you have preferred it was that other man?" he asked. "The one with whom you hoped to make a deal?"

Radrin Blackstar stood a few feet before me, his unscarred features framed by the raised collar of his cloak, the dull glint of his dark blond hair faintly visible in the spectral glow. It was hard to say, with any great certainty, what sort of demeanor he displayed. He did not wear a grin of an infuriatingly smug variety, as Col had done throughout our conversation, nor was his expression particularly severe—as I suspect mine was in that moment. He was much as he had seemed the prior night: focused yet strangely serene.

"What are you doing here?"

This was the next sentence I could muster, and not a very eloquent follow-up to "You?"

Radrin nodded towards me, as if the answer to his question was right in front of us both.

"I've come for you, of course," he replied. And he let that statement rest there amidst the shadowy vapors of the quiet courtyard. The words simply floated in the space, hovering lightly over the broken crates and shattered glass, out of reach of rats and revelers alike. And I, robbed in that moment of my loquacity, replied with yet another monosyllabic gem.

"Why?"

Perhaps it was the sheer size of that question, the wide universe of possibilities and intricate causalities all contained in that simple three-letter word, that finally drew forth a semi-useful response from Radrin Blackstar. He let out a small, tired sigh, as if he were now ready to share with me his many shadowy burdens.

"I have scouted the Three Bay and the surrounding territory rather thoroughly, as instructed, and the results of my reconnaissance are concerning to say the least."

This had been Radrin's task in our preparation day, though, as a point of fact, nobody "instructed" him to do it, for he was the one who came up with the idea. Furthermore, this proposal had resulted in a twenty-minute argument with Fe Gesbon, who finally agreed to the scouting mission under the strictest of conditions. Nervous that the Finisher would arouse suspicions from the target's people, Fe Gesbon insisted that Radrin simply make a cursory pass through the area in the darkest hours and that he should, under no circumstances, attempt to enter any of the buildings. The heart of the Lower City was a truly dangerous place for any uninvited guest, even a trained Shadow Bidder, as it was the exclusive domain of the Underlords. When we called our city Hell's Labyrinth, we were really referring to the depths of that vast, forlorn neighborhood, which, hundreds of years past, had been the crown jewel of the North. Most of my bids ended there, but I was an expected visitor, and I certainly didn't linger. Even the city watch and the imperial constables did not dare to set foot in those dark streets without significant backup. Therefore, Radrin's talk of a "thorough" reconnaissance mission suggested that he had not overly concerned himself with the Line Man's warning.

"As you no doubt recall from your own bids," Radrin continued, "there are plenty of towering structures in the immediate vicinity of the bay; however, upon closer inspection, none of them appeared suitable for the target's intentions. I am not a trained Locksmith, but I am handy enough with simple mechanisms, and over the course of the last twenty-four hours, I either gained entry or conducted outside surveillance of all those buildings, and I'm sure that none of them are the site for our bid. They are either occupied already, or else too dilapidated to seem viable."

I couldn't tell if Radrin was waiting for a response, but since I didn't offer one, he simply continued.

"I also scouted the streets and buildings for several blocks beyond that, and I met with similar results. There were a few spaces that denied me entry, but none of them seemed promising for various reasons. At this point, I would estimate that the odds are low that the target will be using any of the buildings within four hundred yards of the Three Bay. If the bid site is not adjoining our landing area, then we will have to move through the streets as an entourage, suggesting the target is not attempting to be discreet. Perhaps there will be more soldiers. Perhaps the site for his tryst will be significantly more secure than hoped. The variables multiply from there."

And now Radrin did lift his chin in what looked like the semblance of a prompt. However, the only reply that occurred to me was a proper formulation of the question that I had really meant to ask from the start, the very thing that all those stunted little sentences had been driving at.

"Why have you come to me with this?" I asked. "To me, and not the others?"

In hindsight, I realize that I didn't know for sure that I was the sole recipient of this information. But, of course, I was. Everything about this weird, clandestine meeting told me that.

"I am well aware of your reputation, Vazeer the Lash."

"You are?" My tone was suddenly defensive. "I'm not at all aware of yours."

"If you were, then I would have failed in my job," Radrin replied. "By contrast, your reputation actually serves you. It also does you credit, for only the most cursory research confirms some key details about you."

"What details?"

"Stories…about your unorthodox methods on the jobs you run. While I have never been hired for a Grell Running bid, I understand that they are some of the most dangerous and unpredictable Shadow Bids of all. And among Grell Runners, you are said to be the man best adapted to such an environment, to making life-and-death decisions under duress. If the bid suddenly changes, you know how to change with it."

In that moment, I was almost tempted to repeat the very thing that Col had asserted: that I was often the cause of, not the solution to, many of those unpredictable situations. But I bit the comment back, as it hardly seemed useful here.

"Let's say, Finisher, that there is some truth to these reports. It still doesn't answer my question. Why have you come to me, specifically, with your concerns? Your surveillance of the bid site needs to be passed on to the Line Man, and the others."

"And how will that go, Vazeer?" Radrin asked, with the dimmest elements of a smile. "How will the Line Man react to my extensive reconnaissance, which includes entry into over a dozen buildings? Do we really need that sort of schism right on the cusp of our bid? I was not able to uncover much information about Fe Gesbon, but the hours we all spent together last night told me enough for my purposes."

"My purposes." Those two words seemed to detach themselves from the rest of the sentence.

"If this bid goes off track, who will step in and put it back on track?" he continued. "Will it be a constitutionally rigid Line Man, who believes that the sketch must be followed at all costs? Or might it be a man who habitually deals with random events, one who knows how to lead other Shadow Bidders—Blades, Masques, Locksmiths, all of whom have spent time under his command."

"I don't command Line Men. Or Finishers."

"I will take care of the Line Man," he said. "And myself. I am only asking that you be ready to lead the others if it comes down to it. If the bid goes awry, they will look to you for direction. I could see that plainly last night."

I have often reenacted this conversation in my mind. I return to it when I try to solve some of the more perplexing riddles from this whole affair. For instance, did Radrin Blackstar ever actually wish me to be a leader on the Narrow Bid, as he claimed, or was this simply a ruse? His talk of leadership definitely distracted me from the other part of his statement—that he would "take care" of the Line Man. Somehow, that one slipped right by me. I didn't really consider what a Finisher might mean when he used such language.

Even deeper than that ran questions about the Finisher himself. Where in the dark hells did this creepy specter of a man come from? He seemed so damned familiar to me. What was this odd sense of acquaintance, as if he were some ghostly kinsman? After all, I never tried to rebuff his furtive overtures, nor did I particularly bridle at his hints at mutiny. Certainly, I could sense the man's subtle manipulations, even there in that courtyard, perhaps as early as the boathouse. Why was it that when I looked at him, I felt I was seeing some sort of warped reflection of myself, an indistinct but vaguely recognizable image cast upon a distorted mirror?

These are the issues that blow about in my mind like back-alley litter. They disturb me to this day.

"I believe I feel a few drops of rain," said Radrin, glancing up briefly into the pallid blackness. I had been feeling the increasing moisture throughout our discussion, but I had been unsure whether it would result in actual rain. Now that a light drizzle was underway, I pulled up the collar of my own cloak and adjusted my hat.

"With any luck it will continue," I muttered. "Poor weather makes Grell Running unpleasant, but it offers good cover."

"And it will certainly delay the Countess."

To this I merely shrugged.

"I'm going home now, Finisher," I said. "You should do the same. We will meet tomorrow at the east end of the wharf, as planned."

Thus we parted, offering no handshake or final salutations. However, just as I was about to exit that courtyard, Radrin said one last thing, which filtered to me quietly through the wet air.

"Regarding that other man, Vazeer, the one with whom you wished to make a deal. It turns out he wasn't interested in making a deal with you. So I made my own deal with him earlier. I just wanted you to know that, in case you were about to waste unnecessary energy looking over your shoulder as you head home tonight."

And with that, Radrin Blackstar disappeared into the gloomy night, leaving nothing behind but vacant darkness, and the gentle sizzle of falling rain.

PART

II

10

FALLEN REALM

Dawn broke the next morning, cold and dark and wet. The rain, while not torrential, had never let up throughout the night, intensifying into a dreary flow, which, by morning, had begun to puddle heavily amidst the cobbles. The water dripped ceaselessly off of roofs, casings, and doorframes, running in fine sheets down window glass, making a small river of every gutter. By the time six bells droned out sullenly into the evening air, the wind had risen into frigid gusts. It sent citizens fleeing indoors, made streetlamps sputter, and at the docks it caused all loosely tied sails and straps to flap angrily. And under these wretched conditions, the six of us climbed inside Droden's oversized cargo skiff and launched our Narrow Bid.

As promised, Leddy had disguised the boat in the weeds near the mouth of the Grells. With most of the rising moon's light obscured by the foul weather, and saner residents seeking dry refuge, I was quite confident that our launch went unseen. Soon we were paddling out into the heart of the river, with cold drops forming pock marks across the surface, their swishing contact causing the black waters to steam ominously around the boat like lava. Here and there, autumn leaves swooped from the night sky with the spiraling jerkiness of bats, and slowly, yet all too steadily, a freezing tempest was beginning to rise out of the north.

In other cities and in other professions, perhaps, one does not overly concern themselves with the elements of nature, yet in Sullward these things are literally matters of life and death. Two hundred and thirteen years earlier, weather played such a dramatic role in the city's history that the Sullward calendar was actually started anew. Such is the power of a single tragically aligned storm.

As I directed our craft up the sluggish flood tide current, my eyes searching the marsh on the right and the tangle of willows and vines protruding from the high bank on the left, my mind began to assemble the clues that nature was showing me; though, in retrospect, I see that I did a far from perfect job of it. The pieces were not adding up to anything I understood.

"Autumn reaper, perhaps?" Col said, leaning forward to mutter over my shoulder. He pointed his paddle towards the north where, just beyond the marsh, the landscape transformed into an inhospitable moorland and then, many miles beyond that, an immeasurable tundra. I merely shrugged.

We both knew that the rare land-based storms known as autumn reapers never announced their arrival with anything so obvious as a day of harmless rain. Their winds were too fast for that, always outpacing the heavy clouds they dragged in tow by several hours. They also moved in gusts—wicked, roaring bursts of northern air—which always caught the ocean-oriented Sullward by surprise and could literally flip a heavily laden skiff and send a grown man rolling down the street like a barrel. We who worked the waterways and alleys of Hell's Labyrinth had good reason to fear them, perhaps more even than the huge southern typhoons, which always gave plenty of warning and against which Sullward

Harbor had a solid defense in the form of an outer bank and an ancient sea wall.

No, these wind patterns did not belong to either of those storms, and yet, without speaking another word on the subject, I sensed that Col had not dismissed them as the random sputters of a gale. There was one last possibility, though I don't think Col or I even dared to consider it.

Apart from the weather, things were proceeding smoothly so far. For starters, all six members of the team had shown up at the rendezvous site, which, given the stakes involved, wasn't a foregone conclusion. A mere forty-eight hours separated our first meeting in the boathouse from this evening's gathering behind an abandoned warehouse, and yet it felt so much longer, as if the intervening day of tense encounters and troubling riddles had tacked phantom time onto the calendar. In the boathouse we had been six independent agents, unsure what we had gotten ourselves into. Now we were interlinked characters, performing our carefully rehearsed roles, and even those of us who were ostensibly playing ourselves could feel the weight of doing so in a contrived manner.

So, in this new context, I had observed our team. Only a single, distant streetlamp illumined the space behind that warehouse, and rain garments made scrutiny difficult; however, I could tell rather quickly that the relevant parties had done their preparation work. I began with the figure I had seen most recently.

There was something darkly comic about Radrin Blackstar's largely successful efforts at appearing both harmless and unremarkable, which was precisely what one would expect from a lady's steward. He wore a finely woven but rather uninteresting gray cloak, and I could see the hint of a similarly colored silk tunic at his neck. Additionally, he wore a soft dun-colored rain cap (the sort of thing one might see on a stablemaster), and this completed the general look of a humble household servant whose entire mission was to meet his mistress's needs, while drawing no attention to himself. How unassuming he looked, which was funny, because there was actually so much one should assume about him, starting with the fact that he had managed to magically eliminate one of my problems last night. While it was true that I, myself, had been prepared to eliminate that particular problem if it really came down to it, I still had trouble with the fact that this mysterious Finisher had taken it upon himself to intervene. Especially when he had casually threatened to eliminate another potential problem in the near future. This is where my eye went next, to our de facto leader—the man Radrin considered too "constitutionally rigid" to run this bid.

I must give Fe Gesbon some deserved credit, for he did indeed look the part of a head guardsman. I saw metal armor at his collar and down at his shins, along with the scabbard of a longsword poking out below his travel cloak. He had wisely dispensed with a full helmet; however, he wore a lightly armored military cap, and it did appear of sufficient quality to grace the head of a commanding officer. Ironically, the very qualities that Radrin had criticized about Fe Gesbon seemed to assist with his disguise, as he bore a certain stiffness, an air of gruffly assumed authority, which appeared well suited to his role. In that moment I found myself rooting for the Line Man, hoping he could pull it off, hoping that our Finisher was wrong with his unnerving predictions and condemnations. I was determined to give Fe Gesbon a chance.

When I glanced over at Flerra Tellian, I felt some real satisfaction, and perhaps a degree of pride, for my erstwhile Brood sister had overcome her petulance and done quite a good job with her disguise. Extending just below the bottom of her raincoat I saw the ruffles of a light blue house dress, along with a pair of slender suede boots, which certainly looked like the appropriate apparel for a lady's maid. Of course, Flerra's real challenge in her preparation day was to not only secure this outfit but to figure out how to inconspicuously store all of her many burglary implements in her boots, the folds of her clothing, and her travel purse. With her coat on, I couldn't tell exactly how successful she had been in these efforts, but in my heart, I knew she wouldn't let us down. Flerra was a professional, a Shadow Bidder who truly took pride in her work, and if there was one person on this bid I knew I could trust, it was her.

With that reassuring sentiment, I moved on to a place where familial trust was now in very short supply. I'll admit, I was still mad as hell at Col for his final comments the prior night, and perhaps a bit nervous too. The man didn't make idle threats. However, he was also a pragmatist, a mercenary in every sense of the word, and at least for the foreseeable future, the big bastard needed me. He was dressed tonight more or less as he always was on a Grell Running bid, which happened to be more or less like me. Both he and I were decked in leather armor, swaddled in dark outer garments, and festooned with every conceivable weapon we could keep strapped to our body while rowing a skiff or climbing a ladder. Col had a hood over his head, making him look like some sort of huge, outlaw clergyman, and while his size always garnered a degree of attention, the poor weather and the presence of the hood made it possible that he would not be recognized as quickly as expected.

Finally, my gaze shifted over to Nascinthé of Levell. While I did not experience my usual embarrassing flush at the sight of her (the sheer intensity of what we were setting out to do simply stifled it), I still reacted with a degree of warmth as I observed our Countess. Nascinthé wore the finest clothing of all, with a fox skin cape over a dark blue belted coat, along with a wide-brimmed hat of a similar blue color and fabric. I could see the light blonde hair spilling out from under that hat, and I must say it looked extremely natural to my untrained eye. Huddled though she was against the wind and rain, I thought I detected a different bearing in this new aristocratic persona—a formality in her posture, a proud tilt to her jaw. I found myself both excited and nervous to see the coming performance.

I knew this mysterious woman was a talent. She was an exceptional talent, but that was not necessarily the same as a Contract Masque. I didn't know where Nascinthé of Levell had actually come from, what her training had been, but I truly prayed in that moment that she was not some pretty stage actress from the South who had opted to come north in search of an epic payday. If that were the case, she would certainly falter at some point on the Narrow Bid. Inexperience and a lack of mental and emotional seasoning killed Shadow Bidders quicker than anything else. There inevitably came that moment on a bid, a contentious bid at least, when the blood spilled and savagery took hold, and only those acclimated to such environments could keep their heads and make the proper decisions. While there was a part of me that relished the idea of Nascinthé being unsullied by the Labyrinth, free of the taint of our contracted world, such innocence would not serve her tonight, nor the rest of us. Only Shadow Bidders could hope to run this bid properly, and, among them, only the truly hardened professionals were likely to survive.

Up ahead on the river, I saw a blurry, rectangular outline nestled into the weeds of the left bank. We paddled onward through the dark waters, and soon we passed the old, stone boathouse where we had met to receive the sketch two nights earlier. Approximately twenty minutes beyond that, the river began to make a series of sharp bends. As we sliced through the twisting gauntlet of sinuous curves, the windswept marsh on the right began to grow ever thicker, taking on the dense contours of a flooded forest, while the left bank was slowly thinning out, indicating that the Lower City was near. This was never the easiest thing to determine. The silty borders of the river changed month to month, and even distances and timing could be deceptive, for the speed of the current varied greatly with the tides. Add to this the fact that the average Runner usually paused several times on his trip to wait breathlessly in the weeds, or under the protruding riverbank, or even in the dankest depths of the salt marsh where he might crouch for hours in his skiff with his heart pounding, simply because he thought he heard something. It was a misnomer to believe that any operative in Sullward knew the Grells like the back of his hand. Everything about that river was constantly in a state of flux.

Despite the weather, tonight's run was a good deal easier than most because of the information provided by Droden Sailwain. If the constables were not a threat, then we could spare ourselves endless stopping and starting, scouting and listening. Additionally, to make sure we were not accosted by anyone else along this river—ocean pirates who had come ashore for an ambush, marsh bandits, or impoverished vagrants who lived along the riverbanks—I had seated Col and myself up front as a deterrent. I even got Col to slide his hood back until we reentered the city.

At last, a dull aggregation of lights became faintly visible through the branches of the left bank. The weather made things seem a good deal farther off than they really were, but I could approximate our location. So, craning back, I passed this information down the skiff to the stern, where I watched it get grimly absorbed by the Line Man, who was peering through the mist in a rigid posture that easily rivaled some of the marble busts I ferried on my smuggling runs. He held up his hand and had us wait.

We had agreed as a team that we wanted to pull into the Three Bay midway between Eighth and Ninth Bells, as this seemed the most logical time for Shaeyin Odel to arrive. As we saw it, the Countess would likely wait for full dark to start her approach but would not tarry long after that, eager as she would be to get things over and done with. Under current conditions, the entire journey would take a little over an hour, and since Grell Runners tended to start their bids after Tenth Bell, this helped to ensure we didn't cross paths with another team of Shadow Bidders.

Our leader waved us forward a few minutes later, and I was grudgingly impressed to hear eight muffled drones bellow out from the Sullward Clock Tower just seconds after we resumed our run. I was certain that our Line Man enjoyed the opportunity to show off his skills, which I decided to match in turn by locating and steering us into the correct canal with no stops and starts or craning about. I think I made it look easy, but it definitely wasn't.

The geography of Sullward is such that the city appears to rise straight out of a swamp, and this is close enough to the truth that one might easily miss what Aurellis Kaennamin's municipal planners discovered—that between the unstable ground of the salt marsh to the north and east, and the tumultuous Derjian Sea to the south, lay a low but remarkably solid shelf of black granite that served as the bedrock for our city. This is why tall stone buildings were able to rise out of what seemed an uninhabitable swampland. Yet, this shelf of rock had a very abrupt edge where the forested riverbank began, a curved border that left the city hemmed in on three of its four sides by water.

The canal I located was one of dozens of tributaries that the engineers had carved into the bedrock in order to channel flowing river water through an intricate network of urban waterways. Designed primarily as a means of transportation, the waters of the canals were so clean in days of old that children swam in them regularly, and certain bridges and balconies were famously good fishing spots. Now, garbage, human refuse, and, from time to time, rotting corpses floated through these channels, but luckily the planners designed them well enough that water never stagnated, and eventually it circulated back into the river, then finally out to sea.

We paddled carefully down the overgrown furrow, deflecting thorn bushes and weeds that dangled on us from both sides. At the time of construction, these outer canals had all been exactly ten feet in width, but in many places the stone walls had collapsed inward, narrowing the span significantly, and vegetation grew so thick that one was forced to the very center of the route. We kept stroking, slithering though this wet, prickly jungle until, at last, we found ourselves staring up through the last vestiges of foliage at the city itself. It rose precipitously into the rainy sky like a great black range of mountains, a sight that awed me, no matter how many times I gazed upon it.

In the darkness I could not see the thick blanket of fungus and moss. I did not notice all the cracks in the stone and rust on the window frames. Instead, I saw an array of turrets and spires, copulas and crenellations, stabbing the stormy sky like pikes raised in victory. Graceful stone archways spanned the gaps between buildings, and down at the street level, equally graceful bridges bowed over the canals. Festooning it all were the silhouettes of gargoyles and satyrs, dragons and angels thrusting themselves from the mildewed stone in a last ghostly effort to be remembered.

Soon we were among them, sheltered from the brunt of the weather by overhanging bay windows. The three-quarters moon was now fully risen, and while the storm clouds obscured the bulk of its light, there was enough to faintly powder the rippling black waters that surrounded our boat. All the while, by this incidental glow, we paddled our serpentine course into a place that fate itself had killed two hundred and thirteen years before.

They called it a Swell Driver. Nobody living at the time had ever seen one, yet later as they pieced together what remained of the city's historical records, people came to understand the true nature of the catastrophe that had sent the city into two centuries of decline. By far the rarest and most dangerous variety of Derjian Sea hurricane, a Swell Driver approaches from almost the exact opposite direction as the southern typhoons, rolling slowly across the massive stretch of icy ocean to the northwest. Day by day it gathers strength, and when it finally arrives in the vicinity of Sullward Harbor, it drives before itself waves that are as tall as houses. Two hundred and thirteen years ago when the waters came surging through the open northwestern side of the sea wall and barreled straight over the docks and through the streets, the solid stone shell of the city remained largely standing, but its records, its art, its fleet, and much of its sleeping citizenry were literally swept away in the flood. Since then, like an amnesiac awakening from a near-fatal accident, Sullward found itself reborn into a dim, spectral existence connected only tenuously to its history by lonely relics of the past.

As for the relics, they were all around us. On our left I picked out Religan Hall, a cavernous four-story structure with a domed

roof, which had once served as an auditorium for musical perfor-
mances. There was something unearthly about the sight of candlelight emerging from the cracked glass of this mausoleum of
long dead melodies, as if a memorial were carried on each evening
by the musicians themselves. Elsewhere, similar tributes occurred,
in the form of dozens of ashen lights in the panes of dozens of
immense black structures, which overhung our waterway. Through
one of the bisecting canals, I spotted the high arch of Kaennamin
Academy, the original school of architecture in the city. I saw no
lights in the windows of that great building, and for this I was glad.
There simply weren't enough felonious inhabitants of the Lower
City to defame all of its many grand constructions.

The residents of this once-magnificent neighborhood were
now almost exclusively retainers employed by the Underlords:
soldiers, off-loaders, appraisers, envoys, not to mention a sizeable
horde of basic household servants who saw to it that the faux
noblemen lived in appropriate comfort. I had been at my business long enough to meet quite a few of them, and while it was
usually the soldiers, off-loaders, and appraisers that I encountered at the drop sites, retainers of all stripes ventured out of the
Lower City to Dockside and other neighborhoods to spend their
earnings. These men and women were generally reserved in their
appearance; however, there was a certain smug complacency in
their bearing that signified Underlord protection.

A quarter hour later, we arrived at the Three Bay, a small open
section of water where a triad of slender waterways converged.
The Three Bay was bounded on all sides by tall, decrepit residential buildings, and it included a rough boardwalk that jutted out
from the bay's rim. Bobbing just below the southwestern section
of the walk, a floating platform was tied, with a crude six-foot
ladder rising from the water at that spot.

"Over there," I said, pointing. I steered in that direction, and we all pulled for it.

Like most things in Hell's Labyrinth, this loading area had the illusory appearance of being poorly maintained and rarely utilized, just as the city itself was meant to seem a sordid yet ultimately disorganized haven for outcasts and small-time scofflaws. When the agents from Tergon made their intermittent appearances in Sullward to investigate the latest litany of charges— an endless catalogue of allegations arising from angry merchant guilds, free traders, regional governors, and quite a few personally aggrieved aristocrats—the authorities found distinctly unimpressive scenes like this waiting for their inspection: a decaying old boardwalk, jutting over a polluted waterway, and not an off-loader, appraiser, soldier, or Underlord anywhere in sight.

As I say, this was an illusion. The true power in the city dwelled quite close at hand, but not where one would expect. The imperial agents had searched all these towering constructions many times over, and while quite a few were inhabited by Underlord retainers, none contained a vast treasure trove of stolen merchandise. The agents failed to surmise what a handful of us had finally guessed after years of living with the mystery: that there was a labyrinth beneath the Labyrinth, that massive vaults lay far below the bedrock bottoms of the deepest canals. This was the great secret of Sullward. Below the surface of the streets, the Underlords, like the ancient dead, presided jealously over shadowy tombs.

We docked our skiff along the platform, and one by one we stepped onto what turned out to be a remarkably stable surface for a floating dock. The rain had increased only a little, but the wind had continued to rise, and even down close to the wrinkled face of the water we could feel its intensity. Fe Gesbon instructed Radrin to climb up to the street level and quickly survey the surrounding area. Before our Finisher could ascend, however, we saw that our arrival had been noted, for a person appeared at the top of the ladder. This figure scanned us for a moment, and then he gave a brief wave. After that, he swung himself onto the rungs and descended to the platform.

The man's clothing was in keeping with garb worn by all Underlord personnel—a dark gray cloak, high black boots, a soft leather hat that hung down partially to obscure his face—yet as he came off the ladder and approached, I could see immediately that there was something subtly distinguished about his walk. It was as though he was making an effort to stroll politely through the storm. When he arrived directly in front of Nascinthé, he bowed slightly and touched two fingers to the brim of his hat.

"Greetings," he said in a voice that was just loud enough to be heard over the sound of the wind. "Are we in secure company?"

It obviously took Nascinthé a moment to understand what he meant.

"My traveling companions know who I am," she finally replied.

"And would you be so kind, my lady, as to state your name."

"Countess Shaeyin of House Odel."

"In that case, Your Ladyship, I deeply apologize in advance for all the breaches of etiquette that will follow. My name is Jevar, Chief Legate for my lord, and were we not being watched right now, I would remove my hat, give a proper bow, and show you the respect that is your due. In accordance with your own wishes, however, I will do everything possible to protect your identity."

I could not see Jevar's face clearly under the brim of his hat, but I didn't detect any sarcasm. His jaw was cleanly shaven, his skin was unscarred and pale, and there was a certain gentility in the carriage of his mouth and overall deportment that seem unfeigned.

Nascinthé glanced quickly up at the rim of the bay.

"Who's watching us?"

Possibly remembering just how little outsiders understood of this world, Jevar smiled and nodded.

"My lord's guardsmen, Your Ladyship. For your protection, of course."

Nascinthé absorbed this information, as we all did. She was perhaps about to ask how many "guardsmen" we could be expecting tonight, when Jevar asked his own question.

"Once again, Your Ladyship, I must apologize for another discourtesy. It is a security protocol, but it must be followed. Would you kindly tell me the name of the ship by which you traveled to our port?"

Nascinthé waved this question off dismissively.

"I cannot imagine what that has to do with 'security,' Jevar," she replied. "Do you really think that Tergonian troops are waiting below decks, ready to attack your lord? As if I want them or anybody else to know that I have come here!"

"Ah, my lady, I see the confusion," said Jevar. "But no, that is not the issue. Having never met you myself, I need to confirm that you are indeed the Countess Shaeyin Odel."

"Good gracious!" Nascinthé exclaimed. "What other madwoman would come to this place on such a night? Has your lord sent out a bunch of invitations?"

At this Jevar let out a small chuckle, then shook his head.

"No, I assure you, Your Ladyship, you are the one and only. That said, I must get this over with before we can proceed further. So please, if you would, kindly confirm for me the details of the vessel you sailed in on."

Nascinthé let out an exasperated sigh and then quickly rattled off the information concerning the Venture's Gain, the ship which Col and Fe Gesbon had discovered in Lothrum. She made it sound exceptionally convincing, even going so far as to describe how tired she became of the smell of coriander and sapikar root, and also the poor hygiene of Esgierd, the First Mate. As these words flowed, I could see Jevar's posture visibly relax. While I was even less familiar with Underlord Legates than I was with Line Men, I was aware that the two possessed similar skillsets—most notably, the ability to store reams of information without having to write any of it down. Clearly, Jevar had familiarized himself with the manifests of all the ships to arrive along our coastline in the last couple of days. The Sketcher for our bid had been adamant that we cover this base, and it appeared that his concerns were well founded.

"Okay then, Your Ladyship," said Jevar. "Let us start the journey to His Grace's compound. I would like to get you out of this terrible weather as quickly as possible."

He gestured towards the ladder, but Nascinthé remained where she was.

"Jevar," she said. "I must ask you, how many men will be witnessing my arrival here?"

"Quite a few, I'll confess." Once again, he touched the brim of his hat.

"I see," she replied. "So, I am now to understand that you are taking me into your lord's compound—a populated place, I can only assume—where I will possibly be witnessed by…what, dozens of men? Does this seem like discretion to you? How in existence are you going to protect my identity under these conditions?"

This was, I must say, a very clever question. Nascinthé had disguised it behind a need for anonymity, but our pretend countess was clearly trying to figure out the most important information of all: how many soldiers might we face tonight, and where would we be facing them? If Jevar did not quickly refute the notion that we were headed straight into Gueritus's home, guarded by dozens of soldiers, then we were in very serious trouble indeed. Unfortunately, Jevar had a truly clever answer to Nascinthé's clever question, and it only made matters worse.

"My lady, we have a solution to this issue that I think you will find agreeable. None of the men waiting up at the street level will know your true identity, and because of this we can provide you proper security throughout your visit."

"Who do they think I am?"

"They believe you are Lave Kaszivar, Your Ladyship, a shipping magnate from the West who deals with Sullward extensively. She has not yet graced this city with her presence, so nobody here would be able to recognize her. However, at this very moment one of her flag ships is in our port, and this is well known to all of my lord's guardsmen."

Again, Nascinthé paused before replying, and from where I stood, I thought I saw her back stiffen. When she responded she spoke in a voice that contained within it a clear quiver of indignation.

"I see," she said. "That is most thoughtful of you, Jevar the 'Legate.' In order to protect my virtue, you have been so kind as to confuse my identity with the notorious Red Siren, a confirmed pirate and murderess. Were you hoping to add irony to the situation by choosing one of the very criminals that my father has tirelessly pursued through the Tergonian courts? I suppose my coming here wasn't humiliation enough."

I couldn't tell at first how Jevar reacted to this, for his initial response was to reach up and pull the brim of his hat back from his face. Upon seeing the soft, decidedly genteel features better revealed, the expression of contrition was unmistakable.

"Your Ladyship, you overestimate my craftiness and deeply underestimate my sincerity," he said. "I am privy to many of the politics that directly involve this city-state, yet I know little of the doings of the courts in far-off Tergon, and, furthermore, I would never presume to insult your person…in any fashion, but especially with respect to the honorable house of Odel, which is the very name I have promised to protect. No snub was intended."

A sudden frigid gust rumpled the water around our dock and had the group of us crouching momentarily for balance.

"Why did you choose Lave Kaszivar?" Nascinthé asked once it had passed.

"Because she is the perfect cover," he said. "We needed a personage, a lovely, female personage, whose presence here would be plausible yet whose face is largely unknown to us. We hear of Kaszivar only through the surrogates who man her ships, and their descriptions vary greatly. Though she is no doubt older than you, Your Ladyship, the men like to envision her as a young goddess…a myth that is sure to be dispelled the moment they actually lay eyes upon her. Which is in stark contrast to your valuation, Countess Odel, for having myself heard a great many rumors over the years about your loveliness, I see now that the tales vastly understate the reality. You are, in the truest sense, breathtaking."

In the past I had come into contact with the Legates of the Underlords on some of my more sensitive smuggling drops, and while they were clearly men of better refinement than the general populace of Hell's Labyrinth, I had never met one with this degree of courtly grace. Was Jevar truly the chief envoy of the dreaded Raving Blade? It went against everything I had ever heard about the coterie of sadistic operatives who worked directly in Gueritus's employ. Additionally, this encounter was not following the script of a degrading power play, as Holod Deadskiff had predicted.

Nascinthé, too, seemed baffled.

"Your flattery, while appreciated, confuses me, Jevar," said Nascinthé. "I can only wonder why your lord encourages you to carry on with this pretense at reverence."

Jevar shook his head, and I saw a doleful little seizure at his mouth. I had to admit, this sentimental behavior was either a whole new standard in Labyrinth diplomacy or some of the best play-acting I had ever witnessed.

"Clearly you do not understand my lord very well, Your Ladyship," he said. "I can only hope that this visit will change your feelings, for I know that is my lord's fondest wish. That is his deepest, most jealously guarded dream. But please, if you will, my lady, let me lead you and your people out of the rain."

Nascinthé gestured for Jevar to climb first, and as he approached the ladder, she looked back at the group of us questioningly. She understood the moment, understood the dangerous crossroads we had suddenly reached. It was the very thing that Radrin had inferred with his reconnaissance the night before—our target did not fear observation on this rendezvous, and this meant that his entire garrison might be within easy earshot throughout the bid. If it took place deep in the Raving Blade's compound, there was little chance that the four of us who were meant to wait outside would ever storm past the many guards to come to the assistance of our Masque and Line Man.

I slid forward and grabbed Fe Gesbon by the arm. Jevar had begun to climb the ladder, placing him in the direct path of the wind, and out of earshot.

"You two can't go in there alone," I whispered harshly.

"We stick with the plan," Gesbon snapped back, trying to shake off my hand.

"Nascinthé," I said, turning to our Masque. "Get us inside. All of us. Otherwise, you are walking to your deaths."

"Back the hell off, Grell Runner!" our Line Man snarled in a louder voice. If not for the wind, Jevar might conceivably have heard him. He didn't appear to, and he kept climbing, then carefully steadied himself as he stepped off onto the tempestuous street level.

"Col, keep that hood on," said Radrin, stepping between me and Col. "Vazeer, keep your hat down low. If they don't recognize you immediately, we are likely to be admitted as a group."

Fe Gesbon swiveled, a truly murderous expression squeezed across his pockmarked features, and I sensed that he was about to erupt in some desperate manner, possibly jeopardizing our cover. Nascinthé must have sensed it too, for she quickly stole the initiative by pushing past our enraged Line Man and strode boldly to the ladder where she grabbed a mossy rung with one of her blue calf-skinned gloves. This seemed to snap Fe Gesbon back into his role, and he leapt forward to assist her with the climb. He scampered up immediately after, and the rest of us followed.

Once we were up on the howling street level, we could finally see the full scope of the threat. They appeared suddenly out of the storm, a wide ring of gray cloaks and coats fluttering in the gloom like sooty wings. I had no way to determine their full numbers, as the close encroachment of buildings offered far too many hiding places to count. Still, I was able to tally up thirteen men in the immediate vicinity of the boardwalk, not a single one wearing a crest or color of any sort to identify him. This is how it always was in our world: overwhelming force and total anonymity, united like two sides of the same dark coin. Jevar signaled us to follow, and soon we were off, slinking our way through the tight, dark streets of the Lower City, moving ever closer to a bid that had somehow managed to get even more terrifying.

Our journey through wind and rain and dark brought us down thin streets that more closely resembled back alleyways than true urban thoroughfares. If the canal system of the ancients was complicated to the point of being whimsical, then the endless tangle of streets and intersecting alleyways that made up the core of Hell's Labyrinth was downright mystifying. In the days when the city was a popular holiday destination for the Empire's richest families, getting lost in the foggy maze of Sullward's streets was considered an exquisite privilege, and a certain prelude to fabulous storytelling upon return. Crime was all but nonexistent then, and an army of stone washers kept the lovely texture of the granite and marble glistening. I'm sure the cultural elite enjoyed wonderful excursions back in the days of old. Our experience on the night of 28 Dekharven, year 213, was entirely different.

Even in the darkness you could sense the terrible change. If nothing else, you could smell it, that stale odor of decay. In the claustrophobic web of alleyways, the air was as smothering as a horse blanket, textured even, to the point where you could separate out its various threads of sour pungency and dull sweetness. The physical damage was now visible to us in close quarters, for even in the dimmest of lighting one certainly knew the difference between clean beige or gray granite, and walls stained so black by mildew that they appeared as though the whole city had once burned in a fire without being consumed.

When we arrived at the entrance to Gueritus's compound, we found it less than noteworthy—a nondescript sunken door set in the skewed wall of a back alleyway, looking very much like all the others we had passed. The building itself appeared so derelict that I doubted the imperial constables had even bothered to check this one. No wonder it was so hard for the authorities to catch the Underlords. I had been living in this city my entire life and I'd never had a clue where Count Ulan Gueritus resided.

Jevar didn't knock; he simply waited a moment and the portal swung in on its own, throwing a soft torch glow over his face and the faces of Fe Gesbon and Nascinthé. There was a single guard standing just inside, and Jevar brushed past him down a tight, torchlit hallway, with the rest of us close behind. Col and I kept our heads covered and our faces down, and I prayed that our outer garments would be sufficient to disguise us a little longer. Jevar walked another twenty feet, then rapped lightly on the wall of the narrow passage. Seconds later, a hidden panel swung inward.

"Come inside, please," Jevar said politely, and he stepped across the threshold. One after another we followed, walking out of the misleading world of decrepitude, into the dim, clandestine domain of a Sullward Underlord.

11

MASQUERADE

I had anticipated that the space on the other side of that panel might be imposing, yet I was truly unprepared for the sheer elegance of what lay just beyond that secret, undignified doorway. The marble floor caught my eye first—an impeccable white plane with seams so tight and level that only the closest inspection revealed them. The rest of the entry foyer bore the classic octagonal shape known to grace the mansions of the Tergonian aristocracy. The ceiling was domed, and the cornice moldings were plaited in gold leaf, with elaborate swooping curves and dentils. The limestone columns at each of the eight corners of the room bore spiraling flutes and were individually painted in a variety of pastel colors—mauve, peach, lavender, and light blue. A huge crystal chandelier hung overhead, and among the dozens of candles that flickered there, I could not spot a single one that had been allowed to burn out.

Yet again I found myself wondering just what sort of man this Count Ulan Gueritus really was. The pure decorous splendor of the space seemed to belie rumors that Gueritus, while brilliant in a strategic sense, was thoroughly unrefined as a man. It was said that his tastes tended towards the gothic, if one was being very generous, or the downright macabre, if one was not. Either the rumors were wildly off the mark, or Count Ulan Gueritus had undergone some sort of personal transformation of late. Of course, there was always a chance that something entirely different was at play here. I had never completely dismissed the strange rantings of poor eyeless, tongueless Brand from the abandoned orphanage. That sad member of the Raved seemed dedicated to the notion that Gueritus wore two faces—one the visage of a demon, the other the seductive appearance of a nobleman. Brand even made it plain that it was the nobleman who had lured him in, drew him into a pretty hole filled with beauty and splendors. Only then, when he was deep inside, did the terrible demon show himself.

"Your cloaks and coats, if you will," said Jevar, and he signaled the guards.

There were eleven men standing at attention in this chamber, one positioned at each of the pillared corners, and three more who stood in the center of the room. Two of these three came forward to take our wet garments, while the third remained with Jevar and conversed with him quietly. There were no distinguishing emblems or brooches on any of them, yet their clothing was surprisingly uniform—tailored crimson and gray tunics, black trousers and boots, short dark cloaks with hemmed borders, which precisely matched the red color from the tunics. I had never seen the soldiers of the Labyrinth dress with anything close to this degree of coordination, no matter who they worked for. A moment later, as we removed our wet outer garments, eight of these smartly dressed, neatly groomed soldiers drew hidden blades from beneath their cloaks and rushed in at us to spring the trap.

They bore spades, the indigenous North Derjian short sword—a stout, wicked implement rarely more than two feet in length from tip to pommel, which was ideal for gutting a man at close range while still retaining enough blade span to cut and parry. Not surprisingly, they came straight for me and Col, and they were so quick and well synchronized that there was no possibility of threatening them back into a stalemate position. It was either full-out combat or complete passivity, and both Col and I, having spent years making split-second decisions in the midst of a rush, decided that this ambush did not quite have lethal intent behind it. Still, it was imbued with adequate degrees of aggression, and within seconds there were four needle-sharp spade tips against each of our necks.

"Submit!" one of the soldiers roared as the sharp steel poked us. We did, though Col had reflexively grabbed the hilt of his blade. Shortly thereafter, his hands, like mine, came out to the sides with palms up in the recognized gesture of compliance.

"What in the name of the gods is the meaning of this?" Nascinthé barked at Jevar.

"I am told, Mistress Kaszivar," he said sheepishly. "I am told that these two members of your party are in fact natives of this city."

Nascinthé glanced at the one guardsman who had remained behind to confer with Jevar. Incidentally, he was also the one who had ordered us to "submit," and together these factors made it obvious that he was a commander of some sort, though he was attired just like the others.

"Yes, what of it?" Nascinthé asked.

"According to the men in this room, to several of these men…I am told that your two companions are actually Sullward free agents, Mistress Kaszivar. Contract operatives."

"Contract operatives?" Nascinthé exclaimed with distress. "Is that right?"

We had, of course, been anticipating this moment from the start, though the fact that we were now inside the compound raised the stakes significantly. The sketch had provided Nascinthé with a plausible explanation to use at this moment, but it was meant to come while Col and I were still safely outside some anonymous Lower City building, not inside the target's actual home. We posed a much greater threat now. Additionally, Nascinthé's explanation was designed to work if it came from the lips of the virtuous Shaeyin Odel, not from the devious tongue of the pirate financier, Lave Kaszivar. Nascinthé was now in the highly awkward position of playing two roles at once—Countess Odel to Jevar, the Red Siren to the guards—and somehow, as both of these people, she was going to have to keep me and Col from being killed. We were about to find out just how good a Masque Nascinthé of Levell really was.

"Jevar the Legate," she said with exaggerated dismay. "You bring me a most disappointing piece of news. You say these men are free agents…contract operatives, as you call them, yet that's not what they told me when I hired them."

"No?" asked Jevar, looking exceedingly uncomfortable. He had obviously hoped to get the Countess past this set of guards without mishap. "What did they tell you, Mistress Kaszivar?"

"They told me that they were Shadow Bidders, Jevar. I like the name 'Shadow Bidder' so much more than 'free agent' or 'contract operative.' It has an almost sensual ring to it."

And then suddenly Nascinthé turned to me.

"This man, for instance," she said with a smile. "This man is surely a Shadow Bidder and not a contract man."

She came towards me, pressing two of the imprisoning guards lightly to either side so that she could step right up to me, face-to-face; so close, in fact, that I smelled the faint floral whoosh of her perfume. The guards must have smelled it too, and I saw the pair who were holding blades on me from the front glance sidelong at Nascinthé with what could only be described as nervous awe. I myself could not help but be entranced by the elongated motions of that slender mouth—the one that had originally failed to express itself, but which was now dancing with pert abandon.

"Where I come from, we have plenty of paid riffraff," she continued. "Mercenaries, freebooters…this sort of thing. But we don't have Shadow Bidders. We don't have…"

Now she removed one of her gloves, stretched forward, and put her hand on my chest, somewhat possessively.

"What is it that you call yourself again, Shadow Bidder?"

"Vazeer," I replied obediently, as if under hypnosis.

"No," Nascinthé snapped. "I mean the other name, your 'Shadow Bidder' name. 'Whip,' or something of the sort…it was better than that."

"Lash," I replied. "Vazeer the Lash."

"Ahhhh," she said with a virtual moan of delight. "Vazeer the Lash; now that is certainly a Shadow Bidder's name. And this…"

Suddenly she reached up and, to my utter startled chagrin, ran her slender fingers delicately down the long, arching scar upon my left cheek.

"…this is a Shadow Bidder's face if ever I dreamed of one—brooding, dark, maimed by the savagery of others, yet not entirely savage itself…almost sensitive really, in ways that my own soldiers' faces will never be."

Nascinthé continued to trace her fingertips along the pallid crescent that ran from the top of my left cheekbone all the way down to my stubbled chin. My face had grown very hot and felt as though it was vibrating, particularly in the region of the scar itself, affording me the vague and highly absurd thought that my shaking might force Nascinthé's hand into contact with one of the sharp blades that were but inches from her wrist on either side. I glanced again to the guards, and though their spades were still held firmly in place, their gazes were entirely transfixed by the veering tour that the Red Siren's fingers was taking down my face. The man on the left had unconsciously allowed his jaw to hang slack like a starving urchin who becomes riveted before a bake shop window.

"Tell me, Vazeer the Lash," she said in a low, almost hoarse voice. "Was it this particular scar that gave you your name? Is this why they call you 'The Lash'?"

My throat felt very dry.

"That's part of it," I managed.

"I thought so," she said with satisfaction. "And the man who did this to you, did you do him in kind?"

I paused for a moment and looked around at the many rapt faces. They all seemed entirely spellbound.

"That's the other part."

Laughter emerged in a low, quiet ripple, which spread quickly around the room like an infectious cough. My captors were soon chuckling along with the others, and even the dour Commander of the Guard, who had obviously orchestrated this detainment, grinned openly and then turned to Jevar with a shrug. And then suddenly, as I swallowed self-consciously and glanced around at the ruddy faces of the laughing soldiers and saw Jevar let out a quiet sigh of the deepest possible relief, I knew, in a most gut-level sense, that Nascinthé had done it. There would likely be some wrangling over how far into the compound Col and I would be permitted to venture, but the threat of imminent disaster had been diffused. Only later did it occur to me how.

There is virtually nothing written about the subtle Shadow Bidder art known as Ruse Masquerade; however, I do possess several political volumes that touch upon advanced persuasion techniques. Nascinthé had performed what was called a "displaced seduction." She must have come to the conclusion that despite her own physical beauty and personal magnetism, and her near-mythical stature as the alluring "Red Siren," a direct seduction performed on the Commander, or any of his men, would be too overt a tactic in a world populated by maniacally suspicious individuals. So, she did the next best thing. Nascinthé used the full force of her dangerous charm on one of her own people—a "safe target"—and that allowed the soldiers to let down their guard and to slip into a fantasy that on other nights might prove quite repulsive: essentially, being Vazeer the Lash. I doubt if there was one man in that room, Jevar and the members of our group included, who did not feel those wicked and enthralling fingers running like warm honey down the calloused surface of his own cheek, who did not smell her warmth when she stood so close, and who did not answer her questions dutifully in his own head with his own words, with his own images of what might happen after it was all over—when we had finished with the petty business of contracted murder and, freshly emerged from this exquisitely decorated deathtrap, he could not help but hope that she, the Lady Kaszivar, the Siren, Countess, Shadow Bidder, Masque…that one who had traced her creamy white skin along the disfigured crescent of ruined flesh called the Lash; that she might actually mean the flattering words that she had just spoken. That she might be more than just a cold and hollow masquerade.

How foolish these soldiers were to dream.

"Very well then, Mistress Kaszivar," Jevar finally said once the men had stopped chuckling. "I take it to mean that you consciously set out to hire independents, or Shadow Bidders if it pleases you to name them. To what end, might I ask?"

"To what end do you think, Jevar the Legate?" she spat with sudden bitterness, as if appalled that he would dare to heap further indignity upon her by asking another question. "Have I ever set foot in this city before? Do I know my way here? Your lord made it clear that I must make it to that three-sided bay on my own to protect his damned interests. What else would you have me do? Try to follow a map?"

Jevar and the Commander conferred for a moment, and then the Commander looked over at his men and waved them off. Within seconds the blades were removed from our necks and the men retreated to their positions around the perimeter.

"I apologize, Mistress Kaszivar, for the inconvenience," said Jevar.

"Why don't you apologize to them?" she said.

"Indeed," said Jevar, and he looked directly at me and Col. "I can assure you, Shadow Bidders, that my lord will wish to compensate you above and beyond whatever you have been promised, for providing the lady safe conduct here. You can wait comfortably in one of the drawing rooms until Mistress Kaszivar's business is completed."

"They'll do nothing of the sort," said Nascinthé, and she strode forward towards the place where Jevar stood with the Commander. "All of my people, hired or otherwise, accompany me throughout the duration of this errand. That's final."

Jevar looked quickly to the Commander, yet, before anything meaningful could be exchanged between them, Nascinthé butted in.

"I have traveled a very long way on rough seas to get here. I have come ashore with only three retainers, as instructed, under cover of darkness, with no greeting party to guide me—all just to keep our precious business secret. Would it not be considerate on your part to allow me whatever scant means of protection I can muster while I'm here? If you don't permit this pair of armed men to accompany me at least as far as the door to your lord's audience chamber, then I turn around right now and walk out into the stormy night and leave you to sort things out with your lord…who, I'm sure, will understand perfectly why you took it upon yourself to sabotage his business."

This last remark was spoken with the same quiver of affronted distress that Nascinthé had displayed out at the Three Bay, and I had the subtle impression that our Masque had now shifted the emphasis of her Masquerade away from the Commander of the Guard and back to Jevar. This new tactic quickly struck home.

"I will vouch for them," said Jevar. "I'll sponsor the two Shadow Bidders and will assume full responsibility for them while they are here, and I will also take their assurances that nothing that they have witnessed tonight—the location of this compound, its contents, the lady's visit here—will be remembered after this contract is complete. Shadow Bidders, am I assured on this?"

Col and I quickly assented, which seemed to be enough for him. After all, a contract operative's entire use in the Labyrinth was his ability to follow through with his promises, no matter what the circumstances. That said, I did not rule out the possibility that Jevar and the Commander of the Guard were simply humoring their guest, and that in their minds Col and I could always be disposed of after she was gone.

Then suddenly, with no further inquests, suspicions, threats, or violence, we were walking past the Commander of the Guard and his soldiers, venturing through a set of double doors into the heart of a place where no Shadow Bidder had ever tread.

In this way, we passed our first major hurdle, though we knew with great certainty that it would not be our last. A messenger had already been sent ahead to alert guards throughout the compound that we were coming and to make the way secure for our approach.

Beyond the set of elegantly carved double doors, a wide carpeted staircase led us down several flights until at last we reached a long gallery, which was decorated with dark wooden wall paneling, tall standing braziers, and pairs of maroon couches that sat facing each other across the highly polished marble floor. There were no guards in this room, and immediately Jevar and Nascinthé began to converse again, quietly.

"Where did you learn to do that?" Jevar asked in a low, tense voice that was notably drained of its former coquetry.

"From my father."

"Archduke Vodun Odel taught you to play-act?" asked Jevar, making no effort to hide his skepticism. "I'm sure you're joking."

"I'm not joking in the least," Nascinthé replied. "Eighty percent of what you need to know as a politician is the art of pantomime, manipulation, and deceit. I was glad for the opportunity to test my skills, particularly in a place where I am hopelessly out of my element."

"Out of your element, Countess Odel? You could have fooled me."

"Good," said Nascinthé. "Then perhaps I *am* cut out to be Chief Legate to the Emperor, as my father insists."

We passed from the gallery and down another flight of stairs, this time a long, elegant spiral, and though the walls of the stairwell were of finely hewn, carefully grouted sandstone, one could not help but feel the thick oppressive moisture enveloping the air here like a musty quilt. We were headed down,

down, and down some more, into that mysterious subterranean realm about which I had speculated so often yet knew so little. All the while, as I descended each clean, ocher-colored step, I kept hearing a high, thin voice in my head. It was Pippen, the old man from the ruined North Derjian Children's Compassionate Sanctuary, translating the frenzied gestures of his disabled comrade.

"The terrible, noble demon lives in a hole. A dreadful but beautiful hole."

Had I not been warned that this was precisely where I was headed? Was I not, even now, walking into the same horrific fate that had left poor Brand a ghostly shell of a man? There was no turning back at this point. Somewhere deep in this pretty maze beneath the city, beneath even the canals and the river itself, dwelled the terrible two-faced demon. The only choice at this point was to press on and drive a knife through him, before he did far worse things to us.

When we reached the base of the circular stairwell, there were two guards waiting for us, and they unlocked a set of heavy iron-bound doors, permitting us to enter another impossibly long gallery lined with a red rug that must have taken an army of weavers to sew. Once they had let us inside, the guards closed the doors, leaving us on our own. Our group had maintained the same general procession, with Nascinthé, Jevar, and Fe Gesbon at the front, Flerra and Radrin just behind, and Col and I taking up the rear.

I noticed instantly that the air in this massive hallway was warmer and dryer than the atmosphere pervading the stairwell, and while it wasn't immediately apparent how Gueritus's engineers had achieved this, their motive for doing so was soon obvious. The paneled walls of this space were decorated with literally hundreds of pricey artifacts: paintings, sculpted busts, suits of armor, ornamented weaponry, bejeweled court fans, gilded mirrors, tapestries, statues, bronze urns, glass cases filled with jewelry…the display went on and on, to the point where I found myself unable to take it all in. I knew what this gallery was, knew it immediately without an explanation from our host. I had heard many rumors over the years about the fabled Ripening Halls of the Underlords, another great innovation of the current High Lord. It was here that the stolen property was stored until the former owner no longer had a legal claim to it. The "ripening" process also gave the theft victims ample time to grieve for, and eventually forget, their stolen property, at which point it was deemed safe to redistribute back into the Empire.

I could tell at once that walking through this vast arcade of illicit objects was going to bring back a few memories. I already recognized two paintings, a suit of armor, and a set of ivory figurines that I had personally smuggled up the Grells.

"Lord Elmónd Ganes!" Nascinthé exclaimed with a delighted laugh, staring up at a portrait of a rather self-important-looking, gray-haired man. "Funny thing is he looks even more arrogant in person. And there's the Marchioness Ursula of Telea. My goodness, you even have a painting of Admiral Hellard—poor Hellard, look how young he looks there. Where's my father? You must have his likeness here somewhere?"

To this day I don't know exactly how Nascinthé pulled this off. Some of the paintings did, in fact, have small placards at the base of their frames, and it was possible that our Masque's eyes were sharp enough to snap up the inscriptions. Or else, she was such a savant that twenty-four hours memorizing the two books I had given her were sufficient to spin this level of charade. I suppose there was a final possibility, one that only entered my mind later—perhaps our faux Countess had actually come from the courtly world about which she was carelessly prattling.

"I am not well schooled in the art of appraisal, Your Ladyship," said Jevar. "We have specialists for that."

"Appraisal!" Nascinthé exclaimed. "Heavens help me, I almost forgot what this place was. Let me ask you, Jevar, who in the entire Empire *haven't* you stolen from?"

"We haven't stolen from anybody, Shaeyin, as you well know."

The change in Jevar's tone was so distinct that I paused in my strolling and stared. The professional Masque in our troupe was better at disguising her reactions, for she merely shrugged and continued her dallying tour of the Raving Blade's Ripening Hall, pretending that Jevar's new tone of personal rebuke was somehow expected.

"Countess Odel," said Jevar a few seconds later, returning to her formal title yet failing to banish the scolding pitch from his voice. "May I please speak with you for a moment?"

"We are speaking, Jevar."

"Alone."

"There is no need for it," Nascinthé said over her shoulder, as she examined a griffon crest on an elegantly embroidered burgundy flag. "I have nothing to hide."

It was a bold act of feigned naiveté, but she knew she could get away with it. Nascinthé understood that the whole "Lave Kaszivar" charade had far less to do with guarding *her* identity than it did with protecting the life of Jevar's boss. If somehow reports of the Countess's visit to Sullward were to leak to the High Lord, then an assassination contract would be pending within hours, which was, after all, a very logical explanation for this current Narrow Bid.

As I watched Jevar glance uncomfortably between Col, myself, and the woman he thought was Countess Odel, I had my first real insight into the man's consistently "un-Labyrinthine" behavior. Perhaps Jevar was a legate in the basic sense, but he was not a true Sullward operative like the rest of the men in this compound; like the Commander of the Guard, who had ordered the ambush in the entry foyer. This meant that Jevar was performing this task because he was the only one who knew the truth, the only one in whom the Count had dared to confide regarding this perilous meeting with Shaeyin Odel. A best friend, perhaps? He seemed to be a gentleman, a rare Sullward denizen motivated by loyalty and not ambition, by a personal connection to his Underlord and not his own purse. I was beginning to think that the Count Ulan Gueritus was perhaps the most grossly misunderstood man in history.

"Please," said Jevar, and now he sounded desperate. "I requested that the guards clear out of this hall, but they won't stay gone for long. If we delay here, they'll soon check on us…and after we leave this chamber, there will be ever-greater numbers of soldiers watching and listening to our every move. This is our last secure space."

We had now moved about halfway down the length of the enormous gallery, and we were, consequently, at the most audibly private space in the entire chamber, hundreds of feet from either set of large double doors. I had noticed several smaller side doors as we walked, but Jevar had never lowered his voice as he passed them, suggesting that he believed they were unattended.

Nascinthé finally turned to Jevar as she walked.

"What is it that your lord wishes you to say to me that he cannot say himself?"

Jevar took an extended breath, glanced back one last time at me and Col, then seemed to conclude that conveying his message was more important than being discreet.

"He wants you to know that things don't have to change."

"How does he figure that?"

"He figures that, Shaeyin, he figures that even if…even when you inevitably succeed your father as Chief Legate, there is no reason to believe that things couldn't be as they were before."

"Oh, do speak plainly, Jevar," Nascinthé said in a wearied voice. "Your lord could give me this speech himself. What is the part that he cannot say?"

And then suddenly, Jevar smiled. I was still in the back of the group, yet the smile was very clear, clear to all of us, and I believe it was most noteworthy because it seemed so genuine, almost involuntary.

"You are everything he said you were, and more," Jevar said with a light, buoyant laugh. "All these years when he was sneaking off, in a dozen different disguises, I truly believed that he had lost his senses. And when you at last broke it off, Lady Shaeyin, I will admit that I was privately overjoyed. Having never met you, I secretly thanked you for being a flighty and capricious maid who had simply lost interest in something that had become drained of its dangerous mystique. Yet my lord insisted, he insisted that you were merely doing what you felt in your heart you must do for the sake of your family. He knew that, Your Ladyship, despite what he may have said. He knows it now, even as he pretends to coerce you with threats of disclosure…threats that you yourself know he would never carry out. He may act cold and aloof in his audience chamber, yet that is not his true face. That is merely his pride."

Jevar gazed warmly at Nascinthé and spoke a few concluding words with a genial, relieved sigh, as though the burden of his own charge were finally emptied from him.

"These are the words that my lord could not speak, which I have taken upon myself to speak, even though he did not ask me to do so. I alone know the pain…"

Jevar's blood, in a tight needle stream, splattered Nascinthé's white cheek like wine squirting from a punctured deerskin pouch. For a second, she did not seem to understand what it was, swiping at the warm fluid heedlessly as though it were an irritating douse of condensation that had dropped from the ceiling. A moment later, when Jevar's body crumpled limply to the floor like a coat that had slipped off of its hanging peg, Nascinthé looked down, saw it all, and froze. Her formally expressive mouth had now squeezed down into an excruciating pinch.

Radrin Blackstar stood over the body of Jevar the Legate and calmly wiped the blade of his dagger on a small black cloth. His eyes were filled with neither brutality nor any notable measures of humanity. For a moment he stared down at the body of his victim as if curious about the oddly twisted posture in which it had fallen, as if interested in the precise shape of the spill that was now darkening the crimson carpet in a warped, oblong bubble. Jevar's form visibly deflated below us as his life's essence drained from the long slit in his throat.

"What…what did you just do, Finisher?" Fe Gesbon stammered. "What did you just do?"

The Line Man's entire face was locked in a furrow of pure confusion, his scarred forehead growing deeper wrinkles by the second as though he was being pressed in a carpenter's vise.

The group of us slowly formed a circle around Radrin and the corpse, with Nascinthé still petrified in the same spot, splattered cheek and all, Fe Gesbon next to her, and Col, Flerra, and I fanning out to complete the ring. It seemed as if there was a haze filling the surrounding air, like a thin film of pond scum that had become gaseous and was now rising from Jevar's throat. Only Radrin seemed unstupified by its vapors, and he squatted down over the body and began to search it carefully, working his hands along the belt, the folds in its tunic, and finally through the gory items around the neck. Somehow, even in my own baffled state, I knew he was looking for keys.

"What are you doing, Finisher?" Fe Gesbon hissed in the same strangled quaver, though he had now changed his tense from past to present, which at last elicited a response from the Finisher.

"What am I doing, Fe Gesbon?" Radrin asked without looking up from his bloody salvage work. "I'm improvising."

12

IMPROVISATION

It has been my experience on the many, many bids that I have run, in the many, many years that I have been running them, that sudden, unexpected acts of violence reveal everything about the people around you. You can literally learn all of the relevant details about a fellow Shadow Bidder at such junctures. Or, stated more accurately, you can determine who is actually a Shadow Bidder and who is not, which was precisely what was about to be exposed in that newly sullied Ripening Hall. I can't say I was entirely surprised by the results.

"Flerra Tellian," said Radrin Blackstar, still squatting down next to the body of Jevar. "Go try two or three of the nearest side doors and see if any of them are open. I'm sure they won't be, but at least tell me how good the locks are and how long it will take to get us through. The corpse does not appear to carry any keys."

Flerra Tellian's expression was strained, yet it had nothing in common with the malfunctioning implosion that was occurring in Fe Gesbon's face, nor did she even remotely mirror Nascinthé of Levell's stony paralysis. Flerra was simply on guard, already adjusting to this violent turn of events without fully understanding it. She glanced quickly at me, and in those narrow, shrewish features, I saw an astonishing vein of poise running through the bedrock of her character—the same solidity that I had always recognized, and which seemed to intensify when it was needed most. I had always respected her for it, yet now, suddenly, in this moment of bloodied confusion, I felt a great heave of gratitude accompanying the respect. She must have noted this, for her characteristically bloodless cheeks suddenly colored like rice paper back-illumined by a flame. I nodded, confirming Radrin's instructions, and Flerra spun away to find a door.

"Finisher!" Gesbon hissed, the trauma rising to a wheezing pitch. "If you don't…if you don't explain this to me…"

"Then what, Fe Gesbon?" Radrin asked with a trace of amusement, standing up at last and cleaning his hands with his black cloth. "Will you report on me after the bid, explain how I willfully broke the sketch? Perhaps you may wish to include in your report the fact that a crucial piece of information was omitted from our briefing—probably out of ignorance—yet still a miscalculation of such serious dimensions that we are entirely in our right now to abandon the bid."

"What are you talking about?"

"Vazeer the Lash?" said Radrin, turning to me. Yet again I felt him reaching out as he had in the boathouse, as he had in that Dockside alleyway, asking me to stand with him against the Line Man. At the same time, I sensed him enticing me into a less tangible form of collusion, which I didn't yet comprehend.

"You are the man who understands improvisation even better than me. Perhaps you could explain to our Line Man what the problem is here. In the meantime, Col, help me move this body out of the sight line of the main doors. The soldiers will find it, but I'd prefer if it took them a while."

Without hesitation, Col moved forward to lend his assistance, and as he did, I saw in him, perhaps in a far less dramatic and affectionate way, elements of what I had seen in Flerra Tellian. Col was as astute and calculating an operative as you might hope, or fear, to find in the Labyrinth, yet he knew when to keep his mouth shut. He could make decisions under the worst duress, on the edge of a razor, and once he decided, there was no hesitancy. He understood enough of what was going on here not to question the parts that remained mysterious.

I turned to Fe Gesbon and cleared my throat.

"The Raving Blade and the Countess Shaeyin Odel were having a love affair," I said in a monotone voice that was so divested of emotion it sounded as though I was talking in my sleep. "There will be no opportunity to seduce the Count into a vulnerable condition, for he will see at once that Nascinthé is not Shaeyin Odel. Perhaps some of his closest bodyguards have met the Countess as well, in which case we may be spotted before we even get to Gueritus's chamber. The intercepted letter indicated that the Countess had never before visited the Labyrinth, yet, as we see now, that didn't mean the Raving Blade hadn't gone to visit her. We are better off resorting to stealth."

Again, I cleared my throat with the same pretense at apathy.

Gesbon's face had not released itself from the tight vise of consternation, even after hearing my explanation, and in that moment, I felt an odd sympathy for him. I could almost see the sense of purpose evacuating from our Line Man with the same speed that Jevar's fluids had spit out onto the Ripening Hall rug. Without the sketch, Fe Gesbon was just another sword, and probably a poor one at that.

Yet, even as I pitied Fe Gesbon, I felt something closer to tragedy when I stared at Nascinthé of Levell. Our stricken Masque had made no efforts to clean her cheek, and now Jevar's blood had begun to worm its slow course over the hump of her jaw and into the frilled white lace of her collar. I suppose in retrospect the fact that Nascinthé was horrorstruck by the violence, violence committed against her gentlemanly co-star in the night's performance, was the main cause of her paralysis. She was clearly unprepared for such things, confirming my fears that she was not, in fact, a true Shadow Bidder. Yet in that moment I saw something else. I saw the Masque suddenly stripped of her Masquerade, deprived of it as surely as Gesbon had been parted with his sketch, and Jevar had been robbed of his life, and somehow, to a degree that was not far removed from what had been done to the Legate himself, there was an awful, vulgar injustice to Nascinthé's loss.

Radrin and Col had managed to force Jevar's body into a huge urn, and though he did not fit entirely, the urn was set back between two pedestals bearing marble gargoyles, and that was enough to require a guard to travel all the way to the spot in order to confirm the crime. There was little that could be done about the stained carpet, yet the red upon red was hardly noticeable from a distance, something our Finisher had no doubt considered just before he clamped his hand over Jevar's mouth from behind and slit his throat.

Flerra Tellian started jogging back toward the group, and I saw that there was a problem immediately. She had ripped off her maid's dress, stuffing it behind a suit of armor, and now all the many small burglary implements were visible in leather straps around her waist, thighs, and calves.

"You picked a nice place to break the sketch, Finisher," she muttered. "I checked five doors and they're all split-locked. The easiest one will take me ten minutes if I make some noise, even longer if I don't. Didn't it occur to you that this is a Ripening Hall?"

"It did, of course," Radrin replied, "yet there was little alternative. Once the Legate led us through that next set of double doors, we would be under constant observation until we arrived at Gueritus's audience chamber, and that would mean coming under attack while heavily surrounded, with no time to coordinate a strategy. As it is we've wasted too much time here and are at risk now of being checked upon."

"Go to work on the lock," I mumbled to Flerra. "You can do it in less than ten minutes, and you can do it quietly."

"You can jam a skiff paddle up your ass, Vazeer!" she snapped. "And you can do it as loud as you like."

She turned away and headed for one of the doors, drawing slender implements from her thigh and waist straps as she went.

"I warned you, Finisher, not to pull out on us."

Fe Gesbon's eyes appeared a touch less confused now, though his forehead was still compressed into a frightful, wrinkled knot of scar tissue. He was shaking his head.

"This must be why I was hired for this bid, because you like to improvise. And you as well, Grell Runner. The proffer obviously wanted me to keep the two of you in line, to keep all of you in line…and I'll be damned if I'm going to break that trust."

There was something particularly ominous about the way Fe Gesbon spoke this threat, though I couldn't credit him at that moment with anything resembling self-confidence or command. Rather, it was his complete lack of authority, the clenching efforts to compensate for impotence, that made him seem dangerous. Strangely, I saw what might almost be classified as a smile working the corners of his mouth. Coupled with the mashed torture of his brow, this weird half-grin seemed highly deranged. A moment later my fears were confirmed.

"Masque!" Fe Gesbon barked, turning to Nascinthé and gripping her limp arm in his mailed grasp. "Can you bluff us through the guards, get us as far as Gueritus's chamber…just to the door?"

Nascinthé's formerly supple body lurched stiffly as the Line Man pulled her close. She turned to gaze at him tentatively, though not altogether blankly, and the pressed arch of her suspended brows came down fractionally on her forehead.

"I know you can do it, Masque," Fe Gesbon rasped. "Tell the guards something, anything…tell them that Jevar needed to take care of some errand, or that you ordered him to stay behind… because he offended you. It doesn't matter what you choose, just get me close to the Raving Blade. I'll finish this bid myself."

I must admit, I probably would have admired the Line Man for his daring at that moment, had I not suddenly begun to loathe him, which I had. It came upon me in an instant, a blistering hatred that forced its way up into my throat like bile, and though I might pretend the feeling had to do with Gesbon's stupidity, or his inflexibility, or the fact that, for all his other shortcomings, he was most inconveniently imbued with a sort of foolhardy courage, I knew that the animosity was confined to one completely irrelevant section of air inside the massive space of the Ripening Hall. It was the section of air that contained Fe Gesbon's desperate mailed fist gripping Nascinthé of Levell's delicate, silk-clad arm. The sight of that one affront made all the insane words coming out of the Line Man's mouth seem beside the point.

"…can you do it, Masque?" Gesbon was asking, having pulled Nascinthé's face within inches of his. "Just you and I, without any of these sketch-breakers; just you and I…and our target. Can you get me close enough to finish the bid?"

I suppose I shouldn't have been entirely astonished and dismayed by what happened next, but I was. Nascinthé of Levell actually brought herself to nod affirmatively to the Line Man's insane proposal; she twitched her chin up and down rapidly in a series of nervous flutters, and though the motion might have been mistaken for a muscle spasm in another context, here it was quite clear what she meant. She did not turn to look at the rest of us, keeping her gaze fixed instead on Fe Gesbon.

"Now, get rid of this," Gesbon said, and he pulled off one of his gauntlets and wiped his bare sweaty hand upon Nascinthé's cheek, succeeding only in smearing the blood around like poorly applied rouge.

"Fe Gesbon, what you are proposing is guaranteed suicide," said Radrin in a tone that, for the first time, held hints of agitation. "The moment you step through that set of double doors, without the Chief Legate providing you clearance, you are a dead man; or, more likely, you will be taken to one of Count Gueritus's notorious 'Raving Cells' where you and Nascinthé will re-learn the meaning of the word torture. The only legitimate plan is to exit this chamber through another door."

"And then what, Finisher?" Fe Gesbon roared, at a volume that might conceivably have been heard on the far side of those distant, iron doors. "Creep around like rats, resort to 'stealth,' as the Grell Runner proposes. This is the lair of an Underlord, you fools! The only possible hope we have here is to play to our strength, and our only strength is right here."

He shook Nascinthé's arm, causing her to rattle awkwardly, and then a moment later he reached over with the sleeve of his coat and used it to aggressively wipe her face. She remained mute and compliant through it all, and I believe that was the only reason I did not rush forward and bludgeon Fe Gesbon to the carpet. This idiotic plan, on some base level, seemed to be giving her a measure of relief.

And then they were off, Fe Gesbon pulling Nascinthé briskly down the long crimson rug of the Ripening Hall, clearly intent on getting through those tall double doors before the rest of us even had time to exit the chamber.

"I'll take them both out," Col muttered from where he stood just behind me and Radrin. "Neither one is of any use to us now."

"Go then," Radrin replied flatly. "Just be quick and quiet about it. No fencing matches."

"We can't risk it," I said.

Even before the words had left my mouth, I was already pressing Col's advancing chest to a standstill with my forearm, and then I started jogging after Fe Gesbon and Nascinthé, praying that neither of the men I had just left behind would try to stop me. They both stayed where they were, and so I ran down the red rug unimpeded.

It's interesting, but on occasion I have what can only be described as a clear moment of self-awareness. Either I grasp something about myself to which I have been hitherto blind or, as in this case, I suddenly understand that a personal issue about which I am reasonably aware, and which others criticize repeatedly, is in fact a problem. This is never a great moment. I don't like seeing or admitting such things, but in the Ripening Hall that night, as I chased after Nascinthé of Levell and Fe Gesbon, one realization was inescapable. Col was completely and utterly right about me. All of his fears were founded; his instincts, premonition, whatever the hell it was he described in that curtained booth at the Gilded Razor, was in every way correct. I was now, exactly as predicted, going dangerously off script. All sorts of unintended consequences were likely to result, and because this impulse-driven departure wasn't manifesting as an abrupt act of violence, or an ill-advised standoff, I suspect that Col didn't quite recognize the moment for what it was.

But I did. I knew very well that what I was doing was stupid, that Col and Radrin were right—a tight crew composed of the four who had remained behind was best suited to what this operation now entailed. It was also true that by insisting upon a course of action that was jeopardous to us all, the other two operatives should, by all dictates of bid etiquette, be eliminated. Yet there was another, mutually beneficial solution to the impasse, which Col and Radrin hadn't thought of. The only problem was, I hadn't thought of it yet myself.

When I had come within ten feet of Fe Gesbon and Nascinthé, the Line Man turned on me furiously.

"Back off, Grell Runner, or I'll strike you down where you stand!"

He drew his sword, and much to my surprise, he handled the weapon with some degree of competence, whipping the long, finely crafted blade free of its scabbard in one fluid motion. He held the sword leveled in my direction and proceeded to back towards the doors of the gallery, all the while dragging Nascinthé by the arm. She continued to look away.

"I'll make a deal with you, Gesbon," I said, my hands raised in a gesture of peace. "I'll accompany the two of you on the rest of the bid if you give the others time to get out. If they're still here when those double doors open…imagine how it will appear to the guards: the three of us standing here, the three of them standing there, and no sign of Jevar."

"Why would I want your damned company, Grell Runner?" Fe Gesbon spat. "You are one of the main liabilities on this bid. And as to the others…let them hide if they like stealth so much. Let them stuff themselves inside an urn when the door opens. The Masque and I will do better without any of you."

"Fair enough," I replied. "Only, I have one thing more to say before I leave you to your own devices. I have some words for Nascinthé."

Though she did not turn to look at me, there was a reaction. It was in the carriage of her head, which was being held in a brittle, decidedly painful position, as though she were suffering from a sprained neck. Her posture loosened almost imperceptibly when I spoke her name.

"Nascinthé of Levell," I said quietly, walking slowly forward as Fe Gesbon pulled her backwards. "I want you to know something. I want you to know that even though you were performing a role back in the entry foyer, even though you were play-acting as Lave Kaszivar…you saw me truly. You probably didn't mean a single word when you described me, but still, you spoke the truth anyway. For some reason, I felt an obligation to tell you that before you stepped through those doors to your death."

"You must be mad, Grell Runner!" Fe Gesbon roared. "Are you really going to try to ruse a trained Masque?"

We had inched our way within fifty feet of the double doors, and it seemed impossible now that Gesbon's reckless shouting would not be heard outside. I didn't see any easy way to shut him up, so I kept my focus directed instead on the one who had the potential to tip the balance. Sure enough, Nascinthé did finally turn to me, and when she did, I saw in her ethereal features an air of deep, forlorn exhaustion, as though she had just lost a battle waged in the name of something dear to her.

"It only worked because the truth was present," she said in a soft, frayed voice that did not belong to either Lave Kaszivar or Countess Odel. Somehow, I knew that I was now hearing strains of the haunting undelivered communication that had so consumed my attention on the night of the sketch.

"I only succeeded in the foyer," she concluded, "because truth, not deception, is the ultimate weapon in the art of Ruse Masquerade."

I watched the door open behind Fe Gesbon in a sort of numb torpor, the tall right half of the arched barrier fading quietly into gloom like the departing haunches of an animal retreating into the marsh. The line of soldiers who emerged from that opening were so quiet and unassuming they seemed almost polite, apologetic even, for having disturbed our fascinating discourse on the nature of truth, deception, and masquerade, and I was privately admiring of how completely unfazed they seemed by it all. They simply came on, their spades and stilettos gripped with impassive conviction.

I did still hate Fe Gesbon; hated him for several reasons above and beyond his hysteric fingers clenched upon the arm of the mysterious performer-turned-philosopher named Nascinthé of Levell. Still, I simply couldn't watch him die without a fight.

"Gesbon, behind you!" I shouted.

As a final, asinine display, Fe Gesbon actually refused to turn around in that moment, clearly suspicious of a ploy. Only when Nascinthé spun, gasped, and jerked at his imprisoning grasp did Fe Gesbon get it. By then it was too late.

The Line Man managed only to let go of Nascinthé, turn, and raise his blade in a pretense of a parry before taking the first spade in his groin, then another in his thigh, then a stiletto to his ribs, then another to his neck. They jammed him so full of steel he went rigid for a second like a skewered banquet pig.

I got a hold of Nascinthé's wrist even as the first blade drove into our Line Man, and I was already pulling her down the hallway before the final exhalation departed Gesbon's shuddering lips. Gueritus's soldiers were clearly proficient with their weapons, but they made one tactical error—the first three men who came through the door all concentrated on the hapless Line Man, tying their blades up in his body, providing the split-second delay

Nascinthé and I needed to get away. Others followed, but we got the jump on them, and suddenly we found ourselves sprinting back down the red carpet at a terrible clip.

"Flerra, get that door open now!" I screamed as we came.

Col was standing in the middle of the Ripening Hall, ready. Like most combat operatives in Hell's Labyrinth, he carried the indigenous spade. However, he seldom used it as his primary weapon and instead wielded it in his off hand in place of the much smaller Derjian stiletto. In his right fist he bore a large military broadsword, an imposing weapon that might have been considered too slow and unwieldy for Sullward application, except for one well-documented fact. The huge Gosian operative known as Coljin Helmgrinder was the preeminent Contract Blade in all of Hell's Labyrinth, and he made weapons of any size dance and twirl in his fists like circus acrobats.

"I'm going to kill you for that stunt, Vazeer," he said coldly as Nascinthé and I ran past him to temporary safety. "Even if you survive this bid, you're a dead man."

The pursuing soldiers slowed at the sight of Col, and in that tiny lull, I glanced around to see how the others were faring. The door that Flerra was attempting to open was fifteen feet behind the place where Col had made his stand, and I saw our Locksmith's slender back hunched intently inside the small recess, working feverishly. Radrin Blackstar was nowhere to be seen. For a few seconds I scanned the Ripening Hall, glancing at the urns and suits of armor, the statuary and small recessed door wells, trying to figure out where the slippery shadow of a man had disappeared to. A moment later I gave up, as I had more pressing things to worry about.

"Stay with Flerra," I said to Nascinthé, ushering her towards the alcove, and just as I was turning to assist Col, I saw, at the very far end of the gallery, the double doors there being thrown wide. Soldiers, dozens of soldiers, poured through the opening like a rolling gray wave, and at the head of that wave was the Commander of the Guard who had given us so much trouble in the entry foyer. Though hundreds of feet away, I saw, in the man's unequivocal headlong charge, a ferocity and determination that truly terrified me.

"Open that damned door, Flerra!" I yelled. "You've got ten seconds at the very most!"

I looked back at Col in time to see him launch his attack at the soldiers who had killed Fe Gesbon. He had waited for the men to attempt to flank him, and as they advanced past him on either side, he took a stutter step backwards as if trying to retreat, then lunged so quickly to his right it looked as if he had been thrown sideways by a storm gust. He cleaved his first victim down with one backhand stroke of his broadsword, spraying the man's blood up across the pastoral greenery of a large landscape painting. Hundreds of berry-like speckles scattered over the bucolic trees and hedge rows. Then, spinning back the other way, Col spade-parried another soldier's blade, whirled his broadsword overhead, and brought it straight down on the man's collarbone, splitting him all the way down to his stomach.

The following soldier took it in the neck, the next in his side, one actually managed to get a stiletto into Col's thigh just before catching a spade tip under his jaw, and then a follow-up cut to his midsection with the broadsword that sent him rolling over and over again across the darkening rug.

The initial spiraling whirlwind of Col's attack was so devastating that it literally halted the advance of the soldiers. Col had once explained to me that he found the term "Helmgrinder" mildly insulting, seeing as he had so many better ways to kill a man than to simply crush his skull. He was certainly proving that now. Col couldn't hold these soldiers off forever—they would keep coming and coming—but he had provided me the opening I needed to make one last desperate effort to get us out of there.

"Flerra, what's happening with that lock?" I yelled, as I backed towards the door recess, keeping one eye on Col's melee and the other on the heavy, hurtling rush of the soldiers led by the Commander of the Guard. It was a matter of seconds before they arrived.

"Flerra…"

"Shut your reeking marsh hole, Vazeer!" she shrieked.

"The lock, Flerra?"

"Shut up!"

"Where are you…the second split?"

"Oh, black hells, Vazeer…please!"

I heard a sob in her voice, and I knew instantly that she was up against something much worse than a split-lock, which she definitely could have penetrated by now.

"What is it, Flerra? A bar?"

"It's a stinking tri-split, you…you…" Her voice fell off. A second later: "…wait…I think…"

I heard the click even before she said it. Through all of that insanity—Col's metallic cleaving, men grunting and screaming, the pounding inexorable stampede of the Commander of the Guard and his men, and, perhaps most of all, the dreadful *thump, thump, thump* inside my own veins—I heard the final split retract into the cylinder of the lock. I also heard something else—a man's whisper behind the door.

"Back away, Flerra!"

For all of her intransigence, Flerra Tellian knew me well, and she heard the crazed warning in my voice amidst the noise. She leapt aside.

I spun around, drew my knee all the way up to my chest, and drove the heel of my boot into the door with every ounce of strength in my body. The heavy oak portal flew open with a splintering snap and slammed so hard into the face of the soldier who had been crouching there that he literally rolled backwards across the marble floor. The other two who had been waiting just behind him were knocked off balance by his rolling, and they both stumbled awkwardly.

"Stay behind me!" I screamed to Nascinthé and Flerra.

And with that I plunged forward through that doorway, a spade in each of my hands. The time for careful strategies and clever masquerades was finished now. All that remained was savagery, and the violent determination to survive.

13

RUNNER

I can be remarkably dangerous.

I was never formally trained with a sword, nor am I an exceptional physical specimen. Apart from my profession as a smuggler, I have no background in soldiery or subterfuge to draw upon. And yet, just as Coljin Helmgrinder can turn two ponderous lengths of sharpened metal into a graceful, death-dealing windmill, and just as Radrin Blackstar is imbued with the terrifying ability to disappear from view, and then from thought, and finally from memory altogether…until he materializes once again with his hand over your mouth and his blade halfway through your throat, so, too, does Vazeer the Lash possess an uncanny, destructive power.

Ironically, it is the power to protect.

As I charged that night like an enraged animal out of the Ripening Hall and into the vast tangle of corridors that composed the lair of Count Ulan Gueritus, I was, strangely enough, thrust into my element. This was not my signature tidal environment, but the finely hewn sandstone and flickering braziers were details of small consequence. What mattered was the fact that I was now protecting a cargo, a valuable and assailable cargo, and though you might think me valiant for it, I knew in my heart of hearts that I took on this charge out of a selfish impulse to save my own skin. I was just plain hard to kill when transporting a cargo. And so, from that massive Ripening Hall stuffed with literally hundreds of splendorous artifacts, I drew forth two that would most readily serve my needs. Their names were Nascinthé of Levell and Flerra Tellian, and I was going to deliver them safely to their drop point if I had to cleave and butcher my way through every miserable soldier in the Raving Blade's army. It was at moments like this that I had earned my reputation for sheer, unmitigated brutality.

The first two victims were just regaining their footing when I ran them down. I sprinted into the narrow corridor so quickly and at such a low angle that I got a spade up under each of their loosely held guard stances. I took the tip of a stiletto in my left bicep and the hilt of a spade hard against my forehead, but I got through. My left spade found its way into one man's side, and the right straight through the other man's stomach, and though it meant possible death for the first and certain death for the second, I cared no more for them than I did for the door I had just kicked in. All three were obstacles, mere obstacles, which had dared to stand between my all-important cargo and its all-important drop point, wherever in hell that was.

"The door!" I yelled over my shoulder, but there was no need, for Flerra had slammed it immediately and had already gotten a pick into the lock. She evidently slid the bolt back into the strike plate because a moment later there was a heavy thump against the wood from the other side. It held, at least for now.

The first man, whose nose had shattered when I kicked in the door, was regaining his feet, trying to retrieve his spade, but he couldn't quite reach it in time. I brained him furiously with the pommel of my weapon and then checked to make sure the other two were no longer a threat. The door to the Ripening Hall shook hard again, and there was a cracking sound at the frame.

"Come on!"

I started forward down the warmly lit, vaulted corridor. As elsewhere, the walls here were composed of smooth sandstone blocks, well grouted and unmildewed. Behind me I heard the desperate click-clicking of Nascinthé's boots on the granite floor, and a little farther back Flerra Tellian's breathless cursing.

"Shit to this damned bid, shit to it!"

Up ahead the corridor hooked sharply to the left and, rounding it, we drew near to a four-way intersection. As I approached, two soldiers came sprinting around the corner, one wielding a spade and stiletto, the other bearing a hinterland durkesh—a short, multi-purposed axe with a protruding pike and a serrated back edge. There was no time to think it through, no room to maneuver, so I simply drove on, swerving towards the man with the durkesh. When his heavy axe blade descended towards my head, I didn't retreat from the contact but instead rushed to meet it, bringing my two spades up in an X block and bearing the full weight on their edges. The vibrations of the impact slammed through my arms and jarred me all the way down to my hips. One of my weapons shattered outright, while the other lost half of its hand guard as the axe head rushed down the blade and snapped it off. My knuckles took rapping contact as the side of the durkesh grazed them, but I wasn't cut. And now my opponent was vulnerable.

My unbroken blade pushed the durkesh aside, and the jagged fragment of the other spade drove straight at the newly exposed side of the man's head. I caught him just above the ear, and though my weapon now lacked a clean point, its broken edge was sharp enough to puncture the temple and send blood gouting into my own face like mud thrown up by a passing wagon.

The soldier managed to let out a scream, and in this ungodly condition I shoved him at his oncoming comrade. The new attacker's stiletto was impeded, so he cut with his spade, and I was forced to make a cross-parry, taking too much of the impact at the spot where the hand guard had broken. The sorry result was a bad gash across my knuckles. A more skilled swordsman would have spun the blade around and led with the good side of the guard, but, sadly, I wasn't that sort of swordsman. In fact, I wasn't a swordsman at all, and as if to bear this out, my unbroken weapon went wobbling out of my bleeding fingers and clattered across the stone floor.

The attacking soldier's eyes narrowed, and I saw the faith in his own victory ignite there. He had figured it out too, realized the moment my spade left my fingers that I was limited in my training, that I hardly resembled the infamous Helmgrinder who was right now piling bodies around him like sacks of wheat in the Ripening Hall. I wasn't even a Contract Blade at all but a desperate, frenzied man intent on breaking out of a death trap that nobody, the tragically doomed Col included, could possibly escape. Yet in his gloating, the soldier overlooked one, eminently important fact—Vazeer the Lash was Hell's Labyrinth's ultimate opportunist, and he would do anything (use any weapon and any means) to drive back the brigands and pinchers, the predatory operatives, and even the constable's uniformed militia, when his cargo was at stake.

The soldier seemed truly taken aback when, in seeming retreat, I reached to the wall behind me, grabbed hold of the brazier bowl that was set in an angle bracket, and, broiling my fingers in the process, flipped the blistering receptacle right into his face. The bowl struck full on, open side forward, and just to make sure the desired effect was achieved, I trapped the bowl against his head with my forearm. The results were even more grotesque than the gouge I had given to his cohort's temple.

"Don't stand around gawking at them," I yelled. "Move!"

The ferocity in my voice was greatly exacerbated by the pain in my sliced and scalded hand. Nascinthé had pressed herself back against one of the walls and was now mutely gaping at the two soldiers as they writhed and whimpered on the shiny granite floor, a nauseating odor of roasting flesh arising from one, a mottled red lagoon issuing from the other. Flerra was in a far more active posture, crouched with a dagger in one of her hands and a picklock in the other, though even she seemed a bit appalled by the sight. I tore off a section of my own cloak and quickly bandaged my hand.

"Such an animal, Vazeer..." Flerra muttered.

Nascinthé was silent.

"Didn't you hear me?" I snapped. "Move along...and stop staring!"

With that they both edged their way around the dying men, though neither one seemed entirely able to shake the sight.

I took the burned soldier's spade, slid it into one of my sheaths, gripped his stiletto as best I could in my wounded right fist, and swiped up the hinterland durkesh to use as a versatile shock weapon. And then we were off again, running.

It seemed to me that these first five soldiers had been patrolling guards, not members of the Commander of the Guard's force, which was the only explanation for why there weren't more of them. We now appeared to have an open stretch of corridor before us, though it certainly wouldn't last. Once Col went down, a score of men would be freed up to come looking for us, and no doubt the Commander of the Guard had already dispersed messengers in all directions to alert the rest of the compound.

The hallways in this deep, subterranean section of Gueritus's lair were less opulent than the ones we had encountered above, yet still they were vaulted, with quality stonework and regularly spaced braziers. I suspected that the Ripening Hall we had just exited was but one of several in this complex. In fact, that long passageway had seemed more like a display gallery than an insulated storage chamber—to dazzle trading clients, perhaps, or other important visitors. Based on the volume of merchandise that I and the other Grell Runners smuggled each year into the Lower City, I imagined that a figure like Gueritus had multiple, highly secure halls, in addition to the one we had visited. Only the Underlords knew how much wealth was stored down here.

"This one, Flerra."

I pointed to a large arched wooden door set at the end of one of the many sandstone corridors. This particular portal felt promising, as the casing was larger and more decorative than the others, so Flerra squatted down and went straight to work on it. Down one of the nearby hallways, I heard the sound of approaching footsteps, several of them, and I knew they would round the corner in a matter of seconds.

"Quicker, Flerra," I whispered.

She was so fast with this lock that she didn't even have time to return an insult. Unfortunately, there was an additional problem.

"A bar," she muttered nervously. "Maybe I can work it with my slip…"

"Get out of the way."

My companions pressed back against the walls of the corridor. Getting two steps of a running start, I again raised my knee to my chest and blasted forward with my heel. The door shook badly, and there was a cracking sound…but it held.

"Black hells!"

I drew back to do it again.

A cry went up from around the bend, and now the soldiers were running. I lunged a second time, slammed the heavy portal with my foot, heard even more of a crack…but stared in frustration as the door held.

"For the love of the damned gods!" I exploded, and I stumbled back once more, three steps this time, and prepared to give it a final try.

The six guards came tearing around the bend like a team of galloping gray horses, and I didn't even bother to size them up. I either broke this damned bar, or we were all headed straight for the Raving Blade's torture cells.

"Aaaaarrrrraaaagggggg…."

I threw every last ounce of my strength into the break.

The door shuddered violently as the bar cracked and the portal swung ajar, though it did so tentatively, as if hesitant to even suggest that we continue this insane attempt at escape. I wasn't giving up just yet, however. I took these things one bloody confrontation at a time.

I forced the door open, saw at a glance that the small parlor beyond was empty, and then I literally shoved Flerra and Nascinthé inside with the flat of my durkesh. The soldiers had come running very close now, and I spun about, cocked my weapon back, and flung it straight at the lead man. It careened off his shoulder without sinking home, but the sheer weight of the axe knocked him spinning into the men behind. He went down below their tripping feet, cursing and struggling not to take a boot in the head.

I backed my way into the parlor and slammed the door shut on the first arriving soldier's forearm. He yowled and dropped his spade, and as he jerked back into the hallway, I closed the door fully and reached up towards the lock, hoping. Sure enough, this door had a bolt knob that could be turned manually. I locked it and backed away, listening to the frustrated bangs against the wooden surface. I knew it wouldn't hold for long.

"Help me get some of this stuff in front of the door."

The parlor was well furnished with settees and armchairs, two low tea tables, and, on one wall, a tall armoire filled with decorative enameled plates. We went to work on the armoire first, the three of us able to shimmy the piece away from the wall and tip it crashing to the floor. We then lined up behind its exposed base and drove it all the way up against the bottom of the door, just as the doorframe began to splinter.

"Stack it up," I yelled. "Anything you can lift, throw it on."

Flerra and Nascinthé worked with panicked determination, their combined strength more than sufficient to toss the smaller pieces onto the barricade. We piled relentlessly, hoisting chairs, tables, even two small couches on top of the horizontal armoire, until we had placed enough weight upon it that the men outside would require a battering ram to get through.

"Flerra, go try that door," I said breathlessly once we were done. There were two other doors leading out of this room, one at the far end, the other in the right wall, much closer to our furniture rampart. Flerra Tellian jogged to the far one, and when Nascinthé started to follow, I stopped her.

"Stay with me," I muttered.

I gave no explanation for it, for indeed I had none. Nascinthé didn't protest, and she came to stand beside me, her damp cheeks flushed, her blue eyes sharp in their fear, or excitement, or horror—I really didn't know which.

"Wait here," I finally said. "I'm going to try this other door."

With that I entered the deep alcove that housed the room's

remaining door. I listened at it for a moment, and when I heard nothing, I tried the knob and found it open. I stepped through and saw that the space beyond was an empty library, which was only dimly illumined by two torches set in wrought iron brackets. I ventured farther, locating the three exits—two doors and another sandstone hallway—then I turned back towards the parlor, eager to round up Flerra and Nascinthé and lead them this way.

There was a dull, ominous thud, which I heard clearly even before I reached the parlor. A moment later there was a loud curse, then a yell, followed by the sounds of a scuffle. I paused, trying to determine if there was any way I could use stealth to my advantage here, then I heard pounding footsteps, barking commands, and finally a wild shriek from Flerra, which told me I was too late.

By the time I entered the parlor, there were already a half dozen soldiers inside, and even more filing in through the door that I had told Flerra to check. One man lay motionless on the floor, and another was crumpled over, clutching his groin and shuddering. Flerra Tellian was being gripped from behind by her hair, a dagger blade pressing so tightly against her neck that blood was starting to leak down her ghostly skin in tiny runnels. The man who held her was none other than the dreaded Commander of the Guard. I noticed that he had a nasty slice under his eye that was just beginning to drip blood.

I knew what a vicious fighter Flerra could be. It was no surprise to me that she had incapacitated two of the soldiers in a matter of seconds and come close to slicing out their leader's eye before she was disarmed. But my Brood sister wasn't trained to take on a room full of armed soldiers. Then again, neither was I.

"Bidder, drop your weapons and submit," the Commander yelled.

Nascinthé was still standing on the near side of the barricade, so I grabbed her by the shoulder and pulled her behind me.

The men began to advance on me.

And, to the soldiers' surprise, I advanced on them in turn.

"Did you hear me, Bidder?" the Commander shouted, and he pushed forward through his men, wielding Flerra Tellian before him like a body shield. "Drop your weapons now."

It occurred to me as I watched these soldiers, several of them sprinkled with blood, and all of them looking decidedly apprehensive, that they had probably experienced more than enough hand-to-hand combat tonight. In addition to being greeted by the startling ferocity of the diminutive Flerra Tellian, I suspected that these men had faced a much larger opponent earlier. Col, I now decided, must have gone down, but not before putting the mortal fear of Shadow Bidders into these men. I was hardly a match for Col in the art of swordplay, but my reputation as a savage was perhaps a trace worse than his, and at this moment I knew I deserved every bit of it. These men, too, seemed to share that notion, for they hesitated.

"Com'on, you little piss-birds," I goaded. "I'll cripple at least four or five of you before I drop."

To my left the barricaded door splintered again, higher this time, and I knew from the sound of it that they were knocking out the hinges.

"This is your last chance, Shadow Bidder," the Commander rasped, and I must say his heavy, mulish features reflected the sort of resolve that made my ploy here seem difficult, if not impossible. He was clever, this ruthless commander. Seeing that Flerra was not some meek lady's maid, he must have suspected that she was a fellow Shadow Bidder, though he obviously didn't know exactly how much she meant to me. I had to keep it that way, conveying to these men the impression of foolhardy bloodlust, madness even, anything to prevent them from guessing that the only reason I was advancing on them was to see if there was any hope in hell that I might retrieve my cargo, and if not retrieve it, then destroy it myself.

You see, if I could not rescue Flerra Tellian from the Commander of the Guard, then I'd kill her, and make sure I never found her one day with that dreadful mark on her forehead. I could not bear to see her with no eyes or tongue, squatting with Brand in that reeking orphanage where our journey together began. I owed her at least—

The scream was terrible, so deeply terrible that I felt it reverberating all the way down into my bowels as though I were sitting directly on the Sullward Clock Tower when it struck midnight. Never had I heard, or even imagined, Flerra making such a sound.

Her body lurched and then spasmed, as a small white object arched away from her head and plopped unceremoniously to the rug like excess clay thrown from a potter's wheel. Only when the torrent of blood began to wash down the side of her face like muddy rinse water did I realize that the object in question was Flerra Tellian's left ear.

"Do you think I'm fooling with you, Shadow Bidder?" the Commander of the Guard roared. "Do you think I speak idle threats? I'll take her apart piece by piece right in front of you. You've got no idea what I'm capable of!"

Indeed, his dagger now moved up to Flerra's eye, where the tip flirted so closely with her iris that even the slightest twitch might blind her.

Flerra's fingers quietly convulsed, and tears ran freely down her pallid cheeks like drain water down a whitewashed wall.

A tiny breathless wheeze escaped her lips, and her eyes were fluttering, the lashes of the left one tickling the tip of the Commander of the Guard's dagger.

And he, "The Commander of the Guard," seemed almost invigorated by what he had just done, an excited smile squeezing itself between his dense lips. How foolish a name I had given him, as though he were some dignified protector of a royal household. From the moment he flung away Flerra's ear as though it were a useless gob of fat carved from a slab of beef, the "Commander of the Guard" became simply "the Butcher," and would remain that way forevermore. Or at least until I died, which was probably going to happen within the next minute or so.

To tell you the truth, I almost welcomed it. This was agonizing in ways that I cannot put into words. To see Flerra Tellian standing there but a dozen feet before me, the thin curtain of blood running down her skinny neck, the tears greasing the boney ridge of her nose, and to know that even though I was almost close enough to grab her, she was gone. The only question was, could I make it quick for her, or would she meet her end in slow, dreadful increments?

I had stopped moving once the Butcher made his gruesome cut, while the terrible scream that accompanied it had actually startled the soldiers enough to delay their advance. But now they came on once more, fanning out to try to flank me, and I saw very clearly that if I rushed in and drove my spade through Flerra's heart, I would be hopelessly surrounded before I could even retract the blade, which meant that Nascinthé would be theirs too. I tried not to imagine what the Raving Blade would do with the woman who had masqueraded as his Countess.

The moment of indecision hung in ghastly suspension as the soldiers and I faced off, a four- or five-second interlude in which

I literally had the passing thought that maybe I was dreaming. It was one of those strange instances where I doubted, deep in the recesses of my own mind, that this could possibly be happening to *me*, that this horror playing out before me could actually be *my* life and not some awful story I once heard. The sort that always happens to *them*—the pitiable "them," upon whom all of life's worst misfortunes always fall.

This most certainly was my predicament. It was the vulgar end of the tale of Vazeer the Lash, and Flerra Tellian, and Nascinthé of Levell, whose not-so-vulgar subplot had lent passing grandeur to the affair. How I would have liked to see that one resolve itself differently. How I wished I were already dead, like Col or Fe Gesbon, who, though an obstinate fool, had died without a single conflict inside his intractable brain.

The choice I now faced was completely and utterly dreadful.

When the soldiers outside rammed down the barricaded door a moment later, I believe I had already made my decision, though in retrospect it is tempting to pretend I had not. The team in the hallway apparently got a running start and slammed something long and heavy straight into the upper portion of the door, which, with both of the hinges now dislodged, flipped forward like a drawbridge, pressing the whole top-heavy mountain of stacked furniture off of the armoire and sending it cascading into the center of the room like an ornamented avalanche.

The men already inside the room who had come with the Butcher bore the brunt of it, for they had circled wide in their flanking maneuver, consequently passing just a few feet in front of the barricade. One man was struck on the collarbone by the arm of a flipping couch while another was bowled off his feet by a rolling table. I myself fell prey to the pile in a more indirect way, for the soldiers on my right used the occasion to rush me, and, as

I retreated to absorb their momentum, I tripped backwards over a chair that had landed behind my legs. I went down, and within seconds they were on top of me.

Several heartbeats passed beneath a struggling, clenching mass of men, and for some reason I remained alive. It didn't take me long to realize that these soldiers had been instructed to capture, not kill me, which was a very big mistake.

As I've said, I am not a swordsman in any conventional sense. I am not a man who lives and dies by my skill with weapons, and I don't, conversely, become effectively useless once wrestled to the ground or tangled in a clinch. It is in close-quarters combat that my finest skills come to bear. This is my absolute specialty—the mastery of an unsavory collection of dirty tactics that Holod taught me in my youth and that I have honed to great effectiveness in the dark hours of the night, in rank places where nobody gives a damn about swordplay, and especially not fair play, and where the only measure of excellence lies in how often a man survives situations that he has no mortal business surviving. These soldiers would have done well to kill me the second I hit the floor.

The man directly on top of me had gotten a hold of my uninjured left hand, which was now wielding the spade. Despite its wretched condition, my right hand was the real threat, for it was the stiletto-bearer, and while the Sullward stiletto was notably large by Derjian standards—designed to allow for parrying and a degree of edge work in addition to its primary function as a close-quarters finisher—the slim blade was still short enough to work effectively in a ground fight. It had not, after all, been nicknamed the "Organ Drill" for nothing.

I made my move.

I targeted the soldier's spleen for its convenience and sensitivity, and my hand ached as I exerted pressure to get past his leatherguard cuirass. I wasn't able to pierce far through the boil-hardened leather, but a lethal thrust wasn't my goal here. I wanted pain.

The soldier screamed, and his body lurched on top of me as I felt a drizzle of warm saliva spray across my face. I thrust harder with the stiletto, jiggling it in the wound, and though the soldier tried to grasp hold of my wrist, the agony was so intense for him that his body writhed out of reflex. Now I had him working for me, using the full force of his maddened pain, combined with my own efforts, to shift the pile of men above off to the side so that I might affect a turnover. I didn't need much, just a little leverage.

Around me I heard the heavy, unsteady knocking of soldiers climbing over the remnants of the furniture barricade. I also heard a noise that gave me a fleeting, improbable hope: the sound of the Butcher cursing in pain.

"Aaauuooohhh…," he roared, "…the vicious little weasel!"

I gave one final push and felt the pile tip. I had dislodged maybe a body and a half of weight from the mass above, which was going to have to suffice.

"Grab her, grab her!" the Butcher was yelling. "Watch her picks!"

I released both the stiletto and the spade and, using my hands to press off, I launched my pelvis upwards and to the left, managing to lever the pile off to the side a few inches, just enough to slide most of my body out from under it.

"Hells!" another soldier shouted. "Odgen is down…watch her other hand."

"I'll do it!" the Butcher roared. "Hold her down!"

I yanked my legs free, spun over, and got up to one knee before they tried to tackle me again. I was better prepared this time, forming a solid triangle between my knee, planted foot, and uninjured hand to keep myself from buckling completely to the floor. Then I reached down to a pocket in my thigh greave and plucked forth a finger-length triangular blade known in Hell's Labyrinth as a "jack." One of the soldiers was gripping me tightly around the neck, and it was really no trouble at all to sever a tendon below his elbow, causing his arm to go flaccid like a strand of ocean kelp.

It was right around then that Flerra Tellian started screaming. "Aaaaeeeeiiiiihhhhh…nooo…noo…!"

"Hold her still!" the Butcher yelled.

"Nooooooooooo…."

"How does that feel, you little vermin?"

"…noo…Vaz…Vaazeeeerrr!"

I really don't remember much of what happened next. My powers of recollection are strong in general, but on occasion I fall into something that can only be called a void, a state in which my brain decides that the services of memory are no longer welcome. At such moments the great, torturous cryptogram called life puts on a display of its worst colors, possibly its truest colors, and such things are apparently unfit to be remembered even by a disgraceful man such as myself.

I know only that I made a choice.

In the world of Grell Running, we call the decision I was forced to make a "half-jettison" or, in its more colloquial terminology, "a cup of blood for the sharks." In this case the "cup of blood" that I gave in order to keep me and the rest of my cargo from being swallowed was my fellow Broodmate and stand-in sibling, Flerra Tellian. I left her to them. I let them wantonly and methodically torture her to death.

As she shrieked and gagged and cried out my name, I fought like a thing from hell to get away from her, to get away from that awful sound, and the Butcher who was carving her, and the swarm of reinforcements who were now scrambling into the room like a plague of rats. I remember only flashes of the struggle itself—a soldier's red, puffy cheek but inches from my face, first inflating with breath, then going flat as the air left his body. I don't even know what I did to him. But another image is clearer—the sight of my jack protruding at an awkward angle from another soldier's eye. I can still picture the man's arms waving out in front of him, almost comically, as though he was parodying blindness or entertaining a group of children by pretending to be a zombie. I also recall going to the floor again, seeing the green scroll patterns in the tawny carpet and noting that the design was probably of West Kaszian origin. After that I bit off a man's finger, maybe several, for the grinding texture of bone and the salty sting of blood still linger in my memory to this day.

I have never been able to work out the exact choreography of how I got out of there. Clearly, I fought my way to the room's one remaining unobstructed door, and as I did, I must have gained an element of surprise over the soldiers who were climbing in across the collapsed barricade. The only way to surprise a group of men who see you already, who have good reason to know that you are dangerous and who are in the most armed and battle-ready condition imaginable, is to first go down in seeming defeat and then rise again suddenly, more aggressive and determined than before. A person cannot help but become momentarily panicked under such circumstances. It is a primal fear, suggestive of superstitious abstractions, or the occult—ghouls who rise from their graves, or men who make secret pacts with hell, or, on a more rational level, the fundamental terror of anything in this world that can inflict terrible injury but cannot be harmed itself.

Sometimes I truly wonder if my odd indestructibility is a cursed birth gift from the infernal powers, a finely tailored cage that was placed upon my body and then split-locked the moment

I came into this world. I have little faith in the Heavenly Spheres. I have perhaps a shred more belief in the presence of Hell. I don't trust much in this world that I cannot readily see or hear or touch, but still this one idea, this concept of being both charmed and cursed at the same time, by some secret force more powerful than myself, I can never quite shake it. Perhaps I am being absurdly vain to take this feeling personally. I have probably just described the human condition in its essence.

These deeper mysteries aside, I somehow made it out of the parlor that night—that awful parlor, which will haunt and rebuke me till the day I die—and the only part of my escape that gives me any satisfaction at all is the fact that I did not leave empty-handed. I managed to locate Nascinthé of Levell by the door of the room and to drag her at a dead run from the torment, dealing harshly with the soldier who was holding her. Or so I assume. I remember her white dress, soaked so thoroughly with blood that it clung sheer to her torso like hosiery. Yet there she was running unimpaired inside of it, clasping my hand, twisting valiantly through sandstone corridors and vaulted chambers and massive storage rooms filled with sacks and barrels and crates. Even in my befuddled state, I understood that the blood wasn't hers. In all of vast existence, that was about the only thing that I really needed to know.

I recall a few jumbled details of our flight through the Raving Blade's compound: door after door slamming behind me, one stout, iron-bound portal in particular, which I managed to lock and bar. Finally, I remember the backdrop changing from clean, grouted stone hallways to a roughly hewn network of bedrock tunnels and storage chambers. It was here, in this crude, monotonous labyrinth filled with boxes and crates and low rock ceilings, that something very strange happened. I was brought suddenly, and most unpleasantly, back to myself. My consciousness was dragged out of the amnesic void, and the person who caused this to come about was perhaps the strangest medium I could ever imagine for such a healing…if one chooses to call it a healing at all. To this day, I still harbor some resentment at being restored.

"Vazeer," came the calm voice through the murky void.

I'm sure I gawked about foolishly amid the barrels and bins, ready to kill this meddler who had the unconscionable nerve to know my name at a time and place where I did not wish to be known. I don't remember a thing about my own movements or even my own body, just a smooth voice emerging from the gloom.

"Vazeer, are your eyes injured? They are watering heavily. Can you see me?"

There, with that question—"can you see me?"—I believe it was precisely then that I began to recover.

I saw a silhouette first, an indistinct, man-sized shadow, flirting between reality and unreality like a bodiless spirit. I could even see the room beyond this man-shadow, see the stacks of wooden shipping caskets, the row of wine barrels, the huge, tangled cargo net, all of them far clearer than the figure who stood in front of me; though they were shaded somewhat, as if tinted by a dark lens.

"Right here, Vazeer. Right in front of your eyes."

Then all at once the blackout ended. I found myself standing in the center of a large, torch-lit storage chamber, my body throbbing beyond the point of pain, my face streaked with salty moisture, my clammy hand interlaced with five soft, feminine fingers. Nascinthé of Levell was breathing heavily alongside of me, but I wasn't looking at her. I was gazing fixedly at the unruffled figure who stood just beyond the quivering tip of my bloody spade.

14

DEPARTURE

"I see that you have lived up to your infamous reputation, Vazeer the Lash," said Radrin Blackstar, his tone light, possibly even amused. "I'm not sure anybody else in the Labyrinth, in all existence perhaps, would have made it out of there alive."

I simply stood and stared. I gazed at those weirdly unflappable features, set below the orderly sweep of dark blond hair, resting atop a finely woven emerald tunic. It occurred to me, with absurd banality, that this shirt must have been the garment he wore beneath his now-discarded steward's outfit, and I also noticed that the tunic closely matched Radrin's eyes in color, though not in texture. The rich, vibrant fabric contrasted strangely with the flat absorbing emptiness of his gaze. Additionally, he was wearing one of the gray cloaks possessed by all of the soldiers in this compound.

Somewhere in the very back of my sluggish mind a reply formed:

"Nobody could make it out of there but you, you nerveless spook."

But this response never came anywhere near my lips, mostly because I was as drained and numb at that moment as an embalmed cadaver.

"Did you lose Flerra Tellian?" Radrin asked in a voice that was suddenly grave.

The shock of it was so fierce that I jerked my face away, fixing my gaze on a neatly stacked pile of grain sacks near one of the cavern's three rough doorways. I felt an unpleasant sting in my eyes, and I was reminded of Radrin's initial comments: "Vazeer, are your eyes injured? They are watering heavily." I blinked and squinted several times and forced myself not to reach up and wipe the back of my forearm across my face. For a moment I felt the thick fingers of the void tickling the edges of my awareness, though it was immediately obvious to me that I would not be able to escape by that means again so quickly.

As it turned out, the void was not entirely done with me that night; however, we will get to that in due course.

Perhaps Nascinthé shook her head to answer, or maybe the truth was obvious by the way I failed to respond. Either way, Radrin did not pursue it, and in fact he changed his tone entirely, giving me the sense that he was trying to steer my mind away from that worst of all topics.

"Assuming that you didn't kill all of the Raving Blade's soldiers," Radrin said with the slight inkling of a smile, "I suspect that some of the survivors might actually find their way to us. Especially given the unsightly mess you have left for Gueritus's chamber maids."

For the first time, I looked down at myself, and I must say the sight was so grotesque it was almost ridiculous. Taken together, Nascinthé and I were such a frightful pair that, in keeping with my earlier ruminations on the ghoulish nature of things that resurrect, we did in fact resemble two defectors from the grave. There we stood, still clasping hands like children, drenched in gore like corpses, Nascinthé's velvety blonde hair now a haggard mixture of staticky feelers and greasy phlegmatic cords, my own fast drying against my skull like mortar. Then there was our clothing. Few words could describe it, but I'll speculate that with a barrel of crimson paint and a large set of shears, a more wretched effect probably could not have been achieved.

Radrin was right: we had left a trail of bloody splatters on the floor that even a blind man could follow.

"Nascinthé appears to have stopped leaking," Radrin said, "but not you, Vazeer, which suggests that quite a bit of that blood is your own. We'll need to remedy that, but not here. There may even be a way to use it to our advantage. Come."

With that he grabbed one of the room's torches and led us away, displaying no indecision whatsoever in choosing his exit. Displaying no indecision, period, which was what I needed. It appeared that we were, in fact, in some remote, undecorated section of the Raving Blade's compound, for this large storage chamber had clearly been hewn directly out of the city's bedrock. The granite walls and ceiling were roughly chiseled, and condensation was visible here and there, reflecting in the torchlight. There were three jagged tunnels exiting this cavern, and Radrin chose one of the two that was not traced with my blood. Strangely, I had a vague sense of where he was taking us.

"You have remarkable instincts," Radrin said in a hushed voice as we walked at a brisk clip along a tunnel that began to resemble an old mine shaft the farther we progressed. There were wooden support beams spaced every twenty feet, and a fungus-laden ceiling that dripped cold, sulfurous water on us as we passed. In addition to large outcroppings of granite, the walls and ceilings here were also composed of sections of earth.

"Even in the midst of battle you were able to find your way back to the Grells," he continued. "I actually found my way here by following you, or rather the sound and mess of you. I'm afraid I'm not the Locksmith…"

Here Radrin paused. He looked over at me with the mildest hint of an apology, and I quickly figured out what he had been about to say. I also realized that this was the first time that I had heard Radrin Blackstar correct himself.

"I am not a Locksmith," he continued. "Still, I make do when necessary, and I was able to get through a few doors that stopped the guards. The beauty of an Underlord's compound is that the host never trusts more than a handful of his staff to carry keys. A man like Gueritus has more to fear from his own people, on a day-to-day basis, than from independents."

The grade of the tunnel had now begun to rise very steeply, and not far into our ascent a narrow runnel of water came snaking down the center of the passageway between our feet. Radrin squatted, dabbed his finger in it, then tapped the water lightly to his tongue. He nodded.

"There's little doubt where this came from."

I had guessed it already from the smell. This tunnel was fast rising to an exit somewhere within the salt marsh. This meant that we had just passed under the Grells and would emerge on the far side of the river, in very good position to make it out of the city entirely. We began to jog lightly up the shaft, splashing through what had grown to be a small stream.

Nascinthé and I had never bothered to release our clasped hands. As we ran up the tunnel, a few steps behind Radrin's nimble back, I felt those warm fingers and the woman attached to them as if for the first time. The last vestiges of my numbness had retreated. I suddenly understood the full implications of this adolescent gesture between us, and also the reality of having just rescued her from death, and the odd new identity that this bestowed upon me. Admittedly, embracing such an identity was going to be a difficult proposition for me, but, as luck would have it, I didn't have to worry about that for long.

We arrived at the exit shortly after Radrin sampled the rill of marsh water. It was a square, water-tight door with a strip of elastic animal membrane filling the seam. The portal was tar sealed and iron bound with three heavy bolts and three thick hinges, and I suspected, without even seeing the outside, that it was brilliantly camouflaged in some manner. Two tunnels arrived at this exit—the one we had traveled, and another, which approached from a slightly different angle. As soon as I spotted that other tunnel, I remembered Radrin's earlier comment, that he planned to use my messy bleeding to our advantage.

"That corridor won't lead anywhere very secure," he said, as if sensing my thoughts. "But it certainly beats the path we just took."

Nascinthé, who didn't appear to be listening, seemed fixated on that heavy, tar-coated door, and I'm certain I felt her clench my hand a little tighter at the sight of it. Radrin stepped away from the tunnel fork and squatted down in front of the sealed portal, examining it closely. After a moment, he looked up.

"The intestine has worn through in several places, though it's only leaking at the bottom, which is fortunate. I had a fear that the door might be submerged by tidal flooding. Still, just for safety's sake, why don't you stand to the side while I open it."

We stepped away, and Radrin threw back the three bolts in succession. He turned the knob and slid behind the door as it opened.

The storm burst through the small hatch with the delirious anger of a charging bear. Water spilled in across the foot-high threshold and ran in a frothed glaze down the sloped passage and away into darkness. The water level of the marsh outside was still an inch or so below the door's raised groundsill, but it was easily gaining entrance on a steady succession of large ripples, which were being pushed across the dusky expanse of the flooded swamp. The northwesterly winds were shrieking at a pitch that defied anything I had ever heard or seen. Still, I certainly knew my way around that environment, and I saw rather quickly that we were indeed east of the Grells, several hundred yards into the salt marsh, a mere half mile from the coast. With clear directions, even a foreigner could find her way to safety from this place.

Somewhere above all of the sky's madness, the moon's radiance was backlighting the storm, and the resulting effect was a tumultuous landscape traced with the haziest silver outline. Illumined this way, by the moon's faint dusting and the orange sputters of Radrin's torch, whipped by rain, deafened by wind, clutching an angelic hand, but ultimately under the thrall of my own worst demons, I at last came upon the great moment of reckoning for which I was sadly prepared.

"Vazeer," Radrin shouted over the terrible noise. "Let go of Nascinthé's hand. It is time to bid her farewell."

I don't think Nascinthé even heard Radrin's words, and if she did, she certainly didn't understand them. She continued to stare uncertainly at the dark square of the exit, and she tenaciously clenched my hand, as if that storming hole led straight into the infernal abyss and not freedom.

"Vazeer, you know what we have to do now," Radrin called. "Think of Nascinthé. She can hide, but only for so long."

He was doing his best to shelter his torch behind the door; however, it looked as if it might go out if we didn't soon close the hatch. He nodded his chin towards my hand.

"Let her go. Our time is running out."

It took me a moment. In fact, it took several moments to even operate my cramped hand, so blackened with crusted blood that it looked gangrenous, so painful that the sensations had moved beyond hurting and into a broad pulse that remained largely unlocalized. I focused my attention on working the joints, prying the digits loose gingerly as if they might drop off. Eventually, I freed myself, though Nascinthé resisted my efforts every inch of the way. I turned to face her.

"Listen," I said hoarsely. "Listen to me carefully. You are very close to a means of escaping this place, and I'm going to tell you exactly how to get there."

Nascinthé's lips parted into that queer stasis that had so hypnotized me from the start. There it was again, the inner messenger's secret bulk, pressing against the two soft, horizontal bars of its cage. Now, unfortunately, I no longer wanted to hear what it had to say.

"Listen," I said again, though this was hardly necessary, for she was as attentive in that moment as a poised cat. "We are in a very passable section of the marsh. Even with the high tide, you will not cross through water above your waist, if you follow my directions precisely. You need to wade from the outcropping of rock where this door is located and press directly to the east, towards the tree line, which will be easy to see. Move in a direct path, and move quickly. You want to get as far away from the river as possible in case it floods. Nothing will be stirring out there in this weather, no vagrants, no snakes…nothing, so don't be picky about it. Just move fast and get to the tree line.

"Once there, the ground will rise up and should remain above the waterline under even the worst conditions. Stay just within the trees and follow that mound to the right, all the way to the coast. Several hundred feet before the ocean itself you will encounter a long, natural mass of rock. The moment you reach it, follow it to the right, staying well up the face in case there's any sort of a surge inside the harbor. The rock forms a sort of gully, which will keep you sheltered from the wind. Your passage should get easier and easier, until you arrive at last at a tight outcropping of stunted bushes. It is the first vegetation you will encounter along the bank, so you can't miss it. There's one bush in particular that you're looking for. It is much larger than the others and it grows tight against the rock on your left, almost like ivy. It's a fake, a very convincing fake, and once you see that bush, you're home free."

Nascinthé had started to shake her head in protest, but I pressed on, more aggressive now, for I had to make sure I at least got the instructions finished before I had to explain this abandonment to her.

"Listen!" I practically yelled. "Do what I say and you will live. Miss any part of it, especially this part, and you will die. It's that simple; do you understand me?"

This, at least, converted her head's shaking into an anxious nod.

"Once you reach that bush," I continued, "you go to its left side, grab hold, and pull to the right. You'll see it will move, though it will snap back into place if you don't hold tight. Behind the bush is a very well-concealed door, camouflaged to look like the rock. Pound on that door. It shouldn't take much to draw them, but in case they're hesitant to open, keep pounding and call out this name: 'Droden Sailwain.' Droden Sailwain… did you get that?"

Nascinthé nodded, and I could see her digest this name, digest all the information with that same acuity that had fully imbibed the books I had given her.

"They'll open for you, eventually, though they may do it with spade tips to your throat. You tell them you're there to see Droden Sailwain and that I sent you. Tell him you are one of the passengers. It doesn't look like you still have your coin purse, do you?"

She shook her head.

I quickly fished out eight suldots from a secure pocket in my leather cuirass, then added two more for good measure. I thrust them into her hand.

"Give Droden eight total, and keep the others hidden for yourself. You'll have to wait it out until the storm dies, and then perhaps a day or two longer until the seas calm. But once they do, you're a free woman, because Droden has a ship waiting for you in a protected cove. It's a caravel named the Elena's Guile, which is capable of crossing the full breadth of the Derjian Sea. You tell him where you want to go and one of his captains will take you there. Is your contract payment hidden somewhere safe?"

Nascinthé nodded.

"Don't try to get it for at least a year, and when you do come back, come in disguise. Here, take this too, as you should have a weapon."

I pulled one of the daggers from my belt and slid it into her other hand. She took it without protest. For several seconds, Nascinthé and I just stared at each other, our caked hair and clothing shaking in the wind, our feet growing damp as the marsh washed over them. Then finally, she uttered her first word in what seemed like hours.

"Why?"

"Why." That was all she said. Just that one word, but what a terminal sound it had. I knew, of course, exactly what she was asking me, and the true meaning reached all the way into the small, jealously guarded spaces inside of me and pierced them.

"Because it is the only way we will ever be safe again," I practically shouted. "If the Raving Blade lives, then he will dedicate his
life to hunting down the surviving Shadow Bidders from this job.
He will literally stop at nothing to find us, send his men anywhere
and everywhere in the search, and there will never come a day
when he simply grows tired of the pursuit. And yet, worse even
than Gueritus is the threat of the proffer himself. The Sketcher
already promised that the proffer would chase us into the bloody
jaws of the abyss if necessary. He will never rest until our defec-
tion from the bid is avenged, and he won't care that some of his
information was inaccurate, nor will he care that we sincerely
tried. He will care only that the code has been breached, and by
walking out now while it is still humanly possible to destroy the
target, we invite the full vengeance of the Labyrinth upon us.

"That is why I must stay and finish the job, and also why you
must go. Your work here is done, Nascinthé. Mine has just begun."

Nascinthé must have seen the full, awful depth of my lies, for
she gently closed her lips, then turned away.

"All right, our time is up," Radrin said, and I had the distinct
sense that he had just become aware of something. "Say goodbye
to her, Vazeer."

But Nascinthé did not give me the opportunity. She strode
to the open door and paused on the threshold. There she turned
and spoke in a strong, flat voice that just penetrated the noise of
the wind.

"I will wait for you," she said. "Only when you arrive at the
Elena's Guile will I allow her to sail."

Then she stepped through the dark square into the storming
night, and I watched her white form struggling to maintain balance as she took her first few steps through the swamp water and
whipping wind.

"No!" I called after her, and I ran towards the door to make sure she heard me. "Don't wait for me…don't even think of waiting for me!"

But suddenly Radrin Blackstar pressed his whole body against the door, slamming it shut right in front of me. He stood barring my way.

"She will leave, Vazeer," he said. "When she gets the chance, she will leave."

"What the stinking hell do you know about it?" I spat.

"I know that you have a very good chance of accompanying her, if that is your wish. Just finish the bid with me. Then you can choose what you want to do."

But those words didn't help. They didn't help at all, because I knew that I had chosen already. In fact, I chose long ago, and though almost every word I spoke to Nascinthé of Levell in parting was imbued with elements of the truth, more than enough to validate my actions, more than enough to stamp upon my unsound brow the mark of reason, even so, as black Hell itself was my witness, I lied to her more surely than any swindler or confidence man who furnished Sullward Harbor with embezzled goods. I lied by not telling her the most sickening truth of all. Vazeer the Lash was more frightened of leaving his dreadful maze than he was of dying in it. There would be no escape boats for me. Even if, against all measurable odds, I somehow survived, Nascinthé of Levell would be departing the Labyrinth alone.

Radrin stepped away from the door without bolting it, allowing the simple mechanism of the knob to hold it in place so that the soldiers would think we had pulled it closed from the outside. Then he looked my body up and down several times, reached into his satchel, and pulled forth a clean black cloth, which he proceeded to use to dab my bleeding left bicep. I simply allowed him to do it and continued to stare at the shaking, tar-coated door. Radrin bandaged the wound and tied it off, and then we both wiped our feet, so that we wouldn't track any water out of that area. A moment later, without a word spoken between us, we set off down the second tunnel and headed back into the Raving Blade's compound.

In my mind all I could see were Nascinthé's slender lips closing at last, and her blue-green eyes turning away, those curious portals, like windows overlooking a dream, and the more I imagined the sight, the more I felt the crushing weight of my own falsehood.

Just finish this bid, I was already telling myself. *Finish it, then I'm done for good.*

15

THE RAVED

I'll admit, I'm exhausted. I'm tired of myself most of all and, to a lesser degree, the telling of this tale, which has now covered two of the three awful choices I was forced to make that night. Forgive me if I move us along quickly from here, so that we can reach the end of the bid before I run out of strength entirely.

Regarding the journey itself back into the tastefully decorated maze of torture and death, this particular facet of the operation was, by far, the easiest of the evening. It was as if the very forces that had tried so hard to thwart us on our way in had now swiveled about like the capricious winds of spring and were finally at our backs. Or, perhaps, the bid had now become as streamlined as a wind-cutting arrow, freed as it was of men who honored the sketch utterly, and those who would have known enough to desert it entirely, and women who pretended to be noble even though there was no need to pretend, and siblings who never pretended anything, except perhaps that they weren't siblings… which in my heart they would always be.

Yes, it was a very "tight" bid now, just as the Sketcher had wanted. Hell's Labyrinth was stripped down to its evil essence.

My partner in crime and I crept back through the corridors of the Raving Blade's compound like a pair of cloaked rats.

Moving through storage chambers and maintenance rooms in an ever-tightening spiral, we circled in on our target as inexorably as pestilence traveling through the veins to the heart. This, I learned rather quickly, was a Finisher's true specialty, the uncanny ability to reach that which others cannot reach, to elude, deceive, bypass all that might bar him from executing the contract. While always possessed of a certain conviction in his manner, Radrin Blackstar now seemed driven like a religious crusader. His eyes no longer looked flat and empty and instead appeared quickened with a sort of hunger. As we passed through the complicated network of outer-lying corridors and storerooms, he moved with such speed ahead of me that my torchlight hardly grazed the back of his cloak, and yet on the occasions that soldiers approached from ahead, Radrin caught sound or sight or smell of them so far in advance that he had us safely around several bends in an intersecting passageway or back in the preceding storage chamber behind a pile of supplies, with our torch cloaked from view and plenty of time to spare. I couldn't help feeling that we were now engaged in a portion of the mission that Radrin had anticipated from the very start, and which somehow represented for him the true beginning of the bid.

For me, it was a restart as well. After all, how much easier was this business of eliminating things than protecting them? How much smoother the job went when the only duty required of me was destroying something that lay at the end, not the painstaking defense of a cargo along the way. Preservation had gone by the wayside, self and otherwise. This was a whole new way of doing things.

Radrin's earlier use of my bleeding gave us great cover in our final approach, as the soldiers did, in fact, believe that we had done what any group of rational human beings should have done:

run for our bloody lives. We learned this as we hid in one of the many storage rooms that lay at the fringes of the complex, waiting together behind a huge pile of crates and listening to the soldiers as they passed through the space en route to join the hunt. From catches of their anxious dialogue, it became clear that our aborted blood trail at the water door had fooled them. At the same time, the prospects of returning to their lord empty-handed apparently terrified them. A very propitious combination, for the one thing that seemed conspicuously absent from the nervous talk and hurried movements of these gray-cloaked men was the idea that we might actually attempt to complete this insane bid tonight.

But we would. And we'd do so knowing that there was even more working in our favor than the fact that nobody expected us, an advantage that Radrin had the uncanny wisdom to anticipate. As he put it, "Our target bears his doubts alone tonight, and this will cause him to blunder."

I had only known the Finisher named Blackstar for a mere forty-eight hours, and yet in that brief interval, I believe I had already formulated and then dispelled several useless theories about his character. His insight into the confused inner state of our adversary displayed not only tactical genius but a clear working knowledge of the human heart, a striking revelation given that Radrin Blackstar showed no evidence of possessing that particular organ himself. Still, his theory awed me.

What he was alluding to was the complex predicament that our target now faced as a result of the night's mishaps. Gueritus alone knew that it was Countess Shaeyin Odel who was meant to arrive at his quarters that evening, not Lave Kaszivar, and yet he couldn't share this knowledge with the soldiers who were right now hunting her through the marsh. Wouldn't this deception cause our host to harbor terrible private doubts? Having never actually seen the female imposter, might he not begin to fret horribly over the possibility that his own pride and paranoia had led to a ghastly mistake? Perhaps the "imposter" truly *was* his beautiful Countess Odel, and somehow, in their suspicion of Lave Kaszivar, his own soldiers had unwittingly ignited the evening's violent events.

Yes, there was a very good chance that Gueritus was pondering at least some aspect of this theory. And if so, what would he do?

"He'll come out of his more secure chambers to take a look for himself," Radrin explained. "He'll search for something: a little clue, a piece of clothing, a whiff of her perfume, anything that will reveal to him, with absolute certainty, whether or not Shaeyin Odel was in his house tonight. And he'll keep his guards at a healthy distance as he searches, in case he finds something while they're watching."

I observed Radrin closely as he whispered this to me. We were squatting behind the pile of cedar shipping boxes, counting the intermittent groups of soldiers as they passed through the storeroom in the direction of the water door, and as Radrin gauged our odds, I in turn gauged him. I remembered his earlier comment, "The beauty of an Underlord's compound is that the host never trusts more than a handful of his staff to carry keys."

Who among the Shadow Bidders knew a damned thing about the beauty of an Underlord's compound? Only a man who had visited such places, crept about in them as he eluded soldiers and bypassed doors. Could it be that Radrin Blackstar contracted Narrow Bids on a regular basis?

In all my years working the Labyrinth, nobody had ever so much as hinted at the existence of such a profession. Theoretically, it was possible. The lowest tier of the Underlord hierarchy was composed of dozens of lesser figures with relatively few retainers, who were obscure enough that their passing would receive little attention from the general populace, especially if the bid was ordered by a figure whose high rank kept the prospects of retaliation limited. Jobs along these lines would be extremely rare, but that didn't change the fact that I was now working with somebody, and something, that shouldn't really exist. I could only hope that he was as good at this line of work as his confidence suggested.

"All right, this is the best chance we'll get," Radrin whispered to me, after yet another group of soldiers passed below us towards the water door. At first, I wasn't sure what had given him the necessary signal, as my hearing is excellent, and I had picked up little of value from this troop.

"I've counted a full battalion now," he explained. "Even the High Lord would be an easy target after sending that many men away. It's now or never."

It seemed that the Count's strategy, ill-advised though it might be, was to send his entire army out into the storming marshlands to retrieve the fugitives. I even knew why, and I felt an uncomfortable heat in my throat as I spoke it.

"Damned clever woman," I mumbled as we quietly crept around from the back side of the boxes. "She left them something in the marsh, something good enough to drive them on."

Radrin paused a moment, then nodded.

"A piece of her dress perhaps, maybe your weapon too," he said. "So that they'd think we were still with her."

I shrugged and turned away. I wasn't even sure what I felt just then—pride, sadness, anxiety? I didn't have much time to figure it out, as I was rescued by the pressing business of murdering a man. Never had an idea appealed to me more.

Never had an objective so perfectly focused me, for if there had been partial lies in what I said to Nascinthé of Levell at the water door, I was not lying now. The madman who had sent an army out into the miserable swamp to track her down, who was right now following her carefully laid clues, needed to be destroyed, and I wanted to personally do the job.

Our opportunity came quickly, and in an astonishingly easy manner. After leaving the large storage room, we traveled several hundred yards down the passage that the bulk of the soldiers had been using. The sheer numbers filing through this corridor made it obvious that this route led back to the heart of the compound, and, sure enough, while poking our heads into open rooms along the way, we found a pantry that contained relatively fresh supplies. There was no produce stored here, but among the sacks, two had been re-tied, and there was some trampled grain on the floor. Several barrels had been opened as well, and the lids were being held down with stones. Cooking implements and pots hung from a rack over a chopping table, suggesting that a soldiers' kitchen and mess hall lay through one of the large doorways in the far wall.

We first heard the voices growing louder while exploring this room. They were coming along the main corridor, and Radrin quickly ushered us back farther into the pantry. He seemed to know at once that the approaching men weren't soldiers, for he nodded to my drawn spade, suggesting that we would not be hiding this time.

Was this it? Was this the moment that the Finisher had predicted with such clairvoyance? The target, Radrin was convinced, would eventually grow impatient and venture to the water door himself, if for no other reason than to stare out into the dark marshland with his own eyes and try to imagine if his lady could have possibly fled that way.

"It's the aversion to uncertainty," Radrin had explained. "The more painful the uncertainty, the rasher the efforts to dispel it."

He was right. He was right about everything, it seemed. Except, as it turned out, the main thing, and I will hate him till my dying day for that one cataclysmic failure.

The two voices rose into clarity, and it became evident as they approached that these men were engaged in a heated discussion. We positioned ourselves together against the closer, inside wing of the doorway, waiting to ambush them as they walked past. Unfortunately, we didn't get a chance, for one of the men was clearly dissuading the other from going any farther, and his efforts at last prevailed when they were still shy of our hiding place by a good forty or fifty feet. Radrin's jaw set in a sudden grimace, and he appeared uncharacteristically frustrated. Still, he kept us from advancing, and we both strained to hear what was being said. The acoustics in the tunnel created some confusing echoes, but I could still make out most of it.

"...dead or alive, we'll find them. So please, my lord, kindly return to your suites and wait this out."

"Dead?" a voice croaked in deep, rasping dismay. "Did I tell you to kill them? Did I tell you to kill any of them? Alive, Weygrin, I want them alive...no matter what."

The fraught quality in this man's voice was so palpable it reached us easily despite the poor acoustics.

"Yes...the word has been spread. Alive, only."

"Where is he...not out there? I told you not to let that maniac loose on her trail."

"Nestor's been called back already, my lord," said Weygrin. "He'll be here shortly, and then you can upbraid him yourself."

"I'm going to skin the sadistic bastard alive!" shouted the other man. "Or send him to Ulan's raving cells, where he'll probably be handed a branding iron and offered a job. Gueritus would make him a damned lieutenant overnight."

"No doubt, my lord, fast friends immediately! A much better use for Nestor too. Now please, why don't you return to your chambers."

The grip closed on my forearm well before I understood what I had just heard. Radrin clenched me there as if reaching for a rescue line in a rough sea, while his other hand grabbed his own brow in a gesture that suggested either deep concentration or intense pain.

"I'm going to take a look out there myself," said the one with the distraught voice.

"Please, my lord…please," said Weygrin, and I could hear some shuffling about as if the two of them were jockeying for position.

"It's not him," Radrin mumbled, still in the same posture.

"Weygrin, stand aside," said the other man, and there was a sudden transformation in his tone to command. I had never heard the voice of a senior Underlord, but in my imagination I suppose it would have sounded like this: penetrating, incontestable, very much at odds with the apprehension I had heard there only seconds before.

Just then a distant shout arose, calling out orders from the direction of the water door, and Weygrin made prompt use of this interruption.

"My lord, that's probably Nestor. You will no doubt get a full report now…and give him one yourself."

Radrin turned to me, his hand still clawed into my forearm.

"Raved," he whispered, half to himself. "…all of us. Our target most of all."

"Yes, that's him, my lord," said Weygrin. "Please let Nestor be your eyes in the swamp."

"I want to speak to him alone, Weygrin. Why don't you go and get me a warmer cloak."

"…As you wish, my lord," Weygrin answered hesitantly.

Radrin pushed me back away from the doorway into the corner of the pantry, between a pile of grain sacks and a stack of barrels. He grabbed my shoulder, thrusting his face but inches from mine.

"Vazeer," he breathed quietly. "Do you understand what's happening here?"

It took me a moment, but finally I nodded. Dumbly.

For I did understand some of it. My mind leapt backwards through the realization like a staggering drunkard, leading from this weird assertion that our target had been *raved*; that part struck me most of all. Into my mind sprang a vision of the Sketcher of the bid scrubbing compulsively at the hem of his tunic, trying to wipe from the air of the boathouse the intolerable stain of Flerra Tellian's mistake, the dangerous words that had been stated out loud: "Gueritus. The Raving Blade."

Our presumed target.

But stating the target's name out loud, while clearly a breach of etiquette, wouldn't constitute a major disruption of the bid. The only thing that truly threatened a job was to state the proffer's name out loud…which, I suddenly knew with shocking clarity, is precisely what Flerra Tellian had done.

Count Ulan Gueritus, the man who hired us for this bid. To kill himself? Clearly not.

The Raving Blade had deceived us, for he obviously thought the ghastly prospect of targeting him was somehow preferable to the truth, whatever that was.

"But why would—?"

"Vazeer!" Radrin interrupted with a quiet, deadly hiss. "Do you or do you not understand who's standing out in that corridor?"

Here, at last, my powers of conjecture failed me, and I was forced to shake my head foolishly.

"Brace yourself then, Shadow Bidder," Radrin breathed.

My dull-faced gawking in no way indicated that I was "braced," but Radrin delivered the truth anyway.

"The man in the next chamber is none other than Lord Beranardos Sherdane, himself," he said, still gripping my arms and glaring at me from a few inches away. "The High Lord of Hell's Labyrinth."

I couldn't be entirely sure, but I was fairly certain that this was the single worst sentence that I had ever heard in my life. And it remained that way for…perhaps two or three full seconds. Just long enough for Radrin to say something worse.

"Vazeer," he continued, his fingers gouging into my arms like talons, his eyes suddenly cold and malevolent. "Don't even think of lowering your blades. You and I are now going to walk into that passageway and kill him."

16

TREASON

Every civilization, from the grandest civic republic to the most morally debased hellhole, needs to create for itself at least one archetypal hero in order to survive. The people want this, the leaders want it, the very land itself requires such a figure, as if the complex fabric of human society cannot remain properly stitched without the elevation of one thoroughly exemplary individual. I have little personal experience to back up this theory, but I read a lot, and in my readings this theme arises again and again. Every society, with even the flimsiest moral code to define it, must have at least one hero.

In the city of Sullward, we, too, had our hero, a figure who evoked in all of us a quiet form of reverence that almost qualified as love, but which could never quite be love, for gut-level fear does not lend itself to that most exalted of human emotions. Still, we all willingly, even eagerly, submitted ourselves to the authority of this one individual. His name was Lord Beranardos Sherdane, and he was, for all intents and purposes, our King.

My entire life had been spent under the rule of this brilliant and secretive ruler, and every bid I had ever contracted as a Grell Runner had taken place during the grand age of the Shadow Bidders, something that Sherdane himself had ushered into existence. I had never been formally introduced to our monarch, as the protective line between proffer and contract agent was carefully maintained, yet I had furnished his halls with hundreds, if not thousands of beautiful items, while he in turn had coughed up a veritable fortune to me over the course of my career. It was even rumored that I was personally Beranardos Sherdane's favorite Shadow Bidder, and one of the only Grell Runners his Sketchers ever used. The High Lord probably knew even less about me than I knew of him; however, my brutal devotion to my cargos was common knowledge to all, and tales of my encounters along the Grells supposedly gave rise to much toasting and laughter around the banquet tables of the Underlords who saw, in my willingness to maim my fellows rather than disappoint my anonymous employers, the High Lord's original Shadow Bidder vision personified.

"Hail to Lash the Lunatic!" they were said to cheer in private. "Dark Gods bless the Grell Reaper!"

If Sherdane saw fit to bless me in the privacy of his dining hall, then so too did I often bless him alone over a glass of wine in my own fire-lit study. For that study, and all the books and artwork in my home, and the wine in my glass, and the chair below my backside...all of these were because of him. Without the Shadow Bidder code, I would have been just another uneducated street thug, committing crimes at the behest of some low-level racketeer.

Well, no more toasts and blessings for "Lash the Lunatic" around the tables of the Underlords, and certainly no hope of redemption for the "Grell Reaper" in the eyes of his fellows. If Beranardos Sherdane was the closest thing to a hero that any of us might hope to find in our eminently unheroic world, then to be sure, Vazeer the Lash was fast approaching a different pantheon entirely.

You see, I didn't need any coaxing to step through that doorway, and into the ranks of history's villains. I had already given the explanation myself.

"He will literally stop at nothing to find us, send his men anywhere and everywhere in the search, and there will never come a day when he simply grows tired of the pursuit."

I had said these words to Nascinthé at the water door, and though at the time I had been referring to Count Ulan Gueritus, this statement now held true a hundred-fold in reference to the High Lord.

Sherdane would be hard pressed to believe that we had been tricked into this bid. Even if he did somehow accept the story, he'd still have to make an example of us, not to mention the fact that he would want the secret regarding Countess Odel wiped from the face of the Empire. Our deaths would make a nice start to the cleansing. But not before the location of Nascinthé's hiding place had been tortured out of us. As I noted earlier, Nascinthé would no doubt pay more dearly for the crime than any of us, having been the primary vehicle that allowed a team of assassins into the High Lord's home.

If, however, we could kill Sherdane quickly and quietly, and then manage to escape this compound, we actually had a good chance of surviving. Without its leader, the High Lord's organization would fracture quickly. In the ensuing chaos, Ulan Gueritus would take over. War would break out, but in the end the Raving Blade would win, and once he had established himself as the new High Lord of the Labyrinth, all would be forgotten. Compared to his role as the proffer of the bid, the doings of the assassins themselves would be meaningless.

It was quite brilliant, really. When Brand conveyed his peculiar message in the orphanage, he suggested that Gueritus spoke in traps. I don't know if that was exactly what he meant to say, or if Pippen was simply doing his best to translate the idea, but the general concept now seemed eerily prescient. The Raving Blade and the Sketcher he used to spin his deceptive stratagem had put us in a trap that was truly breathtaking in its creative wickedness. The moment we took those contract payments, and certainly once we arrived at the Three Bay, our fates were sealed. Even if we figured out the true identity of the target as soon as we entered Sherdane's compound, everything I described earlier would still apply. The only way to survive the trap and avoid the wrath of the High Lord was to finish the contract. The cunning Ulan Gueritus knew that when this moment finally arose, men like Radrin Blackstar and Vazeer the Lash could be counted on, with absolute certainty, to do the wrong thing.

My co-conspirator was still burrowing his fingers into my leatherguard cuirass like a famished bird of prey when Nestor finally showed up. Radrin had wisely waited for this man, ensuring that he did not arrive while we were in the murderous act. We heard his aggressive footfalls hurry past the pantry, and when he came before Sherdane, he spoke a decidedly gruff "my lord?"

Radrin's hands came off my shoulders. He flipped his chin in the direction of the corridor and the message was clear: "Nestor" was going to be my responsibility. I gave little thought to this duty, for I was completely fixated on the unsettling tone of Sherdane's voice, which began to needle my resolve with the very first syllable.

"Nestor," the High Lord said, his speech quivering less with rage, it seemed, than a deep, forlorn anxiety that again surprised me with its nakedness. "Tell me that you didn't make a horrible mistake here. Tell me that you know, beyond all shadow of a doubt, that the visitors who arrived tonight were here to kill me, that they murdered Jevar for that reason, not because my councilor accidentally insulted…her person. Can you assure me of this?"

Nestor apparently needed a moment to think this over, for he cleared his throat conspicuously.

"The men don't believe me when I say that it wasn't Lave Kaszivar, my lord," he finally replied, hoarsely. "But they are wrong. When she entered the compound, I was focused on the two Shadow Bidders who came with her, but now that I think back on it, the woman seemed too well bred, high born even—"

"That's not what I goddamned asked you, you sadistic moron!" Sherdane screamed, and indeed it was a scream of the most primal, tortured emotion I could ever remember hearing from the lips of a grown man. It literally pierced the dank, underground chamber like the shriek of a wounded bird.

"What the damned hell would you know about courtly breeding?" he yelled. "…about one who soars so high above you that you can't even see the soles of her feet! Would you have taken scalpels and razors to that woman too if you had caught her? Nestor, I am going to have you flayed alive if that woman out there is who she's supposed to be. I'm going to have it done straight away, do you hear me, you psychotic half-wit?"

"M-my lord," Nestor stammered, "all I did…all I have ever done is try to protect you. If I am to be flayed alive, then it should be for failing to be sadistic enough as your master sentinel, for listening to that simpleton Jevar and letting these pretenders into your house. I know you were close with Jevar, my lord, but as your councilor he failed you, badly, just as I did. Now we're both going to pay for the mistake."

Crouched a dozen yards away, waiting for Radrin to give the final signal, I found that I had become utterly transfixed by this interaction. My attention was swept into Beranardos Sherdane's world like a piece of twisted flotsam dragged into the roiling flow of the autumn Grells, and it seemed to me of the deepest fascination how the High Lord would respond to this disclaimer from his head of security. I knew I should try to extract myself. Finishers supposedly trained themselves long and hard to avoid this sort of hypnotic fascination with their targets. But I wasn't a true Finisher. Not yet at least.

"Oh gods…oh great gods, what have I done…!" Sherdane cried, and suddenly his voice changed again, this time into a staggering lament of sorrow and despair that came on with such surprising force that I actually cringed where I waited.

"Please protect her, merciful gods, please…please deliver her to me unharmed!"

There are a handful of moments from my bitter journey through this world that stand out for their sheer existential poignancy. The torture and murder of Flerra Tellian in a pleasantly decorated underground parlor was one of them. The sound of Beranardos Sherdane calling out to the "merciful gods" of some long-dead North Derjian religion, impotently beseeching them to protect the one thing he clearly loved most of all in this cold universe, was another. It literally rattled me down to the hollow of my bones. I also guessed, in that moment, that Jevar had been the only other person besides the High Lord who knew the true intention of this night's meeting. It seemed that Nestor had been fed the same "Lave Kaszivar" story as the rest of the men.

"Damn you, Beran, damn your stubborn pride!" Sherdane hissed, and he said it with such disgust that it took me a moment to realize that he was addressing himself. "What did you think would happen? What in hell were you thinking?"

"My lord?" Nestor probed tentatively.

"Leave me alone, Nestor," Sherdane moaned. "Go away from me."

"I will not. Not unless you come with me, back into the compound."

"Do as I tell you!" Sherdane snapped, but his tone lacked conviction; in fact, it lacked strength or authority of any sort. Seconds later we heard just how overwrought he had become when he let forth first a groan, then a high-pitched wheeze, and finally, to my utter mortified disbelief, a series of choking sobs. Before I knew it, the dreaded High Lord of Hell's Labyrinth was weeping disconsolately like a broken-hearted child.

"No need, my lord, no need," Nestor intoned quietly. He was clearly embarrassed and confused by this episode; however, I noticed that he did not sound even remotely contemptuous. If anything, I detected hints of that same quality that had been ever-so-present in Jevar the Legate and that, until tonight, had seemed all but non-existent in Hell's Labyrinth. What I heard, strange as it is to say, was love.

"Fear not, my lord; we will find them. Whoever they really are, we will find them and retrieve them safely. Now, let's return to your suites."

"Bring her back to me, Nestor…." Sherdane sobbed. "…Please bring her back. All is forgiven if you just bring her back to me… safe and sound."

From where I hid on the far side of that doorway, I slurped up this bewildering drama as if it were a cup of stinging acid, absorbing and then reacting to each new emotional episode with dizzying speed. By the time Sherdane begged his master sentinel to bring back the lady in the marsh, my sense of personal conviction was a total mess. At just that moment I felt a hand tap me on the shoulder, and I looked over to see Radrin Blackstar nod in the direction of the doorway. I knew what he was saying, knew that he had, as usual, chosen the perfect moment to make our move, and somehow, amid all my confusion and moral turmoil, I simply stood up and entered the corridor. Once again, the Finisher of the bid overrode my own uncertainty with his icy sense of resolve.

The stretch of hallway outside of the pantry was like all the others in this outer level of the compound. The floors were lined with roughly grouted flagstones, while the walls were a mixture of granite and packed earth, with shoring beams spaced approximately every twenty feet. The stone here was damp, and there was a light sulfuric odor, suggesting that we were still under a section of the salt marsh.

Forty feet away stood our target, face wet, arms crossed over his chest, while Nestor was planted a few feet from him with his gray-cloaked back turned to me and his weapons sheathed. I had only seen Sherdane a handful of times in my life, for the social establishments he frequented were the exclusive domain of the Underlords. Moreover, when he traveled the city above ground, he was usually in a carriage or a covered gondola, and his men always worked the surrounding alleys ahead of time, forcing loiterers out of the way. Still, I had managed to get one or two good looks at him in my day and knew him to be quite a dashing figure, with a thick silver-blond mane sweeping back off a high forehead, a sharp well-groomed beard that was darker than his hair, and arched eyebrows that were darker still. Older women in Sullward grew veritably faint when they reminisced on his breathtaking good looks from days gone by, while younger women expressed doubts that he could ever have been much more handsome than he currently was. Indeed, when last I saw him, perhaps a year and a half earlier, his naturally ruddy complexion, broad chest, and air of vitality marked him as a man in the prime of his life, with little if anything lost to age.

When I tried to picture Countess Odel involved with the coarse, inelegant Ulan Gueritus, at least as I imagined the man, the idea had been all but impossible to fathom. But not so with the High Lord. Sherdane was probably ten years the Raving Blade's senior, but his radiance and charisma caused the likes of Gueritus (and the rest of us for that matter) to seem as homely and uncouth as a gang of swamp vagrants. Shaeyin Odel would probably be hard pressed to find such a figure anywhere in her own stilted circles of aristocracy.

To tell you the truth, the High Lord did not look overly diminished when I observed him that night, despite his grief. Our gazes met instantly, for he had been staring vaguely in my direction when I entered the hallway, and I saw that his clear brown eyes were moist but still sharp, while his flushed cheeks were only a little puffier than normal. He had on an elegant crimson coat with a black fur trim, and his red hose descended into tall black felt boots—presumably the outfit in which he had hoped to receive his distinguished guest. His mouth appeared to drop open slightly when he saw me, and his posture straightened, but my gut sense was that his reaction was not born of fear. To the contrary, it seemed to reflect some sort of excitement or (Dark Gods help me) perhaps even hope.

As I advanced on him, lowering my blades, I absorbed this marginally hopeful gaze as if guzzling down a draught of poison, so odious to me was the idea that I was somehow prolonging Sherdane's fantasy, even as I came to cut short his life. In those split-seconds I understood what he was thinking, knew that the sudden presence of one of the "visitors" here offered the slim possibility that his Countess might be near at hand. Perhaps the scar-faced, blood-spattered, blade-wielding man who was striding aggressively towards him across the crude flagstones of his own back hallway might, in fact, be bearing good news. Poor smitten old fool.

I came onward, each step taking me closer to the terrible, unthinkable treason, each breath drawing me nearer to the final ruin of my character. Could I really do this thing? Could I kill this man and what was left of my principles at the same time? Could I cleave down the source of my prosperity in this lifetime, the true funder of 27 Fletcher, the one who had indirectly paid for all the artistic and intellectual relics therein? Quite suddenly, and decisively, I knew I couldn't. I just couldn't do it! All the reasons I had given to Nascinthé at the water door, all the cold logic that lay in the plan…it didn't hold up in the face of the act itself. There simply had to be a better way.

At just that moment, Nestor must have registered the look on his lord's face, for he turned in my direction. I was quite close now, less than ten feet away, and my guess is that Nestor lacked the appropriate readiness merely because the High Lord did not seem suitably alarmed. Therefore, I recognized the true identity of the Master Sentinel a split-second before he recognized me. As I look back on it, I suppose it's odd that I didn't clue in on the man's voice before that. Then again, I had never heard him speak without snarling.

Around came that face—hard, brutish, indomitable. His expression was softened somewhat by his exchange with Sherdane, but still I saw the malice hiding there, writhing just behind the severe lines of the brow, twisting like a muscular tic within the thick block of his jaw. I also saw the deep slice under his eye, which had fallen just shy of its mark. This was the man who had diced and murdered my Broodmate Flerra Tellian. This was the dreaded "Commander of the Guard," who later become the "Butcher" in an improvised torture chamber somewhere within this compound.

Someday, I really must learn to control myself. It is true that when my blood is not entirely boiling, I can rein it in somewhat, but not once I cross that line. As soon as that happens there is no turning back, and all plans and good intentions scatter from me quickly like a bevy of startled marsh wrens. So it was when I recognized Nestor; the instincts of a lifetime took over, the brutal habits spawned years ago in childhood brawls, and then borne out over an entire career of Grell Running simply lashed out like my name's sake, and all hope of breaking the bid was lost. I knew only to avenge in that moment. I knew only to cleave and rend and destroy.

My sense is that I would have had a very poor time of it against the well-trained Master Sentinel had the two of us faced off in a duel, using anything resembling the rules of fair play. But I don't fight by such rules, and never have from as far back as my very first boyhood fisticuffs.

As I descended on Nestor, it was primarily the element of surprise that came to my aid, accentuated by a psychotic howl that would have frightened even the most battle-tested brute. Out of my mouth it came, phlegm-clogged and ghastly, loud enough to scare the monster who made it, had I not been so completely choked with hatred at that moment.

My spade connected first, a lateral, arching slash that was aimed for the neck, but which Nestor had the wherewithal to take on the shoulder as a result of some quick reflexes. He had armor there under his cloak, and it buffered the blow enough that he was able to get his other arm up and deflect the stiletto from piercing his throat. He took a grazing cut across his cheek, and he showed astonishing combat instincts in that he didn't fall back in retreat, but rather moved forward and went for a clinch, getting one hand on my tunic and the other on my right bicep. It was a smart move, a much better idea than fruitlessly scrambling to draw his weapons and thereby giving me a second opening. The only problem was he had now surrendered his almost certain advantage in swordsmanship and had thrown himself whole-heartedly into my single favorite fighting position. As explained, close-quarters combat is my specialty, and over the years there have been countless instances in which assailants, often several at once, firmly believed that they had gained control of the fight by grabbing hold of me, only to realize that the truly nasty portion of the encounter had just begun.

Instinctively I reacted to Nestor's grab by thrusting myself against him and driving my knee hard into his groin. He had some padding there, and his legs were closer together than I would have liked, but the blow seemed to catch him largely off guard, enough so that he was left entirely open when I drew my head back and launched perhaps the most savage headbutt of my career straight onto the bridge of his nose. I heard the crack of his nasal bone splintering and felt the pellets of blood hitting my hands before I even pulled back my head and saw the damage. His already unattractive face was now a frightful mess, puffed like dough and atrail with crimson runnels, though, to his credit, the powerful Master Sentinel did not pass out or collapse, as most men would have. Still, he staggered, and his grip on my stiletto arm loosened. That was all I needed, and I slipped my weapon down and then drove it up hard under his armpit where I knew there would be little armor. The long blade plunged deep into the side of his chest cavity like a knit-ter's pin into a cork ball.

I'd like to tell you that the defeat of my nemesis, Nestor, Master Sentinel, Commander of the Guard…the Butcher, was a moment of great satisfaction for me, but it wasn't. Just as quickly as the hatred came on, it dissipated, and the cause was the look in my victim's eyes as he sank down to his knees, trying to staunch the flow of blood. Instead of glowering up at me with loathing, he was staring to his left in terrible regret, and, following his gaze and seeing that it was fixed on the startled High Lord, I was present once again to the strange devotion that seemed to pervade this compound. All this man Nestor cared about was protecting his liege. He didn't regret dying; he regretted only that he hadn't done a better job anticipating the threat or convincing his lord that it existed.

He definitely hadn't, for I saw that even now the truth was not immediately obvious to our target. How sad to watch a dreamer ruinously affix himself to his dream, watch him adjust the narrative to accommodate all troubling pieces of evidence to the contrary.

My stare was locked so completely with Sherdane's I could see every fractional movement of his dark eyes, see his gaze panning over me. What a sight I must have been! I stood panting heavily, my stiletto dripping, my face flushed and no doubt littered with speckles of Nestor's blood, my deranged howl still reverberating in the space of the hallway like the aftershock of the huge rogue swells that broke on occasion against the southern portion of the sea wall. The High Lord, by contrast, still looked rather dignified, though his bearded jaw ground subtly back and forth as if on a hidden current. There was a sharp intensity beneath the thick dark arch of his brows, reassuring me that this was not a man to be easily frightened by spectacles of violence. If anything, he seemed to understand. If anything, he seemed relieved that the terrible dread and uncertainty were now behind him.

The slit opened in the High Lord's throat so quickly that I didn't even see the blade that caused it. One moment Sherdane was standing there, staring at me with his expression of anticipation and relief, and the next he was falling in an unceremonious heap to the floor, dark blood streaming fluidly from his neck into one of the soiled grout channels that ran alongside my feet. For a second all I could do was watch the dark rivulet as it slid towards me, following its gliding path between two flagstones as though watching a tidal surge pour into the narrow, tainted furrow of a Sullward canal.

Then I looked up to face the man who had done this thing.

"You seem entirely incapable of killing quietly, Vazeer the Lash," said Radrin Blackstar, once again drawing a small black cloth from the folds of his clothing and wiping the High Lord's blood from his dagger. "There's little chance of escaping now without a fight."

17

SWELL DRIVER

Radrin Blackstar's ability to disappear from sight and thought and memory has taken up a fair amount of my attention so far in this account. I have focused repeatedly on this unique quality of his, the strange way he evaporates into the ethers at the most unlikely of moments. This is certainly a disquieting phenomenon, but it isn't the real issue. The real issue is the way this bizarre spook of a man suddenly *reappears*. The real problem is that he always, always comes back.

For several seconds I just stood there, glaring at him. I looked at his impassive face, his neatly dressed form, unruffled by the night's butchery, without a speck of blood upon him. I watched him standing in an almost relaxed manner over the disheveled corpse of our murdered king.

In hindsight, there are several things I might have said in reply to this idea that we would now need to fight our way out of the compound. I might, for instance, have asked, "Do you really expect a fight, Blackstar? All I've ever seen you do is poke your knife into men who aren't looking at you." But I didn't say that, or anything else. I was simply too dazed to formulate words.

We could hear the soldiers now, shouting from all directions, and my first guess was that they were unclear as to the High Lord's exact location, which may have been true for the ones deep inside the compound. Not the men who guarded the water door, however. They had something much more pressing to think about.

As I've explained, my entire life has been spent surrounded by three interconnected bodies of water—the river Grells, its adjoining salt marsh, and the mighty North Derjian Sea—and in no uncertain sense do the various essences of these waters suffuse me. Their acrid smells clog the crooked passages of my nose, their saline residues crust my calloused skin, their cold, foreboding boundaries entrap me, reducing my world to a vaporous penal colony from which I have never attempted escape.

As all prisons do in time, the walls of this one finally closed in around me, inflicting punishments long overdue. The night that saw the sentence passed down was none other than *the* night, 28 Dekharven, year 213, the date that everything, and I do mean everything, came apart at its seams like a poorly stitched sail. The Underlords had anticipated a great deal in their constant efforts to avoid eradication. They had, regrettably, overlooked the worst possibility of all.

The dreadful North Derjian monstrosity known as a Swell Driver only vaguely resembles its distant cousin, the southern typhoon, and it was clearly our generation's catastrophic mistake to envision the Great Storm as simply a larger, meaner version of the meteorological violence we experienced on an annual basis. The storm's main threat, we had always been told, derived from its angle of entry into Sullward Harbor, and yet upon review, this information so badly understates the point as to render all common precautions useless. About a century ago, a jetty had been constructed to the northwest just in case the disaster ever struck again. In his endless efforts to secure his creation from harm, High Lord Sherdane, at the start of his reign, had forced the Governor to reinforce the jetty, thereby giving our city an official seal of safety, at least as far as weather-related disasters were concerned.

Unfortunately, a Swell Driver has no respect for official seals, nor does it think much of jetties, for the internal dynamics of this storm are such that it literally displaces huge portions of the ocean with the sustained force of its polar winds, and thus does not create waves in the conventional sense. It brings, instead, massive walls of water that are so thick that they behave more like tidal bores than actual swells. From the descriptions of survivors who watched the beast as it entered our city that night, the entire sea appeared to simply rise up and roll over us, as if somewhere far to the northwest, huge ocean dykes were being released one after another, flooding the North Derjian with far more water than the stony coastline could contain.

The warnings about "angle of entry" were indeed well founded, for the mouth of the Grells is an exquisitely aligned receptacle for a northwestern surge, allowing the flood to snake its way around the entire city and waylay us from three sides at once. Those of us near (or Dark Gods forbid "below") the Lower City bore the brunt of this terror in a way that the other residents did not. The Underlords had learned how to keep their underground palaces safe and dry in the advent of all manner of heavy weather, flood tides, and even occasional storm surges—an unlikely feat of engineering that consigned law enforcement to endless, frustrating searches of high-ground warehouses. After all, what fool would hide his precious merchandise far below ground in an area subject to annual flooding? The part the Underlords had never foreseen was the Lower City's complete and utter submersion, an inundation so deep that only the spires and gables of the tallest Lower City buildings remained exposed at the height of the storm.

None of this was even remotely apparent to me as I stood in a crude underground corridor, listening to a commotion I didn't yet understand, staring at a sad carnage I also didn't understand, even though I had created half of it. This was not where I would have chosen to be when Sullward's second Great Storm struck.

We could now hear a handful of retainers from the compound's interior hastening towards us, obviously drawn by my deranged expression of rage, though it seemed as if they had quite a distance to cover before they arrived. Whether or not Radrin knew what was coming, he definitely understood that we were about to be parted.

"I will take his ring, as proof of execution," he said. "You can have this."

And with that, he tossed me something small and shiny, which I caught out of reflex. When I opened my fist, it was the profusion of blood that I noticed first, streaked over my palm as though I had just crushed a handful of berries. Since my hand was wounded already, I thought that it was my own blood, but then I looked at the object itself and saw a small octagonal brooch with an intricate maze pattern engraved into its gold surface. The little angular turns in the maze all led inward to the center of the brooch, where a beautiful purple-red stone was inlaid—a Gosian diamond, I guessed, though it was a bit difficult to tell in the torchlight. A second later I realized that I was holding High Lord Sherdane's throat brooch and that my skin was now smeared with his gore. There it was, the dark crimson essence running through the furrows of my palm, filling my own injuries and mingling with my blood.

For some reason it was the presence of that brooch that broke me; I'm not sure why. Perhaps it was the physicality of the object, feeling the solid metal in my hand, and the blood flowing into my blood, and also, perhaps, the filthy outrage of its current condition (Radrin always found time to clean that vile dagger of his, but he chose to throw me my High Lord's brooch soaked in our treason)…maybe all of this came together in that moment to push me over the edge. For that was exactly where I went: tumbling, cascading, right over an invisible barrier, pushed there by the betrayal and the loathing, by the many devastating losses, by failing to protect my own Brood sister in her hour of need, and then sending away Nascinthé of Levell when, in truth, this was my own personal hour of need. And finally, the grotesque, ignoble murder of the ever-so-noble Sherdane. It was all too much for me.

When I break, I do so convincingly, but I can rarely report much about it after the fact, for I am the one person who is conspicuously absent from the guest list. As I've said, I have a propensity to enter a void at these moments, effectively blacking out when my emotions, my beliefs, my sense of morality can no longer withstand the barbarous onslaught of reality. I exited the scene at the climax of our Narrow Bid, but it wasn't quite blackness that engulfed me. Instead, I entered what can only be called a dream.

The dream came at precisely the same moment that the waters came, and though this was perhaps some ironic accident, it felt otherwise. I was swallowed by twin beasts simultaneously, and somehow neither killed me nor drove me permanently mad, though I am to this day irreversibly affected by both. Certainly, I should have drowned. That was the logical thing to do (perhaps even the decent thing), for when the North Derjian sea came rushing into the High Lord's compound, there should have been no escape. It is true that Sherdane's magnificent underground bunker was constructed very well, built virtually water-tight in many places, with clever air shafts that reached high above the waterline via ducts in the buildings above. Still, the waters did reach me; they were the last meaningful thing I saw on that bid.

In the torchlight, the flood looked like a glimmering second floor that sliced over the bloody flagstones with the swift momentum of a guillotine blade. The initial surge knocked my feet out from under me and sent me whooshing along like a piece of debris, sweeping me right down that corridor and through a doorway into the base of a flight of stairs. Though the water had only come up to my knees, the force of it was stunning. As a final conscious experience, I smelled the sulfuric stench of the marsh, and since it came from the direction of the water door, I could only imagine that the soldiers in the marsh had made a last desperate gambit to get back inside the compound. The door was probably wide open when the surge struck, and the sheer weight of the water likely tore the vulnerable hatch right off of its hinges.

But that was it. Beyond that I bid farewell to my memories of our house call on our High Lord. The thing that follows does not exist inside that pretty cave of death, nor does it exist above. I cannot even say, with any great conviction, that I actually lost consciousness, for all the while I was somehow vaguely aware of the frigid waters and the torturous struggle to live. These things, however, were so far in the background as to seem like dreams themselves. As to how I got out of there, I'm really not sure. It's quite possible that I climbed that flight of stairs and then slithered up an air shaft into one of the buildings above. It's also possible that I swam in the opposite direction until I finally exited the water door (I have been known to hold my breath beneath the chilly surface of the Grells for several minutes at a time). When it comes to the physical exodus, I'm largely in the dark. But the other thing, the strange, esoteric escape that transpired at the same time, this part deserves some attention.

In bed at night there is no inner signpost that tells us that we are slipping out of the waking state and into the realm of slumber. The transition is seamless, and the mind steps between worlds without questioning the new reality, nor with a sense of what has just come before. This is how it was for me that night when the deluge struck. I was suddenly and effortlessly in another place, a rather familiar place, and I felt no overt confusion about being there. Perhaps this was because I had actually lived this scene, though it had occurred many years in the past.

The memory was of a special day. I would go so far as to call it a seminal day, and it occurred when I was twelve years old. I had escaped Holod's tutelage that morning, making my way out of the northern boundary of the Wags, and, despite my mentor's adamant rules against this, I meandered into the dark, majestic streets of the Lower City. This wasn't the first time. That whole year had been an exciting period of forbidden exploration. I had worked out careful routes through that huge, beautiful neighbor-hood, making the sojourns between the hours of Seventh and Ninth Bell, when the streets were reliably empty.

So, there I was that quiet morning, wandering a looping, whimsical route along misty canals, over high arching bridges, under the weighty shadows of architectural greatness. In the vision I saw the towering Nengriant Basilica, one of the few religious buildings in our city and a true marvel of engineering. It had seen a multitude of secular uses in the four hundred years since the Dawn of Reason, but it still engendered holy awe in my young breast as I stared up at the flying buttresses and high stabbing spires, at the colorful upper sections of stained glass that had not cracked or been pilfered by looters. It was but one of dozens of splendors I gazed upon that morning. Happily, I did not enjoy them alone.

Walking at my side was a pale, freckle-faced girl with auburn hair, and while this girl did not seem entirely transfixed by the sights around her, she listened with some interest to my commentary on the unique genius of the Old Calendar architects. Flerra Tellian was open to my mad ideas back then. Holod had not yet beaten the idealism out of her, and she smiled and at times looked up at me with wide, clear eyes, entranced by my talk of Sullward's eventual revival. Someday, I told her, it would come. Someday the wild vision that drove Aurellis Kaennamin to erect all of this stunning grandeur in the most improbable of places would find life again. When the time was right, those of us who saw what King Aurellis had seen would band together and take up the call.

In my Narrow Bid phantasm, as in real life, Flerra and I made it as far as Kaennamin Academy, the city's original school of architecture. The gorgeous building had some characteristics in common with the basilica, as there were delicate arches coming off of its peak, and while the glass in the high windows lacked the dramatic coloring of the religious building, they were a pleasing amber in hue. We stood on a canal bridge, under the soaring shape of that building, with murky waters sliding below and wreaths of mist slowly curling above, and we found ourselves in a peaceful stasis. We waited in a place outside of time. Flerra and I, who had already known so much trouble in our young lives, simply lingered there, sharing a truly happy moment together.

But, as with all forms of innocence in Hell's Labyrinth, it could not last, for the aggrieved soul of the place deliberately sought out young optimism and strangled it in its crib. The agent who exacted reprisal this day was the man we generally feared the most, and it was on this same graceful canal bridge, in the shadow of the mythical Kaennamins, that he found us.

Holod Deadskiff emerged from the fog that morning like a hulking ape, and the vicious beatings and the raw vitriol that followed ended a thing that had only just begun. Flerra Tellian never again accompanied me on my historical walking tours. In fact, she would not even speak of that day, or the general topic of pre-storm architecture, or, particularly, the ludicrous notion that Sullward might ever know resurrection. Holod had forbidden it, and Flerra was so traumatized by the episode that she eventually came to hold it against me, like so many things. Who could blame her? Even in the far-removed world of my flood-induced dream, I knew I had a habit of always letting Flerra Tellian down.

It was at this precise moment in my hallucination, just before Holod was due to come, that I experienced the first break in the reality of that world. I literally felt it, for the frosty bite of the waters somehow pierced the phantasmal curtain and reached as far as my twelve-year-old limbs. I was not jarred awake, but suddenly I knew pain. It was a cold, frightening pain, twisting through my dream body and telling me that I was, on the most basic level, no longer safe. Some catastrophic thing was now transpiring very close to where I was, but not quite where I was, which was a little too difficult to grasp. Had I probed the mystery deeply enough, then perhaps I would have been ejected from the vision. But something else happened, and my attention was drawn away.

Holod had stormed at us from the direction of Kaennamin Academy, and by the time he was in view, there was no getting away from him, not unless we wanted our lives to be forfeit. So, we just stood there, awaiting judgement. In my Narrow Bid dream, a figure did approach from that exact street, splitting the mist with his thin, robed form, click-clocking the cobbles lightly with his boots, but I could tell right away that this was not Holod

Deadskiff. Flerra definitely would have confirmed this…had she still been there. But she wasn't. Just like that, my Brood sister was gone, and I stood alone on that stone bridge, with the distant cold stinging my limbs and the unlocated catastrophe occurring nearby. The finely dressed stranger made his way to me briskly, striding right up the elegant, canal-spanning arch and stopping before me, tall and reproachful.

When I looked at this man's lanky, clean-shaven face, surrounded by an ermine collar, with a jeweled necklace hanging at his breast, I was surprised to experience recognition. I had seen many drawings over the years, as well as two splendid oil portraits. I was also the proud owner of a marble bust that graced an arched wall niche in my study, the recollection of this last item suddenly reminding me that I was no longer a twelve-year-old boy but rather the full-grown owner of 27 Fletcher Street. And the tall man before me was none other than King Aurellis Kaennamin himself.

What an absolutely shocking turn of events! Also, an honor of stunning proportions. I did not question King Aurellis's presence there. I did not find it suspicious or indicative of some flaw in the reality of my world. I accommodated it, as one absorbs such turns in a dream; however, I'll confess that one trifling detail did snag in my consciousness. Why was my ancient idol glowering at me with such contempt?

He absolutely was. He scowled down that long supercilious nose of his, and he pursed his bloodless lips. There was a disdainful cock to his finely groomed eyebrows that somehow conveyed both incredulity and utter dismissal at the same time. Did he not know how I revered him? Did he not understand that I, perhaps of all people in this city, truly grasped his singular genius? Maybe he mistook me, understandably, for pretty much any other narrow-minded son of a bitch he might encounter wandering these streets. Walk up to another bridge, and you were likely to meet some useless scamp there. But, as luck would have it, Aurellis Kaennamin came to the right bridge, and certainly the right man. For some reason, he didn't see it that way.

"In the bloody name of Eresis," he said in a surprisingly high, nasal voice. "This is no way to run things."

Ah, yes, Eresis, reigning deity of the North Derjian pantheon—known collectively as the Dark Gods. The Kaennamin dynasty was founded before the Dawn of Reason, though this particular monarchy was known to pay only the most cursory homage to the Dark Gods. But...what? What was Aurellis on about with this talk of running things?

"What in existence did you think would happen, man?" he snapped, and truly he seemed irate. Aurellis Kaennamin's face contorted into a mask of disgust and resentment, neither being a good look for him. Beneath his short, thinning brown hair, that long arrogant face became a showpiece of priggish irritability.

This really wasn't going well. Some sort of misunderstanding was afoot, for Aurellis Kaennamin wouldn't react to me in this manner if he understood the mad dreams we shared in common. He wouldn't be mistaking me for...who exactly? I struggled just then to guess what this long-dead monarch was getting at. Did he somehow think me in charge? Did he imagine me a ruler of this city—a civilian governor or, perhaps (Eresis forbid) the High Lord?

Right then, with that chagrinned thought, the cold and pain breached the dream a second time, now with greater force. It whipped through me like an icy cross-draft, quivering into my flesh and joints and blood. It was like a much worse version of those times when I left windows open at night in winter, then needed to run naked from my bed in the morning to close them. In those cases, I always knew that relief was but a few rooms away and that the source of the discomfort could be sealed off, while a re-stoked fireplace would banish the lingering chill. Not so in the half-world where I languished. I couldn't comprehend the source of this terrible ache, nor did I know which hatch to close in order to deny entry to the cold. I was also having trouble breathing, so I grabbed at my chest and tried to stretch it wider.

"You can't build a city in a place like this, you fool."

The words helped to pull my mind from the awful struggle. When I looked back to my companion on the bridge, I expected to see his expression wrung with sarcasm, for this must be some sort of imitation he was affecting—mockery of those who had doubted his vision. However, as I scoured that face, I noticed that it was not the same collection of sallow, patrician features. This figure was robust, imposing, and handsome. In fact, the whole shape of this man had changed, and while he was now not quite as tall, his body was decidedly broad and strongly built. Along with the strapping form, my phantasmal companion had high ruddy cheeks, a powerful bearded jaw, and striking dark eyes that radiated charisma. Most notably, he possessed a great lion's mane of silver-blond hair, which, despite having no crown upon it, in every way painted a portrait of a sovereign. This was no longer King Aurellis Kaennamin. I was standing face-to-face with the High Lord of Hell's Labyrinth, Beranardos Sherdane.

If, but a moment before, I had been infused with a sense of reverence, tempered only by the sting of my idol's misunderstanding, I was now suddenly flooded with a staggering onslaught of guilt, tempered by nothing. Except, perhaps, self-loathing. Staring at the regal figure of High Lord Sherdane, healthy and vibrant, addressing me directly, I was heartbreakingly present to the impossibility of this meeting. The details were hazy, but I understood, on the most core level, that I was the one responsible for destroying him.

"You're crazy to attempt it," said Sherdane, ostensibly picking up where he had left off. This statement was just strange enough to pull me temporarily out of my swirl of self-condemnation.

I was crazy to attempt it? I was a fool to build a city in such a place? There seemed no logical way to interpret this, other than to observe that this king was just as mixed up as the other one. In fact, he seemed to think I actually *was* the other one, for even the most uneducated street urchin in the Wags knew that it was King Aurellis Kaennamin who had commissioned the dramatic expansion of Sullward six centuries earlier. He was the "fool" who had made that decision. How could Sherdane mistake a rogue like me for a great man like that? Damn if this whole dream sequence wasn't getting confusing.

Indeed, I did now start to grasp that I was in a dream, or, as I conceived it then, I was wallowing in some in-between place from which I was soon to be ejected. As to where I was headed next, I could not say. But it was bad. It was unspeakably bad, and it behooved me to stay in this confused place a bit longer if possible. Only pain and cold and cataclysm and death lay in the other place. Sherdane the corpse lay there. Sullward the fallen realm lay there. Vazeer the Lash, the treasonous killer, the one in whom faith had been poorly placed, into whom irrational aspirations had been invested, that godsforsaken man was right now thrashing around in that other place. And who in hell would wish to get back to being him?

Around me, the dream cityscape remained intact, with Kaennamin Academy still soaring in the background, and the crenelated majesty of the other buildings standing strong. However, cracks were forming in my world. From below, the dark waters began to surge and spit, sloshing up over the cobbles of the bridge, rinsing across my boots. And the sky above had changed from a foggy morning gray to ominous black. It veritably broiled up there with billows of threatening darkness churning and heaving over each other, ready to belch out a torrent. My companion was still with me on the phantom bridge, and I threw my attention at him as a shepherd throws a lasso over the neck of an errant lamb. He was the key to my staying tethered to this reality a little longer, to hoisting myself out of a far more terrible place. Or so I thought. Once I looked at him more closely, I really had to wonder if I was better off letting go of the rope.

I was, as it turned out, no longer in the presence of a king, legitimate or otherwise, nor was I face-to-face with greatness. I now confronted a man whose brand of vision did not build cities or rule clever outlaw empires, but which devised murderous ways to eliminate both. Sure enough, my dream companion had transformed one last time, and this change was by far the worst.

The new figure was a bit shorter than both of his predecessors, and his build appeared unremarkable—neither broad and strapping like the High Lord, nor tall and boney like King Aurellis. He wore a deep gray cloak with the collar up, and the two sharp points of it framed a head of neatly combed dark blond hair. He was attractive in a much less dazzling way than Sherdane, with a clean set of features, accentuated by a pair of absorbing green eyes. Having just taken the unpleasant journey from reverence down into a morass of guilt, my feelings made one last torturous maneuver on the night's emotional highway. Suddenly, I found myself completely and utterly enraged.

How and why the infernal spook known as Radrin Blackstar made it to my conference of great rulers, I couldn't begin to guess, but there he was standing calmly before me on that faltering phantasmal bridge. His demeanor in this place was as it always was—placid, vigilant, and devoid of any recognizable human emotion. The mere sight of him filled me with loathing.

"You!"

At last, a sound out of my own lips in this sequence of dream interviews. A rather hoarse and gurgled sound, conveying a single word, which, if my memory served me, was the exact poetic utterance I made the last time Blackstar approached me alone in the Sullward streets. Something about this man robbed me of my eloquence.

"You have received confirmation, Vazeer," said Radrin in that unperturbed voice of his, and he nodded towards my right hand. "I have now completed the first part of our contract."

I glanced down at my hand to see what game this eerie bastard was playing, and I was surprised to find that I clenched an item tightly in my fist. When I opened it, I experienced something close to a vomit reflex. My hallucinatory form was perhaps poorly outfitted for such a base bodily function; however, my mind was well equipped to experience a spasm of pure revulsion. In my palm was a sticky mass of crimson blood, smeared like jam over a small gold object. It took me a moment to realize that I was still holding Sherdane's bloody throat brooch, but once I did, the entire evening came back to me with a thunderous roar. That which had remained nebulous now sharpened into perfect clarity—the exact manner in which the High Lord died and my own role in the affair, not to mention all the painful episodes that had come before it. I also, at last, understood the awful cataclysm that was occurring in that "other place," for in my mind's eye I could picture the icy surge of water sweeping towards me across a bloody flagstone floor. Perhaps I didn't grasp the precise nature of the storm that was right now driving those waters, but it hardly mattered. A great calamity had come, and I was in the middle of it.

Even with my memories restored, I still remained in the dream world a bit longer. Now, however, the black hallucinatory skies finally began to disgorge their watery load, and rain sheared down in livid sheets. A fierce wind rose in the alleyways, beating our cloaks and lashing our hair about our faces. In but seconds, Radrin and I were soaked, and he took a step closer to me, presumably to be better seen and heard in the storm.

"As I said, Vazeer, part of our contract is fulfilled," he said without raising that cool voice of his. I could somehow hear it perfectly.

"But you commissioned more on this bid," he continued. "We must now get on to the next phase."

What in the name of Eresis was he up to now? Was this spook implying I was the proffer on this job?

"The Raving Blade put out this contract, you miserable ghost!" I spat, finally regaining some articulacy. "And you are the one who did his bloody bidding."

Radrin slowly shook his head, which, like mine, was drenched, with his hair plastered over parts of his face.

"Mere transactions," he said. "All just part of your dream."

This comment truly took me aback.

"My dream?"

Radrin nodded.

"None of those awful things happened in a dream," I said, feeling the great sadness returning suddenly to replace the anger. "I wish they had. Then I could awaken, and they would all be gone."

"Oh, but they did happen in your dream," he answered, and there was the hint of an elusive smile on his face. "Your *mad* dream, that is."

Then, quite unexpectedly, that partial smile broke into a full grin. To say the expression was out of character wildly understates the issue, for this customarily staid, unemotional being appeared positively friendly in that moment. In contrast to his former self, as well as the two dour men who had appeared on this bridge before him, Radrin Blackstar radiated a warm, almost familial manner, as if he and I were the dearest of friends, or even brothers.

"Now, Vazeer," he said, in a newly affable voice, "let's you and I summon forth the means."

And with that, Radrin's wicked dagger suddenly emerged from his cloak, and he moved it with such fiendish speed that I simply could not react in time. Up it came, whipping towards my neck, carving the air in a quick dreadful arc. The dagger cut cleanly across my jugular in just the place where the High Lord's had been opened, and, horrifyingly, open it did. I felt an awful clenching pain in my throat, and as I lurched to grab the wound, cold fluid began to flow out. It veritably gushed, spraying in all directions, a gruesome second rainstorm emerging out of my body. Stronger and stronger it grew by the instant. I choked and coughed, staggering and clutching, but the gash could not be closed, and the deluge could not be stopped.

I have read that you cannot die in a dream. I don't remember which book it was, or why this conventional wisdom exists, but I can tell you that on the night of the Narrow Bid, in my flood-induced delirium, I did experience a death of sorts. In fact, I witnessed it. The departing soul is said to gaze down upon the body one last time as it escapes (perhaps this is from that same book), and I must say this is not far removed from what I experienced. Suddenly I was outside of all that was transpiring with that dream body, and while I can't exactly say I was "above" the scene, I had a very clear perspective of the little scar-faced Grell Runner in the black clothing who was wildly seizing his throat. There he was on that graceful stone bridge, surrounded by beautiful buildings, dying entirely alone. Radrin was nowhere to be seen. The others who had come earlier were gone as well. The only other thing moving near that undignified little man was the seething gout of liquid spilling out of his neck. I could see it quite vividly, and the sight was monstrous.

The blood wasn't red. It was a deep charcoal gray, like the river Grells, like the raging North Derjian Sea, and it spewed out of the dying figure with such force that in a matter of seconds the canal was overflowing, filling the bisecting street, submerging the bridge. Soon the little thrashing man was lifted upon the floodwaters, and his body was driven along the rushing canal like waste down a gutter. He was swept right towards the looming majesty of Kaennamin Academy, and by the time his body reached that place, the waters were so high that they slammed into the building with destructive force. Windows and doors collapsed before the onslaught; the flood plowed inside and through the great edifice. Elsewhere I saw other portals succumbing, including the entire row of arched doors to Nengriant Basilica, which caved in simultaneously. The windows above shared the same fate. All around, mighty buildings were breached and battered, glass exploded, wooden doors and outbuildings were swept away like brittle leaves upon the Grells. This terrible deluge was only just getting started.

It was around this time that I awakened. If the transition into the dream world had been a smooth one, then this reemergence was anything but. It was horrible, really. One moment I was in my disembodied perspective, hovering apart from it all, watching the little man getting whisked around the Drover Theater. I saw him spin past the long-vacant playhouse down a narrow side street, which had become like a sucking drain. The surge was now breaching a new pocket of the neighborhood, and the force of the pull was so strong that the scar-faced man was dragged under. Down he went, disappearing quickly below the turbid surface. This time, instead of remaining above it all, my perspective was forcibly drawn under the water, tugged right into the cold, murky depths where that poor wretch floundered. No longer was I the departing spirit. I was, instead, right there in the mind and body and struggles of that man, knowing his panic and pain, trying to hold my breath a little longer, feeling the oppressive weight of the freezing waters pressing in from all sides. I just needed one breath. I just needed to breach that gray, shifting surface, wherever it lay, for that was the only chance I had of survival.

Then I broke free. My face split the surface of the water; my mind shook loose from the dream. I was gasping and coughing madly. My physical body felt beaten, drained, and limp. It has occurred to me subsequently that I did, in fact, die in that flood, at least temporarily. Such things are known to happen, and these episodes are no doubt the source material for that book I can't quite remember. I am aware that people do get revived on occasion, and they are among the few who can report on the first part of the trip to the great beyond. Was my little segment of the journey some strange parade of presumptuous figures who all had me confused with someone else? After all, a pathologically vain man like me would certainly have his dying spirit ascribing all sorts of powerful agency to himself that he does not possess. My living self knows full well that I don't run a damned thing, nor have I ever built a city. And, as the Dark Gods are my witness, I have never put out a contract on anybody, especially not the High Lord of Hell's Labyrinth.

Finally, it goes without saying that I did not summon a freak natural cataclysm, a meteorological disaster that no human being has the power to command. Pure deluded vanity, all of it; with perhaps a hefty pinch of survivor's guilt.

With my mind and body now fully back in the real world, I found that I was being swept along by a terrific current. I was outdoors somewhere, exposed directly to the storm, and, above and around me, the maelstrom howled its black celestial wrath, with rain driving sideways through the dark air and the shrieking wind forming whitecaps on the water as far as the eye could see. In fact, I would have believed myself far out at sea, if not for the fact that all about me I saw the upper portions of grand buildings. I was flowing past them quickly, watching a steady procession of crenelated parapets, tourelles, spiked cupolas, and corner turrets. At one point I came very close to a big bronze eagle atop a coned tower, but it was just out of reach, and I was shuttled along without being able to grab hold.

But that was what I needed to do, grab on to the top of some building, hoist myself out of the surging drink. I recognized several of the building crowns, including that eagle, and as best I could tell, the floodwaters were now pushing me back in the direction of the sea. I had read several accounts of the first Great Storm, and in that event, as appeared to be the case now, the initial surge had flowed from the northwest into Sullward Harbor, where it was funneled straight up the river Grells. Once the river and the salt marsh were fully inundated, the force of the downflowing river pushed the invading waters back into the Lower City from the northeast, which meant I was now flowing towards the center of the city and then eventually back into the ocean. I would, of course, perish from the cold long before I had to worry about being swept away, and though I was considered quite a freak of nature by my fellows, able to remain in unspeakably cold water for unspeakably long periods of time, I couldn't do this forever. The elements would defeat me in the end, just like anyone else. So, I began desperately looking for some tall building, some indomitable structure that would survive this flood and give me refuge throughout the remainder of the storm.

I heard my safe haven before I saw it. Through the screaming wind and the spitting foam, over the sound of my own coughing and gasping, I detected a dull reverberating tone, which called out to me like a buoy bell. As the seconds passed, it grew louder, and somehow wilder, rising from a muffled drone into a steady resonant gonging, and finally a sharp, manic clangor. It didn't take me long to realize what it was. The storm must have snapped the brass chains that shackled the bell to the complex mechanisms inside the tower and, with this abrupt emancipation, the enormous chime was set free to ring out its alarm and heartbreak. I could hear the clapper crashing about riotously inside that ancient iron cone, bawling irately as the city around it died.

Then suddenly it went still. Only the shrieking of the wind remained, and I knew the clapper must have suffered one crazed concussion too many before breaking off. But it had done its job, for I was now in range, and this caused a numb, ailing smile to cross my lips. Rising nobly before me amid the thunderous winds and juddering waters was the iconic Sullward Clock Tower. I could see its square citadel shape looming in the storm, its great spear-like peak rising to the black heavens, and I knew it would only take one last burst of effort, perhaps a dozen powerful strokes, and I could reach it.

Somehow, Vazeer the Lash might actually survive this terrible night. He just had to raise himself up into that beautiful spire, the one that dwelled at the top of his sunken world, where two centuries after the first great disaster, the mighty bell of Sullward had fallen deathly silent once again.

18

RESURRECTION

The strangest of sensations awakened me. It was warmth, caressing my face with an affection and a gentleness that this dark life of mine had never afforded me, that my own mother clearly lacked, for in jettisoning the task before her, she showed how little she understood of the baffling miracle called life. If only some softer woman and some brighter land had greeted me here upon arrival. If only the warmth had reached me from the start, that I might have flourished and burgeoned, standing proud to the sky like a stately oak. Such are the possibilities for the lucky few who are wanted. Such is the vast potential of a human life; a human life that begins correctly.

When I finally opened my eyes that morning, I found it difficult to see anything. I have dwelled so long in a world of thick mists and oppressive darkness, adapting to it like a nocturnal creature from the marsh, yet the veil before me then was of a completely opposite nature. It was stunning clarity and brightness that assaulted me. It was a disorienting onslaught of sight.

With great difficulty, I had managed to make it to the Clock Tower the prior night and, after an arduous climb right up the face of the clock, I had reached the belfry where I sprawled out on the flat sill directly beneath the wildly swinging, clapper-less

Sullward bell. Thus, a good twenty feet above the flood and partially sheltered from the elements, I had huddled up in a tight ball and waited out the remainder of the storm. Somewhere in the wee hours of the morning, as the rain was slowing to a mere drizzle and the winds were starting to die, I finally drifted off into a mercifully dreamless slumber.

But now I was awake. Awake, damp, partially injured, but apparently alive (this last one I say with a caveat). For what sort of place was this where sight itself was blinding me? What was this bizarre brightness that engulfed me when I stared out from the sheltering belfry to the wide space where my city should have been?

Reflections assailed me first—glinting pieces of light and color that spread before my eyes in a myopic rainbow. With enough squinting and blinking, I eventually brought form to the formless, and I detected shapes that, at least in a general manner, made sense to me. I saw winding contours, I saw tall, sharp pinnacles, I saw the tracery of a great city, its towers and jutting edifices, its twisting avenues, lithe arches, all far more visible than they should have been. And how strange it all looked. How heavenly.

Among my sizeable collection of books are several tomes on the religious beliefs of the Mid Derjians. Quite a few sects prevailed in the Tergonian Midlands before the Dawn of Reason, and while their traditions varied somewhat, they were all fairly consistent in their descriptions of the celestial abodes of the gods. These were the grand locales where deserving souls were said to go after death and, for whatever reason, such places were described as vast, resplendent cities in the sky. My imagination has never been particularly captive to religious mythology, reserving its full intensity for those things that have actually occurred, or still might; however, the vividness with which the great ethereal cities are described has had at least a small impact on my psyche. Enough so that on the morning of 29 Dekharven, year 213, I did indeed wonder if this was where I had gone.

What element, I tried to gauge, had been painted here in such abundance? Why were my perceptions so weirdly altered, leading me to believe, if only for a short while, that I had passed on to the next world…and that somehow the process had turned out much better than expected? In the end the answer was quite simple. For the first time that I could ever remember, the sun was shining brightly over my city. It veritably blazed in a perfectly cloudless sky.

And that sky was everywhere. It was above the buildings, it was also below them, it could be seen in sharp slivers through the alleyways, and at the same time it filled the spaces once dominated by the canals. The gray upon gray upon black upon stone that had always constituted mass in my world was now suddenly aerated and penetrated by lovely rivulets of azure blue. Where else could I be if not above the clouds?

So, I looked a little closer, and now I started to solve the odd celestial mystery. What I had been perceiving as sky below was, in fact, water. Five to ten feet of water everywhere, reflecting the gorgeous cerulean awning of the sky. The sheer brightness of it all! It is almost impossible for me to capture in words the full dramatic effect of that strange light splashed across the upturned face of my city. Glazed with the moisture of the sea, each gabled roof, each crenellated tower, each cornice and frieze, each spire and each dome, was like a glistening profile of some greater anatomy. Never had I seen it all at one time in this way. Only in my fondest visions had I imagined the full sweeping panorama of the once and future glory known as Sullward.

That image remains in my mind to this day, though the waters have receded and so much has transpired since then. When I first awakened that morning, I saw none of the true damage, none of the devastating loss of life, none of the ruined homes. Nor could I even conceive of the terrible, dark battles that were soon to be fought, all the vicious scores to be settled. A whole world of skullduggery and labyrinthine machinations were about to unfold in the wake of Sullward's second great cataclysm, but in that moment on that Clock Tower, I saw and knew only that which was before me. I didn't even realize that in less than forty-eight hours the dark clouds and choking mists would return, replacing my new scintillating heaven with the old, gloom-shrouded byways of Hell's Labyrinth.

Reaching down into the collar of my damp tunic, I fished around for an object that had been lightly poking my skin. After some fumbling, I pulled forth a small gold item, one that I vaguely remembered secreting in that spot as I floundered in the deluge. In my hand was the High Lord's octagonal throat brooch. The morning sun was still rising, so its rays were easily reaching me below the eaves of the belfry roof, and as they fell upon the piece, they glinted lightly across its elaborately carved maze pattern, causing the little purple-red diamond in the center to sparkle softly. I realized that this brooch had likely never before been touched by pure sunlight. How clean it was now, without a trace of blood or stickiness upon it. Was it possible that the crime itself had been wiped clean in the same manner? This small token was my proof to the proffer that I had completed the contract, but perhaps nobody else ever needed to know. The Swell Driver had swept away so many things; why not this terrible misdeed as well?

While I was at it, might I dare to imagine that the dark phantom known as Blackstar had been dispatched in the same manner, been cleansed from this world so that his days of seducing me into collusion were over? How delightful it would be if that grotesque dagger of his never again wound up in some poor bastard's throat.

Soon, of course, I would need to scale down from the tower and find out what truly awaited me. I did not relish that prospect. Nor did I wish to leave a stunning vantage where all of my ludicrous ideas still seemed possible, so I gazed out one last time and seared the vision into my mind.

Before me beamed the grinning morning gold of the unhindered sun, setting the intricate byways of my Labyrinth aglow; beneath me swam the misplaced waters of the Derjian Sea, mirroring the sky. Around me lay a city about which I, in my endless, deluded fantasies of resurrection and rebirth, had only dreamed.

Certain dreams, I've since learned, should be handled carefully. For the mad ones, the recklessly grand ones, can sometimes come dangerously true.

PART

III

19

REFLECTIONS

How my home pulls at me.

Separated from it, I recalled its sweet stone and wood anatomy, mollifying and curative, felt it slumbering in its chosen place, its one and only place, where I currently was not. These thoughts consumed me that morning after I shook free of my reverie on the Clock Tower. More than anything in all the world, I simply wanted to go home.

I suppose my situation could have been worse. The surge path along which I'd been shuttled like a piece of debris had driven me straight out of the Lower City and into the municipal Middle City where the tower lay. The ground was higher here. And all around the floodwaters were already retreating, slithering quietly back into the shining monster that had spit them forth. That sea, with all its heaving peril, was at least good at taking back its discharge, and the properly pitched streets and well-constructed canals sent the watery load promptly back to its source.

By the time I finally scaled down from the belfry, then jumped the final ten feet, I splashed heavily into water that only came up to my chest. And it was dropping even as I stood. The water was cold but somehow not terribly cold, and I could only guess that sunshine, that strange new visitor to our land, had already begun to warm it. In this way, I began my trek back to 27 Fletcher Street.

It did not take me long to reach a point in the Middle City where I could get my feet solidly beneath me and start a tired, sloshing walk. To my right was the columned white block of the Sullward Courthouse, and a ways beyond that I saw the imposing gray fortress of the Imperial Garrison. My clothing clung mud-like to my body, and my legs bumped against things below the rippling skin of the water. Taking a deep breath, the fumes of the sea assailed me, their stinging salinity crawling deep inside my lungs, and all around the damage began to make itself known—bobbing barrels, scraps of wood, unidentifiable uphol-stered things that spun slowly in the water like dead animals. There were real animals too, though these mostly lived, and in addition to seeing two bristled cats staring down at me from a balcony, I heard a dog barking fiercely from a rooftop, though I could not catch sight of it anywhere.

I moved on and reached the outer fringes of Dockside, where I encountered my first corpse. She was a thickly built woman, floating facedown in an alley, her hair splayed wide like seaweed. I saw others too, or so I believe, but their sodden, cloth-shrouded forms were far enough away that I could tell myself they were something else. Pedestrians were just starting to emerge from their homes. The waters had receded sufficiently that some of the ground-floor doors could be utilized, but in most cases, people climbed out of windows, and the faces I saw were vacant and stunned. An eerie pall hung over the city.

I made my way to the fringes of White Hill, sluicing through the ever-shallower waters, gripping walls to stabilize myself, feel-ing my weapons catch on things half-submerged. I passed several pedestrians, one of whom was an older man who wept openly as he approached, but he walked past unseeingly as if I were a ghost. I made a turn off my chosen track, my only turn, for there was one thing I needed to check before heading home. I brought myself to the head of the Virtuoso.

Merejin's stately brown building was only a few doors down, and I was able to quickly determine what I had hoped was true: the flood's dark stain line rose only three quarters of the way up the ground floor, as it did on all of these buildings, which meant that Merejin was safe. Despite her aged legs, my dear friend kept her bedroom on the third floor, and she was rather punctual about her bedtime. She would have been nestled away up there when the surge struck. Even her books would have been spared, for her tall front stoop ensured that the main library was well above the street.

Tattered wreckage of all varieties floated in the waist-high water along the Virtuoso, though much of it had likely been swept in from other parts of the city. Still, I could tell the ground-floor shops had taken damage. I didn't need to see Jaspar Marzan's manic form to know he was probably having a fit this morning, as the main showroom of his grand Emporium was only a few feet above the cobbles. Standing artifacts would have suffered a nasty beating, but his wall-mounted items, including my cherished house clock, would have almost certainly survived.

Closer at hand I could see the shattered front window of Wind and Strings where the wrought iron muntins clung to but a few jagged stalactites of glass. The pretty engraved sign hung at a crippled angle. Annaliese kept many of her lovely instruments on the walls; however, this was not universally true, for I had first spotted my captivating and entirely useless harbeen lounging seductively on her maple floorboards. I prayed that the shy young woman had the wherewithal to hoist some of those beauties out of harm's way before the true damage struck. I turned and headed for the most important artifact collection of all.

While I knew 27 Fletcher would survive, it was still a moment of overwhelming relief when I reached the intersection of Fletcher and Gale and first spotted her. Glistening white and wet in the strange brilliance of this day, my home basked beneath the unlikely rays as if she were a granite queen. Her swans and fluting, the gentle curve of her third-floor balcony, and the high arches of her windows were, in that moment, so much more than architectural details. They were friends, my most enduring companions, for the prior night had shown me how quickly all else could be swept away.

I trudged through standing water until I was able to shuffle up the six steps of my stoop. Others were starting to move about on the street, and I saw Cassia Bellim from 31 Fletcher leaning heavily on the railing of her own steps, gazing out over the fulgent new dimensions of our world. Cassia had always been just a little nicer to me than my other neighbors, and when she turned my way, I gestured to her warmly. She exhaled affectedly and slid her hand over her heart, suggesting, it seemed, that relief must be the one and only response for those of us who had chosen this neighborhood as our own.

She was right, for the stain line was even lower here than in the Virtuoso, rising but a third of the way up the lower level of these houses. This meant that only basements would be flooded. When I stared up at my windows, I saw that the shutters had mostly done their job, with only one set having ripped off, allowing the glass in the lower pane to shatter. How differently the Swell Driver had treated White Hill from the treasure-stuffed necropolis where I had endured the night. Without the bludgeoning force of the surge, this neighborhood, and to a lesser extent the adjoining Virtuoso, had simply been subjected to a very bad storm.

I thought of the Wags, and without even seeing it, I knew the devastation that had been wrought upon the neighborhood of my youth. While topographically higher than Dockside, the flimsy structures that jammed the area would have splintered like children's toys before the deluge, transforming that place into a choked field of jagged wooden shards and filthy daub. Of course, this was not true of Holod Deadskiff's Broodhouse. While the water may have come up to the ceiling in the ugly granite barracks where I had been raised, the building itself would have repelled the surge. Holod and all his little Broodlings would have had time to scamper up into the attic before the ground floor flooded completely, and there were always the roof hatches if the waters climbed higher than that. For all these reasons, my mentor's physical safety didn't concern me; however, his emotional condition was something I was soon going to have to face. For now, I put that agonizing thought out of my mind.

Wrangling deep into the recesses of my clothing, I produced my keys—still dutifully shackled to their chain—then set about opening my many locks. Shortly after that, I swung the door open and stepped inside.

I have already described the sweet bouquet that always greets me upon return, and this day it was mostly so. There was the whiff of a rank wetness emanating from the flooded basement, and also perhaps from water damage upstairs where the window broke. But these smells were not overpowering. I locked the door and slid deeply into my home's affectionate embrace, feeling the heavy, granular protection of aged walls. I tore off my wet outer garments and hung them on cloak hooks. I quickly surveyed the first floor, then peeked down the staircase into the basement, which had transformed into a dripping grotto, complete with a dark lake. I secured that door and made my way to the pantry.

I stuffed down an entire smoked sausage, half a chunk of cheese, and pulled some droopy lettuce from the ice chest, along with a pitcher of ice water. I gorged ravenously for a while, then headed for my staircase. I was but a few steps up the first sweeping flight when I paused and leaned back against the curvature of the wall, craning towards the skylight. For years I had paid to have the large octagonal window kept pointlessly clean, an activity that elicited strange looks from the scrubbers, since the only thing that could possibly be seen when one looked skyward was a full and glorious spectrum of dingy grays. This expensive housekeeping detail did improve the incidental light, but I had yet to see anything of note beyond that iron-reinforced pane.

Until today.

Today the multi-faceted glass had become a luminous halo, a portal so vividly radiant that it seemed a source of illumination in its own right. It was as if, during the night, some divine entity had crept to my home, cut a swatch straight from the sky, and affixed it here as an inspirited gem. I simply gawked for several minutes, my eyes swimming upwards into the azure heights before I finally peeled myself from the wall and resumed my climb.

The moment I reached the second floor, I drew water for my bath and sparked a flame in the underlying wood stove. After that I went to check on things, starting with the broken window in my second-floor hallway. I used the partially soaked runner rug to swab up the remainder of the water, and I stuffed the rug into the open window, jamming it so tightly against the bars that I created a temporary buffer against the autumn air. A quick inspection of my art gallery and then my third floor showed that all was well. Then I shed the remainder of my clothing and crawled into the bath.

Slouched in the cleansing waters, growing ever warmer as the flames did their work, my mind began to wander. It was pleasant at first, for the tensions I had experienced in the last twenty-four hours had been so horrific as to defy description. And yet, with this balmy release I felt my thoughts venturing to places unbidden, felt them penetrating the exposed edges of things I was not yet ready to confront. Images geysered upwards from the pressured source—faces that made me flinch, pain that waylaid my passive mind, violence and treachery, cruelty and destruction. And below that, in the bubbling fountainhead where acidic currents spun, I sensed a whole world of personal regrets and sadness. It was down there that my worst fear lived, side by side with a meek and improbable hope. I was not ready yet for that one, so I slid upright in the bath to force my mind back into the room.

Beneath me I saw that the water had turned cloudy from blood. I grabbed a glass jar from an adjoining shelf and dumped a quarter of the powdered green contents into the tub. The sharp smell struck me instantly, wafting upwards into my nose like dock-mopping solvent and causing my eyes to water. A few seconds later I felt the sting set in, attacking my right hand, my wounded bicep, and an assortment of other cuts and lesions that I had not noticed until now.

Nettledown was the single most powerful healing agent yet developed, and it was so prohibitively expensive to those of us in the North that I had likely just dumped a field worker's entire yearly salary into my bloodied bath. The curative mix was an elaborate blend of southern herbs and root compounds that was ground, simmered, and then dried into a form that could be transported and stored without losing potency. Whenever a shipment came into the docks, the wealthiest Sullward physicians descended upon it first, but not far behind them were the Shadow Bidders and the Underlord retainers. I would guess that a full ten percent of my yearly income went towards Nettledown and a host of other restorative materials, not to mention those rare occasions when I simply could not treat myself and had to dump my entire purse into a physician's hand, before collapsing onto the stitching table. The doctors in this city were some of the best in the Empire, but you paid like a nobleman to get their services.

It took several cold rinses to wash all of the blood and Nettledown residue off of my skin, and then I set to work with the ointments. The bicep wound was ugly and would clearly leave yet another scar on the hatch-marked landscape of my body. My guess was that the arm would be back up to full capacity within days; however, my hand would take a little longer, as the combined burn, bruise, and slice was going to make it painful to use for another week at the very least. I applied a series of salves and creams to the spots I could reach, and then I bandaged the two main injuries.

Finally, I headed to my bedroom. The Clock Tower had remained mute since that final battering concussion stole its voice, and I could only guess it was somewhere around First Bell. My room was flooded with sunlight, and the city's sounds were now starting to rise in earnest, with voices traveling from near and far. They were accompanied by splashing and pounding echoes, which shuttled to me via the new acoustics of our flooded streets, and yet, despite all of this light and activity, I fell heavily into bed. I stared up at the faded map on my hearth and tried to read Aurellis Kaennamin's inspired words, which seemed all the more puzzling, and perhaps even frightening, after what I had experienced. But I could not. My eyes closed like weighted shutters, and I slid off into a heavy, deadened sleep.

I awakened suddenly to the spectacle of bright orange flames engulfing my bedroom. I bolted upright, my fingers snatching at the brass edges of the bed, my eyes glancing first at the fireplace to see if this was the source of the crisis. It wasn't. I checked all of the wall braziers but remembered that I never lit them. For an alarmed interval, I sat stiffly in my twined, newly blood-streaked linens, gawking about at walls that were blazing and a ceiling that was rippling with brilliant strips of fire, and I tried to force my bumbling mind to plot an escape. As the seconds wore on and my chest continued to throb, and the rippling seemed to grow ever brighter and redder…nothing happened. None of my roof timbers collapsed, no thick, black clouds of smoke overwhelmed me. I sat in the middle of a dazzling inferno, yet I suffered none of the hallmarks of a true fire.

Was this another bizarre dream? Was this, possibly, my arrival at that final, punitive destination, where I had always belonged in the first place? Duly bewildered, I remained there several moments longer, until, on impulse, I lurched out of bed and over to the western window, throwing wide the drapes. There, at last, I discovered the source of the inferno.

I am aware that most residents of Derjia are blessed each day with an enchanting event known as a sunset. For the denizens of the northeastern Derjian coastline, especially in the vicinity of the misty marshlands of the river Grells, this is unfortunately not the case. We encounter, at best, a pink tinge in the western mists, which does little more than alert us that the deepest hours of Labyrinth darkness are soon to come. Perhaps every few months something resembling a sunset is visible to those who happen to catch it, but certainly nothing on the magnitude of what I saw in the late after-noon of 29 Dekharven, an event perhaps unwitnessed in Sullward since the autumn of Year One, when surviving residents gazed out of battered shutters and from puddled rooftops at a torrentially flooded world that had suddenly caught fire.

How strange it was to see water and flame combusting in this manner. Earlier that day as I sat on the Clock Tower, the synthesis of those two elements included the yellow light of the morning sun, which radiated rather than scalded, casting a beatific luminance upon the world. This thing I now witnessed from my window could only be described as apocalyptic. Flooded east-west streets like Gale raged as they conducted the red horizon all the way from the harbor to White Hill, while segments of the crosswise Fletcher veritably erupted wherever its southward course came unsheltered into the fireball's path. The mighty conflagration crawled up walls and timbers, set glass windows ablaze, caught gargoyles, swans, nymphs, dragons…all manner of statuary in its vermillion flames and finally seemed to leap skyward from hundreds of torched rooftops into the great dome of fire overhead.

Ashland Nuce is widely recognized as the Empire's premier landscape painter, and this is largely because of his extraordinary ability to render natural light. In this building I possessed two of his works, both depictions of the late-day sky glowing beneficently over Midland settings, and I must say (no offense to the departed Tergonian artist) those paintings had absolutely nothing in common with the frightening splendor I now witnessed outside my bedroom window. Perhaps in Tergon, or neighboring Abelein, across the wide expanse of the Tergonian Midlands, where the Empire's pedigreed families lorded over bucolic estates, maybe in these places the sun gave of itself in measured doses. But there was nothing measured about Hell's Labyrinth. After her mad natural laws smote us with the aggression of wind and sea, it was only fitting that she should haul from her arsenal of extremities a newly introduced sun that was of such a scalding red temperament as to set water to burning.

I don't know exactly how long I sat in my bedroom window seat. When the fireball at last submerged itself below the silhouette of the city, all that remained was a brushed yellow glow upon the western sky, coupled with small trails upon my sight from having gazed a little too long at the sun. But this was temporary, for I felt the opposite effect occurring within. The naked sky, torn free of mist, which had this morning awakened me into celestial hopes and this afternoon awakened me into infernal fears, was doing something very strange to my psyche. Obstructions inside were dissolving. An almost imperceptible crust upon my emotional foreground was breaking apart, and as this happened, I felt an unpleasant stinging in my throat, as if I had just gulped down tea that had not been allowed to cool. I couldn't tell exactly what the new feeling was, or which old things had been displaced, but the sting now moved up to my eyes, making them hot and damp. Something acute and painful was coming.

While this occurred inside, I became present to yet another outside phenomenon—a thing I had read about often and seen in paintings, though rarely witnessed myself. The sky became filled with stars. I spotted them first from my bedroom, then quickly threw on some clothes and rushed for a better view from my third-floor balcony.

I dragged out a chair and sat. Above me it seemed that a great net of diamonds glistened, its pattern stretched out across the wide black ocean of the cosmos as if engaged in a massive night trawl. In keeping with the day's earlier mischief with reflections, I could see a section of Fletcher Street that produced a dim recreation of the speckled sky, again lifting me to a soaring perch from which even constellations could be witnessed below.

And here, with this finale in the day's sequence of celestial wonders, the mysterious stinging identified itself. I was, all at once, seized with a profound and overbearing loneliness. It was as if a cavernous hole had opened inside of me, which seemed perfectly mirrored by the dotted blackness above. The sheer distance of those stars, and the cold vastness that separated them, made me all the more present to a crippling feeling of isolation. Into this space arose images of the ones I had lost.

Flerra's face came first. I wanted to picture her as I had usually seen her—annoyed or bored, puckering her mottled cheeks into a rebellious mask. It would have been nice to imagine that Flerra who had always been both unreasonably difficult and impossibly competent, who, despite all the trouble she gave me, could not hide the fact that she prized me as her older brother. But that's not what I saw. Instead, I pictured her ghostly features quivering in agony as the blood drizzled down her pallid flesh.

Suddenly I began to weep. The tears swilled up from inside, and I simply could not stop them, and while I controlled the sounds somewhat, I was unable to suppress the terrible grief that spat from my guts and spewed out of my eyes and gagged at my throat and made me shudder all the way down to my toes. Mixed with my own pain were thoughts of Holod, and how utterly I had failed him. Such a terrible heartbreak awaited my mentor, and the mere thought of it only made my own feelings worse.

At the same time, images that were not as personal came to mind, but these somehow stirred me almost as much. I thought of Beranardos Sherdane. I did not delude myself that the High Lord had been a good man, nor did I imagine that he would have been particularly forgiving had his soldiers actually caught me. However, that wasn't the side of him that consumed me. Instead, I thought of how deeply and hopelessly the man had been in love.

It was love that had brought Sherdane down to the tunnel where he died. It was love that made him foolish and petulant, then disconsolate and lost, and, in remembering his laments and wheezing sobs, I found that I related to it all. The prior night I had been mortified, but not now, for in my stark openness, Sherdane's anguished need for his countess was the most logical thing in the world. She, whom he had coerced into the nightmare by an act of pride, dragged from the shining courts of Tergon where theater and art and literature still thrived, a true aristocrat, not a self-assumed one...how desperately he pined to see her again. How badly he wanted to beg her to forgive him for making such a terrible mistake.

This brought me, at last, to the most disturbing thought of all, something that demanded resolution, even though I knew the resolution might crush me. I needed to find out what happened to Nascinthé of Levell. I had sent her out into that marshland, shoved her into the path of the storm. Had I simply gone with her as I should have, as any sane man would have, then we would have sped quickly to the stone embankment and made it to Droden's protected cove. But I didn't do that, and as a result I suspect my Masque undertook her own heroics, led the High Lord's soldiers on a protracted chase. If this was true, and I was sure it was, then she would not have exited the marsh in time to avoid the surge. Lingering too long, she would have died frightened and alone out there, submerged beneath the cold weight of the North Derjian Sea.

And for what? How, exactly, had I used her sacrifice? To commit a terrible act of treason. To save my own life too, I suppose, but that suddenly didn't seem like such a worthwhile prize. As I sat there on that balcony, sniffling and blubbering, staring up at a measureless scattering of brilliant white sparks, it all seemed pointless. What was the use of witnessing these wonders by myself? How many years had I lived in solitude, hunkered down in my fortified museum, sharing my experiences with no one?

I had only known Nascinthé of Levell for a short time, but already the feelings of connection I experienced at the mere thought of her were staggering. Her ethereal face, haunted and beautiful, evoked a wild mix of terror and elation that was unlike anything I could remember experiencing. No woman of flesh and blood had ever caused this. My magnificent Giradera of Azmoul, poised for conquest in my second-floor gallery, had absolutely quickened my heart for a time. However, Emalia Zeltier's bronze creation had never caused me to fret terribly, nor did she make me flushed and dizzy.

All of these things were happening on that balcony as I recalled my series of enigmatic encounters with the Masque. In the boathouse, and significantly more so during our exchange in the Emporium, I had the unsettling sense that the woman was actually seeing me, seeing through me even, to the guarded things that lay underneath. On the Narrow Bid, Nascinthé told a room full of soldiers that there was a deep sensitivity hiding in my face, just beneath the scarred surface, and while at the time I thought this a mere masquerade, she later said otherwise. My fellow Sullwardians never saw these things. They were, quite understandably, halted by the rough flesh, hooked on the callous bait I fed them. But this foreign woman was not, and that touched me in ways that I simply cannot describe.

As the sadness swaddled my face like a wet bandage, I could only wonder if I would ever have that experience again. Either way, something needed to change, for I could no longer bear to be so alone. Nor could I allow myself to blunder into any further episodes of violence, a trend in my life that had to stop. All of this was as clear to me in that moment as the unobstructed night sky. Painful though it was to see it, I felt a strange sense of calm come over me with these thoughts.

It was somewhere around then that the team of Underlord soldiers stormed into my house and tried to kill me.

20

BROKEN THINGS

The attack was launched from the street directly below my balcony, and these men, unidentified to me at that point, tried to gain access via the very perch where I was lost in melancholic reverie. As I contemplated the starry infinite, and the profound transformation that it was inspiring within me, an improvised grappling hook clanged up over the slim wrought iron handrail that ran atop the parapet wall. It was followed a moment later by another. I was slow to even glance down when I heard the metallic scrape of the two hooks taking hold. Then, well before I became alarmed, my mind fixated on the fact that these weren't proper grappling hooks. They were actually gaff hooks, tied off to lengths of nautical rope, and this made sense really, for Underlord retainers spent much more time snaring smuggling boats and cargo than they did climbing into people's homes. I even noted that they had barbs, which was a smart choice. Most gaff hooks are unbarbed, but when the targeted object needs to be secured under difficult conditions, then some form of a spur is employed.

Interestingly, I know a great deal about this topic, for it was just such an implement that raked the vicious scar down the left side of my face. That one barbed gaff hook, the tool that opened my jaw and released a torrent of retribution and far-reaching consequences, resulted in actual changes to the precise role of the contract operative in Sullward. A whole host of legends were born, and the alias Vazeer the Lash was coined.

But I digress. We will get to that another time.

So, there I was, my swollen eyes squinting at the barbs on those two gaff hooks, listening to the quiet grunting of climbing men, and it took me a shamefully long time to register the sort of danger I was in. After all, didn't I deserve a pass at this moment? Given what our city had just suffered, not to mention my own newly invoked desire for personal growth, didn't this merit some sort of unspoken armistice? The men who came to murder me didn't appear to think so.

I have described many things about my magnificent Sarentine Triplex, presented a picture of its stately features and its artistic and intellectual treasures. What I haven't quite explained is the fact that over the years I have turned the building into a veritable fortress, one that would require siege engines to breach. Therefore, this team of resourceful Lower City killers, likely deterred by the two iron-bound castle-style doors to 27 Fletcher and the solid bars on all the windows, saw the great efficacy of a set of wide-open balcony doors. They must have arrived at some point during the sad musings of metaphysical Vazeer and, seeing no sign of the man himself, slouched back as he was in his woolen evening outfit and a pair of silk house slippers, they thought quick entry could be attained.

By the time my mind fully grasped what was happening, the first two soldiers had climbed within a couple feet of the balcony. They probably scaled part of the way up the first-floor façade before they even tossed the hooks, then sprinted up the ropes after that. I myself am quite a good climber, as a large portion of my profession involves scampering on and off of ships with no help from a gangplank, and I would have to give this team of anonymous assassins high marks for their speed. They came so quickly that I found myself faced with a critical decision before I could sit fully upright in my chair.

I was entirely unarmored and unarmed, having come to the balcony in a dazed state. I had no blade with which to cut the ropes, and the tension exerted on the hooks, coupled with those clever barbs, ruled out the possibility of hoisting the gaff heads off of the railing. So little time remained before those first two men made it up and over the parapet that were I to attempt to free the glass balcony doors from their latched positions inside my study, close and lock them, and then fasten the security bars, I would likely take a blade in the gut for my efforts. Finally, if I dashed inside for my own spade, these men would complete their climb and I would find myself facing them on a level play-ing field. Over the years, I had learned that level playing fields weren't exactly my specialty.

Therefore, I reached for the only weapon available to me on that balcony, which was none other than the chair beneath my backside. Jumping upright, the snotty grief still drying on my nose, I swept the piece of furniture over my head and waited breathlessly for the lead climber's face to appear over the railing. I would shat-ter it onto him first, then use what remained on the others.

Let's pause here a second. I need to say a few words about that chair.

It is true that I take all of my possessions quite seriously (too seriously, it could be argued) and while an original work of art garners a more elevated place in the hierarchy than, let's say, a piece of furniture, it is also fair to say that not all furniture is cre-ated equal. This chair I was holding was not some creaky piece of

Dockside crap that I had snatched up from one of the local vendors. It was an original creation from Havlec Chiselwright, the best craftsman in the best furniture market on the best street in all of Sullward. I had spent hours on the quaint Virtuoso working with Havlec to perfect that design. This chair was arguably the most important seat in my house, dwelling as it did in my third-floor study, and thus the throne upon which I launched most of my cerebral wanderings.

In addition to the clever mechanism Havlec created to allow the chair to lever back into three carefully chosen positions of recline, it was also an absolute beauty to behold. With an elegant wingback top, and slender armrests that had just enough width and padding where my elbows rested to make it comfortable, the shape was grand without appearing stodgy. Yet it was the upholstery that lifted this chair within striking distance of being art. I had searched long and hard in the warehouses of my favorite fabric merchants before I was struck with a moment of inspiration. On a whim, I shelled out a small fortune for an original Kaszian wall tapestry in Jaspar Marzan's Exotic Emporium of Fine Collectibles. The tapestry was meaningful to me, as I had personally smuggled it up the Grells, and I had actually fought off a pack of marsh brigands to get it and the rest of the cargo to the drop site. As far as I know, I didn't kill anybody in that encounter; however, there were a lot of the sorry scamps, and the rumors flowed afterwards that I slew at least four of them and left several others permanently crippled. Sheer nonsense. However, it further enhanced my already exaggerated reputation, and I had quite a bit less trouble with brigands thereafter.

So, when Havlec agreed to upholster my grand reading chair with this now storied red and gold tapestry, depicting a pre-imperial Kaszian coronation, and to set it off magnificently with hexagonal brass nail heads, I knew I was entering unique artistic territory. The project took over three months to complete, and the final price tag, including the tapestry, was an eye-popping thirty-four gold suldots. But it was worth it, every last diven. For, whenever I sat in that glorious red and gold chair, embraced by my shapely wingback, the graceful arms allowing me to effortlessly hold a book at the proper height, all the while with my body hinged back in the perfect state of recline, I was truly and utterly at home. The light musky smell of the tapestry-turned-upholstery reminded me of the risks I had taken to reach that place. The sheer cost and effort of the project told me that the best things in life never came without a sacrifice.

Therefore, you see, as I hoisted this so-called "weapon" over my head, it was about to bring as much grief to the man wielding it as the dirty scoundrel who was hauling his ass up that rope. Using that lovely chair like a common street thug's cudgel was beyond a mere indignity for me. It was a crime.

But it couldn't be helped, and use it I did. When that first suspicious face appeared over my railing—scowling, ugly, ruthless—I clubbed at it like a gaffed shark. Down whooshed my beautiful chair, a streak of night-muffled red and shaded gold, and it connected with a terrible splintering crash. Unfortunately, this lead climber was no fool, and he was not entirely unprepared for a defender on the ramparts. He wore a steel cap, which was highly unusual for an Underlord soldier, and though I couldn't quite imagine how he scrounged up such a piece on short notice, I had seen firsthand that Underlord storerooms were filled with all manner of equipment. This man clearly knew he might have to come at me from below. As a second inconvenience, the climber poked his face over that wall in such a cagey manner that the mere hint of my looming form must have alerted him, and his head instantly sucked back down again like a turtle retreating into his shell. He dropped below the protective buffer of the railing, causing the wrought iron to absorb much of my first strike. It wasn't enough to fully protect him, but it did result in more initial damage to my exquisite weapon than I had anticipated.

Ironically, or perhaps fittingly, it was Havlec's crafty hinged apparatus that doomed that man. I spent a lot of additional money to allow the chair to lever back in recline, so there was perhaps the faintest hint of justice when I saw the expensive mechanism torquing the heavy base around the obstructing railing to deliver the full crushing weight of the blow onto the soldier's back. He was swatted like a bug against the face of my building. Sadly, the entire bottom half of the chair broke off and tumbled to the street below; however, this nasty son of a bitch tumbled along with it. Sometimes we need to be grateful for the little blessings in life.

After that, lucky breaks came in shorter supply, and attackers came in greater numbers. I was left holding the back of the chair, a relatively inconsequential weapon for the remainder of my defense, and a moment later, as the second climber popped up and over the railing, I found myself unable to halt his advance. I whacked uselessly at his armored back as he rolled over the parapet, all the while aware that there was still tension on the two ropes. More climbers were coming, more spades were scraping up my building. My chance of surviving this encounter was shrinking before my eyes, and I needed to do something quickly or I'd be dead inside of fifteen seconds.

With my pulse slamming violently, I gripped the shapely wingbacks of my injured chair and, as the rolling man below me tried to stand, I swung the remains of the device straight into the side of his head. Again, this is where Havlec's ingenious hinges came into play. The twisted metal that had once linked the two halves of the chair now gouged into the kneeling soldier's cheek and sent him spinning into the wall of my balcony, leaking a blotchy trail of blood across my slate.

That was my last victory on the balcony. With the brightly speckled sky winking above, and the nomadic ocean waters twinkling below, I watched as the next two men came over the railing simultaneously. The ropes were spaced about ten feet apart, and there was simply no way to deal with them both at once, so I flung the remnants of the chair at one of them, slowing him briefly, then retreated back into my study with the other attacker directly on my heels.

I still didn't know who these men were. The first four were all dressed in the same nondescript gray and black apparel customarily worn by Underlord soldiers; however, I did note something interesting: the man chasing me through the balcony doors had a bandage around his head, with blood clearly leaking through the gray cloth, while the fellow just behind him had a gauzy white sheet tied around one arm. These soldiers had experienced combat in the last twenty-four hours. Had the battle for High Lord succession already begun?

The man on my heels had drawn a spade with his right hand, and I could see his other hand fumbling for a stiletto at his thigh. He looked like a fighter in his prime, with an angry, weathered face and an athletic build, and I sensed that this would not go well for me if he got that other weapon drawn. Therefore, I did the only logical thing: I grabbed the longest, heaviest object within reach and swung it straight for that bloody head bandage. The attack played out reasonably well; however, it came at a terrible cost, for the object in question was none other than my beloved harbeen.

I have already taken the time to relay my feelings about my

now-deceased reading chair. I won't belabor the other culturally significant casualties of that battle, but virtually every blow I struck that night inflicted a wound in both directions. The gently curved Inland Kingdom instrument known as a harbeen has a long hollow shaft with small finger holes and a heavy solid base, which is meant to rest on the floor while being played. I fell in love with it because of its exotic, quasi-aboriginal appearance; however, after several cacophonous attempts to blow into it, I realized the only way to protect the serenity of my neighborhood was to mount it high on the wall of my third-floor study. Apparently, it was still a threat.

I grabbed the harbeen by its shaft and swung it overhead with all of my might. The soldier raised his spade to block the blow, but this merely broke the instrument's relatively weak shaft and allowed the heavy base to lever down straight at his wounded skull. It made a muffled snapping sound as it struck, a noise not unlike the dull crack I hear when I drop a piece of ice into a glass of lukewarm water. Something underneath that bandage fractured. The soldier went straight down to the floor, moaning; however (and I must give the bastard credit for this), he somehow managed to keep his grip on his spade, while his other hand tried to wipe the blood out of his eyes. On his knees, with a red curtain spilling across his face, the man swiped the spade around in front of him, clearly afraid that I would try to come and finish him off, which I would, because I wanted that spade. The busted shaft of my harbeen was useless. The soldier with the sheet tied around his arm was now shuffling over the step-down threshold of my study. I needed a proper weapon at this point if I had any hope of turning the tide here.

It would have been nice if I had mounted some ornate blades on the walls of my study. I had several pretty swords and daggers, and even an imperial halberd very tastefully displayed in my second-floor art gallery while, in my bed chamber, I kept weapons aplenty, most of them in my wardrobe, but some stashed conveniently near the bed in the virtually impossible event of a nighttime break-in. In the study, however, I had shied away from such imagery, a foolish lapse I have since remedied.

On that evening, all I could do was improvise one last time. I needed something big and heavy that could be rained down on the fallen soldier from several feet away, allowing me to finish him off as I kept away from his sweeping spade. The item I chose was not the most expensive or irreplaceable of the night's artistic armaments (every year or so one of these becomes available on the Virtuoso); however, for some reason it bothered me more than the chair and the harbeen combined. In fact, hoisting this one item over my head and using it to brain a man on the floor of my sacred study might conceivably have sent me into one of my blackouts. Perhaps the reading chair and the harbeen didn't quite rise to that level, but grabbing the smooth, marble bust of my lifelong hero King Aurellis Kaennamin, visionary genius and founder of the once and future cultural nexus known as Sullward, then launching it like a catapult stone at a man's head, might have brought on the void. Seeing that shiny, white-and-gray-veined, cleanly sculpted visage spinning through the air and making sickening contact with an underworld brute was certainly a form of tragedy. Regrettably, I remember it all.

I will spare you a description of what happened to that soldier, as the result was truly disgusting. Suffice it to say that I hit the target dead-on, as the man failed to even see the missile coming. This spelled the end of him, and also my plush tan and gold Engoliese rug, for obvious reasons. After that I dove for his spade, and while this was a dicey proposition with another soldier now in the room, it was worth the risk. I was running out of meaningful artifacts to heave at these men, so I snatched the blade and rolled on one shoulder out of the path of the next soldier's cut. He was somewhat impeded by the body of his fallen comrade, and he did seem to be wielding his spade clumsily, suggesting, perhaps, that the gauzy sheet was on his primary arm, leaving him to grip his blade in his off hand. Either way, he did manage to graze me across my side as I rolled, but it was more of a nasty scrape than a deep cut. Had I been wearing my leather-guard cuirass, it wouldn't have even made it to my skin.

Now we fought each other on equal terms, or relatively so. I wore no armor, but none of my wounds looked quite as bad as what I could now see was a major injury to his left arm, for the man seemed to be wincing as we circled each other. I glanced at his spiky brown hair, his stubbled face, his big, wide nose, and I had a fleeting moment of recognition. I had seen this man recently; in fact, I might have even fought with him. He must have been one of the guards I had encountered in the High Lord's compound, and whether he was among the men in the entry vestibule, or those who killed Fe Gesbon in the Ripening Hall, or quite possibly one of the soldiers who attacked me in the parlor where Flerra died, it didn't really matter. What mattered was that I now understood who these men were, and why they had come. This was retaliation, which was certainly justified.

But I would try to slaughter every last one of them, because what were the alternatives? I was pretty sure that I had blown any chance of diplomacy. I couldn't even imagine what I would say to them if I was given the opportunity (even if I somehow garbled out an explanation about the confused nature of the Narrow Bid, and Ulan Gueritus's trickery, it would leave too many difficult details exposed). These retainers would not easily believe the story of Sherdane's love affair with Countess Shaeyin Odel, and hearing it delivered out of my mouth would probably just make them angrier. No, the best bet was to continue doing what I was already doing, which was fight like a mad thing from Hell to destroy them.

My combat with the man with the wounded arm was not a pretty affair. He poked his blade at me a few times weakly, and I was able to easily deflect these thrusts with my spade. His other arm was obviously in pain from the strenuous climb up the rope, and he had seen the three men before him dispatched in a gruesome fashion, plus I could also only imagine what barbaric behavior he had witnessed in the High Lord's compound. Therefore, when I charged at him with sheer murder on my face and an animal snarl erupting from my lips, he took a step backwards and stumbled straight over the low jade tea table that he clearly didn't see behind him. That table always did have a habit of fading into the background, given the emerald curtains directly behind it. I've since moved it to a place where the subtle detail work can be better observed.

I plowed into the man's midsection, grabbing the wrist of his spade hand as he attempted an awkward, falling counterattack. We crashed together over the tea table, and once I was on top of him, it wasn't too difficult to get the edge of my spade up to his throat. My own hand hurt terribly, but not as bad as his arm seemed to be hurting him, and, in the battle of our respective injuries, his turned out to be worse. With a series of frenzied slices, I put a rather messy end to the fight.

Heaving myself off the floor, I dove towards the balcony doors, as yet another figure was entering my study. For all I knew, a half dozen more were about to come through those doors, so I launched myself at the newcomer with the same intensity I had unleashed on the others. In hindsight, I regret this. In hindsight,

I wish I had paused for a split-second to contemplate the fact that the man with the wounded arm had hardly been in a condition to scale the outside of a building, let alone fight, while the fellow before him with the bleeding head was only a little better off. Had I slowed my bullish charge just a little, I might have noted that the stranger entering my balcony doors did so tentatively, and while he was holding a slender short sword, he wore no armor. He also seemed very winded from his climb.

But my blood was up, so I didn't notice any of that, and I barreled right into him, swatting his sword out of the way with my spade and then driving my weapon directly into his abdomen. He fell back against one of my latched balcony doors, then slid to the floor, dropping his sword and clutching his guts. I pulled my blade free and sprinted onto the balcony, the bloodied spade held before me, but there were no more attackers. Instead, I saw the man whose face I had gouged with the back of my chair disappearing over the railing. I ran and tried to swipe at him, but he slid quickly down the rope, and by the time I managed to cut the thick nautical cord, he was less than ten feet over the ground. He must have felt the rope weakening, for he pushed off the building and dropped with a splash onto the partially flooded street. There was only about a foot and a half of water there, but it was enough to soften his fall, which, it now seemed, must have been the case for the first attacker, the one I clubbed with the base of the chair. That man was just now slowly limping away down Fletcher Street. He waited a moment for his fellow to catch up with him, and they departed together into the darkness.

"That's it?" I screamed after them. "Just five of you? Next time bring a goddamned army, you useless half-wits! Five is a bloody insult."

I'm hard pressed to think of anything stupider I might have said. Challenges issued in Sullward were generally always accepted. But this is just the sort of thing I'm known for, and at that point, with my heart thundering in my chest, and blood starting to leak down my side, and the hot flush of victory burning across my face, I wasn't exactly my most rational self. As I learned in time, that particular taunt, screamed from my White Hill balcony, echoed far and wide. It was heard by most of my neighbors, further cementing the already unfavorable opinions they had about the Shadow Bidder who lived in their midst; but the whispered reverberations also reached the streets of Dockside and the Harbor, and even the flooded byways of the deadly Lower City, where stories of the unsuccessful assault on Vazeer the Lash's home circulated and magnified. By the time I heard the tale repeated back to me, it wasn't five wounded, emotionally broken stragglers from the High Lord's compound who attacked me. It was a half dozen highly trained assassins who, despite attaining the element of surprise and having every possible advantage, were killed virtually to the man. Vazeer the Lash, in his nightclothes, and apparently wielding half of his art collection, found ways to slaughter an entire team of heavily armed killers. You really couldn't buy better publicity.

But I didn't know any of that yet. Once my blood cooled and my calmer head prevailed, I could only imagine that the two survivors would bring my challenge back to those who were in a better position to answer it. I had likely just called the vengeance of hell down upon myself, but, of course, I had clearly done that already, which explained this raid.

I pulled both of the gaff hooks up and onto my balcony, then returned to my study. The final assailant, the one who had taken a spade in his gut, was still breathing. In fact, he was quite alive, though I could tell from the nature of the abdomen wound that he wouldn't be for much longer. He was also bleeding all over one of the room's tied-back velvet curtains.

"You people make a damned mess," I muttered, unlatching the unobstructed balcony door and closing it. I threw the cane bold, then turned to the other door.

"Would it be possible for you to die a little farther to the left?" I asked, as the man was still partially blocking that door. "I've had more than enough fresh air tonight."

"You're a traitor, Vazeer the Lash," rasped my bleeding guest, "to everything you should hold sacred."

I was truly surprised, not so much by the sentiment, which was nothing short of the truth, but by the strength and clarity of the man's voice. It must have been an agony for him to talk. Strangely, I somehow recognized the voice, and though he spoke in a clenched manner, I felt certain I had heard him speak very recently. I stared at his round features, trying to determine if I recognized them. He seemed several years my senior, with mildly creased pink cheeks, light brown eyes, and curly chestnut-colored hair with a few touches of gray. While I didn't experience any overt recognition, his clothing was nicer than that of the other men—a dark burgundy tunic and light gray hose descending into polished black boots—suggesting that he was no common soldier.

"All of these beautiful items that fill your home," he continued, "all of this is because of my lord. And yet you betrayed him. I pray the others will come and finish the job."

"Weygrin, is it?" I asked.

Confusion furrowed the man's pained face. "How is it you know me?"

"Damn," I muttered by way of response. "Damn you, you stupid fool."

Weygrin stared up at me from his slumped position against my door, and I think he was trying to figure out if I was addressing him or myself. In truth, I was addressing us both. Weygrin had been the figure who spoke with the High Lord down in the crude tunnel where he eventually died. Near the end of the bid, Weygrin had attempted several times to draw his liege back into the compound and away from potential harm and had only departed very reluctantly when the High Lord instructed him to go and fetch a warmer cloak. That was just moments before Nestor arrived. While I never saw Weygrin during that conversation, his tone and manner seemed to be that of a devoted household servant—a steward or a personal assistant. In this way he was probably very much like the ill-fated Jevar the Legate, who was the first casualty of that catastrophic night. Neither of these men, Weygrin or Jevar, deserved what had happened to them.

"What were you thinking, coming here?" I said after a moment. "You're not some street goon to go scaling buildings and fighting with the likes of me."

A defiant spasm crinkled Weygrin's features, and he spat the answer back at me.

"And where was I supposed to go? Last night I lost everything; last night I lost my lord. He died because he was down in a damp tunnel, looking for you and your party, instead of in his secure chambers, which endured the flood."

That, I now realized, was exactly how Weygrin had survived. He had returned to the High Lord's chamber to fetch that cloak, and he had clearly still been there when the deluge struck.

"This was really your main priority?" I asked. "To come and invade the home of a Grell Runner? I would imagine that you people have more important concerns."

"Those are no longer my concerns," Weygrin answered, and now he began to cough. I had been waiting for this, and I suspected that bloody spittle would soon follow. But he brought his coughing under control and continued.

"The others are already at it, maneuvering. The power play has begun, but I want no part of that. Beranardos's men were decimated, and a few of us who survived wanted to at least do something useful."

"Take revenge on me," I said, more to myself than him. "I was one of the only recognizable enemies from that night."

"Easy to find, too," said Weygrin. "Sherdane knew all about this beautiful home of yours, and he mentioned it often. I think it was a point of pride with him…that his contract system worked so well that everybody was elevated by it, even the likes of you."

"Damn," I muttered once again. "Damn this whole thing to hell."

If there had been any lingering flush of victory in me from my battle, if there had been a hint of swagger, it was gone now. My mood plunged precipitously. These words from my grievously injured guest delivered pain in kind, and I could tell it would only get worse from here. I knelt down next to Weygrin and gently pulled his hands away from the wound, and though he resisted at first, he eventually allowed me to do it, grimacing the whole time. The burgundy color of his tunic was complicating things, so I pulled the garment up, and with this he let out an agonized yelp. Underneath, his pale torso was covered in blood and continuing to leak profusely.

"I need to staunch the flow of blood before I can get a sense of how bad it is," I mumbled. I pulled off my own tunic and wadded it up, then pressed it against Weygrin's wound. My shirt wasn't exactly clean, but it would do until I found something better.

"Press this tightly against the injury," I said. "I'll be back shortly."

I quickly ran down to the second floor where I stored my linens, all the while dripping my own blood on the winding contours of the staircase. There was a pretty gray and blue runner that circled all the way from the top landing to the bottom floor, and as I saw my blood starting to stain that runner, I thought briefly of sliding closer to the wall so that the drops would fall on the exposed granite, not the carpeted center. But I didn't bother, for I found that I no longer cared. No amount of scrubbing was ever going to scour the dreadful violation of this night out of my home.

I returned with a set of linens and also some water from the bath chamber pump, which I carried in the bath jug. I set to work cleaning Weygrin's wound and the surrounding skin, hoping against hope that I had somehow missed his vital organs with my reckless thrust. After a few moments of doing this, I could see the unfortunate truth. I had stabbed him fairly high on his abdomen, just below his breastbone, and while I am hardly an expert in anatomy, I knew I had likely penetrated his stomach or colon, and quite possibly his liver. Any one of these would lead to internal bleeding, blood poisoning, and ultimately death; that was, if he didn't bleed out first.

"I'm sorry, Weygrin," I said after a minute of administering care. "I truly am."

"Then why?" he asked. His voice was much weaker now, and his face had lost most of its pink color. He had gone very pale.

My mind fumbled to come up with a reply. Only one thing seemed paramount now, and that was making this poor man's passage a little easier, so I struggled to decide what would be the most appropriate thing to say to him. Would it be best to tell him the full truth—about the exact nature of the Narrow Bid, about the relationship between Sherdane and the Countess, about the trickery of the Raving Blade? This might partially exonerate me, but would it help him? Or would the man actually be better off thinking me the true villain, so that even if he had failed in his efforts to kill me, at least it had been the right idea. I was genuinely confused for several seconds, but Weygrin decided the issue for me.

"That woman," he said softly. "She was an imposter, wasn't she? Not Kaszivar."

I paused a moment before answering.

"She was a Masque."

I pushed the linens more firmly against his wound. I felt his forehead, and it was growing cold.

"I knew it," Weygrin mumbled, now with his eyes closed. "The men still think it was the Siren, but I know better. Kaszivar would never plan so poorly…bring just three retainers, and a pair of Shadow Bidders. When she comes—and she will come—she'll come in force."

I didn't reply. It seemed wrong to burden Weygrin's final moments with the fact that his own lord had thought up the Lave Kaszivar story. Let him go to his grave believing his liege blameless in the night's events.

"Which means…," Weygrin muttered, apparently more interested in his inquiry than in dying peacefully. "…which means that you were engaged in a Narrow Bid."

Again, I remained silent.

"One man…," Weygrin continued, with his eyes squeezed tightly shut. "Only one man would proffer such a bid. Only he would be so treacherous and so bold."

I let this sit for a moment. Then, in no way certain it was going to help my victim's peace of mind, I replied, "It was him."

Weygrin took a series of shallow, labored breaths, and then he got a few more words out of his now-crinkled lips.

"But why? You were Sherdane's favorite…certainly you knew that. You epitomized everything he had built, everything he stood for."

"Because I was tricked," I replied miserably. "We all were. The Sketcher implied that Gueritus was the target, not the proffer. I didn't realize the truth…not until the very end, when it was too late to change things."

Weygrin went terribly still for several moments. When he did speak again, his lips opened only fractionally, making his voice garbled and thin.

"Was it ever too late to change things, Vazeer? You were in that tunnel, weren't you? That's how you know my name."

Oh, the bloody awfulness of this thing! Any brief optimism that I had experienced this morning, any hope that the Swell Driver might have swept away the wreckage of the crime, was now irrevocably dashed. It would never be made whole, and though on a conscious level I wished to flee this ghastly topic, I knew also that the wicked secret would eventually kill me. I could no longer even remotely gauge which words might "help" Weygrin or hurt him, so I simply opted for the truth.

"Yes, I was in that tunnel," I said. "And there was a very slight chance that I could have saved Sherdane, though the waters nearly killed me, and I am trained for such things. The High Lord almost certainly would have drowned, but still I failed. I failed in just the way I often do, in just the way I failed you tonight. I lost control of myself. I did not kill Sherdane, but I lost control when I might have protected him, and for that I am profoundly sorry."

Weygrin's eyes were still squeezed shut and his brow was furrowed, but I could see the subtle movement of his shallow breath as he appeared to take this information in. He was extremely still for a long time after my confession, and then his hand slid up fractionally from his stomach to rest on my hand.

"I wanted to tell you…" he softly breathed, "…that you have a very nice home. Beranardos would have liked to see it. I'll make sure to tell him about it, when I see him next."

I took Weygrin's hand in mine and held it, saying nothing. He was entirely motionless for several long minutes, and I thought he had finally moved past the point of speaking. His face had gone as white as my linens. However, he did finally speak again, in a deathly quiet hiss that hardly made it past the frigid gateway of his lips.

"Run," he whispered. "Run, Vazeer. You are not square with Gueritus. Nobody is ever square with him. As darkness follows the day, the Raving Blade will come for you. Running is your only option now; for he will certainly come."

And that was it.

Weygrin never spoke again, and within the hour, he expired. I remained there with him the whole time, holding his blood-covered hand, a scab from my own wound forming upon my side and a terrible, yawning emptiness growing all the while inside of me. The great starry night continued to flicker just beyond that single open balcony door, but within my own heart, the expanse was vacuous, and entirely devoid of light.

21

EASTCOVE

I cannot recall a more unhappy awakening than the one I experienced on the morning of 30 Dekharven, 213. Blood stained my sheets, wreckage filled my beloved third-floor study, and three corpses lay on my balcony; but these were not the only casualties. Damage, possibly irreparable damage, had been done to my sense of resolve.

When I finally pulled my injured body out of bed, I felt such little volition that it was a major undertaking to even make it to the privy. Afterwards, I contemplated crawling back in bed, so burdened was I at the mere thought of facing this new day. I did not wish to head upstairs, where debris and death awaited me. Nor did I have any stomach to eat, which was the only reason I would bother to descend. So, in the absence of a plan, I lumbered into my art gallery, collapsed into one of the chairs, and stared mindlessly at my treasures. My gaze flitted over the blue-glass figurine of a breaking wave on the mantle, past a whole series of ceramic wonders by Mindsk. I took little notice of Lougán's enormous driftwood horse and, shame upon me, I was untouched by the graceful molten tension of my javelin-wielding Giradera, her metallic muscles stretched and frozen at their deadly apex.

My eyes did at last find their way to "Late Day Over Imperial Square," one of my two works by Ashland Nuce. This large piece showed the wide public area at the heart of Tergon—a massive plaza paved with yellow marble and complete with the spraying extravagance of a fountain. In this view, pedestrians thronged the area, making their way in and out of the Capital Gallery on the left, and the Tergonian Imperial Theater on the right, while in the background, imposing and lustrous, towered the dizzying height of the Emperor's Gilded Palace. All of these details—the buildings, the perfectly manicured trees, the diverse faces of the pedestrians, right down to the spitting waters at the marble heart of it all, were bathed in that lovely pastel light for which Nuce was so admired. Soft, calming light, so unlike the blistering fire I witnessed the night before. For some reason this was the one piece of artwork that spoke to me in that moment, so I just sat there staring at it, sprawled out like a limp rag. In this condition, I tried to plan my next move.

By every possible measure, I was in trouble. The trouble ran so deep and was built of such complicated stuff that I had great difficulty separating out its many awful components. There was, first and foremost, a terrible threat to my safety, which should have concerned me most. Weygrin was right. The very thing that might have protected me at this moment—the successful completion of my contract—would be of no help if the proffer disavowed his involvement, which he would, for it was now easy to do. With the floodwaters creating the perfect distraction, and the Lave Kaszivar story conveniently deflecting blame, the Raving Blade could seek the coronation without having to justify his Narrow Bid. To do this, he would first wish to eliminate anyone who might bear witness against him.

The threat that this posed did scare me; however, other things concerned me more. The ghastly burden of Flerra Tellian's death, mixed with the assassination of our High Lord—an act that I did not perform myself, but which I helped facilitate—topped off with the lesser tragedy of Weygrin's death, an act which I did perform, thus making it perhaps the most onerous of the three… this was all somehow much worse than the risk of my own highly imminent demise. My actions of late seemed nothing short of cursed, each generating a host of tragic consequences both big and small (but mostly big, for when death is involved, how small can it be?) and it was making me rethink everything. It started out as a subtle intoning, like the first delicate timbres of a wind chime as a breeze begins to rise, but in time it began to gong inside of me with the somber monotony of a funeral bell.

"Run, Vazeer," it reverberated. "It's time for you to run."

In the deepest sense, this bleak refrain was heresy. I do not deny that I had arranged for an escape boat three days earlier with the ostensible plan to vacate my homeland in the dead of night should things go terribly wrong. But I never behaved like I might actually leave, for I really had no intention of leaving, which I learned at the height of the Narrow Bid while staring at an open doorway leading to tempestuous freedom. The Elena's Guile was a mere contingency. It was relief in the face of ridiculous odds, something that would allow me to put one foot in front of the other as I prepared for the bid. By contrast, this weird droning hymn, the one that rang so loudly without actually making a sound, was of a different order, for it had about it the unsettling resonance of a good idea. It was exactly what I would have told somebody else to do. It was what any reasonable person should do, and while I have not always had the most cordial relationship with reason, even I can resist the miserable power of logic for only so long.

So, with my gaze resting on the painted contours of a distant land, and the inner spaces echoing my chant of exodus, the plan began to form. I mentally inventoried everything I would take with me and figured out how I would pack it all. I also came up with a strategy for traversing the inundated river. Once across, I would make my way to Eastcove, where my escape boat had almost certainly survived the storm. At that point I would learn, one way or another, if my other passenger had also survived, and while the fear I experienced just thinking of that moment was almost unbearable, I worked hard to stuff it down. There was much to do between now and then.

I dragged myself downstairs to the kitchen where I managed to eat a small meal. After that, I set about packing. The goal here was to assemble the most useful of my clothing and weaponry, along with a transportable share of my wealth. Everything else— my sizeable collection of art, the hundreds of books, the bulk of my wardrobe, the furniture, the decorative items—this all needed to be left behind. The fortress-like nature of my building would be its only defense.

The storm had caused significant flooding in my basement, and while I never stored anything of great importance there, I made sure to haul the extra furniture and foodstuffs out of the cellar and dump the ruined material into the alley behind my home. It took me an hour or so, but the process made me feel better. In time the standing water would drain out, and while there was likely to be mildew, I could keep the smell cut off from the rest of my house by means of a solid door at the top of the basement stairs.

There were clear and enforceable rules in Sullward regarding property possession, and years from now I might conceivably return. Terrible things would happen first. Looting and vandalism were imminent—bloody messages scrawled across my walls would no doubt replace the beautiful paintings and tapestries.

But eventually the danger might pass, and 27 Fletcher could become my home again. I wished to ensure that the building itself didn't go to hell, even if all of its many lovely treasures were soon to be hauled away.

By the time the sun set that evening and the stars reemerged, I was ready to undertake the final and least pleasant of my housekeeping chores. The moment had come to address the three corpses on my balcony. My plan was simple: I took my sharpest spade and set about cutting my soiled study rug into three large strips. Into each of these I rolled a body, and once they were spooled off in this manner, I hoisted the first soldier over my shoulder and carted him down my stairs and out the back door. After that, I lugged him through the back streets of White Hill.

I knew I would be quite safe from prying eyes. Even under the best of circumstances, the residents of this neighborhood were seldom out at night, and now, without a single working streetlamp, waterlogged streets, debris littering the alleys, and a good deal of shouting echoing from near and far (no doubt from roaming salvage gangs), I was certain I wouldn't be encountering any of my neighbors. The moon would not be rising for at least an hour and a half, so, in rather heavy blackness, I threaded my way through the most uninhabited route I could find. I did hear some rustling in a few of the alleys and saw the light of torches down one of the streets, but it wasn't too difficult to sneak by unnoticed.

The ground to the southeast of my home sloped gently upwards, and as I made my way through the last of the narrow, cobbled lanes, I was soon clear of standing water. Then I was free of buildings altogether and, with the immense stippled bowl of the night sky above, I trudged towards the sea, my boots slurping the mud. A short time after that I arrived at the coastline to the west of the docks where the elevated land formed a low cliff. There, I uncere-moniously dumped my package over the edge, down into the shal-low, boulder-strewn waters. The tide was still rising, and within a few hours the body would be pulled out into deeper waters where it would join the dozens, if not hundreds, of others that were likely littering our harbor. I returned home to repeat the process.

I purposely saved Weygrin for last. When I finally hoisted him to the edge of the bluff, I unwrapped his body and then squatted down and placed a hand on his head. All of the pink vibrancy was gone from his cheeks, and his skin felt clammy to the touch.

"I'm running, Weygrin," I said. "Just like you told me to."

I paused a moment, my palm resting on his chilly forehead, the edges of his curly bangs pressed back beneath my fingers, and I tried to remember a prayer or appropriate ceremonial passage. A smattering of things popped into my head, but none seemed relevant. They meant nothing to me, and I doubted Weygrin would care about them either; so, I spoke the only words of con-sequence that came to mind.

"When you see Sherdane again," I said, my voice suddenly fighting through a viscid clog, "please tell him how sorry I am, for all that happened, but also that he never got to visit my home. How I would have loved that. I'm grateful…truly grateful that he gave me the chance to live there for a while, even if that time has finally come to an end."

I knelt a few minutes longer, gazing to the east where the damaged docks lay. From my vantage I could see an array of torches and even a few fires, with figures moving about. I could make out the angled masts of ruined ships, jammed up against the wharf, and I was fairly sure I even saw two smaller vessels splayed out like butchered carcasses across the Harborway.

I turned back to Weygrin, gave him a final farewell, then dumped him over the cliff, just like the others. I stood and made my way back home, ready to say a doleful goodbye to my life. It took me half an hour to wander through each room, to visit briefly with all the many meaningful items, before I turned my back on it all. I used the rear entrance, closing and locking that door for the last time, and though I wanted very much to venture around to the front and view that gorgeous façade, I didn't dare. At all costs I needed to avoid being spotted, so I carefully made my way out of White Hill via back alleys and the most circuitous of streets.

Once I entered the maze of Dockside, the conditions deteriorated rapidly. Tying my cloak around my midriff, I waded through thigh-high water, weaving amidst the tattered detritus of ruined lives. The water stain on these buildings was well above the first story, which portended dreadful damage inside. I practically tripped over a half-submerged corpse, and when I looked down, I saw with horror that it was a young boy. He was lying on his back, his colorless, dumbstruck face gaping mutely at the sky.

At last, I broke from the tangle of streets and made it out onto the broad expanse of the Harborway. While I didn't expect to find a usable skiff at the docks themselves, there were several boat-building warehouses that lined this avenue, and I came armed with a durkesh for a discreet break-in. Having already viewed the docks from the cliffs, I knew to expect some activity. Nothing prepared me for what I actually found.

I can only describe the scene on Sullward's grand wharf-side avenue as a sort of wild looting orgy. Lanterns had been hung from the inactive dock lampposts, and many of the figures in the crowd were carrying torches, though the main illumination was provided by four large bonfires. These whooshed and sparked right in the middle of the thoroughfare, consuming piles of hissing debris. At night there were seldom more than a handful of figures loitering on this avenue, but this evening, I don't think it was an exaggeration to guess at over three hundred souls. Half of them were fanned wide at the water's edge, and some of those had ventured out onto the remaining sections of heavily damaged dock, while ropes trailed out into the water. There was a cacophony of shouting and arguing from all corners. This was clearly a crude salvage operation focused on retrieving whatever had gone down with the dozen or so ships in port at the time of the Swell Driver. Not one of the vessels remained intact, and I immediately saw the enormous stern of Kaszivar's Galleon exhibiting its slowly bobbing underside about thirty feet out. Its slick surface was already crawling with parasitic figures who appeared to be chiseling off boards in an effort to get at the treasure inside. Elsewhere, the mangled mast of a caravel slanted upward at a sharp angle, and on the Harborway itself, I saw the two beached ships I had spotted from the cliffs.

A quick glance up and down the line of neighboring warehouses revealed that full-scale looting was underway: doors had been ripped off their hinges, and scraps of unidentified rubbish were splayed everywhere. There didn't appear to be a single Sullward watchman anywhere in sight. Adding to the overall chaos, the crowd had evidently gotten its hands on a stockpile of ale barrels from one of the warehouses, and they had already broken into this stash with delirious abandon. Men and women, shivering orange in the furious light, were slopping away out of lidless barrels, utilizing all manner of improvised device—smaller barrels, kitchen ladles, hats, or their own cupped hands… anything that could transfer a few intoxicating gulpfuls. And it was working. Fights were breaking out at several areas on the

Harborway, while mad, dissonant singing arose from one of the bonfires. Somehow, these people had moved from blunt shock to loutish derangement in very short order.

My chances of finding an unpilfered skiff anywhere seemed slim; however, the general pandemonium helped to keep my movements disguised, so, pulling down the brim of my hat, I ventured through the unruly crowd. I bumped into a short, round woman who was dragging a large sack of grain in the direction of Cargo Street. She snarled something at me without glancing up and continued hauling. I passed several others who were lugging things out of the area, but I didn't look closely at them or the items they carried. They weren't dragging skiffs, which was the only thing I cared about. I kept my head down and continued searching.

I finally spotted my prize down near the eastern end of the avenue. Two men were hoisting an old rowboat loaded with sacks towards one of the alleys that led back into the city, and though I saw at once that the upper sidewall on the starboard side was damaged, I suspected that the rest of it was in good shape. After all, these men were taking pains to lift the vessel a bit each time they pulled it over the cobbles, suggesting that the hull was worth preserving. I headed for them.

"Three tolgens for the boat," I said to the larger and older of the two. Now that I was closer, this appeared to be a father-son team.

"Piss off," said the man, who was bearded and heavily built. "Money ain't worth nothing now, an' this boat's the best way to drag my haul."

"Money will have value again soon, my friend," I answered, "and I doubt whatever you have in there is worth four tolgens… which is my new offer."

The man let go of his end of the craft, and suddenly he squared up on me. He put his hand on the pommel of a long dagger at his belt, and his expression became decidedly hostile.

"Like I said, piss off. Boat alone is worth that. You're wasting my time."

My hat was down low, and in the poor lighting, I was certain this man did not recognize me. It was better this way, even if it did make the negotiation more difficult.

"Five tolgens is my final offer," I said, "and I promise that's worth far more than the boat, and the entire haul. But you keep the haul; just sell me the boat."

The man took a few heavy breaths, then looked over at his young companion, who appeared to be in his early teens. The boy's wide, guileless eyes seemed hopeful, and this perhaps caused his father to relent.

"I'll take six tolgens, and not a diven less," he said.

"Done."

I reached into my purse and drew forth the six silver coins; then I thrust them into the man's hand.

"Now, get your crap out of my boat. You and your boy have some hauling to do."

The two of them worked quickly to unload the sacks, and once everything was out, I saw what I suspected to be true—the bottom was largely intact. I would probably experience some leaking from a single crack I saw near the bow, but nothing that would threaten a relatively quick journey across the Grells. I had no paddle, but there were enough broken pieces of wood around that I was certain I could improvise something.

A short time later, I had hoisted the boat down the remainder of the Harborway, past the final warehouses, and into the lightly forested area that bordered the river. When I finally got the vessel to the water, I wasn't far from the split oak where we had launched our Narrow Bid. I had also found a section of plank, which would work as a viable, if somewhat clumsy, paddle. Using my durkesh, I whittled down one end so that I could grip it easily, and then a few minutes later, I shoved off.

The tide was still rising at this hour, which slowed the outflowing current and made my crossing easier. It didn't take long before I was in the heart of the flow, and I pulled hard to keep myself from being swept down into the harbor. At this point in its waning phase, the moon was rising about a half hour later each night, and though the Clock Tower was not yet operational, I had kept fairly good track of nature's cycles. I expected to see the blurry orb ascending to the east any moment now, just shy of three quarters. Sure enough, I was about midway across when a section of baleful orange appeared through the spindly trees of the salt marsh. Soon after that, it rose to the point where I could observe it clearly.

Unobstructed and unearthly, that warped autumnal disc had little in common with the fog-choked nimbus I encountered most nights. The color was a deep lustrous amber, and it began to dye the surface of the Grells with tinges of dirty gold. My bow cut a swath of gilded ripples through the inky blackness, and the landscape around me became more and more visible. Upstream, I noted many disruptions to the river border—massive root balls from overturned trees, snarls woven out of vines, branches, and trunks, all plaited together like knotted fishing nets. There was also plenty of flotsam in the river itself, and I took pains to avoid logs and other drifting things that bobbed towards my port side. Apart from these inanimate travelers, I was entirely alone out there. No Shadow Bids were being run, nor were there brigands, scavengers, or constables on the prowl. By the time I had made it across, the moon had ascended above the trees, and its ever-whitening radiance revealed the full extent of my solitude.

I am one of the few individuals in the city, aside from Droden and his crew, who knows all the intricacies of this portion of the Sullward landscape. To the east of the harbor, across the widest portion of the delta, there is a tall and surprisingly substantial range of rocky outcroppings. Swaddled in vines and thorn bushes, this imposing feature of the topography is not an easy place to negotiate, and pulling a boat up onto any sort of beach is difficult. However, I know what to look for, and I was able to drag my expensive rowboat through a dense barrier of prickly hawthorns, wedging it onto a shelf of rock. I also know how to scale up the crevices, an otherwise dangerous undertaking unless you know exactly where to place your hands and feet. This night I chose a relatively wide route, as I was wearing the heavy backpack and an assortment of auxiliary weapons and clothing. I climbed slowly but steadily.

None of the guards here were likely to expect some fool to come scampering up the rocks, so I had a good chance of observing the lay of the land before anybody spotted me. Once I reached the top, I made my way through a crown of spiky vegetation and slid around to a position that would allow me to clearly view Eastcove. I slipped off my pack and squatted for a few minutes, scanning the narrow beach below.

Over the years, Droden and his people had done a wonderful job with this protected inlet, dredging the circumference, creating proper anchorage, and greatly expanding a natural cave at the north end of the cove. They had gone so far as to create a fully habitable dwelling there, complete with an office, bedrooms, a workable kitchen, and even an escape tunnel, which exited to the north. Droden and his wife, Elena, generally resided in their tasteful Dockside apartment, but my former Broodmate had been known to spend days at a time in Eastcove, sleeping in his embellished cave complex along with the trusted staff who guarded the area.

Never particularly fond of Grell Running, Droden had counted the hours until he could raise enough money from that hazardous profession to fund his current enterprise. While he earned most of his livelihood from the armada of small boats at the Sullward docks, it was the five larger vessels anchored in this cove that gave him his true sense of pride. Three he had built himself, the others he purchased, and they were a strong testament to how good the last decade had been to Droden Sailwain.

I spotted the Elena's Guile right away, for she was significantly larger than the others. With two tall, willowy masts sporting angled lateen booms, her overall shape was elliptic and elegant, suggesting formidable speed on the open water. This was one of the two ships that Droden had purchased, though he had made a whole series of improvements to her, which he had showed me in great detail. I scanned the boat for signs of damage and saw none. For a while I simply crouched there on the bluff, watching as the tapered hull and the graceful masts grew slowly brighter in the rising moonlight.

I saw some illumination emerging from the excavated cave complex, and there was a single guard sitting quietly on the beach to the west; however, there were no signs of life on the boats themselves. The deck of the Elena's Guile was empty, and she seemed uninhabited. Seeing this, my worst fears returned in a terrible, agonizing rush.

What was I going to do? When I inevitably learned that Nascinthé of Levell had never arrived, how would I react? Would I go slopping through miles and miles of inundated swampland, calling her name, scouring the reeds for a pretty corpse? I'd likely never find her, yet could I really set sail otherwise? The mystery would linger, and the wounds would fester, and peace would become as illusive in my new life as it had been in the old one. I would have to resolve this somehow.

Time passed with me squatting there in mournful anxiety. Perhaps it was half an hour, maybe longer, but eventually something did move on board the Elena's Guile. The door to the cabin swung open, and somebody stepped out onto the deck. The figure was slim, and at first glance I thought it might be Leddy or one of Droden's other dockhands, wrapped in a long wool cloak against the chill. But this person didn't walk like Leddy. They didn't walk like a boy at all, and I watched the slender shape glide quietly to the sterncastle and take up a position there, staring towards the northeast side of the cove. The mishappen globe of the moon was now starkly beaming in the eastern sky. The channel of water to the south was beginning to flicker luminously, and yet the figure did not stare in either of those directions, where there was something worth seeing. Instead, they gazed into the shadowed darkness where a dense knot of bushes obscured one of the walls of the cove, where the secret pass connected Eastcove to the salt marsh. The smallest hint of a breeze arose, and this light gust was just enough to dislodge a few strands from the figure's head. Bathed in the gentle radiance, I saw the softly glinting fibers of a woman's long, blonde hair.

A swoon, I now know, has much less to do with dizziness than it does with losing one's hold (that desperate inner clutching—like the scrabbling grip of a climber's fingers) upon the muscles that administer dignity. Nobody witnessed my inner stumble, yet there was no denying it happened. Before my mind fully identified the figure on the boat, I underwent this strange loss of control, first feeling my facial muscles go numb, a second later noting that they were twisting out their own entirely unregulated concoction, then experiencing a series of short, labored breaths like those of a winded old man who is no longer able to make it up his own staircase.

But far worse than any of this was the spontaneous recitation of words that never passed my lips, yet which clarioned in my own skull like badly played pipes. It was a jumbled mix of deities and divine terms: "Oh Heavenly Spheres, Eresis, Gudros, Yisva!"—entities in which I had only the faintest belief, and all of them strung together blasphemously, for I was conflating two pantheons. I put my hand to my heart as if abashed, and I lurched forward, stopped, forward again...and then finally stopped dead.

"Yisva, Eresis, Heavenly Spheres, Celestials!"

Perched on the sterncastle, traces of bleached moonlight dusting her hair, a female figure stared alone into the darkness, searching. There was no mistaking her now, nor what she was doing. Nascinthé of Levell was standing on that boat.

And she was waiting for me.

22

LOOKING GLASS

Prior to the Dawn of Reason, there were a whole host of far-fetched religious beliefs that held sway in Derjia, most of them too ridiculous to describe. There is one, however, that makes at least a modicum of sense to me. Just a modicum, but I have even gone so far as to leave slips of parchment in several of my books to note the places where this concept is addressed. The idea is this: when a person nears the gates of the Heavenly Spheres, they will be given one final test to ensure they are worthy of entering the realm of the celestials. As to the nature of this test, it is often described as a temptation of some sort, and it always involves a confrontation with one's greatest weakness.

Why have I concerned myself with such an idea, especially when I claim only the slimmest belief in an afterlife? Because, if you simply remove the notion that this sequence occurs after death, I have found, again and again, that these sorts of tests do occur, and that in my own case the results are never good. In fact, were I to actually make it to the gates of the Heavenly Spheres, it is an absolute certainty that I would find some insidious way to foul things up right on the threshold. I've done this at several key junctures in my life. I'm rather good at it.

I lead with all of this because I wish to give fair warning about what comes next. This probably seems like a moment in the story when a fairytale ending of some sort is about to take place. Don't count on it.

I'm simply incapable of having such a moment. I'd like to explain why that is, but I, too, find it baffling. Among those long-departed religious concepts, which now adorn history's scrapheap, there is another that garners no slips of parchment in my library. Stated succinctly, this idea implies that humankind's inherent weaknesses, thus my penchant for spoiling happy endings, is, in fact, a shred of an original mistake harkening back to man's first trial upon creation. Faced with a choice between worship at an altar erected to the gods who created him and fascination with a looking glass in which he viewed himself, the newly assembled creature chose poorly.

To express their displeasure at man's egotism, the gods began to pile ever worse calamities upon their bewildered creation, until, at last, in misery and defeat, he tore his eyes from the looking glass and bent his knees to the divine altar. The lessons were hard won, and the gods decided that the calamities would not be removed, serving as a reminder to the recalcitrant, and spawning the notion that this world might conceivably have been free of misfortune had man not been so irrationally consumed with himself. To me, this story makes no sense at all. Why not build the creature correctly from the start? Did the gods not botch the project, that their self-absorbed prototype failed to make the right choice? It seems divinely unjust to pile the full measure of blame upon the poor wretch's shoulders.

Anyway, seeing as I give no credence to this idea, I will not explain away my worst impulses in this manner. And yet, strangely, as the first cracks began to form in my plan for a fairytale ending, it was indeed a version of the looking glass story that asserted itself. I will describe this as best I can, though I suspect I will earn little sympathy.

There I was, standing on the high rocks over Eastcove, swooning like a playhouse fop, lurching back and forth with my hand over my heart and my mind spewing up celestial garbage, when the first troubling thought arose within me. It was a mental picture, actually. It was the image of my own face.

I envisioned those angry black eyebrows stabbing down over even angrier black eyes, the cracked rudder nose, the weather-abused skin, the long arching scar, which hacks a bushwhacker's path through the stubble on the left side of my face. Even my deeply swarthy complexion—skin tones that seem rich and exotic on the Kaszians who share my bloodline—appeared broiling and venomous on my own face. This exterior had perhaps assisted me in my role as a Shadow Bidder, but it had also been a perfect representation of a vast array of social shortcomings.

Which is exactly where the problem began for me that night. It was the thought of that face, glowering and villainous, the one that gave pause to those who might otherwise attack me on the Grells, and equal pause to those who might befriend me in White Hill…the thought of that visage finally exiting the shadows; the idea of it trying to present itself anywhere outside of Hell's Labyrinth. Suddenly, this seemed the most unfeasible of prospects.

How ludicrous to try to conclude a story such as mine with a romantic, moonlit boat ride. Imagine Vazeer the Lash living on some idyllic Midland coastline with his ethereal countess, or perhaps in the great city of Tergon, trying to pass himself off as a Kaszian gentleman whose scarred face, total lack of decorum, and penchant for spontaneous acts of violence would all be kindly overlooked in the face of his ability to quote obscure literary texts. Had I ever really thought any of this through?

As the moments passed, and the waters of Eastcove grew ever brighter, my mental turmoil expanded. Now other pictures arose, images I thought I had already put to rest. In my mind's eye, I saw 27 Fletcher Street and its many collections: the books, the artwork, the furniture, the clothing. Was I truly ready yet to turn my back on all that I had built there? It was one thing to make that decision while still in the protected confines of my home, but I had since ventured out into the wild streets, seen the mayhem, watched hordes of brainless drunkards singing and looting and fighting. Didn't bronze Giradera, and Nuce's framed masterpieces, deserve better than to wind up in their grubby hands? How about the hundreds of books, which would no doubt be turned into stove fuel by illiterate morons? I could not help but construe, palpably construe, what it would mean once 27 Fletcher was ransacked. It would be nothing less than the looting of my soul.

Wise people tell us not to confuse material possessions with character, and yet in some cases they are wrong. In my case, they are wrong. That building *was* me, or at least the very best part of me, and to lose myself in this way suddenly felt worse than death. The very uncertainties that bedevil human interaction were never troublesome while stretched out in my reading chair, in an artifact-laden study, poring over the texts of long-dead men and women who, ages ago, thought and felt and dreamed as I did. Why take a chance on something so grievously unpredictable as another human being? Why alter an approach that had been working for years? The absorbing closeness of written words, or rendered images, of sensuous architectural lines or carefully worked bronze were sure bets for a man who was about as compatible with his own species as a fighting cock in the killing pit.

On and on it went, the distress growing worse by the second. I can't say precisely how long it took me to talk myself out of doing the right thing, but it couldn't have been more than a quarter of an hour; a measly little interval in which to thoroughly fail the test at the gates of the Heavenly Spheres. The gods didn't need to send a temptation or demon to knock me off course. I took care of that myself.

It was settled then. For better or for worse (certainly worse), I would stay. I would remain behind and defend all that I had accumulated, and at the same time maintain my lunatic dream of Sullward's resurrection, something that could only be pre-served if I were actually there to be a part of it. Which I prob-ably wouldn't be, because I'd be dead. "Dead" was not a useful platform from which to enact change, but neither was exile, and somehow in my disquiet and delusion, the former seemed just a little more helpful. It certainly beat the alternative. It beat scal-ing down these rocks into Eastcove, walking aboard that boat, then sailing off with a beautiful stranger in my arms and a lav-ish fortune in my purse. Who the hell would want that, when violent death surrounded by useless artifacts was still possible?

One issue needed to be addressed first, of course: the beau-tiful stranger herself. On a certain level, I wanted to simply skulk away into the night like the scamp I knew myself to be, hoping Nascinthé would eventually think me dead. This would definitely make things easier. After all, I had already decided I wasn't leaving, and there was no way I was going to allow her to remain with me in my Sarentine deathtrap, awaiting the coming of the Raving Blade. Why not permit the woman to grieve as she might, then sail away unburdened by some ill-advised attachment to me? The problem was this plan would probably fail.

News of my recent battle at 27 Fletcher would soon filter into Eastcove via Droden's network of spies, and Nascinthé would likely catch word of it. Then what would happen? She would put on some brilliant disguise and come looking for me. It wasn't too hard to find me, and once she did, she would become a liability. As one of only two survivors from the Narrow Bid, and also the primary instrument that facilitated the operation, she would be a logical target for those seeking vengeance. But even more to the point, in the interest of keeping the Lave Kaszivar story alive, the Raving Blade would wish to eliminate Nascinthé as quickly as possible. Her very existence undermined the tale.

So, I needed to make sure she left. I had to drive her off, using any means necessary. I would unnerve her, threaten her, reveal all that was abhorrent about myself, that she might see the twisted face that forever glowered back at me in the wardrobe mirror. Whatever false virtues she had projected on me during the traumatic events of the Narrow Bid must now be laid bare. There was simply no other way.

I started down the rocks, which were significantly easier to traverse on the cove side. It took me only a couple minutes, and once I reached the pebbly beach of Eastcove, I began to crunch quietly through the gray stones at the water's edge. Within a short time, I drew near to the guard on the western side of the beach, and as I approached, I saw that it was Habard, a flinty old fighter who had been in Droden's employ for almost as long as I had been running the Grells. He stood from his stool as I neared but showed no alarm, indicating that his eyes were still sharp even in middle age. I pulled up before him.

"I'm glad you're working Eastcove these days, Habard," I said. "Not much damage here, I see."

Habard grunted. His lined face was serious but also somewhat impassive, which was how he usually looked.

"Smallest boat got beached, now has a hole. 'Nother lost the boom. We pointed the ships towards the cove mouth, which kept 'em from keeling when the waters rose. Nothing like what happened at the wharf."

"Did those guards take it hard?"

"Lost two of the lads," he said. "Jake and Marpan. Droden called all hands off, but poor fools were still out on the Harborway when the surge struck."

"I'm sorry to hear it," I said. And I was.

Jake was a dock boy who had prepped my skiffs on countless occasions, and Marpan was a particularly dedicated young guard who never let Droden's inventory out of his sight.

Habard shrugged by way of acknowledgement. He wasn't easy to faze after so many years working protection, though his stony expression did seem a bit graver than usual. He turned and shifted his stubbled chin towards the north where the carved dwelling lay.

"Might be best if ya avoid him tonight. Might be ya avoid him altogether. He don't have the most favorable things to say of ya right now."

This was no surprise, but it still stung. Clearly the rumors had already begun to flow, and some of those must have reached Droden Sailwain. It was bad enough that I had deceived him about the number of soldiers that might come chasing me to Eastcove, but at this point, I had to assume that he knew the High Lord was the target.

"I'll bear that in mind," I said.

Habard nodded, then turned to the water, flipping his chin in that direction.

"Yer woman," he grunted. "She said ya would come."

That took me aback. I gazed out to the Elena's Guile, and though the deck itself was obscured by two closer ships, I could see the twin masts rising above the others.

"She said that?"

"Aye," Habard replied. "Must be she knows what we all know."

"Which is?"

A cool smile crossed the man's grizzled lips.

"Damn near impossible to kill ya."

"Is that what you know, Habard?"

"Seems plain enough."

I sighed and shook my head.

"Try not to believe everything you hear."

Habard again offered one of his expressive grunts.

"Never do."

Then he glanced out towards the water.

"I reck'n ya don't want to keep her waiting much longer."

"I suppose not," I concurred, and I patted Habard on the shoulder. As I made my way past him and started down the beach, he spoke again.

"Vazeer."

There seemed something a bit lighter in his tone.

I turned.

"Not like I know much about women," he said, "but this one seems special. Might be ya try and make her happy, if ya can."

For a long moment I just stared at Habard, listening to the gentle wash of tiny waves at my feet. I finally replied.

"If only I were capable of that."

Then I hurried off down the path of shiny gray stones to the place where the Elena's Guile was moored.

Droden's team had rigged a series of clever floating gangplanks in Eastcove, which allowed at least one heavily weighted individual to walk out to each boat at a time. As I reached the gangplank leading to the Guile, I looked back towards the carved dwelling and noted that there was a tall figure standing up in the high doorway. He was some distance away, and his shape was backlit by the lanterns inside the complex, but I could easily tell that his arms were crossed over his chest. I could also see his lanky build and long hair, and this told me it was almost certainly Droden himself. I waved to him tentatively, but he just gazed at me in return, offering no greeting or acknowledgement. Finally, he turned his back and disappeared through the doorway, removing all doubt as to his identity.

I stepped onto the floating walkway, sending silvery ripples spiraling outward, and I slowly made my way towards my next act of betrayal. This one would be even more difficult than what I had done to Droden. While Nascinthé of Levell wasn't a true Shadow Bidder, she was definitely a Masque, for I had watched her perform acts of elaborate persuasion during the Narrow Bid, which rivaled anything I had ever seen. This made her dangerous. Of all the Shadow Bidder professions, Masques were the least likely to be trained in combat, and this was primarily because their repertoire was so heavily weighted towards diplomacy. Even so, those of Nascinthé's skillset could achieve amazing things when it came to this so-called "diplomacy." On more than one occasion, I had watched Masques convince entire crews on hostile smuggling ships to stand down, even when the crew held a decisive advantage.

Therefore, I would have to be careful not to underestimate her. As I neared the halfway point on the gangplank, I rehearsed my role, which was, essentially, being myself. My true self, roguishly revealed, with no pretense of civility. The clever woman might concoct some ploy to use against me, but that tactic would only prove effective on a soft-hearted imbecile, like the one I had left on the rocks above. It went without saying that there would be no more unseemly swooning tonight.

I could now see the slender form standing up on the stern-castle. Nascinthé had obviously missed my approach around the circumference of the bay because she still seemed to be facing northeast, where the secret path emerged from the salt marsh. Nearing the boat, I tensed up as if ready for a fight, my face so stiff it felt like it was coated with tar.

At last, Nascinthé turned, registering that somebody was approaching. She seemed to struggle with my identity, as she just stood there for a second, staring. Then, apparently, she got it, for suddenly a small shriek rang out into the night, and like a cat startled off of a shelf, she sprang forward from her perch. She flew, it seemed, down the steps of the ship's rear section and began a weaving sprint through the items on deck towards the place where the gangplank intersected the Elena's Guile. I watched every motion of that run, every little twitch of her shoulders as she dodged around barrels and coils of rope, her light hair trailing out behind her like a frayed scarf. Time appeared to actually slow, so that the wraithlike form, leaping and dashing, twisting and gliding beneath the bone brightness of the moon, seemed to exist before me in some kind of suspended dimension. I could hear the skipping rasp of her footsteps, and even those protracted out to the steady clicking tempo of a clock. I saw so much in that extended interval. My mind reacted in kind.

"Oh Heavenly Spheres! Celestials! Eresis! Yisva!"

That's all that remained in my head. Gone were the rehearsed roles, the careful stratagems, any semblance of a plan. The sound of her wild shriek, and the sight of her darting sprint across the deck of the Elena's Guile, shattered the looking glass right before my eyes.

I would not advise anybody to attempt a flat-out run on a floating gangplank, especially when weighted down by a large, over-stuffed backpack, but this is what I did, and I rocked wildly with each stride. I also wouldn't suggest a person leap up a rope ladder in this weighted condition, but this is also what I did, and I swear I was up that climb quicker than I would have ascended a shallow ramp.

And then we were abreast of each other. I had but an instant to see her face—luminous and exultant in the pale lunar blush, her long, thin mouth stretched open wide. Her eyes were clear and reflective, and while the blue color was dimmed by night, the crystalline quality was entirely present and even incandescent before me. After that I could see nothing, for we threw ourselves upon each other like drunken lunatics.

My infamous blackouts, which I have described at length, tend to overtake me when I am faced with a terrible trauma; however, it now appears that the exact opposite is true when in the grip of a rapturous joy. Who knew? As Nascinthé and I went at each other, I could feel every spot on the back of my head where her fingers clawed frantically through my hair, knocking my hat askew. I was viscerally absorbed into the warm gnashing of our two mouths as we sucked heavingly at each other's breath. Bumping first against the sidewall, we staggered back together until we crashed up against the mizzenmast. Eventually, we sank down to the deck on our knees, kissing and clutching each other like a pair of love-lorn maniacs. But more than that, more than any of those stunning details, I was acutely present to one thing in particular. I was ecstatic! I was so deliriously happy in that moment that the sheer explosive force of the joy seemed capable of ripping out of my chest and blowing apart that boat. It was beyond any passing sensual delight I had ever known, beyond any tipsy intoxication. It exceeded the contented bliss of my own fire-warmed study, with some newly acquired tome from Merejin's Books beckoning my mind into a world of cryptic discovery. My reunion with Nascinthé of Levell was an elation that transcended all of those things, and I threw myself into it with complete abandon.

We did eventually make it below deck and into the homey little cabin where Nascinthé had slept the prior night. And here, at last, my cumbersome backpack dropped from my shoulders, followed quickly by my cloak and then my leather cuirass, my weapons, my tunic, my boots, and finally my pants. And Nascinthé tore off her own garments in a similarly hysterical manner. After that we tumbled together into the bed, and what followed was as joyful and intimate as anything I might concoct in my most shameless fantasy. Every feverish grasp, every ardent caress, every passionate, hungry, desperate kiss was so utterly perfect, so entirely natural that I couldn't even recognize myself as a partner in this joining. Or, perhaps, I recognized myself so completely that I was left without a shred of self-consciousness. For in this place our union became graceful and elegant, and the sight of her milky form, kneading up against the scar-hatched darkness of mine, was not incongruous in any way, but rather immaculate and beautiful. It was all beautiful—the sensations and sights, the smell of her skin, the moist feminine taste of her body, the collective sounds of our rapturous cries. Truly, it was the most wonderful thing I had ever experienced in my entire life.

I think it best I stop there. Some things are too sacred to be conveyed in their entirety. Some phenomena lie in places that cannot be reached by simple words.

I have not had many exalted moments in this strange life of mine. But that night, the culmination of a day that had started as poorly as any I can ever remember, I did, in fact, experience something celestial. Even if I fail to ever reach that place again, I shall still consider myself a lucky man to have lived at least one beautiful night such as that.

23

NASCINTHÉ OF LEVELL

Have I been deceptive? Did all my talk of failing tests and blowing chances prove misleading? Perhaps a little. It's true I did not wreck the reunion with Nascinthé of Levell, even though a very real part of me wanted to. But I was far from achieving a "happily ever after" ending. I had no intention of leaving Sullward, and there was no way I would allow Nascinthé to stay behind with me, foolishly throwing her life away. First things first, however. There was still some wonderful reveling to do before we reached that crossroads.

Nascinthé and I spent much of the following day nestled together in the cozy little cabin aboard the Elena's Guile, rarely even leaving the bed. I did venture on deck a couple times just to make sure that all seemed right in Eastcove, and it did. There were always two guards flanking the inlet at all times, and apart from them, I saw nobody else at all. Also, I knew that I would hear and feel the vibrations of somebody approaching the boat via the gangplank, as I am well attuned to such things. So, in bed we stayed, and my extraordinary stint of happiness continued. We made love again in the late morning, and the experience was every bit as new and magical as the first time. After that we sprawled in exhaustion and contentment, then Nascinthé took some time to tend to my injuries, which had reopened during our passion. She used a small portion of the Nettledown that I had brought with me, and she did a reasonably good job with the bandages. All the while, I could not take my eyes off her.

Nascinthé of Levell was just so exquisitely beautiful, so elfin and perfect that I could hardly fathom that she and I could possibly be sharing the same bed. Her unblemished flesh bore no scars or lines, and she had none of the tattoos (either artist-rendered, or constable-branded) that had adorned the bodies of the handful of other women I had slept with in my day. Most of those had been Shadow Bidders, and there was a roughness, a knotty, scarred muscularity to their bodies that was wholly different from what I saw in Nascinthé. Even my beloved statue of Giradera, aside from being bronze and lifeless, was a thoroughly different species, for she, like the women who graced my profession, was a creature bred to the rigors of armed conflict. Nascinthé was not bred to these things; she had come from a different world entirely.

"I was an actress in the Midlands," she told me as we lay together. I had suspected as much, though that was as far as my presumptions went.

"In fact, I became quite famous by the end. If you dwelled anywhere near Tergon five years ago, you would have heard of me."

"I would not have heard this name, I assume?"

"Another," she agreed. "A name that is gone now, for that woman is dead. I prefer not to even speak it. The stage name was assumed anyway."

"But Nascinthé isn't?"

Here she paused, and it seemed she was trying to decide exactly how much to disclose. Finally, she nodded.

"Nascinthé is my given name, and I was born in the southern village of Levell. However, my family moved up the coast to Abelein when I was very young, and I was known as Nassy throughout the remainder of my youth."

Nascinthé was reluctant to tell her story at first, though after some time the details began to flow. Despite the convincing display of courtly manners I had witnessed on the Narrow Bid, she was not from the aristocracy, or even the regional gentry. She was the child of two artisans, a pair who started a successful fabric business once they arrived in Abelein. Her father was a weaver and her mother a seamstress, and they wound up supplying much of the clothing and drapery to the township. Being a busy port in the heart of the Tergonian Midlands, Abelein was a frequent stopover for both waterborne travelers and also those riding the Midland Highway to the Capital. As such, it hosted a steady stream of passing theatrical troupes, and there was a decent theater in the center of town for both local and outside productions.

"I couldn't keep away from that playhouse," Nascinthé said with a wistful smile. "It was my parents' largest customer, and I was constantly being sent to deliver things to the director—costumes, props, curtains…anything requiring fabric, which, in the world of theater, is everything. By the time my mother tried to turn me into a seamstress, the only interest I had in cloth was affecting dramatic capes and gowns for myself with the scraps. Every free minute, I was there. I became such a regular the staff called me the 'wardrobe fairy.' But it was the stage that beckoned me, not the dressing room. Even at a very young age, I knew I was meant to be an actress."

Nascinthé explained how she finally convinced the theater director to try her in a few small roles when she was eleven. This went well enough that by the age of fourteen she was being given leads, and the local playwrights routinely composed parts with her in mind. In this capacity, she was spotted by the director of a prestigious traveling troupe, and at that point her career began in earnest.

"It was during the touring years that I learned much of what I have used here," she said. "I studied makeup, the ability to alter my appearance, age…sometimes even my gender. I learned accents from just about everywhere, and also how to imitate all of the Tergonian social classes. Often, I had to make these changes in a matter of minutes, since I usually played several roles in a single show."

Nascinthé also received an extensive education, which was a requirement for those who spent half their time reading scripts and the other half improvising before crowds on a wide range of subjects. She excelled at all of it, and eventually she made her way to the most prominent stage of all.

"I was admitted to the Tergonian Imperial Theater by my twenty-second year," she explained. "I rose quickly, for I was very good. But I also plummeted spectacularly, because I was a fool, and way out of my depth. Theater life in the Capital is almost as duplicitous and meanspirited as this place. The Imperial Court is even worse. Where those two worlds overlapped, I made a terrible mistake, spurred on by players who wanted to see me fail. I attracted the affections of a duke who would not stop wooing me, no matter how many times I rebuffed him. The man was married already to a peer almost as significant as himself, but the woman rarely ventured out of her family home in Engolia, and the Duke loathed her. I thought the presence of that icy marriage, in name only, would keep our affair casual."

When I asked Nascinthé if this was a mere flirtation or a true affair, she regretfully answered that she allowed it to become an actual relationship.

"At first he seemed charming enough. He was handsome and intelligent and had great appreciation for the theater, and, when I asked my fellow players about him, they said all sorts of complimentary things that turned out to be complete lies. Once his façade came off, I found him to be domineering and wildly jealous. He actually began to dictate the roles I could take at the theater, and the male leads that he was willing to let me play against. I have since learned to be a much better judge of character."

Nascinthé tried repeatedly to break it off but found this far more difficult than she ever would have imagined. The Duke was thoroughly infatuated with her, and he defied aristocratic convention by demanding that she be his wife. She made it plain that she had no interest in assuming that role, but apparently her interests were of small consequence to the man, for he went ahead and annulled his existing marriage in an effort to pressure her.

"At that point the only hope I had of saving my name, and possibly my life, was to give him my hand," she said with resignation. "But I didn't do it. My family said I should accept what was being offered, as it really was an astonishing windfall, but the only thing I cared about was being an actress. I didn't want to be a duchess, and I definitely didn't want to be that man's wife. Afterwards, I was finished."

She quickly became despised by a whole array of parties. The Duke, seeing that he would never win her back, spread vicious rumors about her character. He told the entire court that she had seduced and manipulated him, that she had convinced him to annul his marriage, then walked away, leaving his heart in ruins. The enemies began to emerge from every corner, including the former Duchess and her relations, who were absolutely ruthless. Nascinthé literally fled for her life, and she had to uproot her parents and younger sister, who had moved with her to Tergon.

They tried to start over elsewhere in the Midlands, but word spread fast, and no theater in the entire region would risk the wrath of those two aristocratic families. Playhouse directors were actually threatened.

"Eventually, I did find a director to take me in, in a small town north of the Midlands. He was a true gentleman, and very brave. But…he…"

And here the airy blue of Nascinthé's eyes glossed with dewy wetness.

"He was…"

Her shoulders jerked.

"He was standing right in front of me," she said, stuffing back a sob but failing to halt the quick, flickering scuttle of a tear down her cheek.

I took her into my arms. I rubbed the humid surface of her cheek, I kissed the tousled mess of her hair, and in that moment, I really had no idea what I was doing, or even who was doing it, for once again I did not recognize myself. I had never comforted a woman before. I had never held somebody like this, transmitting through my battered hands and weathered lips some hitherto unrevealed wellspring of empathy. It felt very strange, but it also felt right.

"They killed him," she choked, gagging upon a heavy clot of grief. "I don't even know which family sent the Finisher, but the blood…the blood splattered…"

She could not continue. So, I simply held her and let my improbable ministrations flow, trying all the while to imagine what she had been through. I had no doubt that these terrible feelings were the essence of the haunting unspoken message I had detected in her from the start. Sullwardians carried pain, cargo loads of pain, but they stowed it away in rank places from which it never reemerged, except as a rotted thing. In Nascinthé the pain was raw and fully present, waiting just behind the unsteady quiver of her expressive mouth, poised for release. We clutched each other for several minutes, until Nascinthé's breathing became steadier, and in that time, something else became clear.

"When Jevar died," I ventured, "did you…relive this?"

Nascinthé nodded fervently, the small bump at the front of her throat squeezing as she swallowed.

"Yes," she said, her voice rattled. "I thought I was prepared, thought I was strong enough for the bid. I had worked a half dozen other straight bids before I was approached for this one. But they were easy—meeting new captains in Dockside, one buy operation aboard a ship with a Grell Runner. Tense, but not violent. But this, this was different. It wasn't just violent…"

Her voice trailed off as she searched for the right word.

"The whole thing was a nightmare," I said. "For me as well."

Nascinthé stared up at me, her unhappy face damp and receptive. Her dyed hair had fallen like hay fibers over her forehead, and her cheekbones looked inflamed.

"But you didn't freeze like I did," she said.

"I failed in my own way."

"Did you?"

I shrugged but said nothing.

"I think you failed by not killing me."

I suppose this shouldn't have caught me entirely off guard, but it did. Nascinthé was simply too astute not to pick up on such a thing, and my inability to respond quickly only confirmed the truth.

"I won't pretend I am a real Shadow Bidder," she said. "But I still understand some things about this world. In the Ripening

Hall, you didn't approach the Line Man and me because you wanted to reason with us. The Finisher sent you to kill us. That was the sensible thing to do, before we left the room."

In truth it was Col who had proposed the idea, though Radrin had concurred immediately. But this was of small consequence, for Nascinthé was essentially right.

"Does it look like I regret it now?"

I did not let go of her, but I pulled away just enough so that I could look at her squarely.

"Listen, you had already saved my life that night in the vestibule. Without your remarkable performance, none of us would have made it out of that chamber alive."

"I was simply doing my job," she said, though she smiled weakly and appeared at least partially cheered.

"You wildly outperformed your job. So, consider the Ripening Hall a bonus. And you made good on it immediately. You led those soldiers on a hunt through the marsh, trying to draw them out of the compound. Am I right?"

Now Nascinthé smiled more overtly, and the teeming wetness seemed to retreat back into its source.

"I did, but I took it too far, because they almost got me. In the end, the surge got them."

"It was incredibly brave of you," I said, "and reckless. But it worked. Better than you probably know."

As it turned out, Nascinthé did know, or at least she guessed. She had watched one of the dock boys arrive at Eastcove the prior day, and she saw him speaking urgently with Habard before moving on to Droden's dwelling. Afterwards, Nascinthé convinced Habard to tell her what he had learned, and while the rumors he recited were of a disjointed nature, there was one consistent detail: the High Lord's compound had been attacked.

In this way, Nascinthé figured out the true identity of the target, and by extension, she guessed who had proffered the contract. All of this I confirmed.

While I did not enjoy relaying it, I described everything that occurred after I parted with her at the water door—the trip back into the compound, overhearing the conversation with Weygrin, my bloody encounter with Nester, and finally the killing of Sherdane. I found it extremely disturbing to relive these things. I also did not wish to remind Nascinthé of my own violent behavior, something she had witnessed in such close quarters that her garments had been drenched in my butchery. And while the killing of Weygrin had not occurred that night, I mentally lumped it in with all the other Narrow Bid tragedies, tangibly recalling the clammy feel of his wet hand as he went frigid in my grasp. I was suddenly and acutely overcome with remorse.

"I hope there isn't actually a Hell," I mumbled. "If there is, then I'm likely headed there."

"There's no such place," Nascinthé replied.

She reached up to stroke my cheek, smiling kindly.

"Remember, it wasn't you who completed the contract. Even if Hell did exist, and it doesn't, it's the dreadful Finisher who would go there, not you."

This required a moment's thought.

"Maybe," I finally said. "Though I'm starting to think that's where he came from in the first place."

A part of me wanted to describe the strange phantasmal dream I experienced at the culmination of the Narrow Bid, to finally speak it out loud and try to make sense of it. However, I was afraid that Nascinthé would either think me mad or, worse, actually understand it on some level, and that this understanding might not reflect well upon me. Having failed to fully interpret the dream myself, I did at least grasp that something destructive, even darkly causal, had been revealed there. Something about me, which was best left alone.

So instead, I explained what had occurred the prior night in my home, which I presented as a few injured stragglers from the High Lord's compound, who were easy to drive off.

The gentle arch of Nascinthé's brows lifted in alarm.

"We must leave," she said. "This place is no longer safe for us."

"No," I replied, slowly shaking my head. "*You* must leave, Nascinthé of Levell. This place is not for you, and it never will be."

Then I looked up at the ceiling, for I could no longer meet her eye. My gaze panned over the many knots, the cracks in the wood, and I also noted the small fibrous glimmer of a spider's web in the corner. Some unidentified thing dangled at the end of one of the threads—a wooden splinter, a leaf, the husk of another insect—and I found myself trying to guess what it was.

Nascinthé did not speak for several seconds. She was still pressed against me, but now she shifted, placing her warm palm on my thigh and levering upright so that her head was parallel with mine. After that, she drew back her other hand and smacked me hard across the face. I was so startled I gasped.

In a flat voice she said, "You're not doing *that* again."

Then she slid back a couple feet and sat, watching me intently. My mind spun frantically, struggling to find a proper response.

"You deserve better," I finally blurted. "You deserve so much better than me."

"Do I?"

"Of course you do. Think of the world you come from, think of your extraordinary talents and potential. So many possibilities lie open before you, especially with the money from the contract. You can buy your way back into favor. You can return to the stage, where the world can witness your genius. Relocate to some wonderful place, with a decent man. Someone who doesn't wear a prison brand on his arm, who has a reputable name, not a street alias."

"A duke, perhaps?"

For the first time since I had met her, her blue eyes looked cold and angry.

"Maybe someone from the theater," I said, though I realized my blunder instantly.

"Yes, that should work out well," she replied, in a tone to match her expression. "Now that I'm fully acclimated to men's blood splattering across my face, I should do much better with the next one."

"Oh, damn it all…" I said, covering my eyes with my wounded hand. "I can't leave this place yet. I just can't, and it's hard for me to explain why."

My eyes were still covered, but I could hear her breathing heavily.

"For someone so well read," she said, "you are surprisingly stupid."

I let my hand fall to my side.

"I've been told this my entire life."

We argued back and forth for quite a while, and I tried, from every possible angle, to explain to her how much better off she would be without me. Nascinthé was (and I felt this viscerally) superior to me in every meaningful way. Her one so-called "failing"—the inability to remain detached in the presence of sickening acts of violence—was no failing at all, but rather a clear indication that she belonged in a better place, with better people than the denizens of Hell's Labyrinth. To this she replied that she had tried those other places, and those other people, and the only thing at which they were "better" was masking their turpitude behind the pretense of nobility.

It was a compelling argument, especially when she described how thoroughly everybody in Tergon turned their backs on her: the aristocracy, her fellow players, the theater director, and eventually the entire citizenry, who seemed shockingly open to the storyline they were fed. This magnificent woman, whom they had all adored and worshipped but weeks before, became a cold-hearted, manipulative whore before she even understood what was happening. She couldn't make it down a single street in Tergon without some vile comment being hurled after her, sometimes with garbage to accompany it.

"But in this city, it will be knives, not garbage," I said.

"In Tergon it became knives," she replied, "which is why my family hides in a village too small to have a name, living entirely off my bid payments."

"Bring them my contract, then," I said, reaching over to my backpack where the pouch of Gosian diamonds was tucked away. "You can tell me where yours is hidden, and I'll retrieve it once you leave."

"I've never seen a man so eager to get rid of me in my entire life," she said, and truly she seemed dumbfounded. "Perhaps I'll take your payment, then deceive you about where mine is hidden. Imagine what a cold-hearted, manipulative whore I'd be then."

We made little progress with our discussion after that. Her argument in favor of leaving made excellent sense, while my argument in favor of staying made no sense at all. But I couldn't let go of it, which is the exact behavior pattern that makes me such an irritating person, even to myself. I didn't really need logic. All I knew was that my home was calling me, beckoning me back into the Labyrinth, and for some reason I seemed incapable of resisting the pull. Plus, on a more basic level, I was certain that I did not deserve this sort of happiness. Nascinthé did. She was blameless in her own misfortune, apart from failing to read the full scope of the dangers that lurked in her glittering world. I felt it would be one of my rare acts of altruism in this life if I convinced her to move on. The problem was, she was just as stubborn as I was.

"I'll stay then," she finally said.

When I tried to protest, she crossed her arms over her bare breasts and a long, cynical smile turned up the corner of her lips.

"Why shouldn't I stay?" she asked. "This seems to be the only place where I can still get an acting job. And I must say, the pay has been excellent."

"He's going to come," I said. "The Raving Blade will come, to wipe out the evidence of his crime. I can't let you stay."

"Oh?" she said, her lips still holding the same taunting smile but her eyes now fierce and enlivened in her defiance. "How, exactly, will you make me leave? It will take more than a pouch of diamonds."

"But why?" I exclaimed. "Why in vast existence do you want to stay with me?"

"You really don't get it, do you?"

"No, I really don't."

Nascinthé let her hands fall to her sides. She sat upright on the bed, exasperated and breathtaking. Her skin was flushed from our argument, her high cheekbones a fervent rose color. Like this, she spoke to me in words that were almost impossible for me to grasp.

"In the world I come from," she said, "people all think they are better than others, when in fact they are far worse. With you, it's the opposite. You are an honorable man, who clearly thinks of himself as some sort of scoundrel. The nobility in Tergon are well read and educated; yet they are shunted into these things, with no true appreciation of the knowledge they possess. Here, in the most unlikely of places, you have educated yourself, and it is more than obvious how much it means to you. You could not disguise the way you felt about the books you gave me, about that scholarly woman you so adore, nor could you hide how enchanted you were when you browsed through the lovely items in Marzan's Emporium. I watched you from the moment you entered that store, and the delight in your face was like that of a little boy. This is not a pretense in you. It's who you are."

"But I'm also a savage, Nascinthé," I said. "You saw that part as well."

"What I saw was a man who would stop at nothing to protect me. Who was willing to throw his life away to save mine. Am I wrong?"

Nascinthé was not wrong, so I shook my head.

"And yet, look at you now. Now that you have me, you are more than willing to let me go; because you believe, falsely believe, that I will be free and happy without you. This was not how the Duke behaved. My freedom and happiness were the very last things on his mind."

To all of this I had no response, so at last I rolled over in confusion, staring at the wall of our homey little cabin, which had suddenly started to feel claustrophobic. The emotions grinding about inside of me were so intense and so muddled I truly did not know how to identify them, and I certainly didn't have an answer as to how we should move forward from here. We spoke no more on the matter that afternoon, and hours later when night fell, we ate a portion of the boat's provisions, then tried to get some sleep. It took me a while, but eventually I slipped off into a deep, tumultuous slumber.

It was there, in the eerie world of roiling dreams, that I finally received an answer.

24

DREAM OFFER

It is hard to classify the dream I experienced my second night aboard the Elena's Guile. I can't even say whether it *was* a dream or, instead, another delirious hallucination like the one I experienced at the culmination of the Narrow Bid. Such phenomena had never manifested before in my life, and yet now they appeared to be unfolding in quick succession. I will simply describe what happened.

My sleep at first was as it usually was, an amalgam of regurgitations—bits and pieces of the last few days, with brief appearances by Merejin, Holod, and Flerra. I cannot fully recollect what occurred in those dreams, only that I was in a steady state of agitation, blended with a dim undercurrent of sadness. Vaguely, I recall visiting Merejin's Books, but it was also somehow the Broodhouse, and Flerra was there. Never before had my Brood sister accompanied me to the Virtuoso, so I felt at least mild surprise to have her with me, though I remember nothing about what we did there, and the scene quickly moved on. Those details were soon forgotten, subsumed by the final episode, which turned out to be the night's main event.

In this dream, I returned once again to that familiar, lissome bridge deep in the heart of the Lower City, where so many strange things had transpired. To my right loomed the glorious mass of Kaennamin Academy, and to the left, farther off, I saw the slender buttresses of Nengriant Basilica, bending skyward to meet the building's crown. Below my feet was the canal-straddling granite arch where I had stood all those years ago with Flerra. It was also, much more recently, the spot where I received a parade of ghostly visitors during my Swell Driven phantasm. As it turned out, there was one more visitor to receive.

He came from the direction of Kaennamin Academy, just like the others; however, there was something different this time. There were many differences, to the look of this place, to the atmosphere, to the colors and tones, feeling and mood. All was darker. All was solemn and conspicuously stripped of charm. While never a place of great color, this spot in particular benefited from the amber tint of the upper Kaennamin windows, and also the vibrant panes of soaring glass in the basilica, which could usually be seen in all but the heaviest fog. But not today. Today I felt I was in a place of oppressive gloom, with a distinct hint of foreboding.

The figure moved slowly, tearing the mist in weary curls, pacing towards my bridge with a faint scratch of his boots. He seemed unhurried in his efforts to reach me, but at the same time there was no hesitancy, and as he neared, I sensed a tenacity of purpose that I found unnerving. This figure was neither tall nor broad, but he did seem impenetrably dark, and the sheer volume of that darkness caused his form to appear imposing. Dimmed as they were, I could not make out the features. What I could see was the flowing silhouette of his cape, and a bristling object upon his head, which appeared to be a crown. My attention was also drawn to another detail; two details, in fact. As the figure came closer, I saw a pair of slender metallic objects aslant from his hands, splined out dangerously, flickering as they spun at hummingbird speed. They blurred the fog as they twirled, becoming almost hypnotic, and it took me several seconds to focus my eyes enough to understand what they were. The stranger was carrying two long, wicked swords.

Below me the silty waters flowed; however, as the figure approached, the texture of the canal seemed to change, thickening and blackening before my eyes like lantern oil. Its gentle current slackened to a lugubrious crawl. I also began to feel a distinct sickness emanating out of it, like pus or poisoned blood, and when I looked around me, there appeared to be an infected quality to everything—a gangrenous veneer upon the stonework, a grimy tinge to the low-lying clouds. During the height of my Swell Driver dream, when the maelstrom erupted, I felt the mindless anger of the elements, the impersonal reprisal of the natural world. This experience was different, for the strange illness wasn't a thing of nature. It was an affliction that was somehow emanating out of this approaching man.

He had come quite close now, and those twin blades continued to flash and spin. I could clearly see the crown upon his head, a heavily oxidized iron piece that seemed to be corroding as he walked, and I could also see the straggly edges of his hair. The face, however, remained of the deepest blackness. The sheer malice exuding from him was palpable, and I stepped back reflexively, reaching across to my left side to grab a blade.

I intended to draw one of my spades, but when I pulled the weapon free, I saw that I had somehow retrieved the wrong implement. In my hand was an elegantly shaped dagger, a relatively small blade with a short hand guard, designed to be maneuvered quickly and stealthfully—the sort of weapon favored by a Finisher. Despite its small size, it was still an impressive dagger, of excellent balance and workmanship. Most notably, the knife was forged entirely of black steel.

As I held this fine weapon, something strange happened within me. The dread disappeared, the sense of foreboding lost all substance, evaporating like steam beneath a stifling heat. Vitality surged through my body, enlarging my insides, converting them to capacious chambers unobstructed by fear. I glared at the baleful figure, and my fingers hardened around the dagger like drying cement.

The blade I wielded was intended for finishing, not fighting, but I didn't care. I would plunge that knife home, drive it like a thundering horseman's lance straight into him, no matter what the cost. It was a degree of conviction so complete my limbs veritably hummed as it coursed through me. This was different than the battle frenzy that sometimes overtook me, for I was not angry; I was not consumed with madness or hatred or disgust. I was certain. I was quickened with a focused zeal, and this feeling had such a powerful draw that I found it nearly impossible to resist.

The man with the two blades appeared to sense this, for he pulled up short at the base of the bridge. It was he who now seemed hesitant, shuffling uncertainly, one foot ascending the arching flagstones, then retreating again. While the features were still opaque, I detected a ripple of concern passing through him. Thereafter, his blades stopped twirling, and he lowered them to the cobbles with a light "click, click."

"Shadow Bidder," he said. His voice was raspy and unpleasant, like the grating of a mason's tool or the snarl of a feral cat. "Sheath that blade, Shadow Bidder. We have business to discuss."

The lowering of those two blades ought to have been a relief. The talk of parley should have stood me down, as the threat posed by this figure was unmistakable, primal even, and any path that avoided confrontation was the only course to take. But somehow, that's not how I reacted; or, more accurately, the dagger in my hand did not respond well to these peaceful developments. The blade wanted blood. It jittered in my fist like a venomous snake, animated and unruly, throbbing right up my arm and shoulder and neck.

I tried to stifle it, for indeed I now began to separate out my own needs from the heedless audacity of this dagger. I tried to put the blade back in its scabbard, to comply with the demands of my dangerous visitor, but I found that this was no easy task. The dagger had a mind of its own, a life of its own, and it shimmered ominously on that phantom bridge, glinting with a purple-black corona like some unholy angel. It had no interest in being sheathed. It wanted to yank me forward down that bridge, to thrust me blindly at the enemy like a sectarian warrior from the Old World. If I did not get control of this thing quickly, it was going to drag me straight into its own crusade.

"Put the blade away, Shadow Bidder," the figure said again, now with a distinct note of unease in his scratchy voice. "It is not weapons that you and I need but shovels. There is burying to do."

I truly wanted to hear what the dark man had to say. His talk of shovels and burying was of immense interest, for, in it, I sensed something important, something that might free me from my own impasse. So, with tremendous effort, I levered the dagger down from its raised position and then finally wrestled it back into its sheath. Even then, I could feel it bulging and contracting at my side like a disembodied lung.

"What burying?" I asked.

The dark figure nodded acknowledgment to my de-escalation.

"The secret," he said, his voice somewhat stronger now. "We can bury it, but only if you and I work together."

Something about that statement actually made sense to me—not all of it, but the pertinent details. I understood, at least in a general sense, what secret he was talking about. I also guessed the identity of this man.

"Count Gueritus?" I asked. It was rhetorical, for I was now quite sure.

The figure nodded.

"What do you want from me? Our contract is complete."

"I am offering you a new contract, Shadow Bidder. I need your word this time, not your blade."

And then, quite suddenly, I understood. A great heaving flood of relief doused through me, washing away the uncertainties, tangibly loosening the strain. Even in the dream world, many of the complexities became clear, enough to grasp the essence of what he was asking. The Raving Blade needed me. He needed me alive, not dead. I was the only one who could spin the false story he wanted told.

"That's right," he said, and there was a nasty little chuckle in his voice. "A much easier job than the last one."

I was present in that moment to an extraordinary feeling of gratitude; gratitude to Count Gueritus, for valuing me, for choosing shovels, not blades, and as such, I reached down the front of my tunic and fished around until I found the secure pocket in my cuirass. I grabbed hold of the former High Lord's throat brooch and drew it forth. I eagerly displayed it to him, offering what I thought would be a superb token of peace. What clearer indication was there that I had followed his wishes the last time? What better tribute to offer the new High Lord? When I stared down at my palm, however, I saw that the pretty little octagon was no longer clean and glistening. It was covered in syrupy red-black blood, and that blood all seemed to be oozing out of the diamond in the center.

"I don't want that thing, you fool!" the Raving Blade spat, with a much more threatening edge in his voice. "You must bury it, along with the secret. The others will be looking for a stupid blunder such as that."

I quickly tried to stuff the brooch down into a pocket on my right side. I jammed it into the padded slip in my pant leg; however, when I pulled my hand back out, I was still holding something. This object was larger than the brooch, and it writhed in my grip like an animal's limb. Looking down, I was appalled to see that I was once again clutching that maniacal black Finisher's dagger.

I was certain I had stowed the thing away on the left side, where I had first found it, but here it was again in my hand, this time in no mood to stay put. It jittered and twitched, pulling wildly like a live cod line, and I staggered several feet down the bridge towards Gueritus. It was all I could do to stay on that bridge, to keep the weapon down at my thigh.

I looked up at the Raving Blade, terrified that he would think me faithless before our deal was even underway. But he had already turned his back and was strolling off, carving a dreary rent in the veil of fog. Again, I was awash in relief.

There was still a path open before me, there was a way forward, if I simply did my part. All I needed was to maintain my composure, and to keep that goddamned unholy dagger securely in its sheath.

I awakened with a start, jolting upright in bed. It took me a moment to remember where I was, to see that I was in the dimly lit, comfy little cabin aboard the Elena's Guile. When I looked over next to me, I saw a lithe form nestled in the bedding. In the tawny light of the low-burning lantern, Nascinthé's bare shoulder looked like a graceful sand dune, and her tasseled hair sprayed out like autumn grass. Beneath the linens, her ribs were softly rising and falling, and I felt such a wave of tenderness at the sight it was almost painful.

"I'm going to fix this," I whispered.

Yes, I would fix it, for I now saw the way. In fact, I saw the entire plan, which did not involve savagery and bloodshed, nor did it require me to sacrifice myself in some meaningless swan song. All it required was that I surrender a little integrity, as I would need to tell lies repeatedly and portray myself as a clueless dupe—a Shadow Bidder who had thought he was merely being hired as a guide. Weygrin indicated that the surviving soldiers believed that Lave Kaszivar was the true instigator of the Narrow Bid. From those stragglers, the tale would spread, and I would offer to help it along, because in it lay the key to my survival. Gueritus must have been prepared for conflict when he launched the Narrow Bid, but how much easier it would be if he could avoid that, which is exactly what I could provide him by corroborating the Lave Kaszivar story: release from culpability, the prevention of a full-scale war.

I reached over and brushed Nascinthé's cheek ever so gently as she slept. She stirred slightly and made a light noise, but she did not wake. I slid my hand down to her exposed shoulder where I allowed it to rest, passively receiving her warmth, drawing from her my motivation for the plan. It would work. It would work because I would work; I would do a splendid job with the negotiation, then play my role flawlessly thereafter. I had a purpose now, a powerful incentive to change. I was ready, at long last, to cast off the coarsest and meanest parts of my own character.

Nascinthé's slumbering presence continued to radiate into my hand, like the restorative vapors from a Nettledown bath, like the glowing mouth of my fireplace, ousting the chill on a blustery autumn night.

Yet all the while, I still felt a lingering sensation from the dream. Down at my hip I was present to a faint tremor, like the burrowing of a mole through the mattress below, and this drew my mind back into the gloomy world of that phantom bridge. There, a part of me remained. There something else also remained, restless and dark, throbbing uncomfortably against my side.

Murmuring and writhing, the deadly Finisher's blade kept beckoning me to grab hold.

THE END

ABOUT THE AUTHOR

Peter Eliott melds his love of evocative writing with an intense interest in dark adventure stories. As a devotee of literary fiction, Peter strives to render exciting action stories in a highly vivid style. His earlier career in architecture and design informs his current novels, the Shadow Bidder Series, adding visual realism to the gritty urban setting.

Peter Eliott currently lives with his wife in Amagansett, NY.

www.ingramcontent.com/pod-product-compliance
Lightning Source LLC
Chambersburg PA
CBHW031110160726
47991CB00004B/1309